HER

FATHER'S

DAUGHTER

Novels By
Harris L. Kligman

The Shaolin Covenant
Kill Alexis Markovic
LIFE IMPOSSIBLE
The Profession
THE DARK
Hakoah

Children's Books By
Harris L. Kligman

The Original Alphabet Gang
The Day the Night Did Not Come

HER

FATHER'S

DAUGHTER

ISBN: 9798583541065

Any references to historical events, real people, or real places are used fictitiously. Names, characters, and places are products of the author's imagination.

Cover by Christopher Civale

Follow Harris L. Kligman

https://www.HarrisLKligman.com

Find Her Father's Daughter on AUDIO

*Dedicated to my son **Rob**, whose relentless urging motivated me to start writing.*
And
*To my wife **Nancy**, whose strength and fortitude kept our family intact over the many lengthy absences.*

Chapter 1

Kathy Longrin was again aware of the hand on her thigh and recoiled. Her body language made no pretense about how she felt. It was a liberty that he had no right to take and he had taken small liberties since the evening began.

She threw the contents of her drink in his face, slid off the barstool without a word and walked out to the street.

The doorman's hand went to his cap, two fingers touching the visor, "Do you need a cab, Miss?"

"Yes, thank you."

The doorman walked to the curb and placed a small silver whistle to his mouth. Almost immediately a cab pulled to the curb and the doorman opened the door.

Kathy held onto her skirt as she slid into the back seat. She neglected to tip the doorman...her mind was elsewhere.

She leaned her head back against the seat after giving the driver the address. It was a brutal evening compounded by the press of a day gone amok. Men were all the same. To them a single woman was an easy mark.

How rudimentary was their thinking that dinner and a drink would open the floodgates of pleasure for them. Under the right circumstances sure, but this was not one of those times.

He was a bore and had an attitude that made the night torturous. Blind dates were something that she would have to weigh more carefully in the future.

She paid the cab driver, opened the rear door and walked obliviously past the doorman and toward the apartment building's entrance.

She glanced quickly to her rear, then stepped inside before the doorman could assist her.

When Kathy moved, she moved at a quickened pace and tried to stay cognizant of her surroundings. It was a pattern she adopted since moving to New York. The city, with all its magic, had a darker side.

As she waited for the elevator, she wondered whether the pepper spray she carried in her purse would get her out of a difficult situation. She hoped she would never have to find out.

Remembering that she hadn't picked up her mail, she turned away from the elevator and walked to the small alcove that held the building's mailboxes.

She opened her box and took the mail without looking at it, then she smacked the mailbox door shut and walked back to the elevator, still seething over the evening's events.

Her apartment was modest, but upscale. New York was expensive and comparable to no other city, domestic or foreign, for here was the world's power center and it was here that she belonged.

Graduation from law school was a scant five years ago, but in that time, she devoted her entire being toward establishing a reputation as a smart, hard-nosed attorney, one who represented her clients fairly, but ruthlessly. She had garnered the reputation as a lawyer to watch.

She had little time for others, whether dates, or her fellow attorneys, outside of office business. The goals she sought wouldn't tolerate wasted time.

Everything she did had its purpose. She legally changed her name to Katherine Longrin when she entered law school. She never felt comfortable with her given name, always thinking it was too ethnic in a country that still looked down on certain ethnic classes with abject disdain.

When she was a teenager she unknowingly walked into a room and interrupted a meeting between her father and several other men. She overheard one of the men address her father by a different name, then abruptly stop when she entered.

After she apologized for the intrusion and turned to leave, her father called her over and introduced her to the two men.

"This is my daughter Karta."

She never liked the way it sounded. The name, Karta Buhler, wasn't the way she perceived herself.

She placed the mail on the coffee table, kicked off her shoes and went to the refrigerator. She opened the door and took out a bottle of Perrier, then placed the cold bottle against her forehead, moving it slowly back and forth.

Then she walked to the sofa and fell into it.

She unscrewed the Perrier cap and took a long drink from the bottle, something she didn't normally do. But tonight, she was tired and lazy and a glass wasn't necessary. She placed the bottle on a coaster and picked up the first piece of mail, a letter that she noted had no return address.

She tore open the envelope and pulled out a paper folded in half. The touch of the paper indicated that it was made of fine quality fiber. Kathy rubbed her thumb and index finger back and forth on the paper and watched as something green in color floated past the table and onto the small oriental rug.

She let out a groan as she went around the table and picked it up. She stared at the front and then the back. It was a torn half from a United States one-thousand dollar bill.

Returning to the sofa, she leaned forward and picked up the paper from the coffee table while still holding the torn bill in her left hand.

Kathy read the note several times. The other half will be given to you after our meeting. Please be in the lobby of the Drake Hotel off Park Avenue at six p.m. Wednesday, the twenty-first.

The paper was unsigned. As Kathy moved her hands, she noted the raised monogram initials in the upper right-hand corner. They referred to no one she could place, either male or female.

She took another sip of Perrier, leaned back, and smiled to herself. Then she said out loud, "Why not, counselor? Thirty minutes at most in a public area for one-thousand dollars…seems quite reasonable."

She finished off the Perrier and walked to the bedroom.

Chapter 2

As a criminal lawyer Kathy Longrin represented all levels of the socioeconomic fabric that made up the New York melting pot, from gang bangers to white collar executives with sticky fingers. The only cases she wouldn't handle were rape cases, deploring what she believed to be a continuing travesty of justice erring on the side of the perpetrator – the defendant.

As she sat in the Drake Hotel's lobby, she thought about what the torn one-thousand dollar bill represented. The options were many and if interesting enough she would have no hesitation in accepting the case.

She eyed the various comings and goings that are traditional to any hotel lobby. The Drake was old world, and the guests were moneyed and mostly European.

She played mind games trying to guess which of the men or women crossing her line of sight might be the sender. She couldn't fix on anyone, so redirected her attention away from people and began scanning the hotel's ornate decorations.

A quiet accented voice caused her to turn her attention to her left. Standing in front of her was a man in his late thirties. His black suit, maroon shirt with white collar and white French cuffs, gold cufflinks and a solid black silk tie, projected success well above the average level.

He leaned slightly forward. "Thank you for coming, Miss Longrin."

Kathy thought about his opening remark. He didn't ask whether she was Kathy Longrin, he knew.

"You know who I am, but who are you?"

"Please forgive me Miss Longrin, I am Raphael Duchant. Would you kindly join me in the hotel's Shepherd's Bar where we can discuss a proposition I have for you."

Seeing a quizzical look appear on her face, he continued. "The proposition is quite legitimate," and he smiled. "I have no ulterior motives. If at the end of our meeting you elect to walk away, the other half of the bill is yours and we will never see each other again."

Kathy thought about this being the easiest money she ever made. A shopping spree at Gucci would be in order.

"Okay, Mr. Duchant, I'm all yours, professionally of course." She laughed and he smiled.

He walked toward the lobby entrance to Shepherd's with Kathy following a step behind. She noticed his black, calfskin shoes, highly polished and wondered again, why me? With all the high priced talent in New York legal circles, she was a relatively small fish in a big pond.

When the hostess walked over, Kathy watched as the man handed her something.

"A quiet place in a dark corner please," then he looked back at Kathy and smiled.

Once they were seated, a waitress quickly appeared. He turned to her and said, "It's the end of one day and perhaps the beginning of another, may I offer you a drink?"

"I don't think so," and then looking at the waitress said, "a hot black coffee please. If it's been sloshing around in the pot since this morning, tell me ahead of time. It'll save you a trip to empty it."

"The coffee is perfectly fine Miss. It's brewed every hour."

"Thank you, then coffee will be fine."

"And you sir."

"I'll have a Grey Goose on the rocks, twist of lemon."

When the waitress left, he reached into his suit jacket and took out a black ostrich wallet. She saw that it had his initials in gold lettering at one corner, the same initials that appeared on the note.

He took out a small envelope and held it toward her.

She took it, and immediately felt the same high-quality paper.

"Do you want me to open this now?"

"Yes, please, Miss Longrin."

Kathy carefully tore open the envelope, reached inside and took out the other half of the one-thousand dollar bill.

She looked up at him and pointed to the half bill, "This is a lot of money for a conversation over coffee and vodka."

"Perhaps Miss Longrin, but time is costly, and I've always felt that it should be compensated well, if used beneficially."

After placing the coffee and drink in front of the man and woman, the waitress waited as Kathy brought the cup to her lips. Kathy nodded and the waitress disappeared.

"Okay Mr. Duchant, the money has definitely bought you my time and you now have my attention. Just how much time and attention depends on what you are about to tell me and you are about to tell me something, aren't you?"

He thought she's direct, a no-nonsense type. Let's put plus one on her side of the ledger.

Raphael continued to look at her for another moment before he began to speak. She didn't take her eyes away from his.

"Someone, and for the purposes of this discussion, he or they shall remain unnamed, has appropriated property belonging to my grandfather and father and subsequently me. During the years leading up to World War II, certain interests approached my father about safeguarding his collection of art masterpieces. His collection was vast and included such old masters as Diego Velazquez, William Blake and Peter Paul Rubens. His interest in the Impressionists was a lifelong pursuit. I grew up looking at Manet, Gauguin, Paul Signac, Edgar Degas and Georges Seurat."

The names rolled off his tongue as easily as one would name his playmates. All the names were familiar to her. She had grown up with art and minored in art history. For a while she contemplated making it her life's endeavor.

Her father, a gentleman farmer of some substance, was a frequent patron of the arts and her home reflected this. Modern Masters, Southwestern art and antique French Posters, hung throughout the house. But the works of both the Old Masters and the Impressionists, only hung in a room specifically built in the basement level and accessed by way of a concealed door in the floor of her father's library.

Once in the tunnel, the path led to a fork from which a series of pathways extended, designed to confuse anyone who managed to gain unauthoriz-ed entrance.

Kathy would be taken there often by her father and she looked forward to these times with great anticipation. She enjoyed playing in the pathways as a youngster although her father never seemed to know of her solo visits there. If he did, he never mentioned it.

On several occasions she lost her sense of direction and panicked, but after a while she grew to know every inch of the passageways and the underground gallery. Her father's idea of a relaxing day was visiting museums and galleries and she accompanied him frequently.

She grew up enjoying the rewards of money. There always seemed to be more than enough even though many of the families in their community were losing their farms to foreclosure, some of which had been handed down from father to son for generations.

Kathy possessed a moral side and felt that legal injustices were the root cause of most difficulties. She believed the law should be used to mend these wrongs and there were many wrongs in this society besides those suffered by farmers.

With the encouragement of her father, she made up her mind to go to law school but still held onto her love of art during her undergraduate years. Sitting there listening to the names of the great ones, once again stirred a long sleeping memory within her.

"After several meetings with the interests, my father felt reasonably comfortable to entrust them with his collection for safe keeping until the war clouds over Europe had passed. However, he was in no hurry to turn his collection over, not just yet."

"When the German Wehrmacht (Army) attacked Poland in September 1939 and then Crete in 1940, my grandfather and father felt that it was only a matter of time until France was attacked. He worked diligently in cataloguing his collection. He flew to Switzerland and at the Bank of Geneva secured a deposit box sufficiently large to hold a number of small canvases."

Raphael sipped his vodka while staring over the rim of his glass at the woman.

After placing the glass down, he reached into his suit jacket again and brought out the black ostrich wallet, opened it and withdrew a small piece of folded paper. He handed the paper to Kathy.

She unfolded the paper and stared at the numbers indicated. It read forty-eight million, three hundred thousand dollars.

She looked back at him.

"That number Miss Longrin is what the contents of that safe deposit box are worth in today's dollars and I may be on the light side. But I'm getting ahead of myself."

"Just before the Germans invaded France by way of Belgium, my father turned over the majority of our collection to the interests. The transfer was sealed with a handshake and a note."

Duchant paused and reached into his wallet again, withdrawing another piece of paper and handing it to Kathy. She opened the paper and looked with disbelief at the number.

"Are you kidding, Mr. Duchant?"

"Miss Longrin, I never joke about money."

Kathy stared hypnotically at the six hundred-million-dollar figure. She signaled the waitress who asked whether she wanted a refill.

"No, I like what he's drinking."

Then she sat back in her chair and looked unblinkingly at her companion who stared back at her with a slight smile.

Chapter 3

"The two figures I showed you, Miss Longrin, might seem stratospheric to some, but in the art world, great masters command enormous sums. You've no doubt been privy to reports of staggering prices paid for Van Gogh, Renoir, Pissarro and Cezanne. As I remarked, when you saw the first figure, this may well be under-estimated."

"Let me continue for a moment more and then I'll be pleased to address any questions you might have. The written agreement was either misplaced or lost during my family's struggles to avoid capture by the Nazis. The paintings were crated and taken away by these interests for safe-keeping, but not for the benefit of my father or his family."

"Field Marshall Hermann Goering, Commander of the Luftwaffe, the Nazi Air Force, was the chief architect who oversaw the systematic looting of priceless art collections from galleries, and individuals throughout Europe. Those who signed the note with my grandfather and father, either from pressure or through their willingness to cooperate, allowed Goering to take these master-pieces back to Berlin."

"Many were destined to be displayed in his personal collection. Others were given to Adolph Hitler who hung some of these in a small museum adjacent to his chancellery. Hitler planned for the majority of the art confiscated from the conquered countries to be displayed in a national museum, which would be designed by Albert Speer, the architect for the Third Reich. This museum would glorify his One Thousand Year Reich, and act as a testimonial to what he viewed as Europe's now dead, but once great societies. My father's collection certainly was destined to be part of that display."

"This never came to fruition. With the end of WWII quickly approaching, Goering, working closely with Admiral Wilhelm Canaris, Chief of German military intelligence, the Abwehr, had the art crated and taken to the salt mines located in the Ruhr Valley of Germany."

"The Brandenburger Division, an Abwehr (Intelligence) unit designated for special operations, was charged with the primary responsibility for transporting and safeguarding these treasures. Realizing the end of the war was close at hand, officers of the Brandenburger Division helped themselves to many pieces of art."

"What was left of this hoard of art treasures was found by US troops, many of whom also helped themselves to these masterpieces without fully realizing what they stumbled upon. There were several officers, one a General and one a Colonel, the latter was eventually court martialed, who knew quite well what these salt mines held. They requisitioned many of the finest art pieces, as well as china, silverware, and jewelry. The United States government took many of these as a war tribute, perhaps with the intention of eventually returning them to their rightful owners, or perhaps not."

"In short Miss Longrin, our collection was dissected and scattered around the world. The safe deposit box, whose number was memorized by a select few, was one of the few pieces of linking evidence to remain in my family's possession. The other was the notebook that contained the complete list of our collection which my father compiled prior to the agreement."

"My father and I managed to escape to France and through bribes we were able to secure a visa to the United States. I was very young, but I remember my mother refused to go with us. She insisted on staying with my grandfather who was too ill to travel. Nothing my father could do would sway her. She was a very strong willed woman."

"My father related everything to me before he died. When I was older, I traveled to Switzerland and accessed the box...it was empty."

Duchant paused and looked down at his drink. He stirred his drink unconsciously with his finger, then he looked up.

"Perhaps, Miss Longrin, this might be an opportune time to stop and answer some of your questions."

"Let's start off with a simple one, Mr. Duchant. I assume your family's fortune in its entirety, or the majority of it, was not vested in this collection. Looking at the way you dress, you hardly convey a lifestyle of need."

"Please call me Raphael. If I may, I will call you Kathy."

He waited before speaking further.

Kathy nodded her head yes and then he continued.

"My family maintained extensive holdings in real estate both on the continent, and specifically in the United States. The wealth of the Duchant family stems primarily from diamonds, not from paintings. We were large importers of diamonds from the South African mines from the outset."

"My grandfather and Cecil Rhodes, the founder of Rhodesia, were not only friends, but also business partners. Rhodes and my grandfather made some interesting money from mining the Kimber Diamond Mines in South Africa."

"They formed a company, RD Consolidated Mines in 1888. Our holding company, Duchant et Compagnie de Fils, originally headquartered in Paris and now in New York, continues to this day to be one of the largest importers of diamonds in the world. However, we now specialize in Russian white water diamonds in addition to those from South Africa, Botswana, and Dutch Guyana."

"We have either sold or reclaimed most of our real estate holdings. The exception being in the countries behind the iron curtain. Perhaps someday we may recover those as well, as litigation is being taken in this regard. I believe that should answer your question as to my ability to pay your fee."

"Mr. Duchant...err Raphael, that was not the intent of my question. It was to determine how serious you are to recover the paintings...whether

17

you would exert maximum time and resources to the effort or approach it lackadaisically."

"Kathy, nothing I undertake is done lackadaisically."

"What do you expect from me?"

"In school you majored in art history…"

Kathy interrupted, "As an art minor."

Duchant shrugged his shoulders.

"Major or minor you have an art background, and you are an attorney. That is a combination I cannot find elsewhere. I want to approach those who have many of my father's paintings and recover these through litigation. They consist of museums, foundations, corporate entities, and individuals. I fully realize that this will take up a considerable amount of your time and that your present law firm may be reluctant to give me your time exclusively. As such, I am prepared to offer you a position with my organization. The salary will be three hundred thousand dollars a year, tax free in any currency you desire and payable anywhere in the world."

"What I've indicated to you so far is background. This position will be taxing, difficult, and could be dangerous. I am not prepared to tell you anything further until I have your answer."

"How much time do I have to consider your offer Mr. Duchant…I'm sorry, Raphael?"

He looked at his watch. It was a round gold Patek Philippe with a black alligator strap.

"Five minutes. I'm going to the men's room. Please have your answer ready when I return."

Chapter 4

Kathy watched as the figure of Raphael Duchant walked away from the table. Then she picked up her drink and swallowed quickly.

As she began coughing, she tried to cover her mouth with her hand but some of the vodka dripped and spotted her dress. She dipped her napkin into the water glass and then brushed at the spots. It only made it worse.

She placed the napkin down and raised the vodka glass to her lips. She took a sip carefully and then placed the glass down.

She thought, what do I have to lose? Three hundred thousand dollars tax free is a lot of money by anyone's standards. If what he stated was true… and then her thoughts trailed off as Duchant approached the table.

He slid into his seat effortlessly and took a sip of his drink before he addressed her.

"Well Kathy, it's decision time."

Self-conscious of the spots on her dress, she placed her hand over them. "It's difficult, Raphael, to reach a decision based on the limited time I've had to consider your offer."

"In my world, Kathy, fortunes are made and lost on the timeliness of decisions. This could be a turning point for you. In life nothing is certain, yet all is possible. Success is fleeting for those who are unable to capitalize on its opportunities. The worker bees of this world are afraid to take chances and therefore are relegated to their status forever. Others seize the opportunities as they come and even in failure they are rewarded."

As she listened to what he was saying, she knew it was characteristic of her life so far. She was always willing to take a chance, to push the envelope a little further in her efforts to achieve success. What was she afraid of here? Maybe his last comment, something about even in failure there are rewards. But for failure, what are the rewards?

Kathy took her hand away from her dress and folded them on the table. She leaned slightly toward the man locking onto his gaze.

"Okay. I agree to work for you conditional on several things."

"And what might those be, Kathy?"

"First, I can sever our relationship at any time. Second, there is an element of trust in all business dealings and ours will be no different. I am giving that trust to you, Mr. Raphael Duchant, until such time that you violate it. Everything must be on the table when we interact, and nothing must be held back. Is that agreeable to you?"

Duchant said nothing in reply but extended his hand across the table. Kathy took hold of his hand, gripped it firmly, and then let go.

"If you care to have dinner, it would be my pleasure. I know that today's events have been rather hectic, but I can assure you a much slower pace over a good meal."

"If it's all the same to you, Raphael, I'd like to make it an early evening. Perhaps you'll give me a rain check."

"Of course."

As Kathy stood up, so did Raphael Duchant. He handed her a piece of folded paper. "Please meet me tomorrow at one p.m. at the address on this paper. You can use the morning to tidy up your affairs at your office."

Kathy smiled, placed the paper unopened in her purse and walked toward the exit door.

Raphael sat down and motioned for the waitress to come over.

"Would you please tell the gentleman sitting at the bar in the gray suit to come over."

Chapter 5

Henri Bertrand thanked the waitress and pushed a ten-dollar bill toward the bartender.

He turned and faced the table where Raphael Duchant was sitting. In a few moments he was positioned across from the man.

"How did it go, Raphael?"

"As expected, she's sharp. Whether she'll fit, is quite another thing. Are we prepared for tomorrow?"

"Yes, but I'm still not sure how much we need to reveal to her."

"I've already given her a pretty good background picture. However, what was stated to her were bits of information that are already well known or assumed about the family and businesses. Nothing has been compromised but we'll work on the need to know basis. If she doesn't need to know, there's no reason to tell her. Even if she does need to know, the decision to tell her must be carefully evaluated."

"Are you having another drink, Raphael?"

"Sure, why not."

Duchant signaled to the waitress, pointed to his drink, and held up two fingers. After the drinks arrived, they waited until the waitress left.

"Have you made contact with the Hauptsturmfuhrer, Henri?"

"Yes! The SS-Captain was eager to meet with me when I explained over the telephone that I was a representative of someone interested in purchasing a substantial amount of impressionist art."

"He started by telling me that his gallery featured a number of modern impressionists such as Pollock, Frank Stella, Roy Lichtenstein, and David Hockney. He then asked whether these were of interest."

"I said that they were, but the individual who retained me was primarily interested in works such as Mary Cassatt's Woman in Black, and Cezanne's Still Life with Plaster Cupid. There was an immediate silence. I decided not to speak until he did."

Finally, he said, "Those paintings are priceless works which have been missing from the art scene for many years. There are some who say they were destroyed during the war."

"I simply replied that while they may not have been seen in years, they still existed. He asked me how I knew this. I ignored his question and suggested we meet to discuss these and other purchases. Surprisingly, he elected not to meet at his gallery. Instead, we met at a restaurant of his choice in center city replete with the tourist trade."

"I purposely kept the conversation general and the meeting short. It was his opportunity to size me up. I handed him my business card and suggested he call me to arrange another meeting in a quieter place where we could talk seriously."

"I excused myself and took my time walking to the parked Rolls Royce. I was sure his curiosity would force him to watch me as I made my way into the chauffeured car."

"He called three days later, and we have a meeting scheduled at his gallery for tomorrow at four."

"Everything will check out with you, Henri, as it always does. Shall we drink to continued success?"

"By all means let's drink to success."

They touched glasses as Henri smiled and said, "Au succès continu et aux plaisirs de la vengeance." (To continued success and the pleasures of revenge)

Raphael echoed his sentiments with "A la vengeance." (To revenge)

Chapter 6

Her law firm partners were shocked at her sudden decision to quit. Matthews, one of the senior partners, tried to persuade her to stay. "If it's a matter of money, Kathy, we are certainly open to discussion."

Their attempts, while sincere, were futile. Kathy Longrin had made up her mind. After packing her personal items, including several cherished law books, she proceeded to the office of the senior managing partner, Stanley Randolph Higgins, Esquire.

As the secretary held the door open, she walked toward a man in his late sixties whose once ramrod straight body had now assumed a slightly bent appearance.

She remembered that it was this man who recruited her from law school stating that she was the only one of interest in the entire class.

"I want to thank you Mr. Higgins, for giving me the opportunity to work at this esteemed firm. Your trust in me is appreciated and I hope my performance justified that trust during these past five years."

The elderly jurist smiled and came around to the front of his desk. "Your performance was stellar. We are sorry to lose you, and I am especially saddened by your decision. Should you ever change your mind or need counsel in any way, please do not hesitate to contact me."

He fingered what appeared to be a gold miniature medal, which dangled from the heavy gold watch chain. Then he took out a business card from his vest pocket and handed it to her.

"On the back is a number which can connect to me day or night, seven days a week. Good luck Kathy. By the way, are you at liberty to tell me where you're going?"

"I'm not sure myself, Mr. Higgins."

He turned away, went to his desk and then looked back at Kathy who stood in place for a moment longer.

Then she walked out and closed the door quietly behind her.

Kathy stopped at the desk of Higgin's secretary. "I'll arrange for someone to pick up the boxes in the morning."

Then she went to the elevator bank. As she waited a feeling of sadness overtook her. Once in the elevator, she began to wonder whether she did the right thing. Wasn't a bird in the hand worth two in the bush? Well, it no longer matters, does it?

Her body had an unusual lightness to it. She decided it was a momentary thing and traceable to leaving a secure position for the unknown. She felt like a drink, but it was too early in the day.

Kathy decided on a cup of coffee and thought about the shop around the corner from her office where she was a regular.

Kathy took a seat at the counter.

The owner, an elderly Jewish man with a heavy accent, walked over.

"What, no takeout, Kathy? You have time today? What happened, you lose your job?" Then he chuckled.

"Not exactly, Oscar, but you're close."

"What will it be? We have some lean corned beef. I recommend it."

"Thanks, Oscar, but I'll just have coffee, black and in a big mug please."

In a few moments, the owner had placed a steaming cup of coffee in front of Kathy. He also held a plate with two croissants and jelly.

"These are on me. They're made from multi-grains. The jelly contains no sugar, it's all natural. Try them, you'll like them."

As the man stood quietly holding the plate and waiting for her to say yes or no, she once again saw the A54668, the faded bluish tattoo on the inside of his left arm. While intrigued, Kathy wasn't sure what the tattoo stood for and couldn't bring herself to ask.

She smiled up at the round face. "Sure, Oscar, I'd love to try them."

Kathy finished her coffee and one of the croissants, then placed a five-dollar bill next to her plate. She pointed to the counter and waved to Oscar on the way out.

She hailed a taxi and slid into the back seat, her briefcase placed on her lap.

"Where to, Lady?"

Kathy hadn't looked at the paper since she placed it in her purse the evening before. "One moment, driver."

She moved the contents of her purse around until she found the paper. She opened it and looked at the address. "I want to go to 47th Street and the Avenue of the Americas."

The driver pushed down the flag on the cab's meter and maneuvered into the heavy morning traffic.

On this island, taxi rides were always the same. They passed the same types of people, the same buildings and got snarled in the same traffic patterns, all of which made up the mosaic that was New York City each and every day.

She stared out the window as she had during countless other taxi rides, lost in thought as the cab negotiated its way to the East River Drive, and up to midtown Manhattan.

Her office near Battery Park was now a fleeting memory. She couldn't help wondering however, why she reacted on impulse rather than the controlled systematic methodology she crafted so skillfully when she represented her clients. Was she any less important?

The cab pulled to the curb.

"This is it lady, eight dollars and thirty-five cents."

Kathy placed a ten-dollar bill in the cup-like contraption that was attached to the plexiglass separating the driver's compartment from the rear seating area.

"Keep the change," and she slid across the seat and out.

The heavy cab door closed with a resounding smack drawing a disgusted look from the driver. She mouthed the word sorry, then stepped onto the curb.

She brushed her skirt and once again looked at the paper she held in her hand. Kathy crossed to the other side of the street and looked at her watch. She was about thirty minutes early and decided to window shop.

The jewelry stores that lined the street were numerous and engaging. As she moved from one window display to another, Kathy wondered if anyone really knew how many retail stores, and diamond trading companies existed in this one block radius.

She laughed at the thought passing through her mind at that instant. With all this glitter, sunglasses should be mandatory.

The stores that fronted the sidewalk on both sides of 47th Street contained an overabundance of diamonds, gold, precious and semi-precious stones, all imaginatively positioned to attract the passerby.

Several alleyways intersected the main street and contained what she assumed were additional retail stores and wholesalers.

She remembered reading somewhere that millions of diamonds were traded here every day. She could well imagine how true this was, based on what she saw displayed.

A glance at her watch indicated that she had another ten minutes to go. She liked to be punctual, it was an ingrained habit, so she crossed the street, and walked at a quickened pace toward the address.

Just short of reaching the door, several black-clad Hasidic men entered. If they saw her, they gave no indication and let the door close behind them.

Kathy pushed the door open and saw a large expanse consisting of numerous companies, their owners and employees manning cubicles or display cases. Signs indicating the name of the various firms hung by wires attached to the ceiling above the positioned merchants. It was a kaleidoscope of activity.

Once through the door, she stopped by the first cubicle. A young man with a black skullcap on his head smiled at her.

"Hello. Are you interested in anything particular? We have loose stones as well as mounted ones."

"I'm looking for 977 West 47th Street."

"This is it."

"Where can I find Suite 230?"

"The elevator is about mid-way against the left wall," and he pointed.

Kathy turned and looked in that direction. "Thanks," and started walking.

The man called after her, "When you finish your business, stop back. I'd like to show you several pieces that were created for someone like you."

Kathy maneuvered around the cramped spaces and politely fended off calls to stop. As she waited for the small elevator, she remembered seeing an old movie not too long ago, starring a singer by the name of Tony Martin.

While she couldn't recall the name, the picture had to do with Algeria and a marketplace called The Casbah. This place seemed to duplicate it, at least as far as the noise and activity was concerned, although the merchandise here was considerably higher quality.

The elevator door opened and Kathy stepped in. As she leaned against the back, she watched several Hasidic men enter together with a rather good looking man dressed in a finely tailored tan suit.

She wondered what awaited her in Suite 230.

Chapter 7

The Hasidic men moved quickly out of the elevator when it reached the second level.

Then the man in the tan suit placed his hand against the elevator's frame to prevent the door from closing, as he nodded to Kathy.

Kathy smiled, but said nothing. She took several steps into the hallway, stopped, and looked at the sign on the wall. Room 230 was to her right.

As she reached to open the door, she felt a presence behind her. She turned and saw the man in the tan suit.

"Are you following me?"

"That depends on where you're going."

Kathy tried the door handle again, but the locking mechanism wouldn't yield.

"You have to press the button on the right side of the door frame."

Kathy pressed the black button, waited for the release click and then pushed the door open. As she walked into the office, the man followed. When she stopped at the reception desk, the man continued past her.

The secretary called out, "Good afternoon Mr. Bertrand," then turned to the woman standing in front of her. "May I help you?"

"Yes. I am Kathy Longrin and I have an appointment with Mr. Duchant."

"Please have a seat. I'll inform Mr. Duchant."

Kathy decided on a leather chair in the corner. She crossed her legs and looked around the reception area. It was ornate. The wall was paneled in some exotic wood. There were two paintings, exquisitely framed, hanging on two of the walls. She recognized one immediately as Andy Warhol's Marilyn Monroe and the other seemed to be by Frank Stella.

Her gaze was interrupted by the voice of Raphael Duchant. "Hello again, Kathy, would you be so kind as to follow me."

Before she could respond, Duchant turned and walked toward a door. As he reached it, Kathy heard the lock disengage and watched as the door opened quickly. She noticed there was no door handle on her side.

She followed Duchant past two men who were posted on either side of the door, both armed with what looked to her like submachine guns.

The room was vast and open with tables arranged in a very definite pattern. White-coated men and women were examining diamonds on each of the tables.

Overhead were a number of halogen lights illuminating everything below and a number of black glass pods, that indicated surveillance cameras.

There were several other armed men strategically placed around the floor.

Duchant acknowledged several people as he passed en route to a stairway. They climbed the ten steps to a small landing.

Duchant kept his back to Kathy as he pressed the combination buttons on the doorframe. After the sequence was complete the door swung open. Kathy again noticed there were no door handles on the outside.

She followed Duchant into a well-appointed large office and conference room combination.

Decorating one wall of the office were a bank of TV screens which showed images of the floor below, the reception area, the hallways, the elevators, the main street level floor, the street front, rear, and the roof of the building. The pictures seemed to change every ten or so seconds.

In front of the screens was a large console-type desk occupied by two men. Their weapons were placed above and besides their individual control panels. They neither turned around nor were they introduced to Kathy.

On the conference room wall were several paintings. She particularly liked the Jackson Pollock. His Autumn Rhythm evoked a number of positive sensations.

Seated at the conference room table was the man from the elevator, the man in the tan suit.

He got up as they approached. Duchant began the introduction.

"Miss Kathy Longrin, this is Mr. Henri Bertrand."

Turning for a moment to Duchant, he said, "Miss Longrin and I have met, although we have not been formally introduced." He then extended his hand. "It is a pleasure to meet you, Miss Longrin."

As Duchant motioned to both of them to be seated, there was a knock on the conference room door. Duchant looked at a screen built into the conference table, then moved his hand beneath it. In a moment a man was standing at the open-door entrance. "Will you please excuse me for a moment."

Duchant and the man walked to the office area and disappeared.

Bertrand smiled at Kathy. She stared back at him with indifference. Then he asked, "Are you in the diamond trade, Miss Longrin?"

The question was moot. Kathy felt Bertrand already knew about her. Let's see if I can push the envelope a bit.

"No, Mr. Bertrand, as you know I'm an attorney, the specifics of which were already related to you by Mr. Duchant. Is there anything in my background that interests or confuses you?"

Kathy thought, if I hit a homer, Bertrand isn't giving me the satisfaction.

He reached into his jacket pocket and pulled out a pack of French Balto cigarettes. "Do you smoke, Miss Longrin?"

"No thank you."

"Do you mind if I do? I know it's a nasty habit, but I do enjoy it."

"Suit yourself."

Kathy watched as he lit the cigarette with a gold lighter. He left both on the table.

"I understand that lawyers never ask a question or make a statement unless they know the answer for certain. Can you be certain that Mr. Duchant and I know each other well enough to assume that he has told me anything about you?"

"Absolutely, it's called body language. I am a woman, besides an attorney. Both have a direct bearing on what I am, and how I do what I do."

He smiled, looked up at the ceiling and began talking as if he were addressing no one in particular.

"A diamond is probably the oldest thing a person can own. Give or take, it's about three billion years old. It's formed in the earth's interior and shot to the surface by extraordinary, violent volcanoes. Just below such volcanoes, is a carrot-shaped pipe filled with volcanic rock, mantle fragments and some embedded diamonds. Magmas are the elevators that bring the diamonds to the earth surface. Diamonds are not only a girl's best friend, they are mine as well."

"Forty-seventh Street, New York, is a very interesting area. It consists of about twenty-six hundred establishments engaged in some form of the diamond trade. The United States is the largest importer of diamonds in the world and ninety percent of those pass through 47th Street."

He took a long pull on the cigarette, tilted his head to the right and blew out the smoke from his nose and mouth. Then he looked directly at Kathy.

Kathy clapped her hands. "Well done. Do your students consider you a good teacher?"

"I'm not a teacher, Miss Longrin."

"Well then, why are you lecturing me?"

"No, no, Miss Longrin, I'm educating you," and then he laughed.

Kathy sat quietly watching the man bring himself back to whatever it was that he considered normal. He reached into his pocket and took out what looked like a folded piece of paper. He carefully undid the paper, which was folded and refolded in a geometric pattern. Then he placed the open paper on the table and gently pushed it toward her.

"And what, Kathy Longrin, would you be willing to do for these?"

Kathy looked down at eight loose diamonds, each exceeding three carats in weight. Their brilliance dazzled and she had to admit to herself that they were beautiful. She wondered indeed what she would do for these.

Then she looked back at Bertrand and asked, "What did you have in mind?"

They both laughed.

Chapter 8

Duchant escorted the visitor to the door and watched as he left. Then he turned and walked toward the conference area when he heard the laughter.

"If it was a good joke, I'd like to hear it."

"I think Mr. Bertrand was testing my virtue."

Bertrand smiled. "No, I think it was more a test of wills."

"You're both confusing me..." and then he saw the open paper containing the diamonds. "Are these the ones you spoke about, Henri?"

"Yes, one and the same, or should I say eight, and the same."

Duchant reached around Kathy and picked one up. He took a loupe from his pocket and placed it to his right eye. He studied the stone for several minutes before he spoke.

"It's magnificent...round brilliant. The clarity is top notch, I'd grade this stone as VVS1. It's a D or E in color. Are the others like this?"

"Yes."

"Where did they come from?"

"Suriname via Liberia, war diamonds. I love the terms these politically correct schmucks (Akin to stupid) come up with. If the powers that be want to use diamonds to finance terrorism, revolutions, war, and insurrection, let them do it and in the process kill themselves. They'll be less of them for us to worry about."

Duchant chuckled. "Well at least the Sparrow is consistent with supplying us with merchandise. He's becoming a primary source."

He brought the loupe down and handed both the diamond and the loupe to Kathy. "Take a look."

She repeated what she saw Duchant do and looked through the glass. "What am I looking for?"

"Imperfections, or as the trade terms it, inclusions or blemishes."

"I don't see any, but then again, I'm not a trained gemologist."

"Nicely put, Kathy. Most people don't have the knowledge to use a loupe or what to look for in a diamond. A trained gemologist will use a ten-power binocular microscope after the diamond has been properly cleaned. It would be examined in overhead white light against a dark background. The size, number, location, color, and nature of the inclusions and blemishes are considered when assigning a clarity grade, which varies from FL or Flawless to I 3 where the inclusions are easy to see with the naked eye. Those diamonds look smokey or milky."

"Thanks for the education. Does the imparted knowledge mean that I get to keep one of the diamonds?"

They both laughed. "In time perhaps, but that depends on you, which brings us to the purpose of this meeting."

"At four p.m. today, Henri will be meeting someone to discuss the purchase of several specific paintings. I would like you to accompany him. The so-called poor man's education on diamonds, was to enable you to rudimentarily discuss the subject should you find it necessary."

"We will have some lunch here, then you two will be on your way. Over lunch we will give you some specifics on the painting we are trying to acquire."

The door buzzed again and Duchant looked at the screen. He opened the door as he had previously and after a few moments, two women in black approached.

They placed gold-rimmed plates and silverware, together with several sets of various cut crystal glasses, in front of each of them.

Then one of the women set down a large platter of fish in cream sauce, the way the French prepare it. The side dishes held asparagus in hollandaise sauce and roasted potatoes with a slight tinge of garlic. The wine was a Puligny-Montrachet, primer Cru "Les Folatieres," 1974.

Kathy took it all in.

One of the women poured a small amount of wine into Duchant's glass. He picked it up and looked at it carefully. He sniffed it and then brought it to his lips taking a small amount into his mouth. She watched as his Adam's apple bobbed when he swallowed.

Duchant looked up and nodded.

The woman refilled his glass, then did the same for Kathy and then Bertrand. Then the woman placed the wine bottle in an ice bucket and waited several moments.

Determining there were no further instructions, she left the room with the other woman following closely behind.

Henri lifted his glass and said, "Welcome, Miss Longrin."

Duchant smiled and Kathy said, "Thank you."

Bertrand passed the platter toward Kathy.

"The paintings we will discuss Miss Longrin, will be Cassatt's Woman in Black (Femme en noir) and Cezanne's Still Life with Plaster Cupid."

"We have reason to believe that this individual has knowledge of their whereabouts. Both paintings were part of the Duchant family collection. Once we can ascertain that they do still exist, and our information suggests strongly they do, we will begin negotiations to recover them."

Kathy felt her heart pound and her throat go dry. She wondered if her facial expression revealed how thunderstruck she was at that moment. Hearing the name of one the paintings had seriously unnerved her. She tightened her hands into a fist as they rested on her lap and willed herself to remain calm.

"Now let's enjoy our lunch. Business and pleasure never mix, and this is one of those pleasurable times. Bon appetit, Miss Longrin."

Duchant repeated the toast.

She tried to concentrate on the food, but she couldn't stop herself from thinking about the two paintings. She could recall one of them in minute detail, as she had seen it often.

She saw it as clearly as she saw the food before her. It was hanging on one of the whitewashed walls, in an antique, intricately carved frame that was several hundred years old.

Like so many others, it was prominently displayed in that special room at her father's house.

Chapter 9

The Rolls Royce stopped in the eighties off Madison Avenue and discharged its two passengers. They walked the several steps to the door of the three-story townhouse. The small brass plate to the right of the door indicated that the Hecht Gallery was located on the third floor. Bertrand pressed the bell and the door clicked open.

Bertrand held the outer door open and then followed Kathy into the well-lit, narrow hallway. He stopped slightly to her rear, in front of the single elevator door. The light above the elevator dial indicated that the cab was parked on the third floor. Kathy pushed the down button and watched the arrow dial move to L.

In a few moments, the elevator's door opened and they both stepped in. Kathy noticed, with some surprise, that the panel had only two buttons, reading 3 and L. Then her eyes moved to the two key locks located above the panel.

She started to say something to Bertrand and then stopped.

As the elevator started up, she leaned back against the wall and again willed herself to relax.

The elevator moved silently to the third floor and stopped. When the elevator's door opened, they were facing another door.

Kathy pressed the solitary button and the door lock disengaged.

They entered a large open space. Numerous paintings were hung on the walls, while others were displayed on easels.

The entire left side of the gallery consisted of floor to ceiling windows that flooded the area with light. In the far-right hand corner was a seating area with a plush leather sofa and several leather club chairs. A coffee table made of wrought iron with a crackled glass top was positioned in-between the chairs.

Off to the right was a wooden table with four chairs. The table was covered with art books and catalogs of upcoming art sales and auctions. There was a large parcel wrapped in brown paper and tied with hemp, taking up the center.

Bertrand stood fixed momentarily until he saw the man heading his way. He waved, placed his hand on Kathy's elbow and nudged her slightly forward.

She didn't like being touched that way and held back until Bertrand dropped his hand. She waited in place as he moved forward to meet the man. After they shook hands, Bertrand turned to her.

"Kathy," and he motioned her to come over to where he was standing, "This is Manfred von Hoenshield. He is the gallery owner."

Kathy extended her hand and von Hoenshield took it firmly, bowed slightly and clicked his heels. Although he smiled, the way he looked at her made her uncomfortable.

"While I was expecting only Mr. Bertrand, you are a very welcomed surprise."

Turning back to Bertrand, but still holding onto Kathy's hand, von Hoenshield asked, "Is this the individual you represent?"

"No, she is an associate of mine who will take care of the legal aspects of the various pieces of art my retainer expects to acquire."

Kathy gently pulled her hand away from von Hoenshield's grip, causing the gallery owner to look back at her. When their eyes met again, she felt the same uneasiness.

"Please follow me."

As they walked, von Hoenshield paused at several paintings and inquired of Bertrand whether these up and coming artists might be of interest.

Bertrand's reply was always the same, give or take a word or two. "Perhaps, Mr. von Hoenshield, but my principal wants to initially concentrate on the acquisition of several more prominent works of art."

"Certainly, Mr. Bertrand, I understand."

Kathy, trailing at the rear of the two men, watched with interest as the owner walked in a cadence that had a distinct military bearing. So utterly Germanic, she thought. Although his gray and whitish hair clearly indicated his age well beyond recent military service, his background certainly had a military connection that carried through to the present.

They seated themselves around the coffee table with Bertrand and Kathy taking up the sofa, and von Hoenshield seating himself in one of the club chairs.

"May I offer you some wine or champagne? Perhaps some espresso?" Bertrand looked at Kathy who shook her head no.

Bertrand replied, "Let's wait until the conclusion of our business, Mr. von Hoenshield."

Von Hoenshield nodded, rubbed his hands together and leaned back into the club chair. He again looked at Kathy. "Are you a native New Yorker, Miss Longrin?"

"No. I'm from Illinois."

"Ah, a mid-western woman. How mobile you Americans are."

"It's a big country, Mr. von Hoenshield, but the center is New York."

He looked perplexed for a moment and then laughed. "How correct you are."

Kathy wasn't sure whether his confirmation was with regard to her comment about the mobility of Americans, or that New York was the center of the country, or both. She said to herself, who cares, smiled back and waited.

"I know you speak French and English, Mr. Bertrand, but I neglected to ask you during our first meeting if you also speak German?"

"Yes Mr. von Hoenshield, "Ich spreche Deutsches." (I speak German)

"And you, Miss Longrin, does your expertise transcend to languages?"

Kathy thought quickly whether she should reveal that she spoke German fluently. She tried to determine whether there was any advantage to saying that she did as opposed to saying she didn't. She decided to tell the truth.

"Ja Herr von Hoenshield, ich spreche Deutsches. (Yes, Mr. von Hoenshield, I speak German) I was raised by a nanny who spoke only German to me."

"While my English has improved over these many years, if it's alright with you I will speak in both languages. Now, Mr. Bertrand, you mentioned two paintings your client wishes to acquire. Since our last meeting I have contacted several associates of mine who confirm that these two paintings were destroyed during the war."

"Let's suppose for a moment, Manfred, that these two paintings do exist. My interested party is willing to pay handsomely for them at today's market price. I am empowered to offer currency of the seller's choice deposited anywhere in the world, or an exchange for a precious commodity such as these, or a combination of both."

Bertrand reached into his pocket and removed the paper envelope. He slowly and ritually unfolded the geometric pattern and placed it on the glass surface. The eight diamonds sparkled in the brightly lit room. Bertrand took out a loupe and placed it next to the diamonds.

Von Hoenshield reached for the loupe, then proceeded to study one, then another of the diamonds. After a few moments of concentration, he placed the loupe down.

"They seem to be of excellent quality. How would you grade them, Miss Longrin?"

Without hesitation Kathy answered, "I would grade these as VVSI. They're D or E in clarity. These diamonds would make an ugly woman look beautiful."

Both men erupted in laughter almost simultaneously. Von Hoenshield said, "I couldn't have put it better in any language." Then he laughed again.

"I am interested in trying to accommodate your client, Mr. Bertrand. I will require more time. I will contact you by the end of this week regarding my progress. Is that satisfactory for you?"

"Yes."

"So that your visit here is not considered unfruitful, I have something that may interest your principal."

Von Hoenshield excused himself and walked toward the table. He moved one of the chairs, then picked up the brown paper-wrapped parcel with both hands and walked back.

"Please take this to your principal. It's on loan to him. If he wishes to acquire it, arrangements can be made. Thank you both for coming and I look forward to seeing you again. Auf Wiedersehen." (Goodbye)

Chapter 10

Bertrand carried the paper-wrapped item past the office area and went directly to the conference table where he gently placed it down. He kept his back to Duchant and Kathy as he began to remove the wrapping paper.

Both Duchant and Kathy moved to their right and watched as he peeled back the paper.

"It's a piece of artwork for sure. Let's see what our esteemed gallery owner has loaned us."

As Bertrand lifted the paper covering, Duchant and Kathy moved closer. It was a framed drawing. "I'm not sure I recognize the artist," then Bertrand turned around.

"Do either of you know?"

Duchant moved closer. "Could be a Gustave Caillebotte."

Kathy shook her head. "It's not a Caillebotte. It's by Georges Seurat and drawn in black Conte crayons on Ingres paper. See here," and Kathy pointed to the lower part of the drawing, "he built up the tonal graduations in his drawing by varying the pressure and the density of the criss-crossed marks. And here, here, and there, the white of the paper glows through giving the sensation of light emanating from the painting itself, all of which is characteristic in Seurat's small oil paintings and drawings."

"Would anyone be interested in a cocktail while we ponder what Mr. von Hoenshield intended?"

"If it's all the same to both of you, I've had a long day and I need to repair back to a place I call home. I think I can ponder better there."

Duchant smiled, "If you must, Kathy, but this now makes two rain checks."

She smiled back. "I promise, the next invitation will be accepted. I'll see you both tomorrow. By the way, I'm an early riser and like to get into work early. Will someone be here to buzz me in?"

"Absolutely." Duchant paused for a moment. "Your photograph and eye prints are already recorded in our database. Just touch the buzzer, and stare straight ahead at the door, about eye level where the small black glass is situated."

"I'll see you both tomorrow."

Kathy walked out of the conference area, past the monitors, and toward the office door, which buzzed as she came within several paces of it.

She remembered that the door swung inward, so she took several steps back and watched the door swing open to its complete arc.

She stepped out onto a metal platform and heard the door click behind her. She turned, stared at the door and saw the small round black glass, which Duchant mentioned. She wondered why she hadn't noticed it before. Then she took hold of the railing and started down the ten steps to the main floor.

She noticed that one of the armed men paralleled her movements from the time she stepped onto the main floor until she reached the main entrance. He held back as she walked out the door.

*

"How did she interact with the Hauptsturmfurer?"

"Fine, Raphael. She parroted what she heard about the diamonds. She's a quick study. The way von Hoenshield eyed her, it was evident that he was having a hard time deciding what he wanted more, the diamonds or her, and while we're on the subject, our Miss Longrin is fluent in German. She admitted it to von Hoenshield stating that her nanny only spoke German to her. She neglected to mention anything about her father."

"She's a lawyer and as such, she wouldn't reveal anything that isn't necessary. Why bring her father into it? What do you make of the drawing?"

"It's stolen art, Raphael, his way of telling us that what we want is available. We can make inquiries to confirm this, but it's probably a waste of time. The question we have to decide is whether we buy this to show our purchasing power and intent, or do we hold out for the Cassatt and Cezanne?"

"I suggest we hold out for the other two. If we buy this one, we'll be flooded with additional stolen minor works and these won't lead us to the big-ticket items and their sellers."

"Von Hoenshield indicated he'd call me by the end of the week. He restated that he believed the paintings were destroyed during the war, but he'd check further."

"When von Hoenshield calls you, Henri, suggest dinner. The cache of stolen art is well protected. It's been that way since the war ended. We need to force a crack in that protective wall and von Hoenshield is the hammer and our Miss Longrin our wedge."

Chapter 11

Kathy kicked off her shoes as she entered her apartment. She dropped the mail on the table and went to the Chinese console that she used as a bar and liquor cabinet.

She reached for the Johnny Walker Red Scotch bottle, a short glass, and then walked to the refrigerator. She took three ice cubes, poured two fingers worth of scotch, and then walked back to the sofa. She put the glass down on the coffee table, plopped into the sofa, and leaned her head back. She breathed deeply and then let out the air.

Then she got up, unzipped the back of her dress, and stepped out of it. She folded it once and placed it across the arm of the sofa, then sat back down. Dressed only in bikini panties and bra, she picked up the scotch and took a long sip, coughing slightly as she swallowed.

She wondered whether it was prudent to have revealed her knowledge of German. If Duchant was as thorough as she suspected he was, any background investigation would reveal this. Besides, what was the harm in speaking another language? It was something that most second-generation Americans were incapable of doing.

Kathy wondered about the relationship between Duchant and Bertrand. The explanation that they were associates would have to do for the present, but there was something else in the equation. Something that went beyond mere associates. It had gnawed at her since the introduction. Although the obvious linkage was diamonds and art, it appeared to her that Bertrand was far more the confidant than the employee.

She took another sip of the scotch. There was no doubt that Duchant was in charge. They were both sophisticated and well-schooled. Their appearance and manner conveyed this, but Duchant's image was one of unquestioned wealth.

Others were rich and she herself had grown up with money and interacted in those circles as an attorney, but these two were of a different bent, a different plateau altogether.

She closed her eyes and let her mind continue to wander. She felt queasy when her thoughts drifted back to von Hoenshield. He reminded her of the visitors that came to her father's home during her childhood and teenage years. They occasionally came in two's but mostly alone. They seemed stern, military in their bearing and devoid of sincere feelings despite their attempts at pleasantries with her.

The visitors always treated her father with the utmost respect. She marveled at this and often wondered what he had done to garner this adoration. He was always evasive whenever she asked.

She remembered the many long summer afternoons alone, when her father and his visitors walked into the woods and disappeared for hours. She was never invited along and the nanny, Gerta, always rebuked her when she persisted.

When the visitors came, she had her meals with Gerta. While the woman was kind to her, she was a difficult taskmaster. Her father always dined alone with his visitors. She was never invited to join them, and her requests were always denied when she asked.

In many ways, her childhood was lonely but when she and her father did interact, it was with a total commitment. There was no doubt that he loved her. That was made evident by the devotion he showered upon her throughout her growing years.

She was told her mother had died during the war and at the conclusion of hostilities, she, her father, Gerta, and Udo, the chauffeur, immigrated as refugees to America.

He often spoke to her about his own family, telling stories of growing up in Bavaria, in southern Germany, where his family farmed for several hundred years.

He spoke of the land, which he said was confiscated by the allies at the end of the war. He offered no further explanation regarding the expropriation of his family's property and even after she became a lawyer, offering to litigate the return for him, he wouldn't agree. He would always say, here is my life now. The past has nothing to offer.

When he came to America, he sought out a farming community to start over again. He decided to settle in Carthage, Illinois where he purchased a small plot initially. Then he added more and more land as it became available and as his circumstances improved.

Their farm, which now covered about a thousand acres, grew soybeans, corn, and raised cattle on one quarter of the land. The workers were both seasonal and resident. The manager and work bosses were all German speaking and lived in the nearby town.

She smiled as she thought of her childhood as her father's only daughter, his only child. Then she opened her eyes, stood up, and walked to the small antique French desk.

She picked up the silver frame containing a slightly yellowing picture, which showed a man and woman looking endearingly at each other. The inscription at the bottom read, Berliner Stadtmauer – May 1936. The picture was taken at the 14th Century Berlin Wall, the original Berlin Wall. She had been there once when she toured Europe after graduation from college.

As she placed the picture back on the desk, she wondered if she would ever find a man as loving as her father.

Chapter 12

Dinner was at L'Endroit De Reunion (The Meeting Place) in Greenwich Village. Duchant and Bertrand were at the bar when Kathy strolled in.

"She cuts a nice figure, Henri."

Keeping his eyes fixed on the woman he replied, "Yes, she does indeed," then got off the barstool and walked toward her. He checked her coat, and then they walked back to where Raphael was seated.

"Good evening, Miss Longrin. You look lovely."

Before she had a chance to reply, he turned toward the bartender. "Claude, vous feriez apporter nos boissons a la table." (Claude, would you kindly have our drinks brought to the table)

"Shall we, Miss Longrin," and he started walking toward the dining room.

At the entrance, Raphael was greeted by the maitre d'. "I have your table reserved, Mr. Duchant. Please follow me."

They walked down the three stairs and onto the main dining floor. The tables that lined both walls were discreetly placed and separated sufficiently to allow for intimate conversation.

The center of the room was open, unencumbered by tables, which eliminated the claustrophobic feeling that diners usually get from most restaurants.

All the waiters were attired in tuxedos, with the maitre d' in tails. The restaurant exuded ambience and the clientele projected New York's monied elite.

On the walls hung a number of vintage antique French posters depicting liquor, aperitifs, cigarettes, and cigarette paper. Among the artists represented were Cappiello, Henri de Toulouse Lautrec, Jules Cheret, and Georges Meunier.

After they were seated, the maitre d' signaled to a waiter who was standing off to one side.

After the waiter set their unfinished drinks in front of the two men, the maitre d' looked at Duchant, then Bertrand, and said, "Gentlemen, appreciez votre diner," (Enjoy your dinner) then left.

Raphael was seated to the right of Kathy. He turned slightly as he picked up his glass.

"We are one ahead of you, Miss Longrin. Shall I order you a double scotch?"

"No thank you, I have a feeling that this might be a long evening. I need to start slow." She smiled. "A single scotch will be fine."

"It's Johnny Walker Red, am I correct?"

"Yes, Johnny Red, please."

Raphael looked up at the waiter, who was patiently standing several steps away. "We'll have two more of the same. Claude knows what we're drinking and a Johnny Walker Red for the lady, short glass, three ice cubes, and a twist of lemon."

Raphael smiled and Kathy wondered how he could have known so precisely. I wonder if they know I'm wearing a string bikini and no bra. The bra part would be easy. Then she smiled.

"A thought you'd care to share with us, Miss Longrin?"

"Oh, you mean the smile. Were you staring?"

Before either could answer, she continued.

"Sure, I'll share my thoughts with you since you were right on the mark regarding the scotch, and how I drink it. I was thinking about whether you also knew what lingerie I was wearing."

Both men smiled. Henri asked, "How many guesses do we get?"

"Men as astute as you and Raphael seem to be should only need one guess," then Kathy smiled again.

The drinks arrived, and they waited until the waiter left before resuming.

Raphael picked up the conversation.

"Perhaps we should table our answer, Kathy, until a more suitable occasion presents itself. Our friend, Manfred von Hoenshield should arrive any minute. Germans like to be punctual, so let's review the game plan. Henri will introduce me as the man who controls the diamonds. We let von Hoenshield lead from there. Based on whether the news regarding the paintings is positive or negative, we'll react accordingly. Let's see if we can make some progress."

As they were finishing their drink, von Hoenshield walked briskly up to the maitre d', started to say something, then saw Bertrand and started walking directly to the table with a somewhat startled maitre d' trailing behind.

Duchant and Bertrand stood as von Hoenshield approached the table. Von Hoenshield went directly to Henri first, shook his hand, then leaned over and took Kathy's hand, brought it up to his lips and kissed the back.

Kathy tilted her head slightly and smiled. "Wei tapferer Herr von Hoenshield." (How gallant Mr. von Hoenshield)

Von Hoenshield bowed a little lower, clicked his heels slightly while still maintaining eye contact with Kathy. "It is the only way a gentleman greets a beautiful woman."

"How kind."

Henri interjected, "Allow me to introduce Mr. Raphael La Monde. Raphael is captivated by diamonds."

Raphael held out his hand. After they disengaged, the maitre d'quickly pulled out the chair next to Kathy, and von Hoenshield sat down.

Then the maitre d' turned and signaled the waiter. The waiter leaned toward von Hoenshield and asked, "Your pleasure, Sir?"

He looked toward Kathy and then a smile appeared. He turned back to the waiter, "I'll have Chevas Regal, no ice."

The waiter turned and left. In moments he was back and placed the drink in front of von Hoenshield.

Bertrand picked up his glass. "Perhaps Manfred, you'd care to propose a toast."

The German took his eyes away from Kathy and looked toward Bertrand. "Yes, I would like to make one."

He lifted his glass and turned back toward Kathy.

"Zu freundschaft." (To friendship)

Kathy touched her glass to his, then von Hoenshield looked at Duchant and Bertrand, lifted his glass a little higher and said, "Prost." (Cheers)

The German took a long swallow and placed the glass down a little too hard. He smiled more in amusement than in self-consciousness. Then he placed his elbows on the table and leaned into the center. "I'm sorry Mr. La Monde, it was rude of me to speak in German without first asking whether you understood the language."

"Unfortunately, I do not. I'm limited to French and English."

"In that case may I suggest we keep the conversation limited to English. By the way, are you also captivated by the masters as well as diamonds, Mr. La Monde?"

"I have a passing curiosity, but I prefer diamonds."

"Then you must allow me to introduce you to the masters. They are as lovely as diamonds and unique since there are so few of them."

He turned to Bertrand. "May I have another drink."

Bertrand motioned to the waiter and pointed to von Hoenshield's glass. After the drink arrived, Bertrand told the waiter he'd signal when they were ready to order.

The German took a smaller sip this time, then turned toward Bertrand and said, "I have some good news." Then he looked at Raphael and back to Bertrand.

"Raphael is one of us. Anything you state here, stays here. There is too much at stake to become careless with information, or people."

Von Hoenshield smiled, looked at Kathy who smiled back and then said, "Good. What you have just said is the way our business dealings should proceed. We should never become compromised."

He seemed to lean further into the table, and it appeared as if his head lowered a bit.

"I have made contact with several individual dealers of shall we say, lost art. They have indicated to me that one of the items you mentioned, the Mary one, might still be in existence."

The German paused and looked at each of their faces. They remained expressionless, so he continued. "If it can be confirmed that Mary exists, what would you be willing to offer as an inducement to the possessor to part with it?"

Henri responded quickly, "Eight million US."

"Absurd, absolut sinnlos." (Absolutely pointless)

"Why is it absurd, Manfred, the painting can never be sold in the open market. The art world can never know that it exists since litigation would be instituted to have the work returned to its rightful owner or owners. It's basically worthless unless another private buyer is willing to assume the risk that goes with its possession. It's only value is to someone who will add it to his collection and enjoy it in solitude. My principal is such a buyer, and his offer is very generous."

"My dear Henri, if Mary can be confirmed as authentic, we must induce the owner to give it up. We are coming to him, not the reverse. Therefore, we must make it, "Wert seins wahrend." How do you say that in English? I apologize to you, Mr. La Monde, for reverting to German. My command of English is at times lacking."

Kathy replied, "Worth his while."

"Yes, exactly my dear, worth his while. Thank you. Eight million for a work that could command twice, maybe three times that, will not persuade the owner that you are serious."

"Then perhaps we should meet the owner."

The German stared at Raphael as if he had spoken blasphemy. Then he laughed.

"That's impossible at this stage and perhaps never. As we agreed at the outset tonight, we must exercise care and avoid compromise."

Von Hoenshield turned away from Duchant and looked at Henri.

Henri locked eyes with von Hoenshield and said, "We are very serious Manfred," and then he looked back at Raphael.

Duchant brought out a small gray velvet bag with a drawstring top and placed it on the table.

Then he pushed it toward von Hoenshield, who picked it up with one hand, and opened the drawstring with the other.

He spread the top, looked in and let out a soft purr. He replaced the velvet pouch on the table and rolled the edges down until the loose diamonds were visible. "How much is here?"

Raphael leaned forward. "Roughly eight million, give or take a few hundred thousand."

Then Raphael reached into his jacket pocket, and brought out an ostrich billfold, took out a check, placed it on the table, and moved it toward the German.

Manfred picked up the check and looked at it. "This is a cashier's check for eight million dollars," saying it more to himself than the others.

Von Hoenshield sat quietly as Kathy looked at Duchant and then said, "I need to speak to Manfred in German. Please excuse me for excluding you."

Duchant motioned his head slightly in a nod of understanding and then Kathy began to speak, as Raphael feigned boredom while understanding every word she spoke.

"Manfred, as you can see, we are very serious. Now you must demonstrate that you are also. We would like to meet with the owner of the Mary."

Silence engulfed the table. No one spoke until von Hoenshield whispered, "I will see what I can do."

Chapter 13

Several weeks passed without any type of communication from von Hoenshield. Kathy was kept busy interacting with several European lawyers on retainer to Duchant who were engaged in litigation to recover several identified family paintings hanging in Zelsbach Museum in Althofen, Austria.

Kathy, Raphael, and Henri sat at the conference table, a plate of croissants, cheese, and pure fruit jellies decorated the table's surface. Raphael picked up the plate and held it toward Kathy.

"No thank you, but I'll have more coffee, please."

Raphael replaced the plate, reached for the silver coffee server, and placed the spout over Kathy's Staffordshire bone china cup.

He poured the hot black liquid into the cup and then motioned toward Henri, who shook his head no.

He refilled his own cup and then brought the steaming coffee to his lips, marveling at how delicious the thick French coffee always tasted.

He had his favorite brand, Grand' Mere Bonne Nuit, imported. Despite his many attempts, he never liked the American varieties and he had tried most of them.

Then a thought flashed across his mind...without coffee, the Frenchman was as vulnerable as he was without love or cigarettes.

Raphael placed the cup on the saucer, then looked at Henri and then at Kathy.

"We didn't scare off von Hoenshield. I'll guarantee it. He's having trouble convincing the owner to meet with us. Who can blame him? The art is stolen. Why enlarge the circle."

"And to allay your fears dear souls, the silence is not because of the amount of money we offered. The world moves on the wheels of finance and money is the grease, the energy, and the means to obtain everything and to make everything happen. The only question is the amount necessary. Let's not read more into the situation than it calls for. Give von Hoenshield time to work it out. We'll hear from him in due course. He liked what he heard at our dinner meeting. He'll find a way to arrange the meeting we requested."

Raphael paused to see if either of them had anything to add.

Both sat motionless, perhaps processing what he said, perhaps not.

Then he continued. "I thought about initiating a call even though it might give von Hoenshield the encouragement he needs to up the ante. I wouldn't put it past our friend to come back to us with a new figure in any event. Any amount above the eight million, he'd pocket for services rendered and on top of that, he'd probably ask the owner for a commission for brokering the transaction."

"If you're thinking he's going to come back with a higher number, why not just call him and try to be diplomatic…pushing, or better put, encourage-ing some progress."

"That's not a possibility, Henri, it was just a thought. The idea is never to convey desperation or anxiety. We wait. The human animal is ritualistic. Once he smells the bait, in our case money, his desire to get it will in time outweigh the element of possible danger. The money will neutralize his fear. The same holds true for the owner."

The intercom button buzzed softly.

Raphael pressed the button as he picked up the receiver. "Yes." He listened and then said, "Put him through."

Kathy and Henri watched and waited, as Duchant wrote on the small yellow pad.

He then turned the pad around.

Both saw the name of von Hoenshield printed in upper case letters. A smile came across each of their faces.

"No, Manfred, this is not Henri, it's Raphael La Monde."

"It's quite alright. No, I'm sorry neither Henri nor Miss Longrin are available. May I take a message or have them call you back, or perhaps you can tell me, and I will inform them accordingly."

"There is nothing to apologize for. Under the circumstances three weeks is quite understandable."

"Yes, that is correct. With regard to the money aspect, I am the one you talk with," and then Raphael looked at both of them and smiled.

"That amount, Manfred, is substantially more than our retainer believes the painting is worth, but everything is negotiable."

"That may prove somewhat awkward. Those types of negotiations can only be held in person. May I suggest that you arrange a meeting at a place satisfactory to the seller, where our ongoing negotiations can be conducted safely and confidentially."

"I understand perfectly. Nothing is easy especially when money is involved. Yes, I know you will do your best. Thank you. Your efforts are appreciated. And the same to you, goodbye."

Raphael cradled the receiver and smiled.

"The sum the German now indicates is eleven million dollars. I would guess one million or more of that amount will find its way to an offshore bank account in the name of our friend, but that's immaterial. You both heard my side of the conversation, the bottom line now is we wait again until we know whether the owner of the Mary Cassatt will meet with us."

Henri lit up a cigarette from his pack of Baltos, tilted his head back and blew the blue gray smoke toward the ceiling. He watched it drift upward and then he refocused on Duchant.

"The owner will not meet with us. His identity will be conspicuously guarded as it has been since the end of the war. The mere fact that he controls a piece of artwork such as the Cassatt, would place him in danger should his identity be revealed."

"You're wrong, Henri. The owner will meet with us. Money has that type of commanding power. Manfred has notified him that eight million is a reality and the possibility of more exists through further negotiations."

"Right now, the owner has a painting, a very valuable painting, but one that is, shall we say, of limited commercial value. After so many years, he might now be nudged into rethinking its value, away from the pride of possession and the enjoyable interludes of admiring it. He may well realize that we offer an opportunity to turn this artwork into a substantial sum of money that is clean and unencumbered."

Kathy spoke up for the first time.

"I think Raphael is correct. The recent financial settlements, notably to various Jewish claimants by the Swiss, attest to the changing international climate toward these continuing World War II claims. The multitude of the litigation instituted against governments, cities, banks, and individuals in an effort to recover real estate,

74

artwork, life insurance policies, and bank saving deposits, are meeting with positive results."

"The efforts to specifically recover artwork that is presently displayed in museums worldwide, continues as we speak. We should know since we're one of the claimants."

"I'm sorry to be so long-winded, but he's right, Henri. Raphael is correct in thinking that the holders of stolen art and sculptures might well be of the mind set to consider parting with these looted pieces, in exchange for clean money which would preserve their anonymity and provide them with liquid funds."

Henri took one last draw on the cigarette before he crushed it in the cut crystal ashtray.

"The Nazi thieves don't need money. They have enough of that. Remember the Reich Leaders and Schutzstaffel, the SS, looted the central banks of the conquered countries. Additionally, they had concentration camp gold melted and formed in bars, all of which were secreted away in Switzerland, Argentina, Paraguay, and Uruguay for personal use as well as to finance the building of the Fourth Reich."

"All that may be true, Henri, but when is enough ever enough. Millions of dollars are tempting. They would be to you, Kathy, or me. Manfred and the owner or owners of the painting are no different."

"We strive daily to enhance our bottom line. If we were satisfied, we'd stop, take what we have and party. We, and the owner of the Cassatt are very much alike in our desire to manipulate power and control wealth in its various forms. Manfred will call and we will get our meeting. I'll bet you a dinner at La Colombre de Bleue."

"The Blue Dove is a very expensive restaurant, Raphael. I will enjoy watching you pick up the check."

"I'm on Henri's side regarding the meeting with the owner or owners. I don't think it will happen, so I'm included in this dinner, right?"

"Sure you are, Kathy. We can watch Raphael pick up the check for the three of us when he hits a stone wall. I'm a patient guy. I can wait while my appetite builds."

Three hands reached toward the center of the conference room table and touched. Henri held Kathy's hand just a moment too long.

Chapter 14

Manfred listened to the ringing, agitated that it was taking so long for the phone to be picked up. After what seemed like an inordinate amount of time, he heard the receiver disengage from the telephone cradle.

The voice on the other end simply said, "Yes."

"I wish to speak to the Doctor. Meine ehre heisst treue." (My honor is loyalty)

The voice on the other end replied, "One moment."

As Manfred held the phone, he thought about the words he had just spoken, my honor is loyalty. They were the motto of the SS, one of the first things he learned when he entered SS training as a sixteen-year-old volunteer from the Hitler Jugend, Bund der Deutschen Arbeiterjugend, or the Hitler Youth.

His thoughts were interrupted by the semi audible voice on the other end. "This is the Doctor."

Instinctively Manfred clicked his heels at the sound of the voice.

"Herr Doctor, they are requesting a face-to-face meeting. They want to negotiate the price directly with the owner."

"Why have you deviated from the usual method of contact? This number is for emergencies only. I need to rethink the matter," and the phone went dead.

*

Four days later a man entered the art gallery, as Manfred was about to close. Before Manfred could speak the man asked, "Are you Hauptsturmführer Manfred von Hoenshield?"

Manfred sensed that the man knew very well who he was before he asked the question.

"I'm not sure I understand. Who are you, and why are you addressing me by the rank of Captain in the SS?"

"Because that is your rank and organizational unit. Let's not play games Hauptsturmfuhrer."

Since the war, Manfred, like many other members of the Third Reich's SS, hid their identities from everyone, with one exception. That exception was as a member of a protective group called Organisation der Ehemaligen SS-Angehorigen, or Odessa.

The organization's sole purpose was to rescue their comrades from postwar justice and establish a Fourth Reich capable of fulfilling Hitler's unrealized dreams. The man standing in front of him could well be a comrade from Odessa, or a tracker from Israel's Mossad.

"I still do not understand."

"Then let me tell you a little about yourself Hauptsturmfuhrer. Your name is not Manfred von Hoenshield. You are Friedrich Herbert Alpers. Born in Lingenfeld, Pfalz. You were at the camps. Your longest service was at Dachau as an Obersturm-fuhrer." (Captain)

"Then you were transferred to the SS Division Totenkopf, the Death's Head Division. This Division was formed from both concentration camp guards and men from the unit, SS Heimwehr Danzig. The Totenkopf was officered mostly by men from the verfugungstruppe, many of whom had seen action in Poland. The Totenkopf Division was commanded by SS-Obergruppenfuhrer Theodor Eicke, your commanding officer at Dachau."

"You were again transferred, this time to the 2nd SS Panzergrenadier Division, Das Reich. You fought in the Low Countries, and in France, then the unit was sent to the Eastern Front. During the invasion of the Soviet Union, the 2nd SS fought with the Army Group Center, taking part in the battle of Yalnya near Smolensk and then in the spearhead to capture Moscow."

"You were awarded the Close Combat Bar in Gold, Iron Cross 1st Class, the Winter Campaign medal and the Wound Badge in black, as well as being promoted to Hauptsturmfuhrer."

The man paused for only a moment before he intoned, "Isn't that correct?"

Manfred stood silent. He hadn't thought about his service for many years and now all of it came thundering back. The man's information was exacting, right down to his decorations. Manfred still couldn't decide if this man was from Odessa or was he the enemy?

As he started to speak, the man said, "Meine ehre heisst treue."

Manfred assumed the position of attention, clicked his heels, and replied in English, "My honor is loyalty."

"Thank you Hauptsturmfuhrer. Now that we have established common ground allow me to get on with my business. You are an SS Officer. You should know what it is to follow orders even after all these years. Your unwavering instructions were never to use a certain phone number unless under emergency circumstances. You violated those instructions. I am here to tell you that if such a breach of discipline occurs in the future, it will result in severe consequences."

Manfred tried to speak but was silenced by the look he received from the man.

"The recipient of that call elects not to meet with the potential buyers. All negotiations are to be conducted through me."

Manfred studied the man as he spoke. He was young, too young to have served the Fuhrer, but his military bearing, and manner of speech indicated an officer or certainly a man used to having his way.

Von Hoenshield pointed to one of the far corners of the gallery. "There are comfortable chairs…"

The man cut him off with a waving motion. "This will only take a moment more."

Manfred nodded. "But before you continue, I would like to know who you are?"

"My name is Rudel, Ernst Rudel. Please inform the buyers of what I have just stated and arrange a meeting. I will telephone you within three days time. When you pick up the telephone, I will say only Churchill. Then you will tell me the date, time and location of the meeting. Nothing more. Is that understood?"

"Yes Sir, it is understood clearly."

The man who called himself Rudel smiled. Then touching the brim of his hat, he turned and walked out the door.

Von Hoenshield involuntarily shuddered. The man unnerved him even though he thought of himself as a hardened individual. He had seen a significant amount of horror from combat and the camps, but that was a long time ago. He wasn't a soldier anymore, only a man in his early sixties trying to seize on an opportunity of a lifetime where he visualized making enough money to see his waning years spent in comfort. And now he was being threatened over a phone call.

The more von Hoenshield thought about the situation, the more he realized the seriousness of deviating from standard operating procedures. His overzealousness to get the business concluded had caused him to violate orders.

He walked to a chair, sat down, and pressed his fingertips together in an effort to steady himself.

He was old, but still a soldier. He was sternly reminded of that fact moments ago. That aspect of his life would forever be intertwined with everything he did until the day he died. He had to remember that. To think otherwise was a delusion he had perpetrated on himself.

In a way the visit from Rudel was beneficial. He wanted the money that this transaction would bring him. He was clever enough to pull it off, but now he must exercise extreme caution, no more careless mistakes. No more hurried impetuous reactions. Everything from this point on would be calculated down to the smallest detail. It would be thought out to a conclusion and then rethought. Nothing would be left to chance or happenstance. He was a soldier again and would plan the future with calculated precision.

He smiled, then reached for the telephone and dialed Bertrand's number.

Chapter 15

After four rings, the answering machine picked up. Disappointed, von Hoenshield hung up. After the session with Rudel, he felt it prudent to speak only to Bertrand rather than leave a message, which might be heard by unnecessary ears.

He looked at his watch noting that over an hour had passed since the man walked into the gallery. He pushed up from the desk and stood staring at the door at the far end of the room, as if he expected Rudel to return at any moment.

Then he turned his head toward the windows running along the wall to his right and watched the darkness take hold. He again looked at his watch, then began walking toward the door. He turned the sign to closed, set the alarm and then locked the door.

The elevator reached the lobby floor with an uncharacteristic jolt and von Hoenshield stepped out quickly. Two men in overalls carrying cleaning supplies were busying themselves in the corridor. They nodded to him as he passed, and he returned their silent greeting.

Once outside the building, he debated whether he should stop for a beer or go directly home. He decided on home and made his way down Madison Avenue rehashing the evening's events. Rudel had unnerved him far more than he was willing to admit.

*

One of the cleaners walked through the lobby door to the street and began cleaning the outer glass as he watched the old German walk down Madison Avenue. He remained in place until the figure disappeared and then reentered the building.

A silent signal passed between the two men as they picked up their supplies and entered the elevator. The taller man jabbed the button for the third floor.

Once the doors opened, the same man pushed the elevator's stop button and froze the cab in place.

They brought out their cleaning supplies and placed them to the left of the gallery's entrance. The taller of the two looked at the control panel attached to the right side of the door frame. His mind raced as his eyes darted over the keypad. He shook his head as if he was satisfied with what he concluded.

The man's planned approach would be on the premise that the alarm was a closed-circuit system, which would detect any act of intrusion when the electric circuit was broken by forced entry.

He anticipated that there would also be a number of zones or areas of protection throughout the gallery, such as motion, glass break detectors, and vibration, or shock sensors.

He suspected that this alarm system incorporated an additional piece of equipment into the circuit called a control box, located in an out of the way place to avoid easy detection. The control box would be hooked up to one or more circuits with its own power supply.

Finally, he projected that the system would have an auto-dial system with a prerecorded message giving the address and other relevant information to the police once the circuit was broken.

It appeared to be a simple keypad, one in which a master code of four keys was entered into the pad to activate the system. Reentering the same series deactivates it.

The man reached into his pocket and withdrew a black object about the size of a pack of cigarettes. He held it level with the keypad and depressed one of several buttons with his thumb.

He watched the small screen at the top go through a series of functions which he knew were random numbers, tumbling at a lightning pace. After thirteen seconds, the screen illuminated six numerals in a green hue.

He thought to himself, two more than the usual. Unnecessary, but if it made the owner feel safer, all the better.

Then he chuckled.

He looked back and forth from the screen to the keypad and pushed each number slowly. Then he pushed the enter button and watched as the keypad's alarm light changed from red to green. He smiled at his associate and gave a thumb's up sign.

The door lock was picked in moments. Both men checked for buttons and trip wires around the doorframe, which would indicate a secondary backup system. They found nothing.

On signal from the lead man, they both entered the gallery and stopped.

The taller man removed an electronic device from his overalls and started to scan the room from left to right for infrared beams. The room was clean.

Then he depressed another button and a low vibration started. He moved very slowly to his right aiming the device at the wall. When he moved, it was with deliberate slowness.

After several minutes, the electronic device started pulsating.

He stopped and looked to his right, at a painting subdued by night shadows. He removed the painting, ran his hand over the frame then leaned it against the wall. He took out a penlight, moved the on button with his thumb and scanned the wall where the painting had hung.

There was a small steel plate with two screws. He placed the pen light in his mouth, took out a flathead screwdriver and unscrewed the plate.

He prodded the plate off slowly and saw the green, white, yellow and black wires. He moved them out of the opening, took out a small knife and scraped away some of the rubber coating on the white or neutral wire and the green or ground wire.

Holding the exposed wires with his thumb and forefinger, making sure to touch only the covered rubber part, he took out a metal clamp and placed it on the exposed part of both wires. He then moved his thumb and index finger to where the white and green wires connected to the receptacle and cut them.

He rolled their ends together, reattached the now single wire to the power source, taped them with electrical tape and removed the clamp. Then he cut the black wire, or hot wire, severing the electrical connection.

The current would continue to register to the control center as functional, but the alarm would actually be bypassed. It was incapable of emitting a signal from either motion or shock detectors, or from an interrupted circuit caused by a forced entry.

The tall man removed the flashlight from his mouth, pointed it at his left hand and made an okay sign. The other man proceeded to the table at the far corner of the room. His quick movements indicated that he was aware of the floor plan.

He went behind the table, dropped to one knee, opened his overall jacket and took out several screwdrivers. He unfastened the telephone wall jack, inserted a small monitor and crimped its wires to the existing line.

He then programmed a personal code that would allow his associates to dial into the monitor from anywhere in the world and listen in to whatever was going on in the room. The monitor would pick up every word and every whisper, no matter where individuals in the gallery were located.

There would be no sound or signal from the device when in use, allowing the eavesdropper to listen in with impunity. Only the control operator would be aware when the mechanism was activated.

The monitor would also activate automatically when an incoming or outgoing telephone call was placed on the altered line.

The man moved to the telephone resting on the table and repeated the sequence with the phone jack. Then he stepped away and dialed a number on his cell phone.

He spoke several words in German and then abruptly stopped. He took a few steps, stopped, tapped his finger lightly against his chest and then stood quietly holding the cell phone to his ear.

He turned, walked quickly to the windows, stopped, and tapped his arm. After a few more seconds he placed the phone into one of his pockets, picked up the two screwdrivers, and walked toward the man standing by the door.

"They're all operative."

The taller man smiled, opened the door, then locked it and reset the keypad.

They picked up their cleaning supplies, took the elevator to the lobby and walked out the main entrance to a van that was marked, Professional Cleaners, Inc.

They stowed the cleaning equipment in the back, then drove away from the building, turning right toward the West River Drive.

Chapter 16

The next morning von Hoenshield dialed Henri Bertrand. Once again, the machine picked up. He tried several more times during the morning and early afternoon, experiencing the same result.

At four p.m. he decided to try one more time. If the answering machine picked up again, he would leave a message. He relaxed somewhat as the ring was interrupted with a click, then a voice saying, "This is Bertrand."

"Good evening, Henri, Manfred here."

At the precise moment, the German picked up the receiver and began to dial, the hidden monitor activated, alerting the system's controller that a telephone call was being initiated.

The controller pushed the record button and watched as the tapes started to slowly rotate in a clock-like direction.

Von Hoenshield decided to minimize the fact that the Doctor refused the meeting.

"I have some good news Henri, the primary assistant to the owner is going to meet with you. He is empowered to conduct all negotiations on behalf of the owner. It enables a favorable decision to be reached quickly."

Von Hoenshield felt that only a positive approach would enable the discussions to continue. He had a lot riding on the outcome, and he took certain liberties with the power Rudel might have, but there was little choice at this point. He could feel his heart pounding as he waited for a response.

"I guess one could classify your statement as progress, but I must be very clear, Manfred, we would not take kindly to being placed in a situation where we have wasted additional time."

"I can assure you, Henri, that is not the case."

"We certainly hope not. There are other transactions that we envision in which you could participate handsomely. What are the particulars regarding the meeting?"

"Let us meet at my gallery on Thursday, at one p.m. if that's convenient?"

"Let me check a moment."

Bertrand covered the mouthpiece and looked at Raphael, who was holding a circular black receiver to his ear attached to a thin wire extending from the phone. He nodded yes, and Bertrand said, "Manfred, one p.m. on Thursday, at your gallery will be fine. In addition to me, Mr. La Monde and Miss Longrin will attend."

Manfred tried to control his breathing. "I will see all of you then. Auf Wiedersehen." (Goodbye)

"Goodbye Manfred."

Raphael made a fist with his hand indicating to Bertrand not to hang up. They both heard the click indicating the German was off the line. They listened a bit longer trying to discern if there were others listening in. They heard nothing until the beep signaled that a receiver was off the hook. Bertrand replaced the phone and looked at Duchant.

"Do you think we had company, Raphael?"

"Yeah, I think so. Better to err on the side of caution."

Bertrand just stared as if lost in thought.

Kathy nodded her head yes. Then she started to speak.

"We're in a high stakes poker game, playing at a table with people who represent the embodiment of danger. The painting is stolen, and the owners are perpetrators in that crime, whether willingly, or by circumstances. Either way, they have a lot to lose."

"The painting in question supposedly disappeared at the end of World War II. In many circles this painting is believed to have been destroyed during the final push toward Berlin by the Russians. From what we have garnered from the German, the painting appears to be very much intact."

"Raphael has indicated to me that certain interests have managed to secret away a considerable amount of artwork, most of it priceless in today's market. These interests are fully aware of the present dangers and have been aware of these dangers since the fall of the Third Reich. They have taken elaborate steps to conceal both their identities and the artwork in their possession. It is a safe assumption that they have a phone tap and that we will certainly be recorded during the upcoming meeting. We should exercise caution. We need to proceed on the premise that they will eventually know who we are, if they don't already."

Both men nodded their heads in agreement. Bertrand was the first to speak.

"Well summarized, Kathy, well done indeed." Then he looked at Duchant, who nodded slightly.

"Von Hoenshield's telephone call was routed through a circuit that connects with a San Francisco company by the name of Reed World-wide Shippers."

"If anyone went to the premises, they would find the office situated in a 1920's building, located in a rundown section of the Mission Area. Once through the 2nd floor office door, the one-room office would be bare, except for a telephone sitting in the middle of the floor. Let's not kid ourselves, von Hoenshield and associates will eventually trace us to the diamond district. Maybe that's just an assumption on my part but I'd like to think it's a reality. This ploy just buys us a little time to confuse."

Duchant looked at Kathy for a moment. "I want you to familiarize yourself with the Mary. Please take what time you need. I want you to become an authority on this painting by the time we meet von Hoenshield."

"I've already begun."

"Excellent! Okay then, let's call it a day."

"I feel like having a drink. Are you interested, Raphael?"

"Thanks, but no thanks. I need to crash."

Bertrand looked at Kathy. "I can't drink alone. How about it?"

Kathy wanted to say no, but how many times could she say it without appearing standoffish.

"Okay, Henri, but I'm limiting myself to one double. I've got homework to do."

"That's a deal. I'll meet you at the elevator in ten, make that five."

She smiled. "Five it is."

Then they both stood up. Kathy waved to Duchant on her way out of the conference room while Bertrand leaned over and said, "Sleep well," winked then walked out to the office pausing in front of the monitors. He turned and waited until the buzzer sounded and the door opened. Then he pulled it wider and walked out.

*

Duchant sat motionless at the conference table. He tried to review everything that transpired up to this evening's phone call, but his mind kept going back to Kathy. He wondered about the wink Bertrand gave him. Was it because he succeeded in getting the woman to have a drink with him or was it some ulterior motive?

What difference did it make? She was pretty and educated, but there was a world of differences separating them. Betrand should know that mixing business with pleasure often had disastrous consequences. Duchant made a mental note to watch the future interplay between them.

Duchant pushed away from the table, stretched, and walked into the office. He stood behind the monitors. "Did the phone call originate from the Madison Avenue gallery?"

"Affirmative, sir. The voice recognition confirmed it was von Hoenshield."

"Did you find a tap?"

"Negative, Mr. Duchant. We completed several series, but nothing positive showed up."

"How comfortable are you that the wire was clean?"

"I'm not comfortable, Mr. Duchant. Neither is Dushku," patting the other man on the shoulder. "We can't pinpoint it, but we both think the wire has a rider on board. Until we can confirm it, Mr.

Duchant, I'd be careful with all your calls involving this man. We'll sweep the conference room and check the phones again, but both of us feel sure that there's nothing on our side."

"Thank you, Brent, and you too, Dushku. Keep us whole."

"Will do, Mr. Duchant," then the buzzer sounded, the door opened, and Raphael walked out onto the small metal landing. He placed his hand on the railing but didn't immediately start down. He stood looking over the floor where the activity was slowing down as the end of the workday approached.

His attention was specifically directed at the guards with their Uzi submachine guns who continually moved around the floor in an unhurried cadence. He watched as their heads turned repeatedly left and right. He saw their mouths move as they talked into their headphones, which connected to their duty officer.

Duchant turned around, faced the door. The door clicked open and Raphael walked back into the office and up to the monitors.

Neither of the men turned, but the man called Brent said, "Back so soon, Mr. Duchant. Must mean our shift is over."

"Not quite yet boys. I've got a hypothetical for you. Let's suppose there is a tap on the line and we can't find it. I've heard about electronic bullets, but I'm not really in the know. Can we use one or more of these to disable the tap?"

Brent spoke up. "If we can't find the tap, Mr. Duchant, and you don't care if they know we know, we can always shoot as you call it, an electronic bullet. The better terminology, however, is microwave. What we do is shoot a high-powered microwave beam through the wire. The beam penetrates the electronic component or tap and the rapidly pulsating action of the microwave in the tap internally excites the components, generating intense heat, which in turn causes the components to fuse or melt. I know that's a mouthful, Mr. Duchant. Do you want me to take it slower or repeat it?"

"No, I've got the general picture. Is there a way to camouflage the path so it can't be traced back to us?"

"That's not a consideration, or a worry, Mr. Duchant. The beam moves at the speed of light. There's no way they can avoid it or trace it back to us. If we shoot the microwave too soon after a conversation, they'll know we know. To be honest, Mr. Duchant, they'll probably know regardless of when we use the microwave."

"When does your shift end?"

"We are running the double today – midnight."

"It's only 5:45 p.m.. You have a while to go. Have fun setting it up. We'll decide what to do by the time your shift starts tomorrow. Goodnight again."

"Thanks, Mr. Duchant. We're bored as hell watching the screens. It's a nice diversion."

"Enjoy, as my mother would say, but keep your eyes on the screens," and then Raphael left.

Chapter 17

When Manfred lifted the receiver at his end, the man seated in front of the bank of screens immediately notified both men.

Rudel respectfully stood several paces behind, and to one side of the Doctor. After several movements by the operator, the audio sound of the dial sequence and then the voice was amplified throughout the room.

Both men listened to the brief dialogue, then the Doctor leaned toward the operator.

"Did you run a trace?"

"Ja Herr Doctor," and then the operator handed him a piece of paper. The Doctor scanned it, then passed the paper to Rudel.

"We'll get the address in San Francisco. Do you want someone to visit the location?"

"Yes. When you finish handling the matter, Ernst, please come to the study."

Rudel clicked his heels and stood ramrod straight as the other man left the room. He turned to the operator. "Put me through to the West Coast."

He watched as the operator went through a series of movements, then turned in his swivel seat so that he faced him.

"The party is on the line. Will you take it here, or in the chamber?"

"Put it through to the chamber."

"Jawohl, Sturmbannführer." (Yes Major)

The guard came to the position of attention as Rudel walked quickly past him and to a small room, which he entered by placing his palm on a glass panel. Once inside, he took a seat at the solitary table and pushed two buttons on the telephone case, activating the scrambler. He then picked up the phone.

Rudel watched the pulsating status display, which indicated scramble or clear conditions. The scrambler would allow a clear, natural sound quality, as well as voice recognition of the individual.

In addition, this particular scrambler employed a speech spectrum inversion technique, digitally controlled and offering over fourteen thousand user selectable codes. This enabled the coding system to function over international distances and deny unauthorized interception from any location worldwide.

At the sound of the connection, Rudel said, "This is New York. Are you copying?"

"Yes."

Rudel then slowly said the California address. "We want a visual and a confirmation. The activities report is to be rendered within three days, no later than seven p.m. EST, Wednesday night, the eleventh."

"If contact is made, do we become operational?"

"Negative."

"Understood."

Then Rudel pushed the disconnect button.

He sat back in the chair and ran his fingers over his cleanly shaven scalp. Then he got up, walked out the door and headed toward the study.

He knocked and waited until he heard the voice requesting him to enter. He depressed the ornate 18th century door handle and walked into the book-lined study.

He walked to the front of the desk where the Doctor was seated and stood at attention.

"Please be seated, Major."

"The orders have been passed, Herr Doctor."

The older man smiled. "Perhaps they will supply us with some missing pieces such as the relevance to San Francisco. Is this where the buyer is located?" The man stretched, "Ah well...all in good time, but we can now make certain assumptions with a fair degree of accuracy based on our recent investigations."

"They, a man named Bertrand, and another named La Monde, operate from a building at 977 West 47th Street."

Rudel registered immediately that the address was located in the diamond district. His mind pictured 47th Street and he thought, there are a number of Jew merchants commingling like so many rats in a sewer up and down that street.

Then Rudel watched as the Doctor stood up and looked out the windows toward a garden, seemingly lost in thought. He turned around to face Rudel and continued as if he hadn't paused.

"The two previously mentioned men always take an elevator to the second floor. One of our men followed them to that address and after several days of observation, confirmed that they always exit at the second floor. He was able to observe one of the men look at a security panel to the right of a door, heard the click and then watched as they entered."

"After a few minutes, our man knocked on the door, it clicked open, and he walked into a small foyer where he was confronted by a secretary."

"Behind the secretary's station was a door, but our man couldn't confirm what was behind it. During the brief time he was there, no one used that door. He feigned being lost, was given directions by the secretary, and departed."

"The suite is registered to Duchant et Compagnie de Fils. The company has a long history in the diamond trade, so one can deduce that behind the door is a room or rooms dedicated to diamonds.

We understand that the actual owner or owners have always been in the background of the day-to-day operations from its earliest inception. This apparently holds true today. As such we do not know who actually owns the company. Originally it was a Jew company. Our assumption is that it continues as such."

"There, however, may well be another purpose for this establishment's existence. Shall we say a parallel purpose. While we cannot be entirely certain, we must be prudent and project a worst-case scenario."

"The Jew bastards never give up the hunt. Despite having their hands full with the Arabs and the Palestinian garbage, the Israelis and the New York Jews always have time for us. Both their internal security apparatus, Shin Bet and Mossad, (Israeli domestic and international intelligence organizations) still manage to extend its tentacles everywhere and into everything."

"The Jews have never given up the chase. After so many years they are still trying to capture us, to bring us down and in all cases, bring us to trial. The Mossad, and that old Austrian Jew who refuses to die, Simon Wiesenthal, will always be our primary concern and the reason we must be ever resolute to exercise extreme caution."

"Your meeting should provide some light on these men as well as the young woman. The sale will go through, but it will be far different then they imagine. That is all for now, Strumbannfuhrer Rudel."

Rudel rose to his feet in one swift movement, clicked his heels and extended his right arm straight out as he said "Heil Hitler." Then turned and left the room.

The Doctor watched him leave and thought to himself, with such fine young men, the Fourth Reich is a certainty.

Chapter 18

After Kathy moved into the booth, Bertrand slid in beside her. The maitre d' centered the table in front of them, bowed slightly, then walked off toward a standing waiter.

Bertrand turned to face Kathy. "I hope this place meets with your approval."

"If you're paying the bill, I approve."

They both laughed.

A waiter approached the table. "May I get you a drink?"

Bertrand replied, "Yes," then looked at Kathy. "A Johnny Red, or will you join me in some champagne?"

Kathy nodded.

"Does that mean champagne or scotch?"

"Oh, I'm sorry Henri, my mind knows what I want, but it didn't communicate it to my brain. I'll join you in a glass of champagne."

Bertrand looked up at the waiter. "A bottle of Roederer and two chilled flutes. Also please bring us some caviar. Make it two ounces of Ossetra Malossol."

"Roederer et Ossetra Malossol. Monsieur tres bon, merci." (Very good sir, thank you)

"Drinking champagne alone is an enjoyable event but drinking it while eating caviar is a pleasurable event."

"You sound like a poet, Henri."

"Hardly a poet. I'm simply a person who has become a victim of circumstances that should be enjoyed to the fullest."

"There you go again, a poet and a philosopher," then she laughed.

"I would imagine it's the way I view money. I look at money only as paper. Its only value is to bring into one's life those things that sustain that life or make it more enjoyable. For some, those things are the bare necessities. For others, they are the extravagances of life. For both, money is merely a means to an end."

Kathy sat there watching him and thinking that he was intelligent as well as handsome and while his exterior persona conveyed little, she somehow felt Mr. Henri Bertrand possessed a sinister side. That somehow intrigued her.

She couldn't clearly define why her woman's intuition made her feel that way. Perhaps it was something that had been ingrained since her first days as an attorney. She never went against that instinct, as it had often proven useful, if not downright accurate over time. She would exercise care. After all, she was still working in an unknown world, although it seemed quite real at certain moments.

Her thoughts were interrupted as the waiter placed two bone china plates in front of Kathy and Bertrand with mother-of-pearl spoons resting on the rim. Two chilled champagne flutes were placed to the right of their plates.

As he left, the waiter set down the caviar, which was in a cut crystal bowl seated in a bed of crushed ice. He also placed three small cut crystal trays around the caviar. One tray contained a garnish consisting of crumbled hard-boiled eggs, chopped onion, and crème fraiche. Another tray contained lightly buttered toast points and the third, sliced lemons.

The waiter showed the bottle of Roederer champagne to Bertrand who nodded.

Then the waiter removed the foil from the cork, untwisted the wire securing the cork, and wrapped the bottle's neck in a pale blue linen cloth.

He angled the bottle away from the table and twisted the cork slowly. He continued twisting until the cork eased out of the bottle with a soft pop. Then he poured a small amount in Bertrand's glass, and waited.

After a nod from Bertrand, the waiter picked up Kathy's glass, tilted it slightly and poured the champagne.

Then he refilled Bertrand's flute, placed the bottle into the ice bucket, bowed, and left.

"Quite a show, Henri."

"It does take time to do it right."

Henri picked up his glass. "What shall we drink to?"

"Perhaps a successful outcome to our business dealings."

"Yes, but that's not appropriate for our first drink together. I suggest we drink to love in all its forms."

After a moment's pause, Kathy said, "Why not? Okay, Henri, to love in all its forms. Although I'm not entirely sure what that means, my mind is racing along different avenues of possibilities."

She laughed, and Henri joined in. They touched their glasses lightly and Henri smiled at her over the rim of his.

"Tell me about Miss Kathy Longrin."

"I could say that there's not much to tell, but that isn't the case. There's a great deal that makes up Kathy Longrin, but to use your words, a discussion of me would be inappropriate for this evening. Let's just say I'm anything but a country girl."

Henri smiled, leaned his head back and laughed. He took another sip from the flute and turned toward her. "I'm not carrying a wire. Anything you say is confidential. I'm just interested in the general details, not the specifics. For example, how did you develop an interest in art?"

"I grew up with it, art that is. My father liked to visit the galleries and museums and I was his constant companion. He exposed me to art, and I cultivated a lifelong passion for it."

Bertrand reached for the tray of toast points. "Would you like one, or better yet, may I make one for you?"

"Yes, thank you."

Bertrand picked up his mother-of-pearl spoon and dabbed some caviar over one of the small pieces of toast. Then he took a slice of lemon from the tray, squeezed several drops over the shiny black roe of the female sturgeon and pointed toward the chopped eggs and onion.

Kathy shook her head no.

After placing the toast point on her plate, he repeated the process for himself, adding the crème fraiche and chopped onions.

"Do you like caviar, Kathy?"

"I've only had it a few times before, but I do like it."

"I try to enjoy it as often as possible with either vodka or champagne. I especially like the Russian recipe, caviar on whole-wheat pancakes, with a dab of sour cream. The Russians call it blini. Have you ever tried it that way?"

"No, I haven't, but it sounds fattening."

"Everything is either illegal, immoral, or fattening. It's worth a taste, if for no other reason than to say you've tried it. I know of several places that make excellent blinis."

"Perhaps you can introduce me to blinis at the Blue Dove. It seems you and I are going to pay the tab."

Bertrand feigned a pained look. "It seems our Mr. Duchant called that one right. We won't get to meet the principal or principals quite yet but we will get to meet the representative so I guess we lose...and yes, that might be a good time to introduce you to blinis, although I hope we can do it a bit earlier."

Henri smiled and motioned the waiter over. He pointed to Kathy's glass and then his own. The waiter picked up the champagne bottle with one hand, titled the flute with the other, then started to pour.

They held up their conversation until he left. Kathy didn't answer Bertrand's off-handed request for a date and let it slide. To avoid going back to that exchange, she picked up the small mother-of-pearl spoon and waved it a bit. "What's the significance?"

"Besides being the classic way of serving caviar, if you used a silver or stainless steel spoon, it would give the caviar a metallic taste. You could use a gold spoon, or for that matter, wood or glass instead of mother-of-pearl. Plastic is simply too gauche."

After a moment of silence Bertrand asked, "Did your father collect art?"

"Yes, modestly. He bought what he could afford and what he liked. The latter was his primary consideration."

Kathy's mind drifted to the underground room with its priceless masters.

"And you, Kathy, do you collect?"

"No, what I like, I can't afford. I enjoy those at various galleries and museums around the city."

"You mentioned that your father emigrated from Germany after the war. It must have been a terrible time."

"I would imagine so. My father always avoided questions concerning his former life including details about my mother, other than the statement that she was beautiful, and she loved me very much."

Kathy looked down at the table, then regaining her composure, looked back up.

"Please forgive me, Kathy. The last thing I wanted to do was to intrude into your private life. I was just trying to make conversation and I stupidly let my curiosity get in the way."

She didn't say anything. She sat there and smiled weakly.

Bertrand picked up the conversation again.

"The future is an interesting phenomenon, wouldn't you say Kathy? One can try to predict what it holds, but no one can possibly know. There are some who delude themselves in thinking that the future can be revealed. That's why astrologers and fortune tellers thrive. I've always believed that circumstances play a role. Some people call it luck. Do you believe in luck, Kathy?"

"I believe in change, constant change, I believe that one can exert some pressure to enact change to a degree, but yes, circumstances play a major role, both good and bad. Some circumstances are beyond any individual's control, while others seize upon these circumstances and turn them into opportunities."

"Nicely put, Kathy." Pointing to the caviar, "May I make you another?"

"Yes, but this time just the caviar and no lemon."

As he passed the plate back to Kathy, Bertrand leaned forward.

"Our upcoming meeting is very important. The individual with whom we will meet must be convinced beyond a doubt that we are serious buyers of the Mary. We will rely on your expertise to assist us in achieving this goal. Success is rewarded. Mediocrity…well you know how it goes."

"You can be assured, Henri, that I will do everything possible to move the negotiations forward. Mr. Duchant is my employer, and I am adequately remunerated. I will earn my salary, I always have."

With that Kathy looked at her watch. "It has been a pleasant evening, Henri, and to anticipate your question, I would like to do it again. Right now the best place for me is home, where I'm safe from the temptation of more champagne and caviar."

Bertrand smiled. "Remember you said it, I didn't ask, but I'll hold you to our next…" he searched for the word and finally said, "meeting."

He signaled the waiter who came over quickly and pulled out the table. "I'll be right back. Leave everything as is."

The waiter nodded and Bertrand walked Kathy outside the restaurant.

Palming the doorman's hand, he said "Taxi," as he returned his attention toward Kathy.

"Thank you for accepting my invitation for a drink tonight."

"I enjoyed it, Henri, and I meant what I said. I'll be happy to meet you again for a cocktail."

The cab pulled to the curb and the doorman reached for the door handle and opened the door.

As Kathy seated herself, Bertrand leaned in.

"This was a memorable evening. Thanks for the company," then he opened the front passenger side door and handed the driver some folded bills.

"Take the lady wherever she wants to go and make sure she arrives there safely."

Then Bertrand looked at the New York City Taxi and Limousine Commission certificate posted on the dashboard. He turned to face the driver. "I know your name and ID Mohammed. Don't play games with the lady."

Then he closed the door and watched the taxi merge into traffic.

Bertrand returned to the table noting that his flute was refilled. He finished off the caviar and champagne, paid the bill and walked out to the sidewalk again.

As his cab pulled away, Bertrand was lost in thought about the woman, wondering whether she would be only a momentary challenge, or something more. He smiled at the prospects.

Chapter 19

Kathy thought about what Bertrand said to the cab driver. It was a veiled threat, but it was said in a way that seemed to come naturally to him.

The doorman opened the cab door with a smile and a "Good evening, Miss Longrin."

Kathy glanced at the cab driver before she started out. He seemed relieved that she was leaving.

As she slid across the seat, Kathy looked up at the doorman. "How are you this evening, Arthur?"

"Just fine, Miss Longrin, and you?"

Kathy didn't answer but smiled back at the doorman.

She picked up her mail and took the elevator to the fourth floor. Once in her apartment she kicked off her shoes, dropped the mail on the coffee table, but didn't take off her clothes as she usually would have.

Instead, she walked tentatively into her bedroom as if she expected to see someone. Then she opened the bathroom door and pulled back the shower curtain. She walked through the kitchen alcove then back to the living room. Everything seemed normal and, in its place, but still she felt nervous and wondered why her heart was racing.

She went to the refrigerator and took out a bottle of Perrier. She had a mild buzz from the champagne and was sorry she had the second glass.

She carried the Perrier to the coffee table and sat down.

She puffed up several decorative pillows with her hand, leaned them against the arm of the sofa and placed her head down. She just wanted to close her eyes for a few minutes hoping that it might help the stress she felt building in her shoulders and abate the hangover that was now growing and pulsating at her temples.

*

Kathy reached over to turn off the alarm clock, but her hand brushed against the sofa's arm. She opened her eyes and realized that the ringing was coming from the phone. She went to the desk and lifted the receiver. "Yes."

"Kathy, are you okay? This is Henri."

"Yes, Henri. I'm fine. Why?"

"Well it's ten thirty in the morning and you didn't come to work. We thought something happened."

Kathy looked at her wrinkled dress and realized that she had fallen asleep in her clothes.

The champagne evidently allowed her to sleep longer than her body clock would normally have. "I'm fine, Henri. I apologize for not calling. Something personal came up."

"Now that I know you're okay, take your time. Are you planning to come in?"

"Yes, I should be there in about an hour. I apologize again for not calling."

"See you later, Kathy," then the connection was cut.

Kathy shook her head in disgust. This never happened before and she was at odds with herself.

She went to the bedroom, undressed, and then walked to the bathroom.

She turned on the shower, leaving the cold water build in intensity but ignoring the hot knob.

She stepped in and immediately felt the ice crystals attack her body. She shivered as she lowered her head into the stream of water feeling it cascade off her neck. Her body soon adjusted to the cold and after another forty seconds, the shower seemed invigorating, slowly bringing her body back to life.

When she felt she had enough, she turned the knob to the right but remained standing, letting her body readjust to the room temperature. She reached up and pulled down the large Turkish towel from the upper horizontal frame on the shower door and patted herself dry.

She stepped out of shower and faced the mirror. Letting the towel drop away, she looked at her body. Still not bad, she thought. The hips were narrow and her 36C breasts still hadn't begun to sag. Her body still had its curves and firmness. It was a body any man would want, but that was just the problem. They only wanted the body.

Kathy Longrin wasn't looking for marriage, but if the right man came along, she felt confident that she could balance a career and a husband. She wasn't in the market for lovers, at least not now.

She dressed quickly in a gray St. John wool suit. She loosely tied a blue and red regimental striped tie around the collar of her white silk blouse and put on black Gucci shoes with two-inch heels.

As she was about to step out of her apartment, she hesitated, then walked to the desk and picked up the phone. She dialed and waited.

When the voice spoke, she recognized it as Udo, the chauffeur.

"Udo, this is Karta, how are you?"

"I am fine, Miss Karta, and I hope you are the same."

"Yes Udo, everything is well. Is my father available?"

"He has a visitor, but I'll tell him you are on the line. Ein (One) moment please."

She heard the click and then her father's voice. "Hello Karta, what a welcomed surprise. Is anything wrong?"

Kathy laughed, "No, Father, everything is fine. I just wanted to say hello. How are you?"

"Well, hearing your voice makes me both happy and sad. When are you coming home for a visit?"

"I'm not sure. I just started a new job. It's a challenging one and I'm still getting oriented. I'd like to see you but I'm not sure when I can take a few days off. We'll probably have to let the telephone keep us updated until I can arrange some leave. Any chance of you coming in my direction?"

"Everything is possible, so don't discount my arriving on your doorstep one of these days."

"Ah Papa, you always say that but you never come. You never leave the farm."

"One day for sure," then he laughed.

"Tell me about your new job, Karta."

"It's a combination of art and law, my two loves after you."

"It sounds fascinating. What's the name of the company?"

"It's Duchant et Compagnie de Fils. I've got to run, Papa. I love you. Stay well. I'll see you soon, I promise."

"I love you too, Karta. Goodbye."

Kathy held the phone a moment before replacing it on the cradle. Then she turned and left her apartment.

*

Her father entered the study and walked behind his desk. He picked up the sterling silver frame and looked at the picture of his daughter astride a horse.

He handed the picture to the man standing in front of him. "This is my daughter. She embodies everything noble in German womanhood."

The man gently took hold of the frame and looked at the picture of a woman sitting on an Appaloosa horse and smiling. Her blonde hair blowing in the breeze, her smile radiating from a classic patrician face.

He stared at the photograph for a long moment. "She is beautiful, Herr Doctor, and her Nordic features are very much in evidence," then he handed the frame back.

The Doctor took hold of the frame and looked at the picture longingly. He looked up at the man standing ramrod straight, "Yes, Sturm-bannführer, she is indeed."

He placed the frame down, then took hold of his gold desk pen, tore off a sheet of paper from the pad, and began writing. He folded the paper in half and handed it to Rodel.

Rodel opened the note, and stared at the name, then looked back at the Doctor questioningly.

"We have a complication, Sturmbannführer," and he pointed to the note. "My daughter is now working for them."

Chapter 20

Raphael arrived at the office early, but the two men at the monitors were not the ones he needed. He either misunderstood or couldn't remember if they were on the morning or afternoon shifts.

The two men kept their eyes focused on the screens as he walked past. He decided to take coffee in the conference room and read some of the mail that flooded his computer screen.

After deleting a number of messages or forwarding them to Henri's PC, he locked onto a coded message from the Paris office. It was sent to his security chief and blind copied to him.

He walked to the monitors and requested the code book for Wednesday. He carried the book, a single sheet of translucent paper, and a special pen back to the table. He decoded the message which indicated that several principals had reported to internal security that they believed they were under surveillance on several occasions.

Raphael looked to his right as Bertrand walked into the conference room with a smile on his face.

"Oh no, I won't ask how last night went, even though that baited smile is plastered all over your face."

"Thanks for asking, Raphael. It was memorable to say the least."

"Bullshit, and I won't let you reel me in. Come over here and look at this," pointing to the translucent paper.

Duchant spun the paper around and waited a moment before asking, "Have you noticed anything, like a surveillance of any type? I don't want either of us becoming rabbits." (Targets)

Bertrand looked back up. "No nothing, but in all honesty, I haven't been a hundred percent vigilant. It's unprofessional I know, and I've slacked off a bit, but that's changed as of this moment."

"When you left last night, I hung around talking with the monitor operators about ways to deactivate phone taps. According to them, they can shoot a high-powered microwave beam through the line into the bug. The intense heat it causes will melt, or fuse, making the monitor inoperative. That's the layman's language for destroying the bug. The question is when do we use it? To do it now alerts the opposition that we know."

Bertrand sat quietly resting his chin on the fist of his right hand, while his elbow rested on the table.

"We should avoid doing anything here that will alert them. Let them think we're dumb and happy. They're doing their due diligence and that's expected. We know what we're up against, but we don't know the depth."

"Notify Paris, Henri, but let's keep it simple. Paris is not on the bigot-list (A list of people

123

who are privy to sensitive intelligence) so just tell them that we've made contact with the opposition and the surveillance on their side of the ocean is traceable to this. They've probably already started, but mention dry cleaning. (Action taken by agents to determine if they are under surveillance) Let them do whatever they feel necessary to make themselves as sterile as possible."

"It's a given that the opposition is watching everything connected with Duchant et Compagnie de Fils. Why don't you work up an encrypted message, Henri, and send it to Paris and our other stations."

As Bertrand headed toward the credenza, Raphael reached across the table for the ashtray and pulled it toward him. He picked up the translucent paper and watched as the black ink slowly faded away leaving the paper with a sterile appearance.

Then he picked up the antique sterling silver Ronson desk lighter and pressed down on the horizontal silver tab with his thumb. The small front cover lifted as an internal wheel struck the flint and simultaneously ignited the wick.

Raphael held the translucent paper by the corner and tilted it toward the flame. The paper caught fire and blackened quickly.

He dropped the paper into the ashtray and watched as the fire rolled the charred paper into a candle like form.

He picked up the ashtray, walked into the bathroom and dumped the contents into the toilet bowl. He opened the mahogany door below the green granite sink, took out a bottle of bleach, unscrewed the cap, and poured some of the liquid into the toilet.

Duchant waited for approximately one minute, pushed the handle and watched the contents disappear. He flushed again for good measure and waited to see if any pieces resurfaced. Seeing none, he washed out the ashtray in the sink, pushed on the toilet handle for the third time, and walked out.

Bertrand was seated at the conference table, a cup of coffee and his pack of Blatros cigarettes in front of him.

"So, you have the ashtray. I was looking for it. Maybe we ought to get two in case one disappears again."

Duchant smiled and sat down in a seat across from Henri.

"You want to pour me a cup? I don't feel like getting up again and walking around you."

"Sure, black?"

"Please."

Henri held the cup out for Duchant, who took it and separated the saucer from the cup. He took a sip and then placed it back on the saucer, which was now resting on the table.

"What was that all about?"

"What are you talking about?"

"The cup and saucer bit."

"I didn't feel comfortable balancing steaming hot coffee on a thin bone china saucer with two fingers. My way was better." He laughed. Bertrand just shook his head.

"By the way, where's Kathy? I hope you didn't wear her out, the poor thing."

"I telephoned her. She said she had something of a personal nature to take care of and would be in later."

"I'd like you to get together with Shimon again, Henri. Go over the dossier on what we've developed on Kathy Longrin. I'm especially interested in her father. Copies of his immigration records show that he is one of thousands of displaced persons to get a visa for the States after the war but in his case he came here from Argentina."

"I'm surmising that the only way he could have gotten to South America is through International Red Cross documents or a Vatican passport. Both of these stellar groups were falling all over themselves to help the Nazis escape justice. The Nazis always had enough money from Odessa to get a new identity and buy a local passport."

"There was no photograph attached to the copies of immigration papers we have in our possession. How convenient, right? I'll wager the father of Miss Longrin is someone of interest."

"Maybe he's what he seems, then again, maybe not. He's a recluse but perhaps our associates could get us a satellite image."

At that moment, one of the two monitor operators from yesterday poked his head into the conference room. "We're on shift now, Mr. Duchant, and the matter we discussed yesterday is ready."

"That's what I was hoping to hear, Brent. Keep it warm, we're going to use it down the road a bit."

"Okay, Mr. Duchant. We'll be ready when you are." He waved and went back toward the monitors.

Henri got up. "If there's nothing more, Raphael, I think this is a good time to get together with Shimon."

"Okay, bring me up to date when you finish." Duchant looked down at his coffee as if trying to see something that wasn't there.

Chapter 21

Kathy waited until she heard the click, then pushed the door open.

The secretary watched Kathy as she walked through the door. "Good morning, Miss Longrin, I'll tell Mr. Duchant you are here."

Kathy shifted from foot to foot while the secretary touched several buttons on the screen to her front. It wasn't the wait that caused her to react in this way, it was the unnerving presence of the two tall, armed men who stood on either side of the inner doorway.

Although their heads remained toward their front, the eyes behind the dark round sunglasses were watching her every movement.

By the time she realized what she was doing with her feet, the secretary said, "Please go in, Miss Longrin."

Kathy walked to the left of the secretary and was almost at the door, when she heard it click and watched as it opened. She took a direct route across the floor, not bothering to look to either side, until she reached the metal stairs.

She climbed the stairs carefully. Somehow the notion of slipping came to mind. Heels were always precarious even on flat surfaces, but why was she thinking about something like that. She hadn't fallen in heels since she was a teenager.

She chalked it up to nervousness. Her mind hadn't yet settled itself into a regular pattern since the moment she realized she'd overslept.

She brushed her skirt as she came to the landing, entered the code, and watched as the door opened.

Seeing no one in the office she walked past the two men at the monitors, who knew from the concealed cameras who had entered, and continued in the direction of the conference room.

Both men stood up as she came into view.

Kathy smiled and took a seat on Bertrand's side of the table but left the seat between them empty.

"Do you care for coffee, Kathy?"

"Yes, please. Make it a Texas-size cup."

Duchant asked, "Bad night?"

Bertrand shook his head as he reached for his cigarette noticing a thinly veiled smile at the corner of Raphael's mouth.

He took a long drag on the cigarette, then turned toward the coffee pot and poured.

He placed the cup in front of Kathy and then reached again for the cigarette.

Kathy picked up the cup and sipped several times. Then she replaced the cup and looked at

Duchant. "It was a stimulating night, Raphael. I'm sorry you weren't there."

Duchant looked at Henri whose smile was very much in evidence.

"Perhaps next time I'll make myself more accommodating. I understand you had a problem of a personal nature. Without violating your confidence, is there any assistance we could render?"

"That's very kind of you, but I have the situation under control."

"In that case let's get a few things out of the way. Number one, how are you coming with the European litigation?"

"I'll phone them after we're finished, but as of yesterday, they reported that the museum wants to negotiate a monetary settlement. They do not want to return the painting."

"Let's see what they offer. Next, are you fully conversant with the Mary? Have you done your homework?"

"Yes and no on both counts, but by tomorrow's meeting I will have a reasonably good handle on the painting."

"A reasonably good handle is not what we expect or need. What we want is an expert sitting beside us that can discuss and authenticate the artwork."

"By tomorrow, you'll have that expert beside you, Raphael."

Chapter 22

Kathy sat in the middle with Duchant and Bertrand flanking her. The Rolls Royce pulled to the curb at twelve fifty-five p.m.

Bertrand opened the rear passenger's door and held it while Kathy and Raphael made their way out.

Then he walked ahead of them and pushed on the bell.

He stared at the door listening for the click, then held it open and followed Raphael and Kathy into the lobby.

At one p.m. they were standing at the third floor gallery watching von Hoenshield approach the door.

He shook hands with Duchant and Bertrand as they entered, then kissed the back of Kathy's hand. He lowered his voice as he said, "I know today's meeting will be very positive. I have worked very hard on your behalf."

Von Hoenshield took hold of Kathy's arm and moved her toward the rear of the gallery.

Duchant held back momentarily as he gave Bertrand a look. Bertrand just smiled acknowledge-ing that he understood what Duchant was thinking about von Hoenshield's comment. Then he leaned toward Raphael, "You know what, we forgot to bring…a shovel." Then he smiled and started to trail von Hoenshield.

*

From the moment Rudel had arrived at the gallery, the recording device was activated. It clearly picked up the exchange between von Hoenshield and the others as well as the comment Bertrand made to Duchant.

Rudel was standing when von Hoenshield approached with Kathy in tow.

"Kathy, may I present Mr. Karl Garland."

Rudel bowed slightly and reached for Kathy's hand, which he shook gently.

Still holding her hand and looking directly at her, he said, "Manfred neglected to indicate your last name."

"It's Longrin, like in long grin," and she smiled, showing off her beautiful white teeth.

Rudel gave no indication that he recognized the woman. "Your name should be easy to remember. Names are usually so revealing, but I can't specifically place your origin."

Kathy stared back without blinking. "I'm a mix of different origins, all of them classical, ambitious, and strong, with a smattering of mystery. That's the best I can offer you for now. Too much, and you might write a book about me."

133

Duchant and Bertrand were holding back, enjoying the exchange between the man called Garland and Kathy, and laughed at her last remark. Garland smiled as well.

Releasing Kathy's hand and turning his attention to Duchant and Bertrand, he extended his hand without waiting for von Hoenshield to make the introductions. After a short exchange, Manfred suggested they seat themselves around the table.

"Does anyone care for wine, tea, or perhaps coffee?" No one answered von Hoenshield, but several shook their heads no.

Manfred smiled. "Fine, perhaps later then."

Von Hoenshield looked around the table. "Mr. Garland is empowered to negotiate regarding the matter in discussion."

Bertrand answered by saying, "We need to make sure that the item actually exists. When we can confirm that fact, we are ready to deal."

Rudel waited a moment before speaking.

"Mr. Bertrand, while none of you know me, I can assure you that I am not inclined to waste my time or that of anyone else. The item exists and the owner is willing to negotiate its sale. You have offered eight million in currency or diamonds. How do I know that you are sincere?"

Henri looked toward Duchant who was already reaching into his jacket pocket. He pulled out a folded paper and carefully opened it on the table.

As he spread the paper, the diamonds caught the late afternoon light at precisely the right angles and their brilliance radiated.

With the other hand Raphael took out a jeweler's loupe and placed it next to the stones.

Rudel picked up the loupe and one of the stones and looked at it carefully twisting it around with his fingers. He set the loupe and stone back down and looked up at Duchant. "It appears to be of excellent quality, Mr. La Monde."

"I can assure you, that stone and the others are everything you think they are."

Raphael reached into his jacket pocket again and brought out his black ostrich billfold. He opened it and withdrew the same check he previously showed von Hoenshield. He passed it across the table to Rudel, who picked it up and examined it.

He lifted his eyes from the check and looked over at Raphael. "Sixteen million in diamonds and a cashier's check is an extraordinary amount of money to be carrying around New York."

"For some in this metropolis, it's pocket change."

A thin smile appeared on Rudel's face. He moved his head like he was considering the remark.

"Yes, for some, just pocket change. That combined amount of eight million each in diamonds, and the cashier's check, sets the parameters of our negotiation to a degree. The item we have, gentlemen and Miss Longrin, is worth thirty million."

"To whom is it worth thirty million, Mr. Garland?"

"To those who possess it, Mr. Bertrand."

"But we are on the other side, Mr. Garland. We represent certain interests that are willing to pay a fair and equitable price for an item that has reputably been destroyed, doesn't exist and if it did, would be submerged in litigation as contraband, stolen during the last world war."

"There is no open market for this item, or any like it. Buyers of this type of item are few and questionable at best, both with regard to their sincerity and ability to pay a reasonable price. Shall we therefore say, Mr. Garland, that the item is therefore worth whatever a creditable buyer is willing to pay?"

"That's not exactly correct. The owners, who have had this item for a considerable number of years, feel no pressure to dispose of it, but are willing to consider a sale if the price is realistic."

"And what price would that be?"

"Twenty million."

"On the open market I'd estimate the painting to be worth that and maybe more, perhaps the thirty million you previously mentioned. However, Mr. Garland, to conclude a sale with us, the price of twenty million is beyond the realm of possibility."

"Our offer of eight million is quite generous. What you get, Mr. Garland, is a substantial sum of money for an item that has a non-existent market. Your owners also are relieved from the ever-present possibility that the work will be discovered. The owners avoid the additional possibility of litigation which would follow, rendering the item worthless. Lastly, undue notoriety would be expeditiously avoided."

Kathy intoned, "The Americans have a saying, Mr. Garland…a bird in the hand is worth two in the bush."

"I've heard that before, Miss Longrin. The Americans also have a saying, he who hesitates, is lost. The offer to sell the item will not remain open indefinitely. I suggest that you reconsider your offer. I am quite willing to entertain any reasonable number as close to the twenty million as you'd care to make."

"Will you excuse us a moment, Mr. Garland."

"Certainly. Mr. von Hoenshield and I will take the elevator to the street and get some air. We'll return in twenty minutes. Would that be sufficient time?"

"Yes."

The three watched as Rudel and von Hoenshield walked out the door, locking it behind them.

Duchant put his fingers to his lips and took a folded piece of yellow legal paper from his jacket. He unscrewed the top of his pen and began to write, then turned the paper so that Kathy and Henri could read it.

"The room is probably bugged. Write your comments...responses...say nothing."

They both shook their heads as Raphael continued to write. "We should raise the offer by one point five million to nine point five million. When he balks, we up it to ten million, then walk."

Kathy took out a pen from her purse and turned the paper.

"If we walk at ten million, aren't we defeating ourselves?"

Henri looked over her shoulder as she wrote. When she finished, she turned the paper back toward Raphael.

Raphael started to write again.

No. We can always reopen the matter through a phone call. Let me take the lead when they return.

The two nodded their heads in agreement.

Bertrand was the first to speak.

"Does anyone mind if I smoke?" Nothing was said, so Bertrand turned the pack on an angle, and tapped the bottom until several cigarettes appeared. He pulled one away from the pack and placed it between his lips. He reached into a pocket and took out his gold lighter.

"I don't hear anything, so your silence says no," and then he lit his cigarette.

Raphael refolded the paper, which they used to communicate, and placed it in his jacket pocket. Then he directed his attention to Bertrand and watched as Henri blew smoke through his nose and formed smoke rings with his mouth.

*

Once outside, Rudel made a call on his cell. When it connected, Rudel said, "This is Churchill... status."

The voice on the line came back quickly. "There has been no verbal."

"Understood. Keep me updated," then he pushed the end button.

Rudel stood there thinking, They're guessing about the voice surveillance and they're correct. Probably communicating in writing or through pre-arranged hand signals. The woman is much prettier than in the photograph. She definitely complicates the situation.

Then he turned to von Hoenshield and smiled. "If you are ready, Hauptsturmführer Friedrich Alpers, let's return."

The voice, the smile, and the way he was addressed sent a chill through Manfred's inner soul.

They rode the elevator up in silence. Manfred realized his place was to say nothing and follow orders whether those orders were stated or implied.

Again seated at the table, Rudel looked at Bertrand, then back at Duchant and finally at the diamonds and the check which remained on the table where Raphael had initially placed them.

He smiled and said in a low voice, "Give me a number that will close this business."

"Nine point five million."

"That's still too far from twenty million. Would you like to narrow the gap a bit?"

Duchant looked at Kathy and then at Bertrand and back to Rudel.

"Before I consider anything further, Mr. Garland, we would like to see and authenticate the painting."

Rudel looked at von Hoenshield and nodded.

Manfred immediately stood, walked to a wall, lifted a wooden case and then placed it on the table.

Reaching out with his index finger, von Hoenshield pressed a button at the top right corner of the case. The wooden top opened by way of the spring mechanism and von Hoenshield carefully withdrew a thirty-five by twenty-nine-inch painting.

He propped the Woman in Black against his chair in a way that made it visible to the other four.

Kathy rose from her seat and moved closer. She turned toward Rudel and asked, "May I take the painting to the window. I'd like to see it in better light."

"Certainly. Take what time you need."

Kathy then turned to Bertrand. "Henri, would you help me."

"My pleasure."

He took the painting with two hands and carried it to the wall of windows.

Von Hoenshield went quickly to an easel and removed its painting. He leaned the painting against a wall, then moved the easel to where Bertrand was standing.

"That's very kind of you, Manfred. Would you place the easel perpendicular to the window, and slightly to the right. The light should catch the painting in the right way for me to examine it. Yes, that's perfect. Thank you, Manfred."

Von Hoenshield moved toward the table, and Bertrand began to follow, when Kathy tugged at his sleeve. "Would you get me some paper. I'd like to make some notes."

Bertrand returned with a pad of paper, then went back to the table. "Does anyone mind if I smoke?"

Garland said, "Yes, I do, Mr. Bertrand. If it wouldn't be too much trouble could you do it in the hallway or in front of the building?"

"Sure," and Henri smiled. "It'll give me the opportunity to tell our driver we're running late."

Kathy let her eyes scan the painting trying to get oriented. Then she started to zero in on the characteristics.

The upper left and right hand corners of the painting consisted of background in an opaque pink/gray color. The position of the woman's right arm was moved from the initial position in which it was painted and changed more dramatically to the right. The arm seemed unnatural as if the woman had a pronounced deformity. Kathy knew that Cassett later reworked the arm's position and reversed it back to the original. The finished work still gave the arm an awkward appearance if viewed closely and during any process of authentication, such an observation would always be made.

The woman's head, her right side and the left portion of the painting were highlighted by a strong yellow color. Other colors seemed to be rapidly dragged down the painting.

Near the bottom of the canvas were colors worked thinly into the painting.

Kathy found everything to conform. So far so good, she thought.

Her eyes roamed over the woman's dress. Unlike Degas, and Cezanne among other masters, Cassatt never abandoned her use of black. She studied the dress from the high collar down to where the dress left the canvas.

She began to write on the pad as she moved her eyes back and forth from the painting. After concentrating on the area above the woman's dress for several minutes, Kathy shifted her focus to the woman's hair, hands, and face.

She looked down at her notes, then called to Duchant. Once he was alongside, she handed him the pad.

Raphael began to read the first of several pages slowly.

The flesh hue of the face and hands appears to have been first painted, let dry, and then dragged. The original painting would have been dragged when still wet. The drag marks would be different than those on this canvas. I have considerable concern specifically in the head area. The painting should show gaps or inconsistent strokes. While there are some drag marks, the appearance seems rushed and not consistent with the way the strokes of a Cassatt painting should appear.

The same holds true of the woman's hair. It was most likely painted with a hog's hair brush which Cassatt normally used. But like the hands and face, there is no indication that the hair was scraped downward while still wet.

Cassatt's main characteristic was dragging wet colors. There is some evidence of this, but not enough to convince me that this painting is authentic. Dragging was an old technique, to soften and blur the forms.

The original painting was completed in a standard format - vertical landscape forty canvas. I'm not sure this painting is painted on such a canvas.

It's good, in fact very, very good, but I believe it's a copy.

Raphael looked at Kathy and smiled, "Seems almost surreal, doesn't it?"

Then he turned and slowly walked back toward the seated Rudel and von Hoenshield. As he walked, Raphael tore the written pages and several additional ones from the pad. The extra pages were removed in case a written impression of anything indicated remained on those pages. Then he stuffed them into his pocket.

As he neared the table, he saw the diamonds and the cashier's check and smiled to himself.

Chapter 23

Bertrand leaned through the window into the front passenger's side of the Rolls Royce.

"It's going to be awhile longer, Shimon. Get a picture of a bald man, about six feet tall wearing a blue suit when he comes out. He may or may not be with the Hauptsturmfuhrer."

Then Bertrand walked away from the car and leaned against the brick wall of the gallery townhouse. He lit a cigarette and looked around the general area out of habit, but now more so, because of circumstances.

He pushed off the wall, nodded to the driver who was turned in his direction, flicked the cigarette toward the curb, and walked to the building's door. He pushed the bell, waited for the click, then walked to the elevator.

He was seated at the table a few minutes later trying to catch up with the conversation. He watched as Rudel denied the allegation.

He remained silent and decided not to interrupt just yet.

Then Raphael leaned forward. "I trust Miss Longrin. If she says the painting is a forgery, until it's proved otherwise, I'm going to assume both you and the owners are trying to pull a fast one."

Bertrand listened with some concern, letting his mind speculate on where this conversation was heading. He felt some comfort knowing that his Israeli .375 magnum Desert Eagle was in a quick draw holster under his left arm.

Rudel leaned back in his chair. He looked first at Kathy, then back at Duchant and started to laugh. The laughter didn't act to defuse the heightening situation but seemed to have the effect of escalating it.

Kathy stared at Rudel with a look of bewilderment.

"Please don't look so forlorn, Miss Longrin. It was simply a test to determine if you all were whom you appeared to be. A test, to determine if any of you knew anything about art, specifically the item in question. It seems that you have passed our little test."

Duchant spoke up. "And you, Mr. Garland, what test do we apply to insure you are what you appear to be?"

Rudel turned to von Hoenshield. In a few minutes, another painting was displayed on the easel.

Duchant and Bertrand stood slightly to the rear of Kathy and watched intently as she systematically went over the painting.

After twenty minutes, she turned around, and faced them. "This is the Woman in Black, painted by Mary Cassatt in 1882."

The three returned to the table and took their seats.

"Well, Miss Longrin and gentlemen, what is your verdict?"

"Miss Longrin concludes that the painting is genuine."

"Indeed, it is, which now brings us back to our negotiations. The price for the item is twenty million. Do we have an agreement, gentlemen?"

"I would like to think so, Mr. Garland. To show our sincerity, we will increase the price by another five hundred thousand dollars to an even ten million."

Rudel sat with his arms folded across his chest, looking unwaveringly at Duchant.

"That leaves us about ten million short, Mr. La Monde. The amount you've just indicated would only purchase the upper, or lower portion of the painting and we cannot sell this artwork in pieces, can we, Mr. La Monde?"

Raphael smiled. "Our principal would not be able to enjoy the painting unless it was intact and original. It appears to be both, but it is not worth any more than the offer we've made."

"Then I feel we have reached an impasse. It's a shame, gentlemen, to be so close," and then Rudel paused.

"Suppose I agree to take the cashier's check, and the diamonds as payment. You claim the diamonds are worth eight million. That may be overstated. The diamonds at fair market value could be worth half that amount or less. If we assume the diamonds are worth four million dollars and add it to the check, we have a total of twelve million. You offered ten million dollars, so we are only two million off."

"Interesting mathematics, Mr. Garland, but the diamonds are worth considerably more than four million dollars. It's our business to know."

"Then gentlemen and lady, we have reached the conclusion of our negotiations."

As Rudel moved his chair back and started to rise, Bertrand said, "Perhaps the gentleman on whose behalf you are negotiating would be more receptive to our offer."

"I doubt that, since I am empowered to decide one way or another and I have decided."

"That's a genuine shame, Mr. Garland, since our principal intended to make this purchase the beginning of what he hoped would be considerably more in the future. He was thinking about a dollar amount between one hundred million and two hundred million dollars."

Rudel sat back down, silence engulfing the room. Finally, Rudel started speaking again.

"Let's table this discussion for the time being and consider that the matter remains open. I will inform the owners of the painting and will advise the outcome through Mr. von Hoenshield. Is that satisfactory?"

"Très bon. Ç'a été un plaisir," then Henri repeated what he had just said in English. "Very good. It has been a pleasure."

Bertrand stood up and extended his hand toward Rudel, who rose and shook it firmly.

Rudel followed suit with Duchant and then Kathy.

The three turned and shook hands with von Hoenshield and then left the gallery.

Chapter 24

Kathy, Bertrand, and Duchant stood by the rear of the Rolls.

Bertrand said quietly, "Shimon will take Garland's picture when he leaves the building. Meantime this is as good a place as any to discuss what happened upstairs."

"I thought we'd lost it until Henri mentioned the hundred million. Did you notice the look on von Hoenshield's face?"

"Yes, Kathy, I could envision all those dollar signs dancing around his head. But on a more serious note, there's no doubt that Garland is the superior of the two, despite his younger age. If Shimon gets the picture, we'll run it through our database and try to come up with a match."

Duchant shifted his weight to the other foot. "I've been sitting too long...cramps."

Kathy laughed, "You don't know what cramps are, Raphael. You should have been born a woman and lived through a full moon cycle."

They all laughed.

"I believe we're going to be the owners of a painting shortly and at our price. Since you both owe me a dinner at The Blue Dove, I'm quite willing to go double or nothing with you both so that Garland's message will be positive. Do I have any takers?"

Henri shook his head no. "I'm inclined to agree with you this time."

Then he turned to Kathy. "You're free to take Raphael up on his offer."

"I feel like you do. I think Garland will come back positive. Sorry, Raphael, no takers."

Duchant spread his arms, turned over his hands, palms facing up and moved his head slightly. "You still have time to reconsider my offer."

Before either Kathy or Bertrand could answer, they heard the door open. They changed positions so they could face Rudel.

He waved to them, started walking to his right, then stopped. He took several steps back, then stopped again and faced in their direction.

"I can't make any promises. My suggestion is you reconsider your offer. The next time may truly end further negotiations if we remain far apart."

Then he turned around again and began walking.

Raphael opened the rear door of the Rolls for Kathy and Bertrand, then he took a seat next to the Shimon.

"Did you get a picture, Shimon?"

"Several."

"Good. Let's get them processed quickly and check against the database."

*

Rudel turned the corner and stopped in a doorway. He stayed against the wall and waited until he saw the Rolls Royce go past the corner and head toward Madison Avenue.

As soon as the car disappeared, he went back to the townhouse. When he re-entered the gallery von Hoenshield was standing near the door.

"I've had second thoughts about keeping the painting here. Get me the original."

Von Hoenshield walked to the wall, lifted one of the crates and returned to where Rudel was waiting.

Rudel turned to leave, then stopped and faced von Hoenshield.

"You will be advised within the next several days what we intend to do. Meanwhile keep the reproduction here and make sure it is stored in a secure place. I'll take care of the original," and then Rudel took out his phone.

*

Rudel waited by the curb as the black Mercedes Benz pulled up. The driver went to the rear door and held it open until Rudel entered. Then the driver opened the front passenger's side door and placed the wood crate on the seat.

After merging with the Madison Avenue traffic, the car proceeded to a SoHo address, eventually stopping in front of a business establishment on Prince Street.

Rudel leaned toward the driver.

"Bring the crate in, Bruno," then he opened the Mercedes' door, and walked to the building's front door.

Passing the display tables of leather merchandise, Rudel made his way through a curtained doorway.

He ignored the workers at the worktables and continued until he reached another door. He knocked once, waited, then knocked again.

Nodding to the man who held the door open, Rudel said something in German and pointed to his rear. Then he took the stairs down to the lower level.

The lower level consisted of a large room, well-lit and elaborately furnished. It served as both an office and a communication center.

Rudel stood near the stairs until the driver appeared with the crate. He took it, dismissed the driver and then turned to one of the men standing near him.

"Secure this in the safe, then connect me with the Doctor."

"Immediately, Sturmbannführer."

The man clicked his heels and turned toward the operators on duty. "Get the Doctor."

The reply came quickly, "The Doctor is on the line."

Rudel walked to a desk situated in a far corner of the room, then sat down facing the communication equipment that ran along a portion of the wall. He nodded toward the operator and then picked up the phone.

"Good evening Herr Doctor. You are aware of the meeting, but it is necessary sir, to advise you that the woman called Kathy Longrin and your daughter are the same."

Rudel waited for the reply that did not come. He motioned to the operators and then pointed to his receiver. They nodded in the affirmative and then one said, "It's working, sir."

Rudel spoke into the phone again. "Did you receive my last transmission, sir?"

The reply came back, "Yes."

Then before Rudel could continue, the voice said, "That information was known previously, and I indicated as much to you. Are you losing your senses, Sturmbannführer?"

Then there was another long pause before Rudel said, "Your orders, sir."

"Contact me this time tomorrow," then the phone went dead.

Rudel held the receiver and looked toward the operator. The operator made a slicing motion across his neck, indicating that the connection was terminated.

Rudel replaced the receiver, got up, walked toward the stairs and out to the Mercedes.

Chapter 25

The Doctor replaced the phone and walked back to his study. He sat down and looked at the picture of his daughter. The memories came flooding back and he let them. After all, these memories represented a major portion of his life and he was proud of his service to the Reich and the Fuhrer.

He drifted back over his career as an Officer in the Third Reich. He was on the fast track from the beginning and credited that in part to his advanced education but mostly to his friendship with Reichsführer Heinrich Himmler, head of the SS and Police.

Himmler was a man he knew well and whose life would intertwine with his for almost three decades. Like Himmler, the Doctor was born into a Catholic German family.

A short-sighted individual and physically weak, the Doctor marveled at how Himmler was able to become an officer cadet in the Eleventh Bavarian Regiment during the First World War, a unit in which he served as a Lieutenant.

Himmler's connection to Hitler was parallel to his own when in November 1923 both joined with Hitler and six hundred Sturmabteilung (Brown Shirts) when they attempted to seize power in Munich. They were stopped at the Hall of the Generals, later to become an enshrined placed in Nazi lore.

In 1925, at the urging of Himmler, he joined the Nazi Party. In later years he looked back upon that day as a momentous one, equal to the exhilaration he felt when he received his Ph.D degree from Universitat Bremen.

His career started to accelerate when on April 5, 1934 he became commander of the 46th SS-Standard in Dresden.

A short time later, he was First Adjutant to the Reichsfuhrer-SS, Himmler.

His career continued to prosper with appointments as the SS-Brigadefuhrer and Major General of Police in the Crimea, then Commander of the Selbstschutz (Self-Defense) of Reichsgau, Danzig, West Prussia.

He pushed back in his chair and reached for a set of keys. He inserted one of the keys into the lock and twisted the key to his right.

The red light to the left of the lock immediately turned yellow. He waited for ten seconds and then turned the key back to his left. The light changed from yellow to green.

He pulled the drawer open, reached inside, and brought out a large metal box.

He placed the box on his desk and opened the lid.

After moving the contents around, he found what he wanted and placed the faded, yellowing envelope down gently.

He gingerly opened the envelope and withdrew several black and white photographs.

The first one, which was always on top of the others, pictured him in the dress uniform of an SS-Brigadefuhrer and Major General of Police. Beside him was a woman in a wedding dress, a woman he adored since their days at the Grundschule. (Elementary school)

He placed the picture carefully to his right, then stared at the next photograph. He remembered when it was taken just after the wedding ceremony and pictured the two of them with Himmler and Adolph Hitler.

The third photograph showed his wife holding a baby. There was a yellowing con-gratulatory note with the embossed seal of Himmler taped to the back of the photograph.

He stared at the picture for an inordinate amount of time clearly remembering the day he and Himmler were discussing the roundup of Jews in West Prussia. Somehow the subject of children came up and in a weakened moment, he related to the Reichsfuhrer that his wife could never conceive.

"There is a way to remedy that, Ludolf, if you'll allow me."

He wasn't sure what Himmler was talking about but nodded his head.

Approximately two and a half weeks later, SS-Brigadefuhrer Ludolf Otto Steiger was summoned to Reichsfuhrer-SS Heinrich Himmler's

SS and Gestapo headquarters at Prinz Albrecht StraBe 9 in Berlin.

He walked up the steps and past the black-uniformed SS Guards, who snapped to attention, rendered a salute with their rifles, and stood ramrod straight until he passed.

The pattern of the well-disciplined SS men continued until he was facing a standing male SS secretary who saluted him with his right arm held straight out and said, "Heil Hitler."

He returned the salute. "I am Brigadefuhrer Steiger. I have an appointment with the Reichsfuhrer."

"One moment, General."

The secretary knocked, opened the door and walked through the immense doorway. A few moments later he reappeared and held the door open.

"The Reichsfurer will see you now, General."

The secretary's right arm shot out as Steiger started toward the door.

Steiger continued walking past two SS guards from the Leibstandarte SS Adolph Hitler (Personal bodyguard) who were posted on either side of the doorway. Once inside, the secretary shut the door discreetly behind the General.

The General approached Himmler who came from behind his desk to greet him. After an exchange of pleasantries, Himmler pointed to a uniformed SS Officer whom he introduced as Obersturmbannführer Otto Adolph Eichmann, head of Gestapo Department IV, B4 for Jewish Affairs.

"Colonel Eichmann has something for you. In fact, Ludolf, it is my personal gift to both you and your wife."

Himmler nodded to Eichmann, who walked to a door of an adjoining room and knocked. The door opened and a military nurse carrying a baby approximately ten months old walked through.

She walked first to Himmler who smiled down at the child, then she carried it over to Steiger.

"Ludolf, this child is yours. Its parents have met with unfortunate circumstances and it is orphaned. Note that the hair is blonde and the eyes blue. This beautiful girl should be raised as a true daughter of Germany.

"I have a car waiting for you together with a very competent nurse, a Miss Gerta Underberger. I have arranged for the delivery of a number of useful items that you and your wife will need. These items should have already arrived at your home."

Steiger remembered standing there transfixed, staring down at the child as Himmler patted his shoulder.

"These papers are your official adoption papers. One never knows about the future and its uncertainties. I believe it is in your best interest to have these papers, Ludolf."

"Thank you, Reichsführer."

"No thanks are necessary. After all, what are friends for? By the way, Ludolf, if you feel like thanking someone, Eichmann is really the one to thank."

Chapter 26

Duchant ducked his head around the headrest of the front passenger's seat and faced Kathy and Bertrand. "The traffic isn't helping. Let's have a drink."

They both nodded yes, then Raphael tapped the driver on the shoulder.

"Shimon, please turn left on 56th and leave us off at Il Gato Pardo." (The Brown Cat) Don't wait for us, but make sure the pictures get printed, and begin the trace. We'll meet tomorrow morning to review what you've developed. Anything that's urgent, you know the number to call."

After several minutes trying to negotiate the evening rush hour traffic, the Rolls pulled in front of the Italian restaurant.

As Duchant entered he was greeted by the headwaiter. "Buona Sera, Mr. Duchant. Your table is ready. Please follow me."

They walked to a table against the left wall and one row from the windows, which looked out onto 56th Street. The headwaiter pulled out the chair for Kathy who seated herself quickly. Then Duchant and Bertrand sat down.

"Do you care for a drink?"

"Yes, Salvatore," and Raphael looked toward Kathy, who replied, "A Johnny Walker Red over ice with a twist."

Then Bertrand and Duchant exchanged glances, with Bertrand finally saying, "A dry Beefeater's martini, very dry please."

Duchant followed with, "A Grey Goose over the rocks with a twist."

When the headwaiter departed, Bertrand leaned forward on his elbows.

"The one hundred plus million added a little spice to our effort. Did any of you catch the look on Garland's face? Ever so subtle, but it clearly registered. You know what though, even if that amount wasn't mentioned, negotiations would have continued despite the appearance of an impasse. They want to move the painting, most likely others, too."

Kathy moved her hand away from her hair. "That's speculation, Henri. Garland seemed pretty sure of his position. Ten million to him is an unbridgeable gap and that was the difference between what he wanted and what we offered."

"He's under no pressure to sell the painting. In fact, selling it could open a Pandora's box of problems. Unless the amount is where the owner feels it should be and this amount has no doubt been agreed upon prior to our meeting, Garland would have walked."

"It was only when you, Henri, mentioned the one hundred to two hundred million in future purchases did Garland make a quick decision to continue. Otherwise, he would have left for sure."

Duchant waited a moment before he spoke. "I agree with Kathy. The diamonds and the cashier's check sitting on the table were constant reminders of who we purport to be, but until you mentioned the hundred mil, Garland would have cut us off."

The drinks arrived carried by a waiter and accompanied by Salvatore who made it his business to supervise the placement. Once he was satisfied, they turned and left.

Henri held his glass in the center and said, "To happy days."

After taking a sip, Raphael put his glass down, took hold of the red plastic stirrer and swirled the vodka around counterclockwise as if the movement was habitual, which it was.

He did this after each sip, not paying particular attention to what he was doing, but knowing it gave him the necessary time to attune to what was being stated, processing it or thinking of what to say or reply.

He started to say something about von Hoenshield, then caught himself.

Kathy Longrin was not in the loop, at least not yet. Certain things were strictly on a need to know basis and she didn't need to know what he was about to say. Instead Duchant stumbled over the first word and twisted the rest into something that resembled "...ungry, anyone for dinner."

"Let me try that again. Maybe after a few sips of vodka I'm getting tongue-tied. Would anyone care for dinner and by saying yes and perhaps picking up the check, that doesn't get either one of you off the hook for dinner at 'La Colombre de Bleue.'"

Bertrand feigned pain and Kathy just laughed.

"While you're both thinking about it, I'm going to have another drink. Either of you care to join me?"

"Naw, I'm okay."

"How about you, Kathy?"

"I'm fine, Raphael. If neither of you mind, I'm going to call it a day."

Bertrand started to get up with Kathy. "I'll see you home."

"Thanks for the offer, Henri, but I'll be fine. Why not take Raphael up on his offer for dinner. He looks lonely."

They laughed.

"Henri is definitely not my type, Kathy."

Then Duchant looking back at Bertrand said, "Stay awhile, Henri. I've got a few things I'd like to throw your way."

Bertrand shrugged his shoulders. "Since Kathy has decided to abandon us Raphael, I'm forced to accept your kind invitation."

Raphael looked at Kathy. When their eyes made contact he said, "You were outstanding today. You were everything I had hoped you'd be and more. Thank you for a job well done."

"I second that."

"Well thank you kind sirs. It wasn't that hard." She smiled. "I'll see you both tomorrow morning, arrivederci," (Goodbye) and headed toward the door.

She stopped by the headwaiter and said something to him. He bowed slightly and walked to the telephone that rested at one corner of the bar.

"I sometimes overlook that Kathy is not one of us. What I was about to say when I caught myself, was that we know who von Hoenshield is and through him will get to the others. Garland is von Hoenshield's superior. There's no doubt about that. Von Hoenshield didn't make a peep as Garland orchestrated the negotiation. Maybe Shimon will get us a fix on who our friend Garland actually is."

"It might be a good idea Raphael, if you and I get von Hoenshield alone for another dinner and a few drinks. Try to soften him up. Garland might not come back quickly, then again...who knows? Meantime we can work on the Hauptsturmfuhrer. What do you think about the suggestion?"

"It's not a bad idea. Do you want to make the arrangements tomorrow?"

"Sure."

"Good but leave Kathy out. It'll just be you and me. Do you want another drink, or shall we order?"

"I think I'm ready for some food."

As he watched Raphael signal the headwaiter, Henri's mind drifted to Kathy Longrin and he silently wished she was here instead of Duchant.

Chapter 27

As Kathy sat in the taxi her mind raced over the events of the day. The first painting she was shown was an excellent copy but even with the little expertise she possessed, it was easy to identify it for what it was. She wondered why the original painting wasn't presented for inspection initially. Why the games?

Yet in this world of enormous dollar transactions to which she was now exposed, everyone seemed to constantly jockey for position. The unexpected was normal and normal became the unexpected. She had to stay alert. Events were happening at an accelerated pace.

On the surface everything seemed routine, but she knew nothing is ever as it seems and everything is subject to change. That goes for people, objects, places, and the spoken or written word. She thought, take a few things at face value, Kathy Longrin and question everything. That was the only way. It was her background once again kicking in. Trust no one.

She smiled at the doorman holding the cab door open and walked briskly through her building's entrance. She opened her mailbox, looked casually through the bills and junk mail, and then walked to the elevator.

Kathy kicked off her shoes, placed the mail on the coffee table and went to the bedroom. She took off her clothes, went to the bathroom, and showered. She dried off, put on the terrycloth robe, and went to the refrigerator.

She opened the door, looked in, forgetting why she opened the door in the first place.

After she closed the refrigerator door she walked to the bar and reached for the bottle of Johnny Walker Red. Then went back to the kitchen with the bottle in tow and placed it on the counter.

After removing a glass from the cabinet, she pressed it against the ice lever on the refrigerator door. The cubes tumbled out quickly, overfilling her glass and scattering across the floor.

She bent down, picked up the spilled cubes with both hands, then came back up too quickly and hit her head on the edge of the sink.

Then after shouting out the word shit more times than was necessary, Kathy wrapped some of the cubes in a paper towel, throwing the rest into the sink.

She placed the free-formed ice pack on the top of her head, stared at the bottle of scotch, turned, and walked back to the sofa.

As she sat holding the ice pack with one hand she wondered if she cut her scalp.

Kathy brought her hand away from her head and looked at the paper towel. There were no blood spots. She was about to place the ice pack back on top of her head when she saw the red message light blinking on her answering machine.

She placed the ice pack down on the coffee table and went to the answering machine.

It indicated one message. She pressed the play button and the familiar voice of her father filled the room.

"Your recent telephone call, Karta, stirred more emotion than I thought possible. I do miss you. I wonder if, despite starting a new job, you might be able to fly here for a long weekend. Call back when you can. Love, Papa."

The machine's recorded voice stating, "end of messages" came on. She moved her finger toward the play button, then pulled it back. She didn't need to hear it again. She heard it clearly the first time. A requested visit from her father was out of character.

Her father was a man of inflexible habits. The way he dressed, the times of the day or evening when he ate, where and when he conducted business, what he drank and a host of other complexities that she had grown to accept without questioning. She could not recall any other occasion where he made a telephone call to her. She had always initiated the contact.

Kathy walked back to the sofa and sat down. She placed her right leg on the coffee table and then crossed it with her left leg. She leaned her head back and closed her eyes. So much seemed to have happened in a few short weeks. Her transition to the world in which Duchant and Bertrand lived was taking hold slowly, but as each day passed the uneasiness within her grew.

Her mind reflected to her undergraduate days, to a class in Roman History and something that Julius Caesar had said, as a rule, what is out of sight disturbs men's minds more seriously than what they see.

She felt this was applicable to her present situation and couldn't help but wonder where all of this would lead?

The ring of the telephone interrupted her thoughts. She opened her eyes, stood up and walked to the desk. She picked up the phone on the third ring. "Hello."

"Karta, this is Papa. I thought I'd try you again. I hope I'm not disturbing you."

"No, Papa, you're not. I was about to call you. I heard the message you left, and I was thinking about a convenient time."

"Good. Do you think you might be able to visit this weekend?"

"Possibly, Papa, but I won't know for sure until tomorrow. May I call you then?"

"Tomorrow will be fine, Karta. How is everything else in your life?"

"Ever changing, Papa, never a dull moment. How are you?"

"Well, thank you. I'm looking forward to seeing you soon. I miss you, Karta."

"I miss you too, Papa. I'll call you sometime tomorrow. Bye."

"I'll expect your call. Good night, Karta. I love you."

"I love you too, Papa."

Kathy walked away from the desk and toward the kitchen. She took hold of the Johnny Walker Red bottle and poured an oversized shot into the standing glass.

She placed the glass against the ice lever and pushed gently. Two cubes came out. She pushed again and watched six more tumble out and overfill her glass.

She bent to the floor again, picked up the fallen cubes and tossed them into the sink.

Mumbling out loud, "I wonder if it's worth the effort." Kathy took hold of her glass, and walked toward the sofa.

No sooner had she sat down, the phone rang again. She debated whether to answer it and finally picked it up before the answering machine came on.

Before she could say anything, the voice on the other end said, "I hope I'm not disturbing you."

She didn't recognize the voice, until the caller said, "This is Henri."

"Oh Henri, I'm sorry. My mind was a couple of million miles away."

"Is there something wrong … perhaps something that I could assist you with? You sound upset."

"No, I'm fine. I received a telephone call from my father, and he wants me to visit. It's been a long time since I've seen him. I know that I've just started working with you and Raphael, but I was thinking of asking you both if I could take a long weekend and mortgage that against any future vacation I might be getting."

"That shouldn't be a problem, Kathy. I'll discuss it with Raphael tomorrow. I enjoyed our dinner the other night and I was hoping we might do it again this weekend, but now you'll most likely be leaving for home. That was my underlying reason for the call."

"You were going to ask me for a date? How sweet."

"Yes, I guess I was."

"Give me a rain check, Henri."

"You have it. See you tomorrow. Sleep well. good night."

"Good night, Henri."

She walked back to the sofa, paused a moment in anticipation of the telephone ringing again, then picked up her scotch and took a sip.

When she finished the drink, she walked to the bedroom, took off her robe, set her alarm clock, and crawled under the covers.

She pushed her head into the pillow and closed her eyes, but sleep didn't come. Her thoughts were of her father's underground room full of paintings and artifacts. She felt a chill run through her body, and she brought her knees up and moved herself into a prenatal position.

"No," she said out loud, "it simply wasn't possible."

Kathy got out of bed, walked to the medicine cabinet, and reached for the sleeping tablets. She swallowed one and went back to bed where she continued to toss from side to side and then finally sat up.

She picked up the remote control, thumbed the power button and watched the television screen come to life.

Chapter 28

When the alarm clock rang, Kathy was already awake. What sleep she did manage to get, came intermittently. It was like getting no sleep at all and her body felt it.

She leaned forward in the shower letting the water cascade against her neck. She wondered if it was doing any good.

When she dried off, she felt as bad as she did when she first got up. It's going to be a lousy day.

Wrapping the towel around her body, she went to the kitchen, then remembered that she forgot to set up the coffee pot.

She went through the drill, then sat at the table waiting for the coffee to brew. As she stared at the pot, her mind quickly recalled the telephone call with her father, then images of Garland, von Hoenshield, Duchant, Bertrand, diamonds, and paintings flashed by.

Lost in a mind fog, Kathy didn't realize that the coffee pot had stopped percolating. When she became aware of the silence, she pushed her chair back, walked to the cabinet and took a large mug from the bottom shelf. She poured the black liquid to the rim and carefully carried it back to the table.

She gingerly took a sip of the steaming brew. She couldn't help thinking that maybe two or three days away might be just what she needed. She wanted to avoid appearing, at all costs, as someone who didn't have the inner strength to handle the pressure and complexity of an ever-changing business situation. She knew what she was, but a weekend and a change of scenery might work like a shot in the arm, a quick fix of sorts. Besides, her father had asked her to come.

She finished the coffee, then walked back to the bedroom and started dressing.

*

Bertrand arrived at the office simultaneously with Duchant. He let Duchant press the code buttons, then followed him past the two operators at the monitors, and into the conference room.

Steam was coming out of the spout of the silver coffee pot and the aroma was invigorating. "Nothing like French brewed coffee," and Bertrand started to pour himself a cup.

"How about you, Raphael?"

"Sure, noir (Black) please."

Bertrand handed the cup and saucer across the table to Duchant then sat down. He placed the plate of croissants, marmalade, and jelly at the center of the table, but left the two plates stacked, and off to one side.

He looked at Duchant, who shook his head no.

"They're tempting, aren't they? I spoke with Kathy last night. Maybe I'm pushing it a little, maybe getting too much involved, but it's strictly a biological pull."

Bertrand paused as if waiting for a response. When none came, he continued. "I'd like to think that getting close to her will result in something, but I'm clueless right now as to what."

"Why are you telling me all this, Henri? You're a grown man and you know the rules of that game as well as the ones we play by. If you screw up, it's your ass that's going to fry and I might not be able to pull you out of the fire."

"I wouldn't place myself or the organization in harm's way. I'm too professional for that."

He looked at Duchant wanting some kind of verbal or facial response, but Duchant only stared back.

"She wants to take a long weekend. She wants to visit with her father, and she seemed somewhat hesitant about asking since she's just come aboard."

"I'll let you handle it. As far as I'm concerned, she can go. Her knowledge of us, the company and what we appear to do, only scratches the surface. She has no in-depth knowledge and we'll keep it that way. What she can pass along to anyone curious enough to ask her, is nothing of value."

"While I'm thinking of it, what about the satellite photo?"

"Yes. Central reports that during the infrequent times when her father goes out, he heads immediately for the woods that borders the property. The photographs we have, show a man bundled with a hat and overcoat. So far Central has no clear photograph of his facial features, but we do have a clear shot of someone who was with him recently. Shimon has the photos."

Raphael reached for the phone and dialed.

"Good morning Shimon. Henri informs me that you have some satellite photographs of the subject. Also, if the pictures have been developed from yesterday, bring them into the conference room. We'd like to review these together with any background data you've developed."

Duchant listened, "Sure, that would be fine. Yes, as much as Central can provide," and then he hung up.

"Do you want any more coffee, Raphael?"

"About half a cup will be fine."

Bertrand finished pouring, but held onto the silver pot as Shimon walked in.

"Do you want a cup?"

"No thanks, I'm coffee'd out."

He pulled out a chair next to Duchant and placed several manila folders on the table.

Duchant picked up the phone again and dialed. It rang to the operators at the monitors.

"No one is to enter. No one! Please inform the receptionist and the guard duty officer," then he replaced the phone onto the cradle.

Shimon meanwhile took out several photographs and placed one in front of Duchant and Bertrand.

"The man whose partial right side is revealed in the photograph has been identified as SS-Obersturmbannführer (Lieutenant Colonel) Herbert Kappler. He was born in Stuttgart. His early years were nondescript until he joined the SS. He rose through the organization, reached the rank of Obersturmbannführer, and was posted to Rome in 1939 as head of the Sicherheitsdient. (Security service) In 1944 he became head of the Gestapo. In close coordination with the Fascist police over those six years, he planned and oversaw the deportation of tens of thousands of Jews."

"On one specific day, 18 October 1944 to be exact, he rounded up one thousand and seven Jews, and sent them to Auschwitz. Out of that number only ten returned. Despite my adopted name of Shimon, as you both know, I am of Italian origin. My parents were among those who were sent to be exterminated on that day."

"Additionally, Kappler was responsible for the killing of three hundred and fifty-five Italians, of whom seventy-eight were Jews at the Ardeatine Caves, in reprisal for the killing of thirty-three Germans by Partisans. He was eventually captured by the British and handed over to Italian authorities for trial. Kappler was given a life sentence. He fell ill and was taken to a hospital in Rome from which he escaped. Since his escape, no sighting of him has ever been confirmed, that is until now."

"The other man whose features are hidden by the hat and the turned up collar, is presumed to be Friedrich Buhler, the father of Miss Katherine, "Karta Buhler," Longrin. We have no photographs of Mr. Buhler and as you are already aware, what photographs were attached to his immigration papers have conveniently disappeared."

"With the confirmation that Ober-sturmbannfuhrer Herbert Kappler is alive and the fact that he was on the Buhler's property, leads us to conclude that this esteemed gentleman farmer and the father of Miss Katherine Longrin, is a Nazi or Nazi sympathizer."

Bertrand looked at Duchant and then back to the security chief. He knew better than to question what had just been indicated. Shimon was older than both of them by years and had reached this position through competence spanning many decades. What he reported could be taken at face value.

"What about the other man, Shimon, this Friedrich Buhler? Can we get a fix on him?"

"We're trying, Henri. Our efforts have been stepped up since the Kappler confirmation."

"Here's some information you can use, Shimon. I've already mentioned it to Raphael that Miss Longrin will be visiting her father this weekend. We'll give the okay when she arrives this morning," and then Henri looked at his wristwatch.

"She's probably already here, in the reception area with the secretary, or out on the main floor somewhere waiting to be let into these hallowed chambers."

Shimon folded his arms across his chest and leaned back in his chair. "We'll tell Central and see what we can come up with over the weekend. I'll get someone into her apartment while she's gone, see if she has a recent photograph around, or a dated one that our artists can age on the computer. Let me know if and when her plans firm up and the details of her flight."

Then the security chief reached out for the photographs, picked up the one in front of Duchant, and held his hand out toward Bertrand for the other.

Then he placed both photographs back into the manila envelope and opened the other one withdrawing several photographs of Rudel. He handed one to Duchant and then pushed one across the table toward Bertrand.

"The man you refer to as Garland is an unknown, at least for the time being. He's too young to have served the Third Reich. Our guess is that he's part of Buhler's staff, German born with language fluency. Although we're pushing the envelope a bit early, we feel he's part of the Fourth Reich. That's the neo Nazi's perverted dream of a new socialist thousand year reign, orchestrated by the remnants of the Third Reich, primarily from South America, notably Argentina, Paraguay, Bolivia and Brazil."

"Just for your info, Shimon, Raphael and I are going to try to arrange a meeting with von Hoenshield without Garland. We'll try to massage the Nazi a bit and see what we can come up with."

"At our recent meeting involving all the players, von Hoenshield was as quiet as a church mouse. There was no doubt of Garland's seniority. Maybe pushing von Hoenshield, might result in something concrete. Nothing to lose."

Shimon shook his head, "Could be helpful. Keep me posted and I'll do the same," then he stood up. "Anything else?"

"I think we've covered it for now," and then Raphael looked at Bertrand. "Anything more, Henri?"

Bertrand shook his head no, then got up and followed Shimon to the door. He kept his right hand on the open door, turned around and said, "I'll bring Kathy in."

Bertrand went down the metal steps to the main floor and stopped. Shimon, who was walking ahead of him, raised his hand up and waved it as he continued forward.

Bertrand looked around the floor trying to spot Kathy. It took a moment to find her. She was huddled at one of the sorting tables, watching the white-coated men and women sort the stones. There was an Uzi armed guard in close proximity.

He began walking toward her when she sensed his presence and turned in his direction. She waved and he waved back.

"Were you waiting long?"

"I don't think so. I was enjoying watching these folks sort the diamonds. The receptionist told me you were in a conference and couldn't be disturbed so I asked if I could watch the sorting operation until you were free and here I am."

She smiled and then continued, "I'm ready if you are."

"Fine, let's go to the conference room. I mentioned to Raphael about your request for a long weekend. He doesn't have a problem with it and neither do I, except I'll miss the opportunity of seeing you this weekend."

He waited for what he hoped would be a response of sorts and when nothing came, he said, "We'll have the travel agent that handles our company account make your reservations. Is that all right?"

"That would be helpful. All I need is the number and I'll take it from there."

"I'll get it for you in a moment. Let's see if Raphael has any of that French coffee left."

She walked with him toward the stairs and wondered why the Rolls Royce driver who she saw walk down the stairs with Bertrand, was part of the conference.

Chapter 29

Henri arranged for the Rolls Royce and accompanied Kathy to Kennedy Airport.

After checking her Vuitton suitcase at curbside, Bertrand tipped the porter, then picked up her Vuitton duffle bag and followed her inside the terminal.

"Nothing here as far as restaurants go, so you might as well clear security and relax at the boarding gate. I hope you have a good time, Kathy. I'll arrange for the car to pick you up. If there's any change in your plans, telephone me."

He placed the duffel down, then gently touched her shoulders with both hands and softly said, "I'll miss you."

Then he let go quickly. She sensed he was generally sincere and moved closer until their bodies were only inches apart.

"I'll miss you too, Henri," and then she separated, leaned down and picked up the Vuitton duffle.

"Thank you for coming here. I appreciate it."

She smiled, then turned and walked toward the line waiting to process through the security gate.

Bertrand waited until she disappeared into the boarding area, then he turned, went out of the terminal, and stood near the curb. He waited patiently knowing the Rolls was circling. When he saw the distinctive grill and silver flying lady hood ornament in the distance, he motioned with his hand.

*

Kathy moved surprisingly quickly through security, gathered up her personal items, and headed in the direction of her departure gate. She passed a crowded restaurant, turned toward it momentarily, then continued walking.

Along the route she noticed a small bar with only one customer. She walked in, stopped for a moment, and then continued to the far end, opposite from where the solitary man sat.

The bartender eyed her from the moment she entered and came over as she seated herself.

His smile disturbed her, and she thought about leaving.

"What can I get you, Miss?"

"How's the coffee?"

"As good as it gets."

"Then let me have a cup, please."

He smiled again and then walked back to where the other customer was sitting. The seated man said something, which caused the bartender to lean closer. After several seconds he shook his head, then they both smiled.

Typical men, fantasizing about what they could never afford or possess, even for a moment.

She chuckled to herself and watched as the bartender carried the coffee. The words danced easily in her mind. Eat your heart out little man. I'm way beyond your means.

He placed the coffee down and asked, "Anything else?"

"Not right now. Thank you."

He walked to the register, touched a few keys and a paper tab appeared. He tore it off, walked back to Kathy and placed it behind her cup.

"How's the coffee?"

"As good as it gets," then she smiled and turned her head toward the cup.

She finished the coffee, paid the tab, then picked up the duffel from the next stool and walked out.

When she reached the gate the first boarding announcement was being made. She waited with the other first class passengers and in another few minutes was comfortably strapped into an aisle seat.

After the aircraft reached its cruising altitude, she ordered a double Johnny Walker Red Label and tried to relax. She was excited about going home and yet apprehensive. The uneasiness she felt stemmed from many things, but mostly the underground room.

To complicate matters further, the two men who were dominating her working life were dedicated to the task of recovering stolen art, art that belonged to a family called Duchant and somehow, she knew a family called Buhler was intertwined.

She thought of reasons to justify the room's existence. Safety primarily, but she couldn't disconnect the linkage to a sordid past. She closed her eyes and pictured Bertrand. While she wasn't sure about her own feelings, she liked his gentle ways. Maybe in time she thought, as she drifted off into a sleep which was denied her over the past several nights.

*

The doorman watched as the two men in ill-fitting and rumpled business suits got out of the three-year-old maroon Chevrolet, which they parked with indifference in a no parking zone.

The doorman, who over the years had acquired the ability to quickly categorize the working class from the affluent, deduced that the two men who were now approaching him, were blue collar specials. Their five o'clock shadows became more apparent the closer they got.

The shorter of the two took out a worn black leather wallet, flipped the top open revealing a gold detective's badge embossed with the seal of the City of New York.

"I'm Linington and this is Miles. We're here to see one of your tenants. We know where he lives, and we don't need your assistance. We expect to be here about ten or fifteen minutes, maybe a little longer."

Arthur nodded, "May I ask the tenant's name? I have a passkey for all units."

"The name is confidential and like we said, we don't need your help."

With that said, both men walked to the elevator bank. Once inside the man identified as Miles pushed the fifth floor button. The door closed and the elevator started upward.

The doorman quickly moved toward the elevators and watched as the needle stopped at the fifth floor. He went back to his desk-like podium and looked down the list of names of the fifth floor tenants.

As the elevator doors opened, Linington and Miles stepped out, hesitated a moment, then started walking toward the fire exit stairwell. Linington held the fifth floor fire door open while Miles made his way down to the fourth level. He called up, "It's open."

Linington let the door close, then took the stairs two at a time. In a few moments he was standing by Miles in the fourth floor hallway.

"Her apartment is to the right."

Miles took out a set of keys and the door quickly opened. Once inside both men separated, each moving along opposite sides of the room. "I have one."

Miles walked to where the other man was standing. Linington passed him the framed picture.

"This is it. Take the picture out of the frame and get a couple of shots. The window over there might be a better spot."

Miles nodded, walked to the window, and placed the picture on the sill. Linington watched as Miles took out a small camera from inside his jacket, then he made his way to the bedroom, looked around quickly before moving onto the kitchen. For no apparent reason, he opened the refrigerator door and looked in. Satisfied, he slowly closed it.

Linington went back to the living room and saw Miles still hunched over the window sill. He saw several liquor bottles on a table and walked over. He unscrewed the Johnny Walker Red, brought the bottle to his nose and sniffed. He did this several more times thinking, that's about as close as I'm coming to this, although I could sure use a hit.

He tightened the cap, replaced the bottle and called out, "Aaron, are you about finished? We only need a couple of good ones, not a photographic gem."

"That's what I'm trying to get. I'll be finished shortly if you give me some space."

Linington went to the sofa and started to sit down, when the man he called Aaron said, "I'm done. Let's go."

They locked the door, took the stairs back to the fifth floor and then the elevator down to the lobby.

Linington stopped by the doorman as the other man continued to the car. "I appreciate your cooperation. Have a good night."

Then he went to the car, opened the front passenger door and got in.

Arthur watched as the man entered the car. He noted that there wasn't a computer terminal attached to the dashboard, which was standard equipment for all New York police vehicles, whether marked or unmarked.

As the car pulled away from the curb, the doorman wrote down the license plate numbers.

The two men drove up to Spanish Harlem and parked the Chevrolet in front of a condemned building. They wiped the dashboard, the inside and outside of both door handles then walked away from the vehicle, the key still dangling from the ignition.

When they reached the corner, they stopped. Linington spoke into his cell phone and after several minutes a paneled Chrysler minivan pulled up.

Both men entered the vehicle through the back doors.

Chapter 30

Henri and Raphael arrived at the gallery, shook hands with von Hoenshield and then they seated themselves around the table.

"I'm sorry I couldn't take advantage of your dinner invitation, but the press of business unfortunately prevented me."

As soon as the first words were spoken, the monitoring device was activated. A few sundry comments were made, then von Hoesnshield volunteered that Garland was away for a few days and this was a perfect opportunity to get together and try to smooth out the negotiations.

"Before I received your telephone call, Henri, I was planning to call you."

Bertrand turned to Rahpael. "We seem to have made a timely connection here, Mr. La Monde."

"Apparently so! Quite fortunate as it saves us some valuable time in trying to bring our negotiations to a successful conclusion."

Then Bertrand turned back to von Hoenshield, "There's a great deal of money involved, Manfred. It may well exceed two hundred million dollars, but this initial transaction is crucial to everything else that might follow. If there is no meaningful expression of compromise by Mr. Garland, we may already have reached an impasse which is final. We need you as an ally, not as the defiant opposition. Do you follow this reasoning Manfred?"

"Yes, I understand perfectly well. I will do what I can. This is important to me as well as you, but in the same spirit of cooperation, Henri, your side must also be flexible."

"We are Manfred. Perhaps we can improve our offer. We shall review our options and will present a new offer when Mr. Garland returns. Will that be satisfactory?"

Von Hoenshield smiled realizing that his vision of shared wealth remained intact. Then his eyes shifted from Bertrand to La Monde as Raphael reached into his jacket pocket and took out a black ostrich skin billfold. His eyes never wavered from the billfold as Raphael removed a check and held it toward the German.

Von Hoenshield took the check and stared at it for several moments. The check was made out to his name for twenty-five thousand American dollars.

"What is this for?"

"Consider it as part payment against your commission for the transaction presently under negotiation."

"That is most generous, Mr. La Monde, and thank you as well, Henri. I will do my utmost to earn this and any future amount you care to offer me."

"There is much more where that came from, Manfred. Success has its rewards," then Bertrand smiled, knowing that every word from the moment they first entered the gallery was being monitored somewhere.

Both Duchant and Bertrand knew that von Hoenshield was now compromised and those who were at the other end of the monitoring equipment were aware as well…and at that other end were the Doctor and Rudel.

*

Kathy was awakened by the announcement indicating they were twenty-five minutes away from landing. She stretched and felt rested, happy that she was able to get some sleep.

She opened the duffel and took out a small bag that contained her toiletries. She carried the bag and her purse into the lavatory and in a few minutes returned to her seat refreshed.

As the fasten seat belt sign came on, Kathy removed a half ounce bottle of Opium perfume by Yves Saint Laurent from her purse and placed several drops behind each ear.

Then she sat back anticipating the slight bump of the airplane's tires when it made contact with the runway. When it happened, she let out a soft sigh, glad to be on terra firma once again.

She followed the other first class passengers out the forward door and onto the mechanical ramp.

Once past the boarding area, she turned to her left and followed the signs indicating baggage claim.

As she neared the baggage claim area, she saw Udo and waved. Then she ran toward him and they hugged.

"How was your flight, Miss Karta?"

"Just fine, Udo. How have you been?"

"Busy, Miss Karta. You know your father. There's always something to take care of," then he laughed.

Kathy smiled back.

"Gerta is looking forward to seeing you Miss Karta. If you'll hand me your baggage tags I'll get your luggage. How many?"

"Just one, Udo, and this duffel. The suitcase has the same type of LV pattern."

The conveyor belt began to move, and Kathy spotted her bag almost immediately. "That one, Udo."

"Do you want to wait at the curb, Miss Karta, while I bring the car around?"

"That's not necessary, Udo. I'll come along with you."

Kathy started to reach for the duffel when the German scooped it up. "This way, Miss Karta."

They moved to the elevators, got off at the sixth level and then walked to a blue Mercedes Benz station wagon.

"The door is open, Miss Karta."

Kathy got in while Udo opened the rear hatch and placed both pieces of luggage on the area behind the rear seats. Then he slid into the driver's seat and started the vehicle.

"It should be about forty-five minutes if the traffic doesn't become too congested. Would you like to hear the radio, Miss Karta?"

"Sure, some soft music please, Udo, maybe something classical."

"I have two CD's, Miss Karta, of Richard Wagner's operas. One is Der Fliegende Hollander (The Flying Dutchman) and the other is an old favorite of your father, Der Ring Des Nibelungen." (The Ring of the Nibelungen)

"Let's hear Der Ring, Udo."

In seconds, the station wagon was filled with music from the Harman/Kardon logic 7 sound system with 12 speakers and subwoofer. Kathy leaned her head back, closed her eyes and listened to the pulsating sounds of the Wagner opera.

*

The van dropped the two men off at the corner of 47th Street and the Avenue of the Americas. They walked into number 977 and zigzagged through the main floor arriving at the elevator just as it was discharging its last passenger.

The man called Linington stood in front of suite 230, pressed in the code sequence and pushed the door at the same time he heard the click.

The guard moved to his right letting both men approach the inner door together. After the door's lock disengaged, they entered and walked diagonally across the sorting floor to the security room located at the right hand corner of the floor.

Linington placed his palm on the greenish screen next to the right edge of the door and waited. When the two letters OK appeared on the screen, he opened the door and walked in followed by the man he called Aaron.

Several banks of security surveillance and communication equipment dominated the room. All the personnel had shoulder holsters and several had Uzi machine guns. Without saying anything to anyone, the two started walking toward a desk, which was placed against the far wall of the room.

Shimon stood up as they approached, and Miles handed him the camera. "If there's nothing else, we're out of here." He waited for a reply.

"Any difficulty?"

Linington answered "No, a cake walk. Came upon a photo right away and handed it to Aaron."

Then the security chief looked at Aaron who added, "It was definitely the subject, Shimon, and when you develop the shots, there should be more than one good picture, which the computer boys can work with."

"Okay, good job. There's nothing more for now. Stand down until we call."

The two men turned and retraced their steps. As he walked, Linington's thoughts drifted back to the parked car in Spanish Harlem and then looked at his watch. He thought to himself, should be jacked by now and either stripped, heading south of the border, or gang-banger joy riding property.

Shimon watched them for only a moment and then picked up the phone. He hung up after a few seconds, then leaned back and stared at the camera in his hand.

He looked up as a man approached.

"Get these developed quickly, then pass them to Jeremiah. He knows what to do. Once he's finished, bring them back here."

The man nodded and disappeared from view.

Shimon debated whether to telephone Tel Aviv or wait. He decided to wait. The transmission would be rapid, and it was better to have conclusive proof that the photograph was usable before initiating contact.

He started drafting a message, then stopped. He brought himself into check refusing to give into the impatience that was taking hold of him. He reached for the coffee cup and brought it up. Once the cold liquid touched his lips, he cursed silently, placed the cup down and willed himself to sit there quietly.

Shimon stood up and came around the desk as the man approached. He took the manila envelope from his hand and opened the flap. He looked at one and then the other photograph before nodding to the man as he walked to the monitors.

The operator he approached remained seated, but looked up at Shimon, waiting for the senior officer to speak.

"I need a pad, Joel."

The operator handed him a pad and pencil and Shimon began to write.

"Photo number one is subject (Male) in 1936 Berlin. Face enlarged and cleaned. Woman presumed wife.
Photo number two aged to project present day likeness. Request data system confirmation and match on male subject soonest.
Photo number three is a man who uses the name Karl Garland. Request data system confirmation and match on male subject soonest. This is a repeat subject trace request. First was unsubstantiated. Requesting redo...Redwing."

Shimon handed the pad and pencil back to the operator. "Get this coded and transmitted immediately. It's to be sent as a priority one, with these photographs."

Shimon stood by and watched as the operator opened the code book applicable to the day and month. He typed in the data sequences and scanned in the photos. He looked at the screen preview and, satisfied, turned around to Shimon and motioned him toward the screen.

The operator pressed several keys and the screen gibberish became readable. Shimon read slowly, looked at the scanned photographs, then patted the operator on the shoulder.

"I authorize transmission."

The operator turned back to the monitor, touched several more keys and the screen returned to gibberish. Satisfied with what he saw, he touched several more buttons and watched as the screen began moving rapidly, carrying the transmission data over the wireless bridge that connected it to the terminals in Tel Aviv. In seconds the screen became whitish and blank.

The operator turned his head in Shimon's direction, pointed to the screen and said, "Confirm transmission sent and received. Anything further, sir?"

Shimon patted the operator on the shoulder again. "Thanks, let me know when a reply is received."

The operator nodded, then Shimon walked back to his desk and picked up the phone. He dialed Duchant.

"If you have a moment, I'd like to show you a few pictures."

Chapter 31

There was little conversation as the Mercedes Benz wagon cleared the city traffic and sped along the Illinois 94 Interstate.

Kathy felt the transformation from her state of anxiety into a relaxed state of mind. The transformation was derived primarily from the music and watching the planted fields of wheat, soybeans, corn and sorghum, the barns, the farmhouses, the horses, and cattle drift by her window.

She felt comfortable with all that she saw. Familiar sights offer a security blanket of sorts and this was no exception.

Udo turned onto the gravel road that led to the main house and passed several patrolling sentries. She never really noticed them in the same way they registered now.

As the house came into view, she forgot about the armed men as her heart pumped with anticipation.

When the car stopped in front of the pillared alcove, Kathy opened her door and stepped out into the waiting arms of Gerta.

After their embrace, Gerta said, "Let me look at you Miss Karta. Ah, so beautiful. Welcome home."

"Thank you Gerta, is Papa here?"

"Yes, he heard the car pull up and will be here in a moment as soon as he finishes with his assistant. Udo will bring in your bags...why don't you come into the house?"

Kathy followed Gerta onto the large Victorian porch, then stopped and looked out toward the heavily wooded area that surrounded the house.

She remembered the hours spent walking in those woods until she knew every inch of it. On one side of the woods was a lake where she learned to fish, swim, and row. She made up her mind that she and Papa would have to take a walk there before she returned to New York.

Her concentration was broken by the sound of her father's voice. She turned and ran into his open arms. Despite herself, she felt the tears run down her cheeks.

Her father looked at her and smiled. "Dry those tears, Karta, I much prefer you smiling and happy."

"I am happy, Papa. My tears are tears of joy at seeing you again and knowing you are well."

The Doctor bent down and kissed his daughter on the forehead, then embraced her again.

"Have you eaten, Karta?"

"No, Papa, and I'm famished."

"Good. The kitchen staff has prepared a welcome luncheon for you."

Kathy looked at Gerta and smiled.

"Pardon me, Karta, I've neglected to introduce you to my assistant." The Doctor stepped to his right, revealing a smiling Ernst Rudel. I believe you have met Mr. Karl Garland recently."

The Doctor saw the surprised look come over his daughter's face. "Please don't look so shocked, Karta. I will explain everything to you over lunch."

Rudel walked up to Kathy, took hold of her hand gently and bowed slightly.

"It is a small world, Miss Buhler. It is a pleasure to see you again," then he let go of her hand and stepped back, taking a place several paces away from the Doctor.

"Come now, Karta my darling, don't look so confused. It's rather simple and we'll discuss everything to your complete satisfaction shortly. Why not go to your room and freshen up? We'll dine in about thirty minutes."

Kathy smiled back at her father but said nothing. She turned toward the ornate curved staircase and started up familiar steps toward her room.

She sat on the bed trying to understand what just happened, when there was a knock on her door.

"Just a moment."

She stood up, brushed her skirt and walked to the door. When she opened it, Udo was standing there with her two bags.

"Just place them on the bed, Udo. If you'll tell Papa that I'll unpack first, then come down I'd appreciate it."

"Certainly, Miss Karta," and he began walking toward the door.

"One thing more, Udo, how long has Papa had his assistant?"

"For several years now, Miss Karta. Mr. Rudel is usually traveling, which might be the reason you haven't met him before today.

"Will there be anything else?"

"No, Udo. Thank you. I'm very happy to see you again."

"And I'm happy to see you also, Miss Karta."

He walked out closing the door softly behind him.

Kathy went to the bathroom, bent over the sink, and splashed cold water on her face. She reached for a washcloth and let it soak under the cold water. She then squeezed the cloth and placed it on the back of her neck.

She looked at the mirror and didn't like what she saw staring back.

Slowly walking back to the bedroom, Kathy stopped when her knees came in contact with the bed, then after a moment, turned and sat down.

She sat with her eyes closed, letting her mind play out the sequence of events since her arrival.

Then she remembered what Udo had answered in response to her question about her father's assistant. "Mr. Rudel is usually traveling…"

She heard the name correctly, there was no doubting that Udo said Rudel not Garland. He probably didn't realize he'd said it. Obviously, it was the assistant's actual name and Udo inadvertently revealed it.

She went back to the bathroom, brushed her hair and reapplied her lipstick. She opened the medicine cabinet and saw the Bayer aspirin. She turned on the cold water tap and placed the glass under it until one-quarter of the container was filled. She popped two aspirins in her mouth and emptied the glass.

Then she picked up her purse and took out the bottle of Opium perfume. After applying several drops behind her ears, she walked out and down the stairs, pausing at the bottom for an instant.

Hearing muted sounds coming from the dining room, she started walking in that direction.

As she entered the room, her father turned away from his assistant and came toward her. He took hold of her arm and escorted her to the table.

"Please sit on my right, Karta, and Karl, please take the seat across from Karta."

Both men remained standing as Kathy seated herself, then they took their seats.

Kathy looked toward the entrance and saw Udo positioned just inside the door. Her father's bodyguard, driver and trusted friend, was unwavering in his loyalty. Wherever her father went, Udo was in close proximity and now that she was again home, he would shadow her as well.

Although he had aged, he was still the massive, but gentle man she remembered from her youth. She knew that his disposition would change to ferocity if her father or she were placed in danger.

"We are having a Puligny-Montrachet 1983. I trust both of you will like it."

Then he nodded to a man standing at his left who then proceeded to pour a small amount into the Doctor's glass.

"Delicious, and perfectly chilled, Klaus, thank you."

The man bowed slightly in acknowledgement then filled the Doctor's glass, poured for Kathy, and then finished with Rudel.

After he placed the bottle into a standing ice bucket, he resumed his stance several paces away from the table.

"Will you excuse us, Klaus. Udo will let you know when we're ready for lunch."

The man bowed again and left the room.

"I'd like to drink to your homecoming, Karta, I've missed you."

Their glasses touched and Kathy smiled. She took a sip and thought how correct her father had been about the wine. It was chilled perfectly. She took another sip, then turned to Rudel.

"I must admit, Mr. Garland, I'm surprised to see you here," then she looked at her father.

Her father didn't move, nor did he offer any response, but Rudel, after placing his glass on the table, looked back at her.

"I wasn't at liberty to reveal whom I was representing when we met at the gallery. I knew who you were from the moment we met, as I had previously seen a picture of you, which by the way Miss Buhler, doesn't do you justice."

Kathy smiled, but didn't take her eyes from the man seated across from her.

"I had my instructions, and those instructions were not flexible. I knew that you would accompany the two men from Duchant et Compagnie to the negotiations. Mr. Manfred von

Hoenshield had already indicated to us that a woman and the two men would attend. Just prior to our meeting, I learned from your father that you were employed with the Duchant company and by deductive reasoning, I knew that woman would be you."

"I was impressed with your knowledge, Miss Buhler, regarding the painting in question. You were very astute, since despite the obvious flaws you noted, the copy is considered an excellent reproduction completed by one of the master forgers peddling his trade in the art world today. I will contact him in the near future to critique his work using your criticisms."

"For a brief moment, I would like to defer as to why I presented the forgery at our negotiations. I, first, need to clarify for you that my duty was and is, to secure the maximum amount of money possible for this painting. Now back to the forgery. I needed to place your art knowledge into play and through this knowledge, secure your position with these two men. That was successfully accomplished."

"My sole role is as a negotiator. I am in no way an owner nor do I know who the actual owner, or owners are. I receive my instructions from your father," and then Rudel looked at the Doctor who began to speak."

"I know you are somewhat perplexed Karta, but the explanation is very simple. To continue from where Karl left off, the instructions that I passed to Karl were given to me by the owners of the painting. What is taking place is purely a business transaction."

"The painting, as represented by the other side, your side," and then he smiled and touched Kathy's hand, "is purported to be a stolen work of art. Nothing could be further from the truth. This painting was never stolen from any family, museum or gallery. It was never war booty claimed by the Germans as their armies swept across Europe. This painting and others were sold to the present owners, whom I represent, legitimately. Money was exchanged and a bill of sale was written."

The Doctor reached into his pocket and took out a yellowing envelope. He handed the envelope to Kathy who carefully removed the pages.

Her eyes immediately focused on the date at the top of the first page, 7 April 1941.

Then she slowly moved her eyes down the list of paintings, noting the amounts and the final tally on the last page. Below the tally were four signatures, all legible.

Kathy saw that one of the signatures was Duchant's father.

She placed the envelope and the pages on the table and looked back at her father.

The Doctor began speaking again in slow articulated German, "As you are aware, Karta, I speak a number of languages fluently having received my doctorate in linguistics. I have always been interested in art. My family collected art and I was exposed to art, as you were, from an early age. When I immigrated to the United States to start life over again after the war, I maintained my art contacts on the continent."

"Eventually I was contacted and asked by one, then another of the collectors in the post war art world to assist them in disposing of some of their paintings. Please remember, Karta, that Europe was devastated after the war. People were concerned with rebuilding their lives and businesses. Art was of no value when survival was a prerequisite. That survival depended on money and the only way that many had to secure those needed funds, was to dispose of their art collections. I became a broker, albeit a very specialized one. I was able to negotiate with the potential moneyed buyers in various countries directly because of my language abilities. The owners never had to reveal themselves."

"I would never handle a painting unless it was authenticated and documented. The sellers in many cases would come here to the farm and place their works with me for safe keeping. The volume of paintings grew and I, out of necessity, built an underground room which you have seen, my darling, on many occasions."

"Some of the original owners of the work stored with me have died. The ownership has passed to family members with whom I maintain contact. Some have elected to retrieve their paintings, while others have left them with me for eventual sale."

"The owners and I agreed at the beginning, that we would sell only those works that would provide them with the money they needed immediately. In a few cases it was only one painting, but this was the exception not the rule. Most had numerous paintings in their collections."

"After they received the money, which in many cases was quite ample for their immediate and future needs, the remaining works of art were sequestered away here. They resurface now only if the art market rises sufficiently to maximize the return to the owner, or owners, or their heirs."

"This is such a time, Karta, and with the owner's authorization I have allowed Mr. von Hoenshield to make it known to one, maximum two selected buyers, that the painting, Woman in Black, is available for sale. The sale, of course, is predicated on a negotiated equitable price and this is where Mr. Garland comes into the picture. If a sale is consummated, accompanying the painting will be a document of authenticity and a signed bill of sale."

"Discovering that your new employment was with a company whose several principals were negotiating with my representative, in no way altered our intention to continue toward the prospective sale."

"What has happened, Karta, is that you are in the middle so to speak. You have loyalties to both sides, but I must tell you now that your first loyalty is to your employer. All that I have just related to you is simply background, which will enable you, with a clear conscience, to continue assisting your employer."

"Is there anything that you would like me to clarify further?"

"Papa, you've read my mind. I have only one question. If these works will be sold with a certificate of authenticity and are not stolen art, why can't you just offer the paintings for sale on the open market?"

"The owners and their heirs want anonymity and to avoid litigation at all costs. Both will happen the moment any of these works come onto the open market. Because the art world has not seen these paintings for decades, the natural presumption is to conclude that they were stolen during the war and hidden away. Litigation is costly and the owners have stipulated that these pieces can only be sold discreetly so as to avoid the unnecessary and costly defense of ownership. I must abide by their wishes."

"Okay, Papa. I think I understand. Thank you for explaining this to me, I was getting very confused."

Her father smiled and reached for her hand, which he squeezed gently. "There is one thing more, Karta. I assume Katherine Longrin is more American. Wait…please wait before you say anything. I am not in the least bit upset. To me you will always be my daughter whatever you decide to call yourself."

Tears welled up in her eyes as Kathy turned toward her father and kissed him.

He placed his two hands on her shoulders and smiled at her.

Chapter 32

Kathy returned to her room after lunch. Her father and his assistant went back to his study.

She walked to the window, unlocked the latch, and pushed it up as far as it would go.

The cool air rushed past her and into the room. She took a deep breath and liked the woodsy smell that filled her lungs.

She pulled the suitcase and duffel off the bed, took off her clothes and put on her robe. Then she propped up the pillows and rolled onto the bed.

Again, her mind returned to her father and his assistant and then she thought about what her father revealed over lunch.

For the most part the explanations made complete sense, but when she recounted what Raphael Duchant had said about his family's stolen art, she couldn't dispel the inconsistencies.

She was confused and that confusion made for inaccurate observations and decisions. Her lawyer's mind couldn't provide the answers she still needed.

Kathy closed her eyes and tried to get her mind to relax. The mind like the body, reaches an impasse, where it craves a time that is unencumbered by worldly motions, thoughts and activities. Sleep eventually came to Kathy Longrin.

*

"California has reported, Herr Doctor, that the telephone trace resulted in a location that was inactive. Our personnel watched for several days. No activity was reported. Specifically, the line was traced to an unused room which according to the building's management was paid for two years in advance. The space was leased by a rental agency. When contacted they indicated that the details were handled by mail and the money wired from a Bank in Canada."

"Further, Herr Doctor, the man I met as Raphael La Monde is Mr. Raphael Duchant, the managing director of the company bearing his name, and a Jew."

"He is the grandson of the founder. The man Bertrand is a Christian. His ancestry is Belgian and our investigation shows he has been in the employ of Duchant et Compagnie for over ten years."

"A rather clumsy attempt at deception, wouldn't you say, Ernst?"

"I'm not sure, Herr Doctor. They couldn't be naive enough to believe we wouldn't check their backgrounds. It's so amateurish to border on stupidity, but I wonder."

"One must never either underestimate, nor over estimate the opposition. Like in war, Ernst, preparation is a key to victory. We must be prepared for the unexpected. When are you returning to New York?"

"This evening, Herr Doctor."

"The amount indicated by Duchant that would be available for the purchase of future paintings is an interesting amount worthy of our attention. Please do what is necessary to sell the painting, Ernst, but do not agree to their offered price. The Jews bargain hard, it's in their blood. Let them have a small victory while we shall win the war. Once this sale has been concluded, we can move on firmer ground toward getting the one to two hundred million from the Jew. I wish you a good flight, Sturmbannführer."

Ernst Rudel clicked his heels, nodded and left the room.

The Doctor busied himself until his attention was interrupted by a knock on the door.

"Kommen Herein." (Come in)

Kathy entered and her father stood up to greet her. "Did you take a nap?"

"Yes Papa, I guess I was more tired than I thought, a combination of the stress from work and the flight here. I was thinking about taking a walk through the woods to the lake. Would you come with me, Papa?"

"Of course, Karta. Wait on the porch for me. I'll get my coat and hat and be only a minute."

While the air was brisk, the temperature didn't require the heavy coat or hat her father wore.

"Are you coming down with something, Papa? Why the heavy coat?"

"You can never be too careful, Karta. The chill in the air at times can be deadly."

Kathy shrugged her shoulders and moved closer to her father. She intertwined her arm with his and began walking the short distance toward the woods.

As they walked the Doctor kept his collar up and hat pulled down to a point just slightly above his eyes. He projected a difficult target to describe, or photograph, whether by visual, camera, or satellite. Trailing behind them was Udo, who continually scanned the general area.

As they started to enter the wood line, Kathy noticed several men walking on their right and left flanks. She recalled this type of security from her youth and paid little attention to it then, but now wondered why a gentleman farmer and a member of the landed gentry always required such protection.

She decided not to question his motives, or reasons, and instead inquired, "How long, Papa, has Mr. Garland been your assistant?"

"A few years now, Karta, but he is in continual motion. I keep him moving and with your infrequent visits here, you and he have not met formally until today. By the way, he is a bachelor and a very intelligent man."

Kathy laughed. "There you go again, Papa, always trying to get me married. I'm still a young woman and I have embarked upon a career that shows promise, thanks to you. Without your help I would never have become an attorney."

The Doctor pulled his daughter close and kissed her on her cheek. "I love you, Karta, and there is nothing I wouldn't do for you. I hope that I'll have grandchildren someday," then he laughed.

"I promise you will have them, Papa, but I have to be married first and I haven't found the right mate yet."

She decided not to bring Garland into this personal discourse. She clearly heard what her father had said, but the man, while not unattractive, was frightening in a way she couldn't quite explain. The body chemistry would never be there. He was sexually unattractive.

"I seem to have caused you some difficulty, Papa…I mean with the new job. It seems so surreal at times and now that you've explained the background to me, I feel that I am working against my own father."

He stopped walking and stared at her but said nothing. He saw the confusion and sadness in her eyes.

"Please try to understand, Karta, that if it wasn't you, then it would be someone else on the other side negotiating against me. In a way I'm pleased that it is you because I know your honesty and dedication will result in the best for your side. As far as I am concerned, Karl Garland is a very capable young man and a formidable negotiator. He will not let our interests be compromised or taken advantage of in any way. See…there is nothing to fret about. I think it's wonderful that we are," and he paused, "how should I put it…ah, friendly antagonists," and then he smiled broadly.

"Those are interesting words you used, Papa, and antagonists translates into hostility and even though you used the word friendly before it, I hope that you and I will never, ever become antagonists."

Chapter 33

Bertrand was seated to the right of Duchant, with Shimon on his left.

"We have received a rybat (Communication where the subject matter is extremely sensitive) from Tel Aviv. The man in the photograph from Kathy Longrin's apartment has been identified as Ludolf Otto Steiger."

"Steiger is evil personified. The Nazi was tracked to Argentina in 1948, then was sighted in La Paz, Bolivia in 1950. He went underground without a trace, until now. He's been in Illinois for several decades using the name of Friedrich Buhler. Sometimes the best places to hide are in plain sight."

"SS-Brigadefuhrer Steiger directed the mass murder of Jews in Crimea and West Prussia. When he assumed the position as First Adjutant to the Reichsführer Heinrich Himmler he oversaw the Reichassicherheitshauptamt (RSHA Reich Security Head Office) and the Einsatzgruppen (Special Mission Groups) in Poland."

"The infamous Reinhard Heydrich, who chaired the Wannsee Conference which formalized plans for the deportation of Jews to extermination camps, was appointed by Steiger to carry out the plan as rapidly as possible using Poland as a testing ground. Steiger is responsible for the death of millions of men, women and children, mostly Jews."

"I could go on, but I believe you gentlemen have the general idea. Steiger has escaped justice for far too long. Speaking of pictures, one of our computer technicians aged the photograph of Steiger and these are three renditions of what he'd look like today.

"The first one is without facial hair. This one shows him with a full beard, and the other one, with just a mustache. It provides a fairly good ID if you ever meet him in person."

When Shimon finished, he handed the report and computer renditions of Steiger to Duchant. Duchant looked at it briefly, passed it to Bertrand, and then said to Shimon, "What's your take on the woman, Katherine Longrin?"

"According to the immigration papers, she was very young when she entered the US. I'm giving an educated guess that she has no actual knowledge of who her father really is. If she does, she's an awfully good actress. However, I suggest caution. She is a member of the enemy camp and we should not lose sight of this fact."

"If there's nothing else gentlemen, I'm going back to my office."

Shimon looked at one then the other and when neither responded, said, "Call me if you think of anything."

Raphael turned to Bertrand, "When is Kathy returning?"

"When I left her off at the airport, we agreed that she would telephone or email me if there was any change in her ETA. She's due to arrive in New York at four p.m. today…at JFK."

"Are you going to pick her up?"

"I thought I would. I must admit the information related by Shimon puts a damper on things."

"I know what you're referring to, Henri. Maybe it's just as well. Office romances are complicated at best but in this case it might be deadly."

Bertrand turned his head sharply in Duchant's direction. "For me it's a biological thing, Raphael. A challenge to see how long it would take to get her to bed. I hadn't planned to take it any further than that. There are too many differences in our backgrounds and now, well it's become a lot more complicated."

The telephone on the conference room table buzzed. Duchant pointed to Henri who was closer to it. Once he had it in hand and up to his ear he said, "yes."

He listened and then said, "Put him through."

Bertrand covered the mouthpiece, looked at Duchant and mouthed Manfred.

Duchant nodded, leaned back in his chair slightly but kept his eyes on Bertrand.

"Fine, Manfred, and you?"

"Yes, that should be okay. At the gallery, two p.m. tomorrow. I'll telephone you later today if we have a conflict, otherwise we'll see you tomorrow. No thanks are necessary, Manfred, there's plenty more where that came from."

There was a long pause as Bertrand listened, then responded with, "Yes, yes, of course we know that you will...okay and the same to you, goodbye."

"Garland's back in town and wants to meet tomorrow. How do you want to play it?"

"We'll move up our price a bit and see how much Garland counters. The fact that he wants another session so soon indicates that he's met with his principals and has a revised figure to throw our way. I know that the mention of two hundred million was passed along and it definitely helped get this ball game restarted."

"Tell Kathy, when you meet her, that she will accompany us. Through Miss Longrin and Garland, we'll get to Steiger, Kappler and their associates. Once the net is thrown, the fish, both large and small, get caught."

*

Kathy sat in first class holding the scotch glass in her hand. She let her mind reminisce about the long weekend. A smile came across her face when she thought about her home, its familiar surroundings, her father, and her surrogate family of Gerta and Udo, but she also felt the anxiety of returning to New York. This vibrant city was part of her now, a place she considered her permanent home.

Then in an instant the smile disappeared and her thoughts drifted to what her father and Rudel had revealed about the art that was displayed in the underground room. She tried to balance what they stated against what Duchant had told her. She tried to be objective, to allow her legal training to take hold and sort out the facts from fiction.

There was no way her father could be involved in the trafficking of stolen art. He was a refugee from the horrors of Nazi Germany. He came to the United States as a penniless refugee and built a good life for himself and her. It was un-imaginable that he could be involved in anything that Duchant had told her during their initial meeting. It was simply not possible.

She knew her father to be a kind and considerate man, someone who had prospered here because of his hard work ethics and his skill as a managing owner/farmer. His farm provided seasonal work to many migrant workers and their families, as well as the many permanent residents of the community.

The frequent visitors he entertained were no doubt the owners of the art work he was com-missioned to sell. It was all so logical, but this now presented a significant dilemma, and she felt an urgent need to confront Duchant and Bertrand before she could continue in their employ.

She was torn between loyalty to her father, and loyalty to Duchant et Compagnie de Fils. Then the question of what loyalty does she owe Duchant came repeatedly to her mind.

Like an inner voice playing off the thoughts resonating inside her head she heard the words clearly...even though there is an impasse of sorts, you know clearly where your loyalty lies.

She nodded her head yes to the unspoken voice, but despite the affirmative movement, she started to analyze what she owed her present employer.

She felt that she had earned her keep so far, but now the equation was more complex than that. After a few moments, she knew full well what she owed to Duchant and it was something that might be impossible to give him…absolute dedication and unwavering loyalty.

She thought about simply telling Raphael that she was resigning without necessarily giving him an explanation. She had made that a verbal condition when she agreed to come aboard. Sure, just cut the relationship off cleanly now and walk away.

She could get another position at most of the upscale law firms in the city. She smiled when she thought of her previous law firm. She probably could ask for her old job back. She hadn't been away that long and she felt with a degree of certainty that Mr. Higgins would welcome her back with open arms.

Her situation needed to be resolved one way or the other today, if at all possible, tomorrow at the latest. She looked at her watch and saw the ETA in New York was about thirty minutes away. She looked up as the Captain's voice filled the cabin announcing their pending arrival at JFK.

She caught the attendant's eye and pointed to her glass, then rethought her request and asked for a strong black coffee. She needed to be alert and functioning if she was going to meet Duchant today. Another drink wouldn't help.

Kathy leaned her head back and closed her eyes. The image of a building tumbling to the ground was the only thing her mind pictured. She opened her eyes quickly and realized her heart was racing.

The stewardess smiled as she unlocked the seat back tray and brought it to an open position. She placed the coffee down and then returned to the galley.

Kathy looked at the steaming black coffee and felt her mood change to utter depression.

Chapter 34

The stewardess removed the untouched coffee, as Kathy sat quietly thinking that meeting with Duchant today was now an absolute priority. She stared out the plane's window, watching the New York skyline as the aircraft banked for its final approach.

After what seemed like an eternity before she disembarked, Kathy was relieved to be out of that silver tube and walking toward the baggage claim area.

As she stood at the turnstile waiting for her luggage to appear, she felt a touch to her shoulder. Startled, she instinctively took a step to one side, before turning around.

"I'm sorry if I startled you, Kathy. You seemed deep in thought and I didn't want to say anything. Please forgive me. In hindsight I should have said something."

"It's alright, Henri. I'm happy to see you. Thanks for taking the trouble to meet me."

Bertrand thought about saying something clever about wanting to be here, or he missed her, but sensed she was agitated and decided to wait in silence until she spoke.

"There's the bag, Henri."

Bertrand moved in front and took hold of the bag with his left hand. He reached for the duffel, but

Kathy gave him a clear indication that she would carry it.

As they waited curbside, the Rolls Royce Silver Shadow edged in between several idling vehicles.

The driver held the door open as Kathy and then Henri entered. While the driver placed the luggage in the trunk, Kathy shifted her position and faced Bertrand.

"I'd like to go to the office. Is it possible for you to contact Mr. Duchant and advise him that I'd like a meeting with him before he leaves today?"

"Sure, but can't it wait until tomorrow?"

"It could, but I'd prefer to meet today."

After the driver seated himself, he turned toward the rear compartment. "Where to, Mr. Bertrand?"

"The office, Micha."

Bertrand took out his cell phone, touched the menu button, and then pushed the speed dial.

"It's Henri, please connect me with Raphael."

"No, there's no problem, we're already in the car. Kathy wants to meet with you today. Is it convenient?"

"Okay, we should be there in about forty-five minutes."

He turned to Kathy. "The meeting is set," then he paused. "I'm tempted to ask why and if there's anything I can do, but I sense it wouldn't do any good. However, I'm still going to ask. What's up?"

"I'd rather not go into it here. Let's table it until we're at the office."

Bertrand shrugged. "Fine, but if we're not talking maybe some music will help both our moods."

Henri leaned forward with his left arm resting on part of the passenger's seat back. "Micha, hand me some CD's please."

The driver lifted his armrest, pulled out five CD's, then passed them over his shoulder to Bertrand.

Henri handed them to Kathy. "Like any of these?"

"Not particularly, I'm not in the mood for rock and roll, or show tunes. I have a CD that I borrowed from my father."

She opened her purse and took out the CD. "Perhaps the driver could play this one."

Bertrand took the CD and without looking at it passed it to Micha. In moments the car was engulfed in sound. "Do you like operatic music, Henri?"

"Sometimes, but I'm a novice when it comes to the works and the composers. What is this CD?"

"It's an opera composed by Richard Wagner entitled Der Fliegende Hollander or translated in English, it's The Flying Dutchman."

Bertrand hoped that his facial expression didn't reveal anything. The name Wagner registered clearly. He knew Wagner was a virulent anti-semite. His music was a favorite of Hitler and inmate orchestras were forced to play his works at Auschwitz, while their fellow Jews were being herded into gas chambers. He hated the thought of listening to a Jew hater's music, but he forced himself to relax.

They rode in silence until they reached 47th Street. Bertrand leaned slightly forward toward the driver, "You can pop the CD now."

Micha placed the CD back in its plastic cover and passed it to Bertrand with a slight roll of the eyes. Bertrand gave him a half smile and then turned to Kathy and handed her the CD.

"I'll leave the luggage in the car until you're ready, Miss Longrin. Have someone call me at the garage and I'll bring the car around."

Kathy nodded to the driver and then walked toward the entrance. Bertrand followed slightly behind as she made her way to the elevator. They said nothing during the ride up.

Bertrand pressed the keypad and waited until Kathy entered, then followed. The secretary said nothing but pressed the inner door's release button. The two armed guards moved slightly away as they passed.

In a few moments they were seated at the conference table. The silver coffee service was in the center and a large plate of Italian cookies consisting of Biscotti, Amaretti di Saronno, and Anise Tosties were placed alongside.

"How was your mini vacation, Kathy?"

"Never long enough, Raphael, but it was nice to be home even for a few days."

"I'm going to have some coffee. It was just brewed. Do either of you care for a cup?"

Bertrand looked at Kathy who replied yes.

"Me too, Raphael, and don't hog the cookies."

Duchant filled Kathy's cup, stood up, then leaned over and placed the coffee in front of her. Then he reached for the cookie plate, but Kathy shook her head no before his hand made contact.

"I insist, Kathy. They're delicious and even if you only have a small piece, you must try one."

Kathy reluctantly reached for a cookie, took a small bite, then placed it on the edge of her saucer. Duchant passed Bertrand his cup and held out the plate of cookies.

Henri took four and looked back at each of them. "Hey, they're good and I'm hungry."

Kathy couldn't help but smile.

Duchant lowered his head and shook it from side to side. Then he looked at Kathy. "You wanted to meet. What's up?"

"I'm thinking seriously about terminating our relationship."

Neither man said anything, but kept their eyes focused on the woman.

"It has nothing to do with either of you. It's not personal, at least not where you're concerned. It's just that circumstances make it impossible for me to continue here."

Duchant sipped his coffee, then placed the cup back on the saucer. He looked at Kathy with a slight smile, which was not confrontational and asked, "And what might those circumstances be, Kathy?"

There was heavy silence that enveloped the room as Kathy remained silent, her eyes never wavering from Duchant.

When she finally responded to Duchant's question, she said only, "It's complicated."

"You were trained to handle complicated matters, Kathy. Every trial before a jury is complicated. Your relationship with us is probably the most complicated one you could ever encounter.

This relationship is beyond the norm of anyone's imagination. It involves attitudes. It involves ideologies, conflicts, misrepresentations, human parasites, and thievery. It involves stratospheric sums of money, among so many other facets, that it's a never ending equation of complexities."

"We work in a rarefied environment, which is a world unto its own. The diamond business is dangerous, complicated, and highly rewarding. Our quest to recover what is rightfully ours, the paintings, is another dangerous and complicated matter."

"I remember quite clearly, that evening not so very long ago, when you stated that one of the conditions of employment would be that you could leave anytime. That still holds true, but I want to go on record that we want you with us. I am sure we can resolve whatever conflict is causing you to consider resigning. If we're wrong and can't resolve the matter satisfactorily with you, we will make no further attempt to persuade you to stay. Your full salary of three hundred thousand dollars, tax-free, will be paid in its entirety and immediately."

"Why not give us the opportunity to hear your reasons. I think we're entitled to that, but whether you want to or elect not to, that's entirely your decision. If you feel that you'd like to think it over without saying anything now, that's fine by us."

Duchant reached for his cup, but kept his eyes on Kathy.

Bertrand said nothing. His body language said it all.

Kathy looked at Bertrand, then back to Duchant. She breathed in deeply, then let the air out slowly, but she still said nothing.

Neither man moved. They waited patiently for Kathy to indicate something that would define which way she was leaning.

Duchant said all that could be said for the moment. There was nothing further that he could add to influence the situation until the woman revealed how she was disposed.

Raphael knew that the woman's litigative mind was analyzing what he said. She was now sorting out what fit and what didn't fit and matching it with the other side of the equation, that part of the equation that was giving her the reasons, the causes, to reinforce her decision to resign.

Duchant saw that Kathy seemed to relax somewhat. He watched her as she now breathed in a normal, unhurried pattern. His training told him that she had reached a decision or was very near to one.

He decided to move his hand toward his coffee cup as a distraction...a move that would cause her mind to focus on him and away from her immediate thoughts. The movement might get her talking.

He picked up the cup and brought it up to his mouth. He sipped the coffee slowly and then placed the cup down. Then he looked at Kathy and almost on cue, she began to speak.

"I may not be the right person to assist you in these negotiations." As if anticipating Duchant's question, she continued. "The position of lawyer and art advisor requires someone who can be completely devoted to the task without conflict."

She quickly realized that she was treading on quicksand and had to be extremely careful with her choice of words. She didn't want to compromise her father in any way. By electing to speak out here because of some sense of perverse loyalty, which she now regretted, she had committed herself.

The two men watched and waited for her to continue.

"I believe there is an element of danger involved in what has been happening since I joined you. I can't put my finger on it specifically, but I know it exists. There seems to be a veil of secrecy that has deprived me of information that could be relevant to my job. There are a number of instances that give me cause to believe that you have not been up front with me and not totally honest with me."

"If I'm expected to work in a vacuum without being privy to everything, how then am I supposed to function professionally? How am I to make value judgments that could help with the business at hand?"

She sat quietly, looking down for a moment and then at each of them before she let her eyes focus on Duchant.

Duchant pushed his cup out of the way and folded his hands together on the table.

"Everything, Kathy, that is relevant to the business of recovering what rightfully belongs to my family, was told to you. The art in question belongs to the Duchant family. That is a fact, an indisputable fact. It was stolen, with considerable dexterity through the violation of a trust that my grandfather and father placed in several unnamed parties."

"I want to recover these paintings. That is my unwavering intention no matter how long it takes. I have both the time and money and am not hesitant to use either to accomplish this goal. Those artworks, which can be identified in private, or public collections, will be litigated. Those that cannot, because they supposedly don't exist, will be repurchased. That is what we are now attempting with the Woman in Black."

Kathy heard the words resound inside her head. "Those that cannot, because they supposedly don't exist, will be repurchased through negotiations."

"We are in one of those negotiations, Kathy, concerning a painting that doesn't exist, but we know it does. You know it does and the people who possess it, know it exists. It's interesting, perhaps the word is curious, that a painting which the art world believes was stolen or destroyed during World War II, is now for sale by other than the rightful owners."

Duchant reached again for the coffee cup, but stopped halfway. He was about to speak, but before he could, Kathy said, "You state that this painting and others were and continue to be, the property of your family. Yet you are unable to provide any refutable proof to substantiate this. You relate that documents have disappeared, people directly involved have died and records have gone astray, yet we're to assume your ownership at face value."

The hostility was evident in her voice. Duchant let some moments pass to defuse the situation.

When she didn't continue, he began slowly and just loud enough to force her attention toward what he was saying.

"The Nazis began their systematic looting of art in early 1930 and continued it through to their defeat in 1945. In the 1930's Hermann Goering, then a top aid to Adolph Hitler, came to my father's gallery in Paris to view the artwork for sale, as well as some of my family's collection, which was on permanent display there. He was unceremoniously asked to leave by my father, which set the stage for what followed. Goering's hatred toward my father over that incident never abated."

"The Nazi's concerted campaign was aimed at confiscating valuable pieces of art and collections from prominent Jewish collectors and dealers, beginning in Germany and continuing through the conquered countries. The Nazis stole and looted at will from collections, galleries and museums."

"At the conclusion of hostilities in 1945, US Army Intelligence units and other US Government agencies coordinated their efforts to identify, recover and return a portion of the looted art to their rightful owners. Despite their efforts, thousands of pieces of art were never returned to their rightful owners."

"Part of the reason was simply that almost all of these owners were dead, victims of the Nazi's final solution. It is estimated that twenty-five percent of the world's most significant works of art seized by the Nazis are still missing today. Many other art pieces and antiquities found their way from post war Europe into the hands of museums or dealers who asked few questions concerning their origins. If they knew, they were quite willing to turn a blind eye."

Duchant leaned slightly forward, but not so far as to appear intruding into Kathy's space.

"When we discover a painting, which was owned by my family, and suddenly becomes available for sale, we have to assume that the people who hold that artwork do so illegally."

"Proving original ownership is a near impossible task since most records have been destroyed during the war. The list I showed you survives and is a testament to my family's ownership."

"Recovery of stolen, or looted art, is very difficult and in many instances, the only way to reclaim the art in question is through a negotiated purchase in secrecy. We are not interested in how the owners acquired the art. We can never be entirely sure and besides that venue is for others to pursue. We are only interested in paying a reasonable amount of money to purchase the underground art and place it back where it belongs...in my family's collection. We are not interested in personalities or how or why they have the painting for sale. The object is to get them to sell the painting, or paintings, to me for a price, period."

"I would like you to stay with us, Kathy," and he smiled. "Whatever is causing you concern, I hope that what I've stated regarding our position, assures you of our intentions. Please delay making an immediate decision. Sleep on it. There's a lot to digest. Please come back tomorrow with your decision or your additional questions. If for any reason you'd rather telephone me regarding your decision, that's fine."

Kathy began to stand up and Bertrand followed her lead. She looked at him but said nothing.

"I'll tell the driver to bring the car around." He reached for the phone, pressed one of the speed buttons and was connected to the garage.

"Please tell Micha to bring the car around," then hung up.

Kathy just stood quietly watching Duchant before starting to leave the room.

She stopped, then looked back again at the seated Duchant.

"I appreciate your time, but I must tell you in all honesty that I'm still leaning toward resigning."

"You're a lawyer, Kathy, decisions should be made with the head, not the heart."

She continued to stare at him for a moment, turned again, then walked out.

Bertrand nodded once to Raphael then followed Kathy out. When he reached the bottom of the metal stairs, he called out her name.

"I'll see you home, Kathy, if you don't mind."

Before she could answer he added, "It's important to me. I hope you won't object."

Chapter 35

Bertrand was ever the gentleman, walking her to the street entrance door, but no further, nor did he make any attempt to touch her in any way. He said "goodnight," and returned to the Rolls.

After picking up her mail, Kathy went to her apartment. She checked the answering machine, noting that there were no messages. She stared at the red zero in the message window and briefly thought about her lack of a social life.

Then she went to the bedroom and undressed. She showered, put on the terrycloth robe and returned to her bedroom.

She sat on the edge of the bed and let her mind freewheel for a while. Then she walked to the living room, took a legal pad of yellow paper from her briefcase and went to the kitchen table.

She drew a line down the center of the page and wrote at the top of each column, pros and cons. Then she began to write, switching back and forth between columns. She went over what she had written numerous times, making the necessary adjustments to words and phrases.

When she finished, she sat back in her chair, dropped the pen on the pad and rubbed her eyes with the back of her hands. She needed to clear her mind. She had reached an impasse and struggling with it further wasn't going to change anything.

She stood up, walked to the refrigerator, and took out a Perrier. She removed the top, thought about a glass, passed on the glass, and then settled on the sofa with the bottle in hand. She took a long sip and felt the liquid coat her parched throat. Kathy reached for the remote and touched the power button.

The television screen filled with a paid advertising spokesman, hawking his wares at a level many decibels above normal. She forcibly pressed the down volume button and let out a sigh when the voice dropped to inaudible.

Leaving the volume purposely low, she surfed the sitcoms and cable news, then past what appeared to be a documentary on one of the public broadcasting system's channels.

The momentary images caught her attention, and she pressed the down button on the controller repeatedly until she returned to the PBS channel.

The screen showed images of what appeared to be a concentration camp. She increased the volume as the announcer described the place, "As a chamber of horrors where mass murder was conducted on an industrial scale."

She was captivated by the moderator's voice, which was slow and methodical.

"The Auschwitz-Birkenau complex, Nazi Germany's largest concentration camp and extermination facility, was located near the Polish town of Oshwiecim in Galacia. It was established by the order of Reichsführer Heinrich Himmler on

April 27, 1940. SS Brigadefuhrer and Major General of Police, Ludolf Otto Steiger, First Adjutant to the Reichsfuhrer SS, was directly responsible for the implementation of the order."

A picture of Himmler appeared on the screen in his black uniform, his wire rim glasses, and bird like features. Then a picture of Steiger flashed across the screen.

Kathy froze. She stared at the picture, unable at first to comprehend what she was looking at. While the picture had a resemblance to her father, there were facial characteristics that didn't apply.

All too soon the photograph left the screen and was replaced with a series of old people. The elderly men and women interacted with scenes from captured German movie footage and photographs that relived memories too horrific to relate, but needed to be told.

The wrinkled face of an old man appeared on the screen and in heavily accented English he began to speak.

"He stood there, his thumbs interlaced in his pistol belt, feet slightly apart, his uniform immaculate and his black riding boots polished to a high gloss. He stood arrogantly surveying the Jews assembled in front of him. These were his prey and he went about his task of selecting those who would die immediately, those who would be forced to participate in his insane medical experiments, and those who would be assigned to the work details.

He conducted the selection with the utmost pleasure."

The old man wiped the tears from his eyes, then with a cracking voice began again.

"The Angel of Death, Dr. Josef Mengele, pointed to a mother clutching her thirteen-year-old daughter, indicating that she was to move to one group and her daughter to another. The mother refused to be separated from her daughter. When an SS Guard tried to separate them, the mother clawed at his face, scratching, and biting him. Mengele took out his pistol..." then the old man again began to sob, "and he shot the mother and her daughter in the head. The incident made Mengele so angry that the entire transport, even those who had been previously selected for the work detail, were put to death."

The moderator's voice overplayed the still pictures, which now took over the screen, showing crematoriums and piles of naked victims waiting for disposal in the ovens.

Then footage of children appeared, mostly twins holding hands with rolled up sleeves showing their tattooed arms to the camera. Behind the children were smiling women SS Guards.

The moderator continued, "...nine out of ten victims were Jews, many of these children. Josef Mengele had a special hatred for Jewish children who were often put to death upon arrival. Children born in the camps were killed on the spot. Mengele, however, kept some alive so that he could inflict intolerable suffering on them by placing them in pressure chambers, testing them with drugs and bacteria, castrating them, freezing them to death, and exposing them to a host of other unimaginable trauma."

A picture of the ovens again appeared on the screen as the moderator continued to speak.

"Near the end of the war, as a cost saving measure, an order was issued by SS-Brigadeführer Ludolf Otto Steiger to place living children directly into the ovens so that expenses could be reduced by saving on the amount of gas that would otherwise be used to kill them."

The same picture of Steiger reappeared, then disappeared as the screen filled with other images.

Kathy pressed the power button, stood up and walked directly to the bathroom. She leaned on the sink and thought about what she had just seen. The picture of the man named Stieger kept flashing back. She leaned further into the sink and threw up.

Chapter 36

Despite the sleeping pills, her night was anything but restful. Her throat felt raw and her head throbbed.

She looked over at her alarm clock, groaned and after several explicatives, got up and went to the bathroom. She held on tightly to the rim of the sink, as she leaned over, not sure whether she wanted to throw up again.

After a few moments Kathy lifted her head and looked at the mirror. She didn't like what was staring back.

Reaching over the sink, Kathy turned on the cold water knob. Then she cupped some water with both hands, brought it to her mouth and rinsed.

Not satisfied, she repeated the exercise with her toothbrush. The mint taste in her mouth seemed to ease, somewhat, the feeling that she needed to regurgitate again.

She took off the t-shirt and silk boxer shorts she had worn to bed and turned on the shower.

The water felt good, and she let it play against her body. She lifted her face into the center of the shower head, then turned around so that the water could cascade off her neck. She refused to move, liking the feeling of the water riveting her body.

After some minutes passed, she finally turned off the shower, stepped out, and dried herself. She went to the kitchen and started brewing coffee.

Kathy pulled out a chair and sat down at the table. Her eyes locked onto the yellow legal pad with her notations.

She reached toward the pad with her right hand and moved it closer. She scanned what she had written, then pushed the pad away.

For the first time in her life, Kathy felt like running away...far away from Duchant, the paintings...everything. All of it was becoming overwhelming.

As she sat thinking about the events since she started working for them, the images from the documentary started to play out again.

Suddenly, a feeling of foreboding came over her and her body shook.

When her body stopped shaking, she sat perfectly still...her mind in a trance-like state.

She slowly became aware of the silence signaling that the coffee had finished brewing.

She lifted herself into a standing position with the aid of the chair back, then hypnotically moved to the coffee.

Filling a cup to the rim, Kathy started back. With each step coffee spilled on the floor. After what seemed like an inordinate amount of time, she reached the table and placed the cup down.

The coffee helped.

After minutes passed her mind clutter was replaced with images of herself...her accomplishments and the struggles that they entailed.

Running away accomplished nothing and it was just a girlish thought, one that was very uncharacteristic of her. She had never run away from anything and she chastised herself for the momentary thought.

She realized that nothing was to be gained by making a decision without hard facts. In order to get to the bottom of what was happening to her and around her, she needed to stay put. It was as simple as that. It was always better to work from the inside out, rather than the reverse.

What was on the table was a potential business, with two different background stories. She would continue to be part of the buying side, the Duchant side. She would stay as neutral as possible, while letting the events unfold.

She went back to the bathroom, tilted her head back and squeezed a drop of red eye remover in each eye. She closed her eyes, then opened them and looked back at the mirror. Satisfied, she began to carefully apply the minimum make up she used.

After a light touch of lipstick, Kathy went back to the bedroom to dress. She decided on a black pants suit and a white silk, cufflink shirt, with a wide collar whose points were extended so that they spread smartly over the jacket's lapels. She wore black Ferragamo pumps with short heels.

*

"You're out early this morning, Miss Longrin."

"Yes, Arthur, couldn't sleep. Would you flag a taxi for me?"

The doorman walked to the curb and blew several times on his metal whistle.

In a few moments, a cab pulled to the curb. Kathy placed some money in the doorman's hand and seated herself in the cab.

She gave the address to the driver, then sat back. The traffic was light, and she was in front of her old law firm building before she realized it. She paid the fare, stepped out and watched the taxi pull away.

Kathy walked past the building's entrance and headed for the small coffee shop around the corner. She saw the lit neon open sign and walked in.

She was alone and took a seat at the counter.

A voice called out from the back area, "One moment."

Oscar walked out fidgeting with a starched white apron. As he adjusted the apron his eyes focused on his customer. He called out "Kathy," and then walked over grabbing her outstretched hand with both of his.

"Hello, Kathy, what a nice surprise this morning. What brings you here so early besides my good home cooking?"

"I couldn't sleep, Oscar, and to be perfectly honest with you, I saw something on television last night that disturbed me, and I thought you could help me."

A perplexed look came across the man's face and then he smiled.

"If this old man can help a lawyer like you, Kathy, I'd be glad to try. But first, what will you have?"

"How about some black coffee and whole wheat toast Oscar?"

"That's not a good breakfast for a young woman like you. Suppose I scramble some eggs and we can talk."

She hesitated a moment then said, "Okay."

The old man smiled and then walked to where the coffee was brewing. He called out, "Decaf or regular?"

"Regular, Oscar."

The owner placed a cup of steaming coffee in front of Kathy, then went to the grill, cracked several eggs and asked, "Now tell me how I can help?"

"I saw a documentary last night about one of the German concentration camps. It was called Auschwitz and…" but before Kathy could continue Oscar turned around with a look of horror on his face.

Kathy wasn't sure whether she should just end this conversation, forget about her coffee and leave.

Before she could decide, Oscar began speaking.

"I didn't mean to startle you, Kathy. I just wasn't expecting that to be the subject of our conversation. The name, Auschwitz, brings back many memories to me, all of them beyond human understanding unless you've personally experienced it. Every day without fail, the memories come flooding back. There is something…a smell or a sound, even a look on someone's face, that reminds me of the camp. This tattoo," and the elderly man pushed up his left sleeve, "is a never-ending reminder."

Oscar stared at the tattoo, looked back at Kathy and then again at the tattoo.

"I was one of the later arrivals. The earlier ones had the tattoo applied to their left chests."

He rubbed several fingers over the faded tattoo before he turned back to the grill and scrambled the eggs. In another moment he placed the plate in front of Kathy, took a cup of coffee for himself and seated himself on a stool on his side of the counter.

"Now ask me anything, but first take some food."

Kathy didn't feel much like eating, but to please the old man she took some of the eggs and smiled at him. "Delicious, Oscar."

The man smiled back and took a sip of his coffee.

"I saw several photographs on the program... the TV program last night. One in particular intrigued me. His name was Steiger. Do you know anything about this man?"

Without hesitation Oscar replied, "Yes, I know of the man."

Then he said nothing for several minutes. Kathy watched his eyes as they glossed over and took on a far away look. He then began to speak as he moved his head and eyes slightly away from Kathy.

"I remember arriving at the camp entrance. Above the gates was a sign that stated, "Arbeit Macht Frei." (Work will make you free) I can still see the buildings clearly...the gas chambers and crematoriums, the Gestapo camp, the medical experiments center, and the gallows. I remember the selektion, (Selection process) where those who were considered unfit for work were always sent to the left. Those who could be worked to death were sent always to the right."

"The execution area was located at the southwest corner of the camp…the prisoners were killed by lining them against the wall and shooting them. I was one of the prisoners selected to live a little longer and was assigned to the detail that placed the bodies in gravel pits around the main camp."

The old man brought his hands up to his face. Kathy saw the tears run through his fingers and reached out to touch him.

He brought his hands away from his face, picked up a corner of his apron and wiped his eyes.

"Yes, I remember the man whose name you mentioned. He was the man, along with Himmler, who was responsible for the camp in the first place, a place where the rationalization of murder was exemplified. Under Steiger's direction and implemented by the camp commander, Rudolf Höss, the Nazis murdered over a million Jews, Poles, Roma, and Soviet POWs. The majority of the murdered were Jews."

"Steiger came often to the camp on inspections tours. He enjoyed watching the gassing and firing squads in operation. It was Steiger who helped introduce Zyklon-B to the extermination process."

He saw a questioning look come over Kathy's face.

"Zyklon-B, Kathy, was a cyanide gas originally manufactured for pest control. The camp's commander, Rudolf Höss used it to speed up the killing. At one point, twenty thousand victims could be gassed and burned in the ovens in a single day."

"Steiger and the Angel of Death, Doctor Josef Megele, were always seen together. Steiger was present on a number of occasions when the doctor conducted his experiments on twins and dwarfs."

Then there was a very long pause.

"You see me here now because I am one of the few fortunate enough to survive. I was young when I went to the camp and it was near the end of the war. I am living testimony of man's hatred toward his fellow man. It was not because we Jews did anything that deserved such punishment, it was simply because we existed. Our existence was sufficient reason for the Nazis to blame us for Germany's problems, real or imagined. On that perverted premise, they killed us in numbers never imagined possible. I am, Miss Kathy, one of only sixty-five thousand that survived the camp…from over a million who were deported there."

Kathy reached out and patted his hands. "It's over now, Oscar. You're safe here in America and I'm sorry for forcing you to remember so much pain."

She pulled her hand away, opened her purse and placed a ten-dollar bill next to her unfinished coffee and plate of eggs. She stood up and walked to the door. As she held it open, she instinctively glanced back at the man who was now standing with his back toward the counter.

She turned and took a step through the doorway, but before the door completely closed, she could hear Oscar crying.

Chapter 37

Kathy sat alone at the conference table. After leaving the coffee shop, she decided this was the best place to be. The French coffee was already brewed so she helped herself to a cup.

The two men at the monitors gave her a cursory nod when she entered, otherwise she was alone with her thoughts.

As she sipped the coffee, she felt a void. She never knew much about Jews. She had come in contact with a few in the legal profession, but there were no Jewish attorneys at the Higgins law firm.

During school and church, she had been exposed to the usual stereotype comments. Despite these, she remained neutral, at least she thought she was.

What few Jews she did come in contact with, were a mixed bag. All in all, they were pretty much the same as all the other races, some good and some bad.

Her knowledge of the Holocaust was minimal. She knew many died during the war, but her knowledge of the death camps was nil, at least until last night.

Then her mind framed a picture of Oscar...a survivor of the camps who brought the documentary to life. Now she faced a perplexing problem with regard to the man known as Steiger. Could this man be...and then her mind refused to let her finish the thought. It was beyond the realm of possibility. The man described by Oscar was devoid of human traits. That was not her father! The picture was a mere resemblance. Many people looked like others and it is said that each of us has a double somewhere.

She relaxed somewhat as she forced her mind to consider the possibility of a lookalike. That man whose photo captured her attention and the description provided by Oscar, was not anyone she knew. The man who was her father was a gentle and kind man. She felt her body relax further, as she thought about how wonderful her father had always been to her. She never remembered him in any other way, even when he was disciplining her.

She turned as she heard movement to her rear.

"Hello, Kathy. You're here early."

"Couldn't sleep, so I decided this was as good a place as any to get some coffee."

Bertrand helped himself to a cup, pulled out a chair, and sat to Kathy's right.

"That's a smart outfit you're wearing."

"Thanks. It's new, and black is the color of my mood."

"Can't be all that bad, or is it? Have you reached a decision?"

"Yes, but I'd rather wait for Raphael. That'll save me from doing it twice."

Bertrand nodded his head in agreement and reached for his cup. They sat in silence, each realizing that there was nothing to say and trite comments would only agitate the situation.

Duchant appeared a little after eight a.m. somewhat surprised to see Kathy sitting there.

After saying good morning and pouring a cup of coffee, he seated himself directly across from her and smiled.

"Well, Kathy, while I'm surprised to see you here, I'm happy you are, regardless of your decision. What have you decided?"

"I've decided to stay. I have issues, but I think they can be better resolved in time by working with you. I believe I'm correct about that. If not and I've made a mistake, well then I'll have no one to blame but myself."

Bertrand was tense as Raphael asked the question. He slowly released an inaudible sigh, pleased that she would still be part of the team.

Then he looked over at Raphael who was leaning forward on his forearms.

"Kathy, we look after our own. If something is bothering you, give us the opportunity to help you. We, Henri and I, have no ulterior motives. What we are, you see clearly from our company's operations here and in Europe. We want to recover what is rightfully ours. We have no hidden agenda."

Duchant waited, hoping that the woman would open up. After a long pause he decided he would bait her and see whether it would be enough to get her talking.

"Kathy, perhaps I've overlooked something in giving you the background of my family. It is not something that I discuss, unless the subject is brought up, but I never deny it either. In fact I'm rather proud of my lineage since it goes back to before the French Revolution. In fact, it goes back over three thousand years to Abraham, Issac, and Jacob. I am a Jew."

Both Duchant and Bertrand watched her reaction. Her face was unexpressive. She just stared back at Duchant. It seemed that she was processing the information. Then she spoke.

"Have any of your family died in the camps?"

For Duchant, it was a strange first question. He pondered her reason for asking and then decided to inquire.

"Before I answer your question, I would like to know why you asked it?"

Kathy bent her head slightly and brought up her left hand. She rubbed her eyes with her thumb and forefinger. Then she ran her fingers through her hair and looked back at Duchant.

"When I went home last night I couldn't sleep. I turned on the TV and started watching a documentary, which was about a death camp called

Auschwitz. The images and commentary were horrifying."

"This morning I had coffee near my old office building. I wanted to go there, in fact I had to go there because the owner has a tattoo on his left arm, just like those at the death camp. I felt the overpowering need to ask him some questions and after it was over, I left him sobbing."

"I am upset at this very moment by everything I saw and heard. I guess that's why I asked if you had lost family there, after you indicated to me that you are Jewish."

Kathy purposely left out the part about seeing Steiger's photograph in the documentary and the uncanny resemblance to her father. It would serve no useful purpose in this discussion.

"Yes, Kathy, I have lost family during the Holocaust. Some were sent to Auschwitz and other camps. None came back."

Kathy looked toward Bertrand. "And you Henri, did you lose family as well?"

"No, I'm a Catholic. We were spared to a degree. Only political Catholics not in step with the Nazi occupation government, or members of the resistance were eliminated."

She looked toward Duchant thinking he was not one of the stereotypes. He was cultured, maybe the word was distinguished, and his persona was absolute class from the way he dressed, to the manner in which he carried himself and spoke.

He saw the way her eyes looked at him and anticipated her next question, which didn't come, so he began to speak.

"We're meeting Garland and von Hoenshield this afternoon at two p.m. at the gallery. We want you to accompany us. Garland called for the meeting and we anticipate that he'll present us with a counter-offer."

"Of course, I'll accompany you. I'm still part of the team, right?" She asked the question more for reassurance than from doubt.

Bertrand answered, "An integral part of the team."

Kathy smiled, stood and said, "I have some work to do. I want to check with our attorneys in Europe to see what progress they're making. I'll have an update for you both shortly."

She left and went to the secure phone room which Shimon and his staff operated off the main floor.

Once she was clear of the area, Duchant said, "Something set her off, triggered her consciousness and it wasn't a few images on a television screen about some poor Jews in a death camp. I want you to call the station, probably the Public Broadcasting System station in Garden City, and get a copy of the documentary. They're always for sale. Send one of our men to pick it up and bring it back here."

*

A little after eleven a.m., Bertrand handed the video to Raphael. They walked to the monitors where Brent and Dushku sat. Anticipating Duchant, Brent asked, "Ready for the bullet?"

"Not yet gentlemen. I don't want you to have too much fun too soon. What I need is this video placed on the conference room screen. We may need some copies of various frames."

"Okay, Mr. Duchant, I'll watch it with you. Just signal and we'll copy the frame for you. When you're seated, let me know and I'll drop the screen."

Duchant and Bertrand went back to the conference room, signaled Brent and watched as a ceiling screen, fifty-two inches, dropped into place. In a moment images began flashing across the screen as the film's moderator began speaking.

After fifteen minutes of interviews and captured German film showing arrival transports and camp buildings, photographs of both Himmler and Steiger flashed across the screen.

Duchant signaled the console operator. "Brent I want a large still of the man shown after Himmler. The one the moderator identified as Steiger. Also get me some of Steiger with Mengele, and Steiger at the gravel pits."

"Consider it done, Mr. Duchant. Anything else?"

"No, that's it. Cut the video and store it."

"Yes, Sir. Be there in a minute with the copies."

"That's it, Henri. Our Miss Longrin saw the man identified as Steiger, noticed a resemblance to her father, and went into some sort of semi-denial. She's rattled, as well she should be. Her comfortable world has experienced a few cracks, and we'll use them to our advantage."

"She's still with us because there's no other place she can be now. With us, or better put, through us, she hopes to find out, one way or the other, whether her father is the Nazi mass murderer, Ludolf Otto Steiger."

Henri Bertrand sat there hearing Duchant's words but thinking of the turmoil that was raging inside Kathy Longrin.

A different torment was stirring inside him, as he realized there was nothing he could do to help her.

Chapter 38

They seated themselves around the table in the far corner of the gallery. Von Hoeshield offered wine, coffee, and tea.

Kathy, Duchant, and Bertrand politely declined, while Garland took coffee.

Von Hoenshield poured a glass of wine for himself, then proposed a toast.

"To a successful negotiation," then he sipped the wine and placed the glass on the table.

Kathy looked at Garland, who gave no hint that they had ever met. His eyes moved quickly past her and Duchant and settled on Bertrand.

"The owner is not willing to see this work of art leave his possession for under fifteen million dollars. It is a generous offer and considerably below his twenty million price. There is no further compromise. Please consider this offer, gentlemen, and lady, and give me your answer."

"We need a few private minutes to discuss your offer, Mr. Garland. Would you please excuse us," and Bertrand began to rise.

Rudel put out his arm. "Please, it is we who will leave you for…is fifteen minutes sufficient?"

"Yes, that should be adequate."

"Good," and he looked toward von Hoenshield, "Manfred please follow me," and they both walked out of the gallery.

Duchant took out a piece of paper from his jacket, pushed the pen top with his thumb and began to write.

"Remember the room is probably bugged. Let me counter at eleven million, move up to twelve and if they don't accept, we walk…the two hundred million along with us. If they let us walk, we'll use von Hoenshield to get the negotiations re-started again. Ready?"

They both nodded yes.

Duchant began to speak knowing that his words were monitored.

"Fifteen million is still too high. Let's make an offer at eleven million. If Garland doesn't budge, I'll up it a bit and then we walk. There's other art that two hundred million will buy and we're spending too much time on this painting. Do both of you agree?"

Kathy said yes. Bertrand followed with, "I agree also. I'm getting tired. These negotiations are going on far too long. That painting isn't saleable unless it's to an underground buyer. If Garland can pull another buyer out of the woodwork, I'd wager the price would be below our eleven million offer."

"Okay, we all agree, eleven million, or we walk away."

Outside the gallery, Rudel's cell phone rang.

Fifteen minutes later, Rudel and von Hoenshield walked back into the gallery and took their seats.

Rudel looked at Bertrand and asked, "Do we have a deal?"

"Yes, if the price is eleven million."

"I'm getting the feeling, Mr. Bertrand, that no matter what price my side offers, it will continue to be too high. We have taken five million off our price and yet that's not sufficient. I'm wondering if you are negotiating in good faith."

"The price we've indicated, Mr. Garland, is a substantial sum for a work of art that doesn't exist."

"But it does exist. You have seen it and Miss Longrin here," and he moved his head in Kathy's direction, "has substantiated that it is the work of art it is represented to be."

Duchant ceremoniously withdrew his black Ostrich skin billfold from his jacket pocket and removed three cashier checks. Then he reached into another pocket and removed the small velvet bag that contained the diamonds. He watched as the four sets of eyes were drawn to his hands, as he placed them on the table.

"Perhaps these," and he pointed to the checks and diamonds, "will convince you that we are here in good faith. We would like to conclude this initial transaction so that we can move on to other possibilities. The offer Mr. Bertrand indicated, eleven million, is a fair price."

Duchant moved the checks and diamonds toward the center of the table, then leaned back in his chair.

"Mr. La Monde, eleven million is on the light side, but in the spirit of cooperation I am willing to reduce our price somewhat, if you will increase your offer."

Duchant moved his body forward a bit. "We'll offer twelve million for the Woman in Black."

Rudel looked back at Duchant, but said nothing. Von Hoenshield shifted in his seat. The others sat motionless as they waited for Garland to respond.

When he did, he said, "Still a bit light, Mr. La Monde."

"It's our final offer, Mr. Garland, made in, as you say, the spirit of cooperation."

Garland sat in a way he had before Duchant made the offer, staring but giving no indication of what he was thinking.

Duchant knew that Garland was aware and briefed fully regarding their conversation. What he was now doing was for show purposes. Well, let him have his moment.

After several minutes, Garland extended his hand toward Bertrand. "Let us consider this business concluded."

After shaking Bertrand's hand, he stood up and reached toward Duchant and then to Kathy. He squeezed her hand a little too hard and she tried to read something into it but couldn't.

"Now, Mr. Bertrand, the payment."

Henri looked toward Duchant.

"Mr. Garland, we have a cashier's check in the amount of twelve million," and he moved one of the checks toward Garland.

"Alternatively, we can pay half that amount in diamonds together with a check for six million, or we can deposit twelve million in any bank account you indicate, anywhere in the world."

"The cashier's check would be adequate. By the way you had three checks. One you indicated was for twelve million, and the other for six million. What was the third check for?"

"The third check, Mr. Garland, was in the amount of five million. If you agreed to eleven million, we would have handed you the checks for five and six million. It was always a possibility you'd agree to that amount," and Duchant smiled.

Garland reached for the check, but Duchant placed his hand on top of Garland's and the movement stopped. "Mr. Garland, may we see the painting?"

"Of course," then he nodded to von Hoenshield who rose and went behind the curtain.

In moments he returned with the painting, which was wrapped in brown paper and tied with a string.

Von Hoenshield carefully removed the string and wrapping and then placed the painting on the table. Then he lifted the painting and angled it so that it would be in full view of everyone.

Duchant turned to Kathy. "Take a closer look and let me know."

"Oh come now, Mr. La Monde, do you think we'd try that ruse again as we embark on our first business venture?"

"I trust you, but for twelve million, we bought the inspections rights."

Rudel smiled at Kathy as she moved forward to examine the painting.

She was trying to decide whether that squeeze was a signal for her to indicate that the fake painting was real or the real one fake. She wondered which one of the paintings von Hoenshield was holding.

She bent down and looked closely at the painting. She knew immediately what it was. Her thoughts focused on her father and then back again to Duchant. She turned toward the table.

"The painting is authentic."

Duchant rose and walked to the painting.

Kathy stepped aside so that he could stand in front of it. He looked at the bottom right hand corner and noted that the oatmeal color of the ground was left exposed. Then his eyes moved to the face, and hands, where he looked carefully at the flesh colors. The strokes were dragged while the paint was still wet, leaving an identifiable pattern, as Kathy had indicated was Cassatt's style. He tried to remember other points that Kathy had mentioned when examining both the fake and the original, but his memory couldn't bring forth any additional facts.

He placed his hand on Kathy's elbow and nudged her forward and away from the painting.

He said softly, knowing that even a whisper would be picked up by the monitoring station, "Are you sure?"

The stern look on his face said more than the words he spoke.

Kathy looked at Duchant, her eyes steadfast and unblinking and nodded her head yes.

They both moved back to the table. Once seated, Duchant pushed the cashier's check toward

Garland, who picked it up, examined it, then folded it in half and placed it in his pocket.

Garland nodded and said, "That concludes our business. If you will excuse me, I have other pressing business that requires my immediate attention. We are interested in selling other works of art. I will compile a list of several which may be of interest to your principals."

They all shook hands again and then Garland turned and walked out of the gallery.

Von Hoenshield seated himself in Garland's chair and turned toward Bertrand.

"This has been a very good afternoon, gentlemen and Miss Longrin. May I offer you some champagne to toast the conclusion of our first transaction together?"

Henri looked at Duchant, then Kathy and back at von Hoenshield. "We'd love to, Manfred."

The German bowed and stepped behind the curtain. He reappeared with several bottles of Dom Perignon. After he placed them on the table, he went back behind the curtain again.

He came out carrying an ice bucket and four champagne crystal flutes. Von Hoenshield placed one of the bottles in the ice bucket and proceeded to open the other.

He filled all the flutes and then said, "To success."

The three responded with, "To success."

Manfred finished his drink quickly and without asking the others, refilled his flute.

"The champagne is delicious, Manfred, an excellent choice. May I ask what year?"

"It's a 1978, and I'm pleased it meets with your approval, Mr. La Monde."

Manfred was thoroughly enjoying himself. The more he drank, the more inebriated he became. The three were nursing their drinks and watching the German consume most of the first bottle, encouraging him when possible.

It took only thirty seconds after ingestion for the first amounts of alcohol to reach Manfred's brain. Once there, the alcohol started to act on his nerve cells, located deep within his brain.

Champagne, like other alcohols, is a depressant. It began acting on von Hoenshield's central nervous system almost immediately. The more champagne the German consumed, the more it affected his nerve cells which controlled his breathing. This resulted in the impairment of his judgement and coordination, two vital processes of the central nervous system.

The first bottle was emptied and von Hoenshield was trying to uncork the other.

Bertrand reached across the table. "Let me help you with that."

The German smiled and handed him the bottle. "Seems I'm all fingers at the moment," then he laughed.

Bertrand removed the wire, then eased out the cork. There was a soft pop sound and then Henri leaned over and refilled von Hoenshield's flute. He looked at Kathy who shook her head, then at Duchant who nodded yes.

They raised their glasses and touched.

Von Hoenshield drained his flute and held his glass to Bertrand who filled it up again.

"I am very happy that we have reached this point. As Mr. Rudel stated we will have a list of additional paintings for you shortly. I know that these will be of the same quality as the one you have just purchased."

Duchant and Bertrand glanced at each other briefly when the German spoke the name Rudel. Kathy tensed and hoped it wasn't noticed.

Bertrand asked, "When do you think Mr. Rudel will have the list ready?"

"I would say sometime next week," and he took another sip of champagne. "Mr. Garland is very prompt when he commits to something."

"We appreciate all that you have done to assist us, Manfred," and then Bertrand looked back at Duchant.

Raphael took out his wallet and removed a check. "I believe this will be satisfactory compensation for your assistance, Manfred."

He handed the check to von Hoenshield, who stared at it through watery eyes for a number of minutes.

"I am at a loss for words. This is a very generous amount gentleman. I am overwhelmed. Thank you...thank you."

Duchant and Bertrand nodded, Kathy remained rigid, and the man listening in Illinois raged inwardly.

Chapter 39

The Doctor's tone of voice dictated the physical position Rudel assumed in front of the massive desk.

He stood at attention, eyes straight ahead and head unmoving as the Doctor paced back and forth.

"This matter should be concluded as expeditiously as possible, Sturmbannfuhrer. Use what personnel you deem necessary from the New York cell. This traitorous schwein (Pig) could compromise much of what we all have worked so hard to build these many years. He's a threat to us all. You have your orders."

Rudel's right arm shot out and his heels clicked as he intoned, "Ja Herr Doctor."

He turned and went out of the room relaxing only slightly as he made his way to the Mercedes Benz station wagon.

"The airport, Udo."

Rudel opened the rear door behind the driver's side and slid in. He closed the door and waited, lost in thought as Udo finished loading his bag in the rear compartment.

As the Mercedes Benz's tires crunched on the gravel roadway, Rudel's mind replayed his report to the Doctor concerning his daughter.

"She did, Herr Doctor, what her position called for her to do. The look on her face, for just a split second, revealed clearly that she was experiencing some difficulty in trying to determine where her true loyalties should be placed. I believe, Herr Doctor, that your words stating that she should do what is necessary for her employer, was the deciding factor in the way she acted."

"In future negotiations, Herr Doctor, you may want to elicit her assistance in besting these damn Jews."

The look that appeared instantaneously on the Doctor's face told Rudel that his suggestion was completely out of bounds.

Rudel said nothing further as he watched the Doctor try to subdue his anger over the liberty he had just taken.

*

Rudel spotted Bruno at the baggage claim and walked toward him.

"Nothing more. I'm carrying it all."

Bruno turned and led the way out of the area and across the street to the short-term parking lot. Once they were both seated, the driver asked, "The hotel or Soho, sir?"

"Soho, Bruno."

*

He sat at his desk with only the communication center operators and a small guard contingent keeping him company.

His mind kept returning to the premise of simply walking into the gallery and blowing von Hoenshield's brains out. The traitor deserves nothing less.

He shook his head wondering how a man like von Hoenshield, an SS Officer and an awardee of the Iron Cross First Class, could betray his blood oath.

Rudel eliminated a number of complicated scenarios, but one thing was certain, von Hoenshield had to disappear.

A simple approach was the best and he felt comfortable about what he finally decided.

He looked at his watch and motioned to Bruno.

*

The Mercedes Benz was waiting at the hotel entrance as Rudel came out.

He carried a small bag and placed it on the seat after he entered the car.

Once Bruno was settled, Rudel leaned forward and asked, "Do we have the materials?"

"They have been delivered to the shop, sir, and the truck is waiting at the service station on the corner for our call."

Rudel sat back, the look on his face revealing little of what he was thinking.

The phone call was made to von Hoenshield only minutes before. Despite von Hoenshield's questions, Rudel simply repeated the name of the Soho shop and its address.

The telephone call lasted only thirty-five seconds at most and ended with Rudel hanging up while von Hoenshield was in mid-sentence.

The East River Drive was crowded with rush hour traffic. Rudel stared out his window but saw only von Hoenshield's image. The man disgusted him. He closed his eyes and thought, it would have been a simple matter, more expedient to pick him up en route, but there was no way I could tolerate sitting next to that disgusting creature. No, it was better this way. Let the traitor find his way to us.

Then a thin smile formed, as he leaned his head back against the soft leather seat.

"Put in a CD, Bruno, something that's soft and relaxing."

The sounds of chamber music immediately filled the car as it slowly maneuvered its way toward the Soho area.

Bruno held the door open, as Rudel made his way out. "Park the car, then wait inside for von Hoenshield. I'll be waiting for you downstairs."

Bruno's body stiffened and he nodded his head slightly. He waited until Rudel entered the shop before he re-entered the car and pulled away from the curb.

Rudel walked past the retail portion of the shop, went through a door marked emergency use only, and then walked down a flight of stairs.

The smell of animal fat, fish oil, glycerins, and tallow used in tanning leather were immediately apparent. There were racks of leather pieces hanging and waiting the stretching and tumbling stage required in the processing sequence.

Indifferent to it all, Rudel made his way down a narrow center aisle until he reached another door. He turned the handle, pushed the door open and was quickly confronted by several men.

Acknowledging him with a shake of their heads, they backed off as Rudel took several steps into the room, slipped, then regained his balance.

He looked down and saw the floor was covered with heavy gauge plastic sheeting. The men were dressed in rubber wetsuits and each had a rubber silicone, glass scuba diving mask resting on or above their foreheads.

Off to one side was a fifty-five gallon drum placed on a wooden pallet. Next to the pallet was a small hydraulic hand truck with a capacity to lift fifty-five hundred pounds. Since tanning leather produces no toxic fumes, there was no need for a specialized ventilation system. The building's central air-conditioning unit was sufficient.

*

Von Hoenshield was surprised and unnerved by the telephone call. It was a combination of hearing Rudel's voice and the curt manner in which the few words exchanged between them were spoken.

He thought about the words...a matter of some urgency and then he heard the name of a store and its address, which he hurriedly jotted down on the corner of a newspaper.

Rudel repeated the name and address and hung up as von Hoenshield was about to ask if there was anything specific he should bring along.

He decided to take the subway to West Broadway and walk to Prince Street. It was quicker than trying to find a cab and fighting the morning traffic, cheaper, too.

Von Hoenshield caught the F train and found a seat. The subway car was filled with the usuals, a few businessmen and women, blue collar workers coming and going from their menial jobs, and groups of school kids with their arrogant ways and indifference to anything, or anyone, but themselves.

He laughed to himself as he thought how quickly their attitudes would change if the camps still existed. So many sub-humans in the world, but we did what we could, yet so many still remain.

His attention was quickly redirected to the closing doors as he suddenly realized this was his stop. He bolted from his seat grabbing the rubber door closures and squeezing his shoulder in between.

He pushed on the right door until it opened wide enough to maneuver out and onto the platform.

He brushed at his suit jacket and cursed, as he watched the train pick up speed and disappear into the darkened tunnel.

Then he turned, got his bearings, and followed the exit sign to West Broadway. He went through the metal gate and up the stairs to the street level where he paused for a moment. The air outside smelled good compared to the damp, rancid air of the New York subway system.

He walked south along West Broadway until Houston Street, turned left and walked two long blocks to Prince Street. At the corner he turned left again. The address he was looking for was the third building in from the intersection of Houston and Prince.

The first two buildings housed art galleries. He paused, automatically drawn to the artist's work on display. He thought that he might stop in after his meeting with Rudel.

As he approached his numbered building, he stopped again to window-shop. He was admiring the various leather accessories when he heard a door open. Directing his eyes to his left he saw a man dressed in a black suit holding the door back with one hand while beckoning him with the other.

"Danke (Thank you). Where can I find Mr. Rudel?"

"I'll take you to him, sir, please follow me."

Bruno took the same path as Rudel had, leading von Hoenshield to the stairway. He held back as he motioned with his hand for von Hoenshield to proceed.

"Walk through the center of the hanging pieces of leather until you reach a door then knock. Mr. Rudel is in that room. I will wait here until your meeting is over then drive you back to your apartment."

Von Hoenshield smiled weakly, turned and began walking down the stairs. The smell of leather became stronger as he descended. At the bottom he walked slightly to his right, found the so-called center aisle and walked until he came to the door described by the man in the black suit.

He knocked and it opened. The lights were blinding, but he heard Rudel's voice. "Your eyes will adjust to the light in a few minutes, Hauptsturmführer. Please step into the room."

Those were the last words Captain Friedrich Alpers ever heard. Rudel aimed the Walther titanium coated P99 pistol with the attached silencer at the left rear of his head and squeezed off two 9mm rounds.

Von Hoenshield toppled forward. The left rear part of his skull disintegrated as the mushrooming and expanding effect of the bullets interacted with the bone and soft tissue.

Rudel began unbuttoning the raincoat he was wearing, as he watched the two men in the rubber suits separate von Hoenshield's personal belongings and clothing from his now lifeless body.

The two men moved the body to a metal table and placed it face down. One of the men picked up a chain saw with a twenty-five inch cutting bar and began to dismember the body.

As each piece separated from the torso, the other man placed it in the fifty-five-gallon drum, half full of sulfuric acid. The acid began eating away at the pieces of flesh on contact.

When the dismemberment was completed, Rudel walked to the fifty-five-gallon drum and looked in, wanting to remember the minute details of the final chapter of von Hoenshield's demise.

He turned to the man covered in blood and still holding the saw.

"Top off the drum with enough acid to insure all pieces are submerged," and as an afterthought Rudel added, "Make sure the lid is fastened as tightly as possible."

He paused again. "Bring up the drum by the elevator. I'll arrange for the truck to be outside. Wash and roll the plastic and bring these along with the drum."

Rudel walked to the door and after opening it, took off the rubber boots and tossed them toward the center of the plastic covering.

He shut the door and started walking up the stairs. At the top landing he nodded to Bruno and they both walked through the retail section and outside to the sidewalk.

Bruno used his cell phone to call the truck which arrived within several minutes. As he was talking to the driver a buzzer alerted them to the momentary opening of the elevator doors positioned in the sidewalk.

The driver went to the rear of the truck and opened the roll top rear door, then rejoined Bruno and Rudel off to one side of the sidewalk. The fan-like doors of the elevator began to open and in moments a small caged elevator appeared.

When it was even with the sidewalk it stopped. One of the two men opened the gate, as the other man moved the pallet with the fifty-five gallon drum onto the sidewalk with the hydraulic hand truck. Rudel noted that both of their rubber suits were now clean, not a trace of the bone, flesh, or blood that covered them just a short while ago.

The pallet was pushed to the truck's rear, then jacked up until it was slightly above the truck's cargo deck. Both men then climbed up and onto the bay and rolled the drum off the pallet.

They strapped the drum to one of the side-walls and anchored the pallet in front. Then one of the men pulled on the strapping, making sure it was taut. Then he tried to move the drum, but it held securely in place.

Satisfied, both men jumped down, grabbed hold of the hand truck, lifted it up and onto the bay, bracing it against the pallet.

They disappeared back down the elevator, then reappeared from the door way with rolled and bounded sheets of plastic flooring, several pieces of two inch woven hemp rope, and three shovels. They loaded these onto the bay, signaled the driver, who then closed the roll top.

The two men waited as the driver secured the door with a lock, then moved into the pass-enger's side of the truck.

Rudel walked to the driver. "Call Bruno when you've unloaded."

The man snapped to attention, clicked his heels, and bowed slightly. Then he re-entered the truck's cab and started the ignition.

As he pulled away from the curb, Rudel and Bruno walked back into the building through the retail shop, but this time took the other stairway to the communications center.

The truck proceeded across the George Washington Bridge and headed to a landfill on the Jersey side. The site of a 1960's chemical complex, it was cleaned and reclaimed by the state government as a landfill. All hazardous waste had been banned, but this made no difference to the three men in the truck.

As they took the off ramp leading to the landfill, one of the men said, "Stop here, let me get in back with the drum to make sure it doesn't shake loose."

The driver nodded, went to the rear of the truck, unlocked the lock and opened the roll top door.

The man got in, and the driver closed the roll top, but left it unlocked.

The truck ambled along the rough road past several city sanitation trucks emptying their day's garbage and trash. As the truck moved forward, the sea gulls scattered only to nosedive into the mounds of refuse seconds after the truck passed.

The truck proceeded to the northern edges of the landfill, using the logic that most haulers would opt for a space as close to the entrance as possible, so they could empty their truck and leave quickly.

The far end of the landfill would provide some degree of protection, at least for a while. All they needed was a little time to allow the sulfuric acid to render the pieces of the late Captain Friedrich Alpers, aka Manfred von Hoenshield, completely unidentifiable.

When the truck stopped, the man inside the bay opened the roll top. The driver and the other man came around and waited as the hydraulic truck was removed from the bay.

Once the drum was placed on the ground, the three men took the shovels and began digging. The drum was moved to the hole and lowered, using the hemp rope.

The ends of the ropes were tossed in and then the hole covered.

They walked a hundred yards from the hole and began digging a horizontal pit. When they finished the two men hurriedly stripped out of their rubber clothing. Underneath they wore moving company overalls. They threw in the plastic sheeting, followed by the rubber pants, gloves, shirts, Rudel's raincoat, and three sets of boots.

Then they covered up the pit and piled a mound of debris over it, making sure it blended in with the immediate area.

The truck moved off thirty feet before the driver braked. All three men got out and looked back at the landfill. They couldn't be sure where their handiwork was located. One of the men nudged the other, "Let's go."

*

Back at the communications center, Rudel listened to the report. He hung up without a response, then he signaled the operator at the monitor and in moments the Doctor's voice came on line.

Chapter 40

They admired the painting, now hanging on the wall of the conference room.

"The Woman in Black is once again in the possession of its rightful owners."

Duchant spoke facing the painting, then turned toward Henri and Kathy.

"We should let the word filter out to the art community that this painting, long presumed to be lost or stolen during the war, has now been recovered. I am not willing to secrete this painting away, nor should I have to."

"I think this calls for some champagne. Will both of you join me?"

Without waiting for an answer, Duchant picked up the phone. Several flutes and a chilled bottle of Roederer champagne were soon placed on the conference room table.

Duchant lifted his glass and moved it toward Kathy. "We couldn't have accomplished this without you. Both Henri and I are pleased that you've decided to continue working with us."

Their glasses touched, then Duchant turned toward Bertrand.

"To my associate and friend. Our quest has just begun."

Henri replied, "To a successful end," and smiled.

"By the way, you two owe me a dinner at La Colombre de Bleue. Are you willing to pay up tonight?"

Henri looked at Kathy, who raised her shoulders in a makes no difference to me movement.

Henri looked back at Raphael and said, "Okay, but we get to choose the wine."

Raphael laughed. "Trying to hold down the price of the dinner, are you? It won't do either of you any good," then he laughed again, and they joined in.

*

Kathy felt the trepidation as she dressed for the evening. Her mind refused to allow itself to rest and continued to project the images of the camps, her father, Duchant, von Hoenshield, Rudel aka Garland or whatever, across her brain in slow motion. No matter what she did to allay her doubts and her fears, they persisted.

So far, she remained as neutral as possible under the circumstances, but categorically refused to believe that her father could in any way be involved with the camps.

Everyone has a double somewhere and the photograph in the documentary was far from a perfect resemblance.

She stood still, her mind now churning with a need to know, to place the pieces into the pattern that would make sense for her.

She called out, "Okay, not now...but soon."

Then she realized what she had just done, and shook her head in disgust, thinking, all this is having a negative effect on me. Get a hold of yourself, Kathy Longrin, or else.

She finished dressing and called down to Arthur to have a cab waiting.

*

As she walked into The Blue Dove, she saw several of the men at the bar glance in her direction as she passed. It does wonders for the ego, she thought.

As the maitre d' approached, Kathy said, "Mr. Duchant's table please."

"Right this way, Madam."

She followed, aware of the stares that accompanied her as she made her way to the table. This double ego trip was making it easier for her to relax.

Duchant stood up and waited as the maître d' pulled a chair away from the table.

Once Kathy was seated, he sat down.

Kathy noticed that Henri was not there. She started to speak when Duchant interrupted.

"Henri will be a wee bit late. I've asked him to pick up something for me. Meantime you and I can enjoy some champagne, which I've taken the liberty to order."

He signaled the waiter who poured the Roederer into Kathy's flute and then refilled Duchant's.

After the waiter discreetly disappeared, Ralphael said, "To friendship," then smiled as he sipped the champagne. Kathy smiled back and took a sip from her flute.

A few moments later, the waiter reappeared carrying a bowl of caviar nestled in a larger bowl of cracked ice along with condiments and mother of pearl spoons.

Duchant placed some of the black roe on several toast points and without asking added a small amount of egg and a touch of onion. Then placed them on a china plate and held it toward Kathy.

She took the plate with a slight bow of her head. "Thank you again, Raphael," and then smiled at him and held the smile for several moments.

"You look beautiful tonight, Miss Longrin."

Kathy tilted her head slightly. "Thank you, Mr. Duchant."

She thought about the clothes she wore. They weren't wasted on this man. Her Chanel dress set her back a pretty penny, but after all, she was a three hundred thousand-dollar woman, tax free. She wore a single strand of 8mm pearls around her neck, and a Hermès silk scarf in a white and tan horse pattern draped over her shoulders. Her Judith Lieber evening bag in red, silver, and blue semi-precious stones in the shape of an apple, added just the right touch to her ensemble.

She looked back at Duchant. "As always, Raphael, you look very well-attired."

"That's kind of you to say, but it's always much easier for a man to dress than it is for a woman."

"I don't necessarily agree. Plenty of men I see have the money to buy the best, but don't know how to put an outfit together. You on the other hand, seem to know what goes with what and the overall effect is outstanding."

"Thank you again, but you're making me feel self-conscious."

"I doubt that I could ever do that, Raphael. You seem to have all things well under control," and she thought about how true that last statement was. He never seemed to get ruffled. He was poised and collected, never rushing a statement, or a motion.

His clothes were always immaculate. The white shirt with a light blue collar, and matching French cuffs offset the dark blue suit with the thin chalk white stripes. His neckwear was a blue Hermès tie with white "H's" interwoven throughout. Mr. Raphael Duchant oozed class, wealth, and everything that went with it.

Kathy followed Raphael's head movement and watched as Bertrand's hand moved forward toward the maitre d'. After the maitre d' discreetly took what was handed to him and after an exchange of a few words, she followed Henri's movements as he made his way to their table.

He sat down next to her, pulled in his chair and placed the small bag he was carrying on the table.

"How many drinks am I behind?"

Kathy replied, "One," and Duchant, almost in the same instant, said, "Two." Then they laughed.

Duchant followed up with, "Take your choice, but if I were you, I'd opt for two."

That brought a few more laughs.

Henri waited until the waiter had filled his flute and then turned to Kathy. "You look terrific tonight."

Kathy shook her head. "This must be my night. I'm getting compliments galore from two very charming gentlemen, champagne, and caviar. I should hang out with you guys more often," then she laughed and soon both Duchant and Bertrand were caught up in the laughter.

As Bertrand set his flute down, he looked longingly at Kathy.

"Raphael and I would like to thank you in a more formal way than simply with words. We are grateful to you for your help in assisting us with the purchase of the Mary Cassatt painting."

Kathy started to mouth a reply, but Bertrand held up his hand.

"We would not have been able to complete this purchase without you. Your assistance was significant, and we are excited about what the future holds in the recovery of additional works of art. Raphael and I would like you to have this small gift."

Bertrand reached for the bag and removed a horizontal red, nine-inch box and handed it to Kathy.

She stared at it for a moment, then looked back at both men. She moved her thumb and pressed the gold toned button at the center of the bottom portion of the box then lifted the lid gently. Her head moved back slightly as her eyes focused on the diamond bracelet resting on the red velvet cushion.

The six carats of diamonds were set in a platinum herringbone pattern and sparkled even in the dimmed light of the restaurant.

"It's…" and Kathy tried to search for the words and finally said, "extraordinary, beyond beautiful. Thank you so very much. I am truly humbled by your generosity."

Duchant thought about what the woman had just said. She didn't protest, feigning not wanting the bracelet. She accepted the gift with the understanding that it was given willingly. Her choice of words added to her character. Too bad her background doesn't fit her outward demeanor.

Duchant watched as Henri helped Kathy secure the bracelet. Then she held out her wrist so that Duchant could see it.

He took hold of her hand gently and leaned forward. "It's a beautiful piece and now it's become more beautiful because the new owner adds such elegance to it."

He let go of Kathy's hand and smiled.

Dinner consisted of grilled steak with olive butte, celery with roquefort cheese. The wine was Chateau La Tour, and dessert, chocolate and nutella truffles. They had a round of Remy Martin Cognac, and Duchant called for the check.

"I thought we were picking up the check?"

"But you are. I'm just helping you along a bit."

When the maitre d' began to present Duchant the check, Raphael pointed to Kathy and Henri.

The maitre d' hesitated a moment and then handed the leather binder to Bertrand.

Henri opened the leather case, looked at the bill and then reached for his wallet. He placed several large denomination bills inside and passed it to Kathy.

She opened it, looked at the total indicated and let out a gasp that was slow and audible.

Both men laughed and Raphael said, "The national debt, isn't it?" and then they laughed again.

"That's what happens when you lose a bet with types like yours truly. It's never cheap. Ask Henri, he's had to pay up quite a few times."

Kathy opened her small Judith Lieber evening bag and slipped a credit card on top of Henri's five, one hundred-dollar bills.

Henri reached for the leather binder and took out his money. "Take this money, Kathy, and pay the check with your credit card. It might be a bit easier that way instead of dividing the check."

"By the way dear folks, before we adjourn, let's schedule another meeting with von Hoenshield. Let's dangle the two hundred million in front of our new best friend."

"Okay, Raphael, I'll phone him tomorrow first thing."

"Good, Henri, now if you two will excuse me, I must leave. I've thoroughly enjoyed this evening, especially since I didn't have to pay for it." Duchant got up, waved, and headed toward the entrance.

Henri held out the binder for the maitre d' and as he walked away Bertrand turned back to Kathy. "I know a little place in Soho that plays some great jazz, interested?"

Kathy thought for a moment, "Why not, sounds like it might be fun."

Henri was pleasantly surprised with her answer. He expected her to ask for a rain check again.

*

The taxi stopped in the middle of the block, in front of a building wedged in between an art supply house and a psychedelic store selling everything from water pipes, to cigarette rolling machines, plus a few hard to get toys for the S and M crowd.

The music filtered out onto the street as Kathy and Bertrand walked past the idlers lounging near the curb and stopped next to the bouncer, who was positioned half in and half out of the doorway.

The black bouncer acknowledged Bertrand with a firm handshake and a pat on the back. "I like that grip…ya been liftin' a bit, I bet."

Bertrand smiled back, "The only heavy lifting I've been doing, Marcus, is with my right elbow and you know how heavy a vodka glass can get."

The bouncer laughed and stepped aside, as Bertrand and Kathy made their way into the darkened interior. Once past the doorway, the din of voices became noticeable.

The room opened into a wide expanse, with candle lit tables placed around the center of the room and along two walls. The flickering candle lights encased in various colored globes on the tables danced on the walls and ceiling in an ever-changing array of kaleidoscope patterns.

Directly to the front was a small stage, which was lit now by the beams of several stationary spotlights in light blue and yellow hues. That would change when the musicians began their next set, but for the moment recorded music played through hidden speakers keeping the assembled crowd more or less content.

The man straddling the floor in front of them extended his hand. "Nice to see you again, Mr. Bertrand. If you and your guest will follow me."

Kathy looked around as they followed the man. The place wasn't upscale, nor was it seedy, somewhere in between. The term shabby chic came to mind.

They walked to the right and entered a small elevator. The ride to the second floor was quick. The man held the door open as Bertrand and Kathy stepped out onto a balcony, which overlooked the main floor.

The balcony consisted of only eight tables surrounded by leather club chairs that were reserved for what the establishment considered its special customers.

The balcony was slightly tilted toward the main floor, which conveyed an eerie sense of vertigo. However, once seated the feeling dissipated and the view of the stage and the main floor was spectacular.

"A waiter will be over shortly, Mr. Bertrand. The next set should start in about eighteen minutes."

"Thanks, Lewis." Bertrand placed a folded bill in the man's hand and turned toward Kathy.

"Do you like jazz, Kathy?"

"As a matter of fact I do. I like him..." and she moved her right hand, fingers curled and thumb sticking out in a motion away from her body. The movement was made as if she was pointing to some non-existent person, whose only identification was from the music being played. I've always liked John Coltrane."

"I would have made a stab at it...the musician that is. I might have gotten it right, but you're definitely on the mark. What would you care to drink, Kathy?"

"How about another Remy Martin?"

"Sounds good to me."

Bertrand caught the waiter's eye and signaled him over.

Two cognacs later, nursed through a forty-five minute jazz set by the on-stage musicians, had mellowed Kathy and she felt relaxed for the first time in days. She looked at Bertrand while holding up her brandy glass. "Do you know any place where we can get an espresso, or a cappuccino at this hour?"

"I do indeed."

Henri settled the bill, and they rode the elevator to the street level. He palmed another bill to the maitre d' and another for the bouncer. The bouncer placed the money in his pocket and called out, "Now don't be a stranger, ya hear."

Henri raised his arm and waved without turning around, as he and Kathy walked arm in arm down Prince Street toward the intersection with Houston Street.

As they passed a leather gallery, Kathy stopped and pulled on Bertrand's arm. "Wait a minute Henri, I'd like to window shop for a second."

They walked back and viewed the merchandise. Kathy pointed to several exotic skinned bags. "Those look beautiful even now. I'd like to come back when they're open and see them in the daylight."

"Let me know when you're game. I'd like to join you."

Kathy thought that his subtle way to find a reason to be with her was cute. She wondered whether she should let him get closer to her, to allow whatever was possible, to happen. But then her thoughts returned quickly to her father, the camps, and her mood changed abruptly. She suddenly felt adrift in a sea of turmoil.

"Henri, would you mind terribly if we skipped the coffee. I'm suddenly feeling tired and I don't want to spoil what has been an absolutely extraordinary evening, even if I'm somewhat poorer."

She smiled and Henri laughed.

"It's perfectly alright. It gives me another opportunity to buy you a cup of coffee."

They walked silently to the intersection each engrossed in their respective thoughts. Bertrand let go of her arm and stepped off the curb. He raised his arm and waved at a passing cab.

The cab braked and pulled to the curb. Henri opened the rear door and got in beside her, perhaps a little too close as their bodies touched.

He straightened a bit, but didn't move away, nor did she. He turned his head to the right about to say something when Kathy duplicated his move-ment. Their faces were inches apart as Kathy leaned and their lips met.

Chapter 41

The answering machine at the gallery picked up the telephone message. The operator at his monitor in Illinois also began recording the message the moment the connection was made.

"Good morning, Manfred. This is Henri Bertrand."

"Our principals would now like to begin further negotiations. Please advise us as soon as possible if your group would be interested in working with us again. We have up to two hundred million to spend. Auf Wiedersehen."

The operator printed out the message, translated it into German and called over to an associate standing near the door. "Hans, please deliver this to the Doctor."

The man took the envelope and left the room. As soon as the Doctor nodded, the man clicked his heels and returned to the communications center.

The Doctor read the note, placed it on his desk, then picked up the telephone and dialed.

When the voice came on the line the Doctor spoke rapidly then hung up.

In moments he was in the communications center walking toward the secure chamber. He waited before he opened the door, waiting and watching the operator. When the operator nodded, he opened the door and walked in.

The operator in the communications center below the Prince Street store signaled Rudel who was sitting at his desk. "The Doctor is on the line."

Rudel picked up the phone and listened to the static noise. In moments the static cleared, and the operator moved his head up and down several times.

Rudel spoke one word into the phone. "Yes."

"A message will be transmitted to you momentarily. It is self-explanatory and taken from the gallery's answering machine. Proceed with additional negotiations. The second sheet contains a list of items that will be of interest to them," then the connection was broken.

Rudel replaced the phone and walked to the monitor. "I'm expecting several message sheets, signal me when the transmission begins."

"They are coming in now, sir."

Rudel looked toward where the operator was pointing. He walked to the machine and watched the two sheets of gibberish print.

The operator then walked over. "It needs to be decoded, sir. It'll only take a moment."

Walking to another machine the operator fed the papers into a slot. He then handed Rudel the transcribed sheets.

The sheets contained the phone message left by Bertrand and a list of twenty-one works of art, and their respective artists.

He jotted a number on a pad of paper and handed the pad to the operator. "Connect me with Mr. Bertrand at that number. Put it through to my desk phone."

The operator nodded and in moments he signaled Rudel that Bertrand was on the line.

"Mr. Bertrand, this is Karl Garland. The message you left for Mr. von Hoenshield has been passed to me. Regrettably, Manfred has resigned as managing director of the gallery effective immediately. It was totally unexpected."

"No...the gallery will continue in operation for the foreseeable future. Despite the loss, no one man is irreplaceable, and we are interviewing for a replacement as we speak.

"I have already been in contact with my principals and they are willing, in fact anxious, to continue our business relationship. May I suggest we meet at the gallery tomorrow at say two p.m."

"Perfect...I look forward to it, Mr. Bertrand...will Mr. La Monde and Miss Longrin accompany you?"

"Yes...until then, Mr. Garland."

As Henri replaced the phone, Duchant took out his earpiece attachment.

Henri motioned with his hand, "Well, you heard. They evidently retaliated against von Hoenshield. Saves us the trouble and we were only a day or two away anyway."

"That's one Nazi bastard that the world is better off without. The kraut had the smell of death on him after he accepted the last check from us. His handlers monitored everything we said and did from inception on. They knew what was happening every moment along the way and the catalyst to his demise was pure and simple greed."

"He'll never know that the two Zurich checks we handed him were purely air, no such accounts existed at the Anker Bank. Do you think he was aware at the end, that his own people were doing him in?"

Raphael smiled. "You can be sure of it. Keep in mind, Henri, that we're out twelve million, but it gets us a little bit closer to the center. Has Kathy arrived yet?"

"No."

"When she does, advise her of our meeting with Garland, but nothing about Manfred. Let Garland tell her or let her find it out from some other source. She's a bit scrambled now. The news of von Hoenshield's departure should and probably will, rattle her a bit further. It will be one more inconsistent element in her ever-growing world of uncertainty."

"While our Miss Longrin is beautiful and everything else that goes with that, she is primarily a pawn in a very high stakes game. She is to be used to further our end. What we are and what we do, cannot be placed in jeopardy because of individual feelings. Feelings have no business in our world. They don't exist. Do not allow yourself, or the mission to become compromised. The consequences are dire."

"You are a friend, Henri, and a colleague. A dangerous liaison is the last thing you need, and the repercussions are the last thing we need."

With that, Duchant excused himself and left the conference room.

Bertrand had heard the words before. It bothered him considerably more now then when Duchant had first lectured him. Despite the anger that he felt within, he remained seated in stoic silence, until his attention was refocused on the standing woman across the table.

"Hey there! I said good morning twice. Whatever it was you were thinking about, your concentration was absolutely superb."

"I'm sorry, Kathy, I was preoccupied thinking about a course of action."

"And did you reach a conclusion?"

"Unfortunately, no, but I'll eventually reach one."

"How about some coffee?"

She nodded her head yes, placed her purse and briefcase on the chair to her right and watched as Bertrand poured the coffee in the china cup.

"Thank you again for a wonderful evening and this," she pointed to the bracelet.

Bertrand just smiled and watched her pick up the cup. Then the thought, this is going to get complicated, as his eyes scanned her face and then glanced down to her chest.

"We're meeting with Garland at two p.m. today. We'll see what his side has to offer, then we'll make a judgement whether we move forward."

"Do we know what is being offered? I could do some research prior to the meeting."

"Don't know, but I think it's more exploratory. In any event we're not going to make any commitment until we have a chance to discuss among ourselves what's offered."

"Then I guess we'll kill time until the meeting. That'll give me a chance to check with my counterparts in Europe to see what progress they're making. I'll brief you both in a memorandum before we leave for the meeting. By the way, where is Raphael?"

"He's here, somewhere."

"I have some things that need taking care of. Excuse me for a while. I'll be back shortly."

Kathy sipped the coffee, wondering what this next meeting would hold for her. She had more or less decided that once this new business was concluded, she would resign from Duchant and Company.

Then she thought about a timeline. I should be able to clarify my concerns by the time these negotiations conclude. After that, I have only one obligation and that is to myself.

She purposely left out any thought reference to her father. She wouldn't do anything to compromise her relationship with him, even at her own peril. But why was she thinking like this... peril, what peril? No one was in danger of anything and...why did she think of the word peril?

She wanted to move away from these thoughts. A recurring negative pattern was developing that seemed to take hold whenever she was idle.

Kathy moved her briefcase to the table and opened the latch. She pulled out the large black leather address/telephone book, then flipped pages until it was opened to a name and telephone number in Paris.

She asked the monitor operator for a secure line, had him dial and when the line connected, she was all business.

*

Bertrand walked across the sorting room floor toward the security area. As he was about to enter, Duchant came out.

"I was going to look for you. I phoned the conference room, but Kathy said you just left. Come on in, we need to talk."

Once they were seated, Duchant began to speak.

"Shimon and I have a tentative plan that we'll bounce off you. It concerns Garland or Rudel, take your pick. The short of it is to eliminate Rudel after we've agreed on another purchase and before any money changes hands. With Rudel out of the way, we have a more realistic chance of getting to Steiger. Shimon will arrange Rudel's untimely death. We'll also use Kathy to the maximum benefit possible. If there's any doubt about who her father is by that point, we'll make sure that the doubt is replaced by fact."

At the mention of Kathy's name, Bertrand stiffened. He was sure that Duchant or Shimon or both saw the change, however slight, in his body movement.

He quickly said, "How do you..." then he paused, thinking that he should have used the word we, "...plan to use Longrin?"

"That's not finalized yet," Shimon replied, "but we're thinking that she could be used to arrange a meeting which will involve Steiger."

Shimon knew that the woman would be at worst a hostage, a pawn, to get Steiger to a meeting, or at best a willing but duped participant.

"And what happens if Steiger refuses to move from his lair and his antenna tells him that Rudel's death is more than just a coincidence?"

Duchant picked up the conversation from Shimon.

"That's a possibility, a very real possibility, but we can only react to what we believe is perceived by the other side after the event has taken place. We'll know pretty much how the situation is unfolding based on what we get, or what we don't get, from the other side. The death of Rudel is not going to bring these negotiations to a halt. Not when they're so close to two hundred million dollars. That money is far in excess of what anyone's life is worth, regardless of whose life it is. Besides, if they suspect we're behind Rudel's demise, they'll be planning a number of convenient hits on us, but not until they get their hands on the money. The fact is we, you and me Henri, are already on their hit list. Caution is the keyword here…no compromising situations for either of us."

Bertrand sat, eyes fixed on Duchant, but no body movement or changes in facial expression occurred to indicate how he received what was being said.

He just sat there as Duchant again made the innuendo regarding what he perceived as a blossoming relationship with the enemy.

Chapter 42

The new gallery director was a man several inches taller than Rudel. He was slightly younger in age with dirty blonde hair and a one-inch scar on his left cheek which ran up to the corner of his eye.

The scar accentuated the pale blue eyes through which Wendel Miller watched the other man intently.

As Rudel discussed the pending meeting, unknown to Miller, every word was being monitored in Illinois.

Miller was not privy to the events leading up to and including von Hoenshield's disappearance. He was told only what Rudel had related to Bertrand.

Miller was a blood German and an SS-Obersturmfuhrer (1st Lieutenant) of the Fourth Reich. The man sat perfectly straight in his chair watching and waiting for Rudel to continue speaking. When he did, he seemed to stiffen more.

"This gallery, Miller, is useful to our organization. The position of Director is a responsibility of considerable importance. Your initial duty will be to assist me in certain negotiations, which I outlined to you previously. The Jews have a considerable amount of money to spend and we will help them spend it. You have been selected to replace von Hoenshield because of your dedication and promise to our cause. Do not fail us, Obersturmführer."

"Herr Sturmbannführer (Major), you need have no concern about me. Meine ehre heisst treue." (My honor is loyalty)

Rudel let a thin smile briefly cross his mouth. As he was about to continue, his attention was redirected to the gallery door. Rudel looked at Miller, nodded then stood up and began walking toward the three people who entered.

After introductions, the five walked back to the table.

"May I offer you some coffee or tea, perhaps?"

Bertrand looked at Duchant, then at Kathy and then back to Rudel. "Thank you, but no thank you."

"Okay, but if you change your mind, you'll of course let me know." He smiled, but it seemed an empty gesture.

Duchant's eyes were fixed on Kathy when Rudel made the introductions. After Rudel mentioned that Miller was the Gallery's new director, he watched as a look of bewilderment clouded Kathy's face.

Now that they were seated, Duchant saw that the same facial expression remained. He decided to ask the question he knew Kathy was thinking about, but for some reason held back.

"While we're pleased to meet Mr. Miller and wish him success, we are curious as to what prompted the sudden departure of Mr. von Hoenshield?"

"The negotiations covering our initial business seemed to cause Manfred some physical distress. He wasn't the youngest of men and was nearing retirement anyway. We accepted his request to be pensioned. He is most probably enjoying a well-deserved vacation somewhere in South America where money seems to go so much farther. He always spoke of someday retiring to Argentina or Paraguay. Perhaps he'll drop us a card."

Duchant stole another glance at Kathy. She seemed more relaxed than before Rudel's explanation, but he wondered what was churning inside of her head.

Four sets of eyes focused on Kathy as she said, "Mr. Garland, may I take you up on your offer for coffee?"

"Of course, you can," and this time his smile was genuine. "Do any of you gentlemen care for a cup?"

Both Bertrand and Duchant shook their heads no.

Rudel didn't bother to look at Miller who rose from his chair and walked behind the curtain. After several silent minutes, he returned carrying a tray with one cup of coffee, a creamer, and a glass bowl of packaged sugar and sweeteners.

Miller carefully placed the entire tray in front of Kathy, then removed the items and took the tray away.

After Miller seated himself, Rudel began speaking.

"I'm pleased we've reached this point. My principals have additional paintings for sale, and they are willing to negotiate with your group prior to contacting others."

Duchant watched Rudel carefully choose his words. He made eye contact with Bertrand and wondered if he was thinking the same thought, what others?

Duchant tilted his head in a motion that indicated, we are appreciative, while thinking, nice try Rudel, but the smell of two hundred million US is too strong a pull. You, and your kraut associates, won't cut and run anytime soon.

Then as if Henri was reading his mind, Bertrand said, "That's appreciated, Mr. Garland. Do you have a list of what is available?"

Rudel turned to Miller, who was already reaching into his jacket pocket to retrieve the list.

He handed the papers to Rudel, who opened them, studied the sheets, then held them out for Bertrand.

"This is a very impressive list. May we have a copy?"

"Certainly."

Miller stood up and went behind the curtain. When he returned, he handed the photocopies to Rudel who in turn passed one to Kathy and the other to Duchant. He kept one in front of himself.

As Duchant scanned the list, he saw that there were at least six that had belonged to his family, among which were a Camille Pissarro, Claude Monet, Paul Gauguin, Georges Seurat, and two Edvard Munch, an artist from Norway, and one of the major precursors of Expressionism.

"A very impressive list, Mr. Garland. I note several that should be of immediate interest to the buyer we represent."

Duchant took out a gold antique Waterman pen and unscrewed the cap, placing it on top of the barrel. Then he methodically checked six paintings and slid the paper to Bertrand.

Henri scanned the list, turned his head so he was looking at Kathy, and then moved the paper in her direction.

After Kathy scrutinized the checked paintings, she held out the paper toward Duchant.

"Please pass it to Mr. Garland, Kathy."

Rudel reached out and took the paper.

His eyes focused on the check marks.

"An interesting selection, Mr. La Monde. I realize that you will need to review the entire list with your associates before we can begin serious negotiations."

Bertrand spoke up. "Where a significant amount of money is involved, Mr. Garland, we'll need more than a little time. Would it be convenient to meet again on Friday? That should allow our side sufficient time to review the entire list and decide on an amount they are willing to pay, individually or collectively for the paintings. Will that be satisfactory?"

"Quite satisfactory. We'll meet again at two p.m. on Friday."

At that point Rudel pushed his chair back, stood up and extended his hand to Bertrand, then Duchant, and finally to Kathy. He smiled at her as he let her hand go. "Does your quietness, Miss Longrin, mean that I can expect a difficult negotiation when you return?"

"Let's say that I am obligated to see that a benefit is derived for my side. I will pursue that end with vigor."

"In that case, let's hope that I am up to the task. I too have a side that requires some...how should I say it...some sense of loyalty."

At the mention of the word loyalty, Kathy's mind focused on her father. Again, her mind clouded and a rush of nervousness took hold.

"Goodbye, Mr. Garland."

Then she looked at Miller, smiled, turned, and began walking toward the door.

Bertrand spoke hurriedly to Rudel about looking forward to beginning negotiations on Friday. He nodded at Miller, extended his hand and after releasing the handshake, watched Kathy exit the gallery.

Duchant was more reserved. "I believe that our negotiations will be stimulating, and, in the end, both our respective sides will have what they want. In fact, I'm positive of it."

Duchant smiled and then looked at Miller who was still sitting in his chair expressionless.

Rudel walked around the table, patted Duchant on the shoulder. "That is a very positive attitude. By the way, is there anything wrong with Miss Longrin? She seems on edge and I hope that I've done nothing to offend her or cause her any anxiety."

"On the contrary, Mr. Garland. She's overworked. I'm afraid it's entirely our fault. Certainly, these negotiations are a contributing factor, but our business, after all, is a hard one. I'm sure that whatever is bothering her is temporary. I thank you, however, for your concern."

Rudel turned to Miller. "I'll walk Mr. La Monde and Mr. Bertrand to the door. I'll only be a moment."

Chapter 43

Kathy was waiting by the Rolls when Duchant and Bertrand exited the building. Bertrand opened the door and she moved in, followed by Henri and then Duchant.

As the Rolls picked up speed and maneuvered into the heavy traffic, Kathy shifted uneasily, prompting Bertrand to ask, "Is there anything wrong?"

Kathy didn't answer but continued to stare out the window. After a few minutes she turned and faced Henri. "I'm sorry, Henri, I'm fine. I was just..." and her voice trailed off.

Duchant, sensing a difficult situation brewing, suggested that they call it a day.

"It's almost three. Let's all have a drink. Do I have any takers?"

No one answered. "Your silence speaks volumes. In that case would you mind if I went back to the office, then you two can take the Rolls wherever you'd like."

*

Duchant was huddled with Shimon and several of his crew.

"We meet with them again on Friday. Does it allow you enough time?"

Shimon nodded yes.

The five men huddling around the desk discussed the initial concept that Shimon presented. They continued to modify and refine the plan, trying to eliminate open-ended possibilities that would be left to chance.

Everything was considered and discussed, no matter how minute or seemingly inconsequenttial.

They substituted, modified, expanded, and went through the timeline numerous times, until they were all in agreement.

Duchant stretched, opened his mouth, and yawned.

"I'm not going to look at my watch. It's been a long day and I feel the need to crash. I leave you all to your pleasant world of good and evil. By the way, Shimon, I'll need an Anker bank check in the amount of five mil by Friday morning."

"Consider it done, Raphael."

"Okay, goodnight to you one and all."

Duchant started walking away from the security room, when he turned back. "I'll send Bertrand to you for a briefing tomorrow morning."

Shimon nodded and went back to the three men still sitting around a table.

*

The lack of parking space in front of Kathy's building forced the driver to double park the Rolls. The doorman angled his way through the parked cars and opened the rear door.

"Good evening, Miss Longrin. I'm sorry about the car," and he pointed to the black Cadillac limousine parked directly in front of the building.

"The car, it's Mr. Taylor and his guests. They said they'd only be a minute."

"Nothing to concern yourself about, Arthur."

The doorman smiled and touched the visor of his cap.

He had to back his way between several parked vehicles, which was again causing him some personal embarrassment.

Once on the sidewalk, the doorman took up a position next to the entrance doors waiting for Kathy to head in his direction.

Kathy turned and faced Bertrand. Their ride here, after Duchant left, was in silence.

"I'm sorry for the attitude, Henri. It's just that I feel overwhelmed lately. It has nothing to do with you," but she knew it did. It had everything to do with him, Duchant and the paintings, and a host of other factors.

"I'd like to come up."

Realizing that he spoke the words too loudly, he lowered his voice. "Please."

She looked at him, her mind racing. Did she really want to be alone now, at this very moment when everything was so convoluted?

"Okay, I think we can both use a drink."

Bertrand went back to the Rolls and told the driver to call it a night. As the car moved forward, Henri walked back to Kathy and followed her through the door, which Arthur was now holding open.

She stopped to get her mail, then walked slowly with Bertrand to the elevator.

Once inside the apartment she placed the mail, briefcase and handbag on the coffee table and then kicked off her shoes.

"I'm going to change. Help yourself to whatever you want. There's some Absolut Vodka in the freezer compartment of the fridge. Lemons are in the door tray to the right as you look in. Make me one, too. Be back in a moment."

Kathy walked to her bedroom and closed the door. She took off her dress, pantyhose, and un-hooked her bra. She shook her head several times causing her blonde hair to dance in the air and fan out like a ballerina's skirt.

She walked to her bureau, took out a yellow t-shirt, and put it on. She opened another drawer and took out a pair of white walking shorts. Then she ran her fingers through her hair before she picked up her hairbrush. The final touch was a dab of perfume behind each ear and along the left side of her neck. She looked back at her image in the mirror and then opened her bedroom door and walked out.

Henri had picked up the mail and then placed it together with her purse and briefcase on a chair next to the small desk. He looked at the photograph of Ludolf Otto Steiger and felt a wave of revulsion take hold.

He walked back and seated himself on the couch. The two drinks rested on coasters and he began to reach for his as Kathy appeared.

She was stunning. Her body was trim, well-proportioned and athletic. Her legs, muscular at the calves and thighs as he followed them up until they disappeared beneath her shorts. She was breath-taking and Bertrand could feel himself getting aroused.

"I hope I didn't make them too strong."

He handed her one of the drinks and watched as she came around the coffee table and seated herself next to him.

"Let's drink to nothing, since nothing is a stateless venue."

"Is that legalese, or are you testing my intelligence quotient?"

"I don't know," then she brought the glass to her lips and took a sip.

The vodka burned, but the fire felt good. She brought the glass back up quickly and took another sip. She held the liquid in her mouth while she replaced the glass on the coaster, then she swallowed the liquid slowly, trying to prolong the fire as it went down her throat.

Bertrand watched her, marveling at how stunning she was. She was a classic beauty and with brains, someone he could envision spending the rest of his life with.

She had leaned her head back and closed her eyes.

He turned so that his left arm rested on the back of the sofa. He looked at her wondering if she felt him watching. Suddenly she opened her eyes and turned toward him.

"Thanks for being concerned. Just so you know, I'm perfectly fine. Nothing at all to worry about."

"If you say so, Kathy. I'm not pushy. I just want you to realize that I'm here for you, if you need my help. If ever you want me to back off, just say so."

She smiled at him. "You're a sweet man, Henri, maybe too nice. Sometimes nice people get hurt."

"I don't understand, get hurt in what way?"

"There are many types of hurt. There's the physical hurt, the mental hurt and the hurt from one's heart. There are many more types of hurt and all of them are painful. It simply boils down to the degree of that hurt. I know. I'm an attorney and I've seen most of it."

Kathy got up, walked to the CD player, and looked at a few titles. She removed one, placed it in the slot and stood there listening as the raspy voice of Chet Baker began to sing.

"Who's doing the singing, Kathy?"

"It's Chet Baker, a jazz trumpeter of the 1950's. He died overdosing on heroin. Too bad, he was a good one."

The song Baker was singing was "Time after Time" and Kathy looked at Henri. "Care for a dance, Mr. Bertrand?"

"I'd love to."

Bertrand moved toward the woman, tentative and anxious. He took her left hand in his and placed his right hand on her left hip, then they started moving slowly to the music.

Bertrand then shifted his right hand from Kathy's hip to her back and gently moved her closer. Soon their bodies were touching as they remained in place swaying to the music.

Kathy lifted her head from its resting position against his and looked at Bertrand.

After a long kiss where their tongues found each other, exploring, and searching for something as yet unrealized, Kathy took his hand and led him to her bedroom.

Chapter 44

A run through, over several hours, took place on Thursday night. Satisfied, Duchant left Bertrand, Shimon, and his crew in place to tie together any loose ends.

He went across the sorting floor, up the metal staircase and into his office. Brent and Dushku were at the monitors. "When does your shift start tomorrow?"

"We're on the twelve to six, Mr. Duchant." Brent nodded his head in agreement.

"Tomorrow, Friday, you'll get your chance to shoot the bullet. Yeah, I know it's not a bullet, it's a high-powered microwave beam, which will emit intense heat and cause the tap to melt. How about that for remembering one's lessons?"

"Very good, Mr. Duchant," and both the operators smiled.

"Shimon will give you the specifics at the end of your shift. Have fun!"

"You can count on us, Mr. Duchant."

Raphael patted both of them on the shoulder and left the room.

*

The Rolls was parked near the end of the block, away from the Con Edison gas crew working in the tunnel underneath the street. The large manhole cover was off to one side and an orange curtain was set up concealing three sides of the manhole. Safety cones were in place and a policeman directed traffic.

As they walked toward the gallery, Kathy pointed to the work crew. "Typical for a Friday afternoon in New York. That should foul up the traffic pattern when the rush home begins in a few hours."

"Let's hope we're out of here by that time," then Bertrand pressed the bell and reached for the door.

They rode up the elevator to the third floor, then walked to the Hecht Gallery door where Bertrand knocked, and the door clicked open.

Garland and Miller stood as they approached the table.

Garland put out his hand. "It's nice to see you all again and we hope this meeting will be successful for both of us. Can I offer you some refreshments?"

"If it wouldn't be too much trouble, I'd like some coffee."

"No trouble at all, Mr. La Monde and you Miss Longrin, Mr. Bertrand?"

They both shook their heads no.

Miller returned with Duchant's coffee. Once he was resettled in his seat, Garland asked if the list had been modified.

Bertrand responded that the six originally checked off were increased by five more and that there was one particular painting which was of immediate interest.

Rudel and Miller watched as Duchant reached into his jacket pocket and brought out his black ostrich wallet. He pulled out a check and placed it at the center of the table facing toward Garland.

"We are interested in acquiring Georges Seurat's The Can Can. This is our principal's offer," and Duchant pushed the check toward Rudel.

Rudel picked up the check and looked at it carefully. "This amount seems to be on the light side. And what about the other paintings, may I see your list?"

Duchant reached into his jacket again as a look of mild anxiety crossed his face.

"I believe I've left the list in the Rolls. Kathy, would you please go downstairs and see if it's there. I might have dropped it on the floorboard when I was getting out."

Kathy smiled weakly, rose, and started toward the door.

Once Kathy appeared outside the building's entrance, the driver signaled the monitor operators at 47th Street and the microwave beam was sent.

Duchant turned to Rudel. "That amount is hardly insignificant. Fifteen million can never be considered insignificant."

"The check, Mr. La Monde, reads five million."

"Please hand me the check," and Rudel held the check toward Duchant's outstretched hand.

*

Kathy had turned and began walking toward the corner where the Rolls Royce was parked. She noted the above ground workmen and one of the police officers engaged in conversation. The other cop was directing traffic around the manhole. They didn't seem to notice her as she passed hurriedly toward the car.

The Rolls driver, who was leaning against the front passenger side door, straightened up as she approached.

"I'm looking for some papers that Mr. Duchant may have dropped when he left the car."

The driver moved to the rear door and opened it. "Excuse me, Miss. It'll be easier if I look first."

The driver crawled onto the back seat and moved his hands into the seat crevices. He checked the floor and behind the tray tables, then called out, "I don't see any papers, Miss. You're welcome to look for yourself."

Kathy hiked up her skirt and made her way onto the floor of the Rolls. She duplicated much of what the driver had done and came up empty handed. She backed out and stood facing the driver.

"I'd better go back up and tell Mr. Duchant that the papers are not here."

"That's not necessary, Miss. I'll call him on his cell."

Before Kathy could say anything, the driver had his cell phone out.

Duchant's cell phone rang. "Sorry about that, gentlemen."

He looked at the cell phone screen and back at Garland. "I have to take this."

"Yes, this is La Monde?"

"Sir, I have Miss Longrin standing with me. I'm passing the phone to her."

Kathy took hold of the cell phone and asked, "Raphael?"

"Yes, Kathy, did you find the papers?"

"No, despite the best efforts of your driver and me."

"Will you please return to the office. It won't take very long and see if they're on the conference room table. Call me on my cell one way or the other. I know it's a pain, but right now we can't begin without them. The notations and the indicated dollar values are an integral part to these negotiations. My copy was the only one that had these."

She replied with an agitated, "Sure."

Kathy was perturbed and it was evident to the driver. "Please drive me to the office. I need to see if Mr. Duchant left his papers there."

The driver held the rear door open and Kathy got in. She thought to herself, lawyer and gofer, some combination.

*

Duchant looked at the check, then back at Rudel.

"You're correct, we have ten million dollars missing and my papers to boot."

The ring of the gallery's phone interrupted Duchant.

Miller got up. "Please excuse me." He called out, "Mr. Garland. The call is for you."

Rudel stood up and looked at Bertrand and Duchant. "I'll only be a moment."

Miller handed Rudel the phone then returned to the table. Rudel turned his back on the seated men and said quietly, "Yes."

At the sound of the voice on the other end of the line, Rudel braced slightly, then relaxed. He listened then replied in German. "Everything is okay at this end, I don't understand why you're not receiving…yes, understood…yes, as soon as we're finished, which should be very shortly now. Yes, Miller and I will wait for them."

Rudel hung up the phone and walked to the table.

"Mr. Garland, would you mind if I had another cup of coffee? I think I could use the caffeine rush."

Duchant looked at Bertrand, "How about you?"

"Sure, why not?"

Miller stood up and then walked behind the curtain. As soon as Miller disappeared, Bertrand reached into his jacket and pulled out an Israeli .375 Magnum Desert Eagle pistol and aimed it at Rudel. With his left hand he moved his index finger to his lips.

Duchant quickly moved to the curtain and stood to one side as Miller came out holding a tray.

Before Miller could react Duchant placed the Israeli Jericho 941, 9mm Parabellum into the

334

small of his back and at the same time said, "Don't drop the tray."

"Bend your knees and bend your body over. Slowly place the tray on the floor. Move an inch in any direction and I'll kill you."

Miller bent over and placed the tray on the floor.

"Now lie flat and place your hands behind your back. Do nothing else."

Miller did as he was told and Duchant bound his hands together with plastic loop handcuffs.

Miller moved his head to one side and looked at Duchant as he walked behind Rudel.

"Place your hands behind your back and keep still. You heard what I told Miller. The same applies to you."

After Rudel was bound, Duchant moved back to Miller, rotated him to a standing position and pushed him toward Rudel. Then both men were blindfolded.

As the elevator door opened, Rudel and Miller were pushed against the rear with their faces pressed against the wall.

"Do nothing, unless we tell you to."

At the main floor, Duchant hit the stop button, which kept the elevator door from closing.

He pulled on Rudel's arms and moved him out of the elevator.

Bertrand did the same with Miller and followed Duchant along the hallway.

After Rudel and Miller were braced against the foyer wall, Duchant went outside. A minute or so later he returned with one of the Con Edison workmen who carried a large, quilted work jacket and a yellow hard hat.

Duchant pulled Rudel off the wall, wrapped the jacket around his shoulders, placed the hard hat on his head, then moved him out to the street.

"Keep your head down and move straight ahead until I tell you to stop."

The chance of anyone, independent of the cop and work crew, noticing the bound and blindfolded Rudel was slight to none.

As they reached the manhole, Duchant said, "Stop."

"Okay, now take another small step."

Rudel followed the instructions and fell through the manhole opening, hitting his chin on the street surface, and knocking himself out as he went plummeting down.

The thud of Rudel's body hitting the bottom of the underground street cavern was louder than the noise from the silencer that placed two bullets into his head.

The same sequence was repeated for Miller. After he was shot, the shooter placed his weapon in his pocket, then started climbing up the metal ladder. In a matter of seconds his head and shoulders appeared at the manhole opening.

One of the workmen extended his arm, Shimon grabbed hold and was through the manhole and standing in the street as the manhole cover was being rolled back into place.

In less than four minutes the policeman, the three ConEd workers, their equipment and truck were gone. The street had once again assumed its former self and traffic along Madison Avenue flowed unencumbered.

Chapter 45

Duchant looked at the screen as he pressed the green button and saw that the 47th Street number indicated. He answered, "Yes, Kathy."

Her voice came on the line. "The papers aren't here either. I'll start back."

"No need for that, Kathy, we ended our meeting early. It didn't make sense to continue."

There was silence, then Duchant asked, "Kathy, are you there? Did you hear me?"

"Yes, Raphael, I did hear you."

"We'll be at the office in about ten minutes. Can you wait for us?"

Again, there was silence before her answer came. "Yes, I'll wait," then the connection was disconnected at her end.

He turned toward Bertrand sitting beside him in the taxi. "How do you feel?"

"I'm fine. In fact, quite relieved. It's been a good day's work."

Duchant couldn't help but smile, looked at the back of the Indian driver's head and then back to Bertrand.

"There's our girlfriend to consider. She is both a known and an unknown factor."

Bertrand looked at Raphael, then turned away without saying anything. The remainder of the taxi ride was in silence. Duchant didn't press. The rear seat of the taxi was not an opportune place to discuss anything.

Duchant paid the taxi fare and slid out the left side onto the pavement of 47th Street.

Bertrand followed and then started walking toward the entrance.

Duchant reached out and tapped his arm. "Can you wait a minute? It's better to talk here, than inside with Kathy around."

Bertrand nodded and moved against the building's wall. He waited for Duchant to speak.

"Henri, we're friends, associates and we share similarities in our backgrounds. We have a vested interest in seeing a particular mission...this mission, through to its successful conclusion."

"We knew where our feelers would lead once the other side took the bait. The specific fish were unknown, but we always knew they would bite. We have seen the end come to an old Nazi and two younger ones. We have the opportunity to catch another mass murderer of our people, an enemy of mankind, who looked at us then and still considers us to be sub-humans."

"When we accepted what was offered to us many years ago, we knew that our lives would become secondary to the cause. It was something that we agreed to. Perhaps you and I will not survive this, but if that's our fate, let it happen by circumstance, not by carelessness. Better, Henri, the error of co-mission, than the error of omission."

"The woman..." and before Duchant could continue, Henri blurted out, "I think I love her."

Duchant stared at his friend who dropped his head momentarily and then looked back.

Raphael waited to see if he would continue. When a silence enveloped them, Duchant spoke.

"The woman is the daughter of a Nazi SS-General and a man closely connected with Heinrich Himmler, architect of the final solution for our people. She is a pawn, nothing more and nothing less."

Bertrand struggled against the onslaught of reason. All of what his friend said was true. It was the way it should be, but despite these truths, his mind refused to acquiesce to its logic.

Bertrand decided, here on a busy street, to advance the matter to another level. He turned his head away momentarily to watch as two Hasidic Jews with their beaver hats, long black coats and beards entered the building. These seconds gave him the opportunity to contemplate a change of heart, a chance to remain silent.

Then he looked back at Duchant with an intensity that propelled the words out.

"I've been with her in the most intimate way. If I thought for a moment that she could be what her father is, I would eliminate her myself."

"From what you just told me, Henri, you are beyond the point of no return. Your ability to render an unbiased decision when it comes to this woman is compromised. I want you off the mission."

Bertrand stood there stunned, refusing to believe the words spoken by his friend and his immediate superior. His eyes glazed over and then took on a far away look as if something in the distant corners of his mind refused to process what he couldn't understand and what he refused to believe.

"Wait for me in Shimon's office. I'll meet with Longrin and then come over."

Duchant moved off to his right and entered the building. Bertrand remained fixed in place, as his eyes followed the back of the man who had just ended his career.

*

The same two cleaning service men made their way to the third floor and knocked on the gallery door. After tapping the door several more times without a response, one of the cleaners turned the doorknob and surprisingly found it unlocked.

A quick canvass of the gallery revealed that no one was anywhere within the premises. He used his cell phone to brief Illinois and was told to fix the monitoring taps and depart.

A few moments later the taller man called out, "Come over here and take a look at this."

"Yeah, it's the same with the wall unit. Someone used a high-speed microwave beam. It's the only thing that could have caused this type of meltdown damage. Let's clean up this mess, get the new monitors installed, and get out of here."

The other man nodded.

They unhooked the wires from the destroyed system and systematically cut back one-half inch on each wire to ensure the reconstituted connections wouldn't malfunction. They reset the taps into the wall and table phone, tested the current to each tap and then replaced both housing covers.

A second telephone call was placed to Illinois. After speaking several words slightly above a whisper and receiving the okay, the two cleaning men gathered their equipment and left, locking the door behind them, but leaving the alarm system unset.

Chapter 46

Kathy was seated at the conference table when Duchant entered. He patted both Brent and Dushku's shoulders as he passed by, raised the thumb on his right hand and waived it back and forth several times.

The two men turned and high fived each other.

Duchant took a seat across from Kathy, who looked bewildered by his antics.

Reading into her facial expression, he said, "Oh that, it was just something personal between the boys and me."

"You don't seem upset about the papers."

"Why should I be upset. If we can't find them, I'll rework them tonight and we'll meet with Garland tomorrow, or the next day. I'm sorry to have given you a gofer's job today, but there was no one else, Kathy. I trust you understand."

She looked at him and smiled weakly. Then she asked, "Where's Henri?"

"He's with Shimon. In fact I'm going there about now. Can I ask you to wait until we're finished? We shouldn't be long."

"Sure, Raphael, I'll wait. It'll provide me some extra thinking time."

Duchant moved the chair back from the table and stood up. Kathy's eyes didn't leave him as he walked out and passed the monitors. He went down the metal stairs, across the sorting room floor until he reached the security alcove. He nodded to the guard and walked in.

Betrand was seated in front of Shimon's desk and looked up as Duchant took a seat to his right. Both men stared at Duchant, but said nothing, waiting for him to start.

"Henri is no longer part of this mission." Raphael paused and watched for Shimon's reaction.

When there was none, he continued. "As mission leader, I have the final say," then he turned to Bertrand.

"I've notified Paris that you'll be reassigned there. Your ticket is being arranged and will be waiting for you at JFK. You have seventy-two hours to pack and leave."

"Now please hand your pistol to Shimon."

Bertrand moved slowly as he removed the .357 magnum from his holster and handed it to Shimon.

"Anything that you leave open ended, such as your apartment, we'll handle. Is that under-stood?"

"It is understood clearly. If there is nothing else, I'll need some personal things from the conference room and then I'll head for home. If necessary, you can reach me there."

Without another word Bertrand stood up and walked out. There were no handshakes, no smiles nor any additional words.

After Bertrand was past the door guard, Raphael leaned into Shimon. "He isn't the first to fall because of a woman and he won't be the last. What did he tell you?"

"He said only that he was no longer part of the New York contingent. Nothing more."

"There is considerably more. He's involved with the woman, Steiger's daughter. I consider the involvement detrimental to the mission. He can no longer be trusted on this assignment and maybe never again on any mission. He needs to be sequestered far away from this area of operations."

Duchant reached up and rubbed his eyes. "It's been a long day." Then he brought his hand down and looked back at Shimon. "You and your men did well. Congratulations."

Shimon smiled and nodded.

"I plan to telephone the gallery later requesting another meeting. Steiger and his crew will have their antennas quivering regarding the disappearance of Rudel and Miller and they'll suspect us, but they'll have nothing definitive. I doubt if their bodies will be discovered anytime soon, so we buy some time."

"They still want to get their hands on the two hundred million and they'll find some way to reconnect. Once they have the money, I'm expendable. Could be, I'm fair game already." Then Duchant let a grin take hold. "Nothing new about that – huh?"

"I'll keep you updated. I'm going back to the conference room if you need me."

Shimon waived his hand, then looked down at the papers on his desk.

*

"That's the way he wants it, Kathy. Please don't be upset. We'll still see each other."

A quizzical look came across Kathy's face. "How will we…" then she stopped, then started again. "I'll talk to him, Henri. I'll leave. Maybe that's what Raphael wants anyway."

"He doesn't want you to leave. If he did you'd be long gone. He needs you, trust me, I know. You are very important to him."

"And you, Henri, am I important to you?"

Bertrand reached for her hand and pulled her gently up. She moved into his arms, and they kissed.

One of the operators looked to his left then tapped his associate who motioned to Brent and Dushku. The four men smiled at one another as they stared, then Brent and Dushku picked up their bags, waved, and headed out as the next shift of monitors turned in the chairs, and faced the screens.

Chapter 47

Kathy remained in the conference room after Bertrand departed. She didn't want to stay, but she wasn't going to revert to juvenile antics and leave like a hurt schoolgirl.

From what Henri had related to her, their budding relationship was no longer private information. She wondered if it ever was. Office romances develop their own feeding frenzy.

Duchant walked toward her in his usual positive and commanding manner, then stopped and walked to where the silver coffee service was positioned. He poured himself a cup, turned toward the table and as an afterthought asked, "Do you care for coffee?"

Kathy shook her head no.

Once he was seated Kathy said, "I'm leaving."

"You are free to go at any time. I have no hold on you. But that decision should be reached based on merit and not emotions. Right now, your system is shocked...shocked that I have transferred an associate, a colleague and a friend because of a romance between two consenting adults."

"Nothing could be further from the truth. What I am trying to do requires complete focus. There are hundreds of millions of dollars involved. You are aware of how difficult and encumbered these negotiations are. There is no room for laxity or ineptitude. On several occasions, Henri has compromised us. I cannot afford another more costly instance."

"I see the questionable look on your face and I am unable, at this moment, to go into specifics. I'm sorry. I will clarify everything for you in due time."

"I believe you have witnessed my dedication to this quest. Henri's transfer is necessary, there is no personal sentiment involved. It is strictly a business decision, based on a rather wide horizon. However, now more than ever, I will need your assistance and I'm asking you to stay."

"You do not have to make this decision now. Sleep on it, but please let me know by tomorrow morning. Right now, I'm going to call Garland and set up another meeting. Please excuse me."

Duchant got up and went to the office part of the complex.

Kathy picked up her purse and briefcase and left.

When she reached the sorting room floor, Raphael watched on the monitor as Kathy crossed the floor and went to the elevator. He followed her movements as she walked across the retail floor and out to the sidewalk. After she got into the cab, he went back to his desk and picked up the phone.

The monitor in Illinois began recording as the answering machine in the gallery connected.

"Hello, Mr. Miller, this is Raphael La Monde. I apologize for yesterday. We have everything now in place. I would like to meet with you and Mr. Garland as soon as possible."

As he hung up the phone, Duchant pondered his next move. The woman was the pawn to be played willingly, or unwillingly and expendable… always expendable.

*

The man stood at attention waiting for Steiger to respond.

"Have Rudel or Miller been located?"

"No, sir."

"Tell Schwimler to report to me."

"Ja Herr Doctor."

*

Bertrand walked calmly toward the wet bar in his apartment. He opened the refrigerator cabinet, which was at eye level, above the granite countertop. He placed three large ice cubes into his short glass and then took out the vodka bottle. He poured the liquid until the glass was half-full, opened a drawer and took out a lemon. He peeled part of the skin and flipped it with his thumb into the drink.

With the drink in hand, he walked back to his living room and sat in one of the leather chairs. He propped his feet up on the matching ottoman, then leaned back, comfortable for the first time in many hours.

He thought about Kathy, the future, and wondered where this was all leading. The alcohol burned on the way down. He looked at the glass trying to decide if he really needed any more or was just drinking for the sake of doing something.

Finances weren't a problem. He could have retired years ago. He placed the drink down, took out his cell phone and dialed Kathy's number. There was no answer on the landline. He touched the memory button and then hit the speed dial button for Kathy's cell phone. On the fourth ring she picked up.

"Kathy…"

"I'm glad you called, Henri. I told Raphael that I'm leaving."

Her voice somehow lacked the conviction to back up what she had just stated. It was as if the finality of her statement was more a momentary thing, instead of an irrevocable decision.

"Are you sure this is what you want to do?"

There was a long pause, as if his question was challenging her to rethink the matter. When she did respond, she said, "He asked me to stay, but that may not be possible."

"Why Kathy?"

Again, there was a long pause. "I don't want to speak over the phone. Maybe I…we should just forget about everything."

"No, I don't want to go there. We're past that point. May I come over? We'll talk."

When there was no response, he said, "Please. It won't go beyond talk and when you've had enough, I'll leave. That's a promise, so help me."

He knew the silence that took hold again was a result of the debate raging within her. Finally, she began to speak again.

"Okay, Henri. I'm not sure where this will take us, but let's talk. The door will be open, just walk in."

Chapter 48

As he entered her apartment, he saw Kathy sitting on the sofa with a drink in her hand. To the right, on the coffee table in front of the leather chair was another drink.

"That's thoughtful," pointing to the drink. "I need it."

He sat down without approaching her. He sensed it wasn't the thing to do, at least not now. She looked edgy.

Letting his mind freewheel, he wasn't sure if this was the right move after all and briefly considered a quick exit after finishing the drink.

She looked at him, her eyes reflecting what she was thinking and then she asked, "What are you going to do now?"

"Go away with you," and he smiled. "Far away and enjoy life with you by my side."

"How romantic, Henri, and how so impractical. Two educated people wandering off to some tropical paradise to become beach bums and live off coconuts, grapefruit, and pine nuts. How quaint."

She wasn't smiling.

With a grin forming on his face, "You forgot the lobsters, crab, and shrimp."

"It wasn't meant to be a joke, Henri. I'm not in a joking mood. I've gotten myself into something that I think for the first time in my life might be over my head."

"Do you want to elaborate, Kathy, or am I supposed to guess?"

He saw the hurt look on her face.

"Oh Kathy, I'm sorry, really sorry, forget that last crack. I didn't mean to be rude. Please allow me in…" Then Henri paused. Seconds later he said, "Let me try to help? My interest in you is well beyond friendship."

As he stared at her, she seemed to be reflecting as if she was trying to decide whether she should let this man into the caverns of her private thoughts and feelings.

Sitting there and watching, Bertrand second guessed himself and thought that her far away look might have nothing to do with her mood, but instead his curt remark and her hurt feelings. He wanted to say more to bolster his position but forced himself to remain silent and just wait until she was ready.

He reached for his drink.

The movement caused Kathy to refocus. She stared at him in an unnatural way, as if she was trying to see something that would provide a direction for her.

When she saw nothing, she shook her head as if to clear it, or to convey a negative response. Since she didn't speak, Bertrand assumed the latter.

Then she said, "This is all a bit much."

Bertrand wanted to reply, to ask a question, but willed himself still. Cupping the drink in both hands, he sat there waiting. Finally, she started to speak again.

"My dilemma is rather complicated. Initially working for Duchant and Company was exciting. It opened a two-pronged world for me simultaneously, one in which two loves, art and law, could be merged. It additionally opened up a shadow world in which stolen art and ruthless men of various persuasions existed side by side."

"As the days became weeks, I was supposed to adjust to fast pace situations, while the situations were attacking the very foundation of my beliefs."

"Perhaps I am not strong enough. Perhaps my senses of right and wrong are misguided. Perhaps the tenants of my belief system are so shocked, that my ability to objectively understand people and circumstances can no longer work in tandem with each other."

She never took her eyes from him and what she said next shocked him.

"I don't think you can help me."

He thought about moving closer, to take a seat next to her on the couch, but he was afraid of

355

the consequences. She placed the drink in front of the chair because that's where she wanted him to sit. If he tried to change this, he felt she would rebel and everything would be lost.

"I can help you. The only thing I'm interested in, on this entire planet, is you. Give me something that will let me help you."

Again she surprised him with her question. "Do you know anything about the camps?"

"The German death camps? Yes, I know about them as you do… through school. I was born in Belgium, but after the war was over. My parents, who were Catholic, never spoke about those years."

"Did you ever hear of a man named Ludolf Otto Steiger?"

Bertrand considered saying yes, but replied no and asked, "Who is he?"

"Some German I saw in a documentary about the camps. Raphael told me about his family's art collection, I was just wondering whether someone like this man could be involved."

"If he was a high-ranking Nazi, he was most likely involved. The upper echelon of the Nazi hierarchy all shared in the spoils of war. Art and artifacts, silver and jewels were bounty that the Nazi regime considered theirs for the taking. Herman Goering, who commanded the Luftwaffe, the Nazi Air Force, was the architect behind the looting of the occupied countries."

Kathy seemed like she was poised to ask another question, but instead looked down at her drink as if considering whether she should take a sip. She brought the glass to her lips and sipped at the vodka, now diluted by the melting ice. It didn't provide the jolt she was anticipating, and she placed it back on the coaster.

"Raphael told me that he is trying to arrange another meeting with Garland. I couldn't find the papers he wanted so today's meeting ended early."

Then she said, "Damn. What's happening to me? You knew about the meeting. You were there. Why am I telling you this?"

Then in frustration she got up from the couch and walked around the coffee table toward her desk. Bertrand stood up and took several steps in her direction, then stopped.

Hearing the movement behind her, she turned and then walked to the standing man. When she was a step away she reached for his hand and squeezed it.

"I feel so alone, Henri. It's like, I'm adrift. I guess I should let someone into my boat...maybe help me row it," then she smiled at him and he pulled her close. Their lips met and their urgency seemed to electrify their very beings.

She lifted her head away, momentarily, to look at him. Then she felt herself drifting in and out of an euphoric state again as their lips met. Their tongues explored each other and when their frenzy was heightened beyond what she imagined possible, she stumbled toward her bedroom. As they moved, they awkwardly clung to each other afraid to break away and lose the moment.

Chapter 49

They lay intertwined in each other's arms, spent from their love making. Henri softly said her name. When she didn't respond, he shifted his position slightly and saw she was asleep.

He carefully disengaged himself from her arms and got out of bed. He reached for his jacket, which was sprawled on the floor and pulled out a pack of Baltros cigarettes and his gold lighter.

He walked to the living room and sat down on the sofa, with his head resting on several pillows. He lit the cigarette and blew the smoke into the darkness, rethinking what had taken place with a woman who gave as much as she took.

She was captivating and he was captivated by her. She was a woman who possessed the best of attributes, but unfortunately, she came with considerable baggage. It was this baggage that was causing him concern. He was a professional and his involvement with this woman wasn't some high school infatuation nor was the opposition amateurs. They were lucky so far. The opposition would eventually strike and then…well then, we'll see.

The business that consumed him up to this point was always deadly and their happenings were always in real time...quick with dire consequences. He wanted to believe that she was unwittingly involved in all of this, otherwise she was one hell of a good actress.

He wondered whether it was possible for a girl to grow up in such a cloistered environment, without knowing her father was a Nazi.

Steiger was educated, a Ph.D and came from a solid Catholic background. Why would he buy into this Nazi stuff, a regime so cruel that it engulfed the world in a war that resulted in over sixty million deaths?

He heard the movement off to his left side and then saw her. Soft rays of moonlight, which penetrated through the two small, curtained windows, silhouetted her. The moving shadows that enveloped parts of her body, only added to the erotic scene.

Henri sat up, as she moved toward him.

This time their love making was fast and their climax was reached quickly.

After minutes passed, they returned to the bedroom.

After they were spent, they drifted in and out of sleep, as they lay intertwined.

Henri was awakened by the rays of dawn creeping through the curtains. His first thoughts were of the love making. He had never experienced such a night. He was in love with this woman and from the way she responded, she was in love with him.

Then his thoughts changed. What if she was using him? Women needed sex as much as men.

With them, the timing had to be right. Maybe with all her problems, she used last night as a release, something to change the status quo and give her an interlude…a time frame to put things back into perspective.

As he moved away from her, she turned, pulled on the pillow, and curled up. He looked down at her naked body and marveled at what they shared during the night.

He went to the bathroom and showered. Then he went to the bedroom and saw the bed was empty.

Dressing quickly, he returned to the living room. She wasn't there either so he called out and she answered, "In here…I'm in the kitchen."

He was surprised to see she was still naked. There was something very erotic in the way she carried this off. As she moved, she seemed completely at ease with her nakedness, something he couldn't have imagined a scant twenty-four hours ago.

"Coffee will be ready in a moment. Want some eggs, or a whole wheat muffin?"

"Coffee will be fine."

She brought two cups to the table and sat down. Her breasts were firm, and her nipples were reddish brown.

He picked up the coffee cup and took a sip. "It's good coffee. Do you want to get showered? I don't mind being alone if you won't be too long."

"I'd just like to sit here and look at you. Do you mind that I'm naked?"

"No, I don't mind, but it might lead us back to the bedroom."

"What's wrong with that?"

"Nothing. In fact, it's an interesting possibility, but I'm not sure I have the strength."

She laughed. "I thought you men were inexhaustible."

"Whoever told you that probably died at an early age."

Then they both laughed. He reached across the table and took hold of her hand.

"I think I love you, Kathy. I've never said that to any other living person. You now have a partner," and his words trailed off for a moment, then he added "if you want one."

She didn't respond right away. She sat there sipping coffee. Then she looked back at him,

"You may not understand what you're getting into. Things seem one way now, but they may turn out quite differently later. I'm not sure myself."

She looked pleadingly at Henri.

"I just can't make a commitment now, Henri. I'm sorry if that hurts you. It certainly isn't my intention. I would never have done what we did last night unless my feelings for you were more than just casual. I just simply can't give myself freely to loving anyone until I know…know about a lot of things that are confusing me and scaring me. Can you understand?"

He nodded his head yes. "I want you to love me, as I love you…unconditionally, but I can't make you. Let's see what the future holds for both of us. Do you want to tell me about what's troubling you?"

"Let me take a shower and get dressed. It'll give me some time to think. There's more coffee, help yourself," and then she turned toward the bathroom and his eyes watched as the curves of her body moved in a way that happens only when a woman walks.

*

She sat down at the kitchen table, dressed in shorts and a white undershirt. Her nipples pressed against the cotton material, pushing it out in a sensuous way.

"Where to begin. Yeah I know…at the beginning, right? But there is no real beginning."

"Then start anywhere."

363

"Okay, anywhere it is. Duchant told me a story about his family and stolen art, Nazis, and diamonds. Is the story true?"

"I've known Raphael for many years. We have been colleagues for all of that time. If he told you something, it is the truth. The collection amassed by his grandfather and his father was entrusted to certain parties for safekeeping as the Nazis approached France in the early days of World War II."

"However, these interests cooperated with and allowed his family's collection to be confiscated by the Nazis. I am not privy to the exact details. Raphael may have gone into these with you when you were interviewed. Since he was a young man, his obsession has been to recover all, or the majority, of this collection, regardless of the cost."

"The hierarchy of the Nazi party, Himmler, Goering, Goebbles, and Generals like Steiger, would have taken whatever it was that they wanted. They, or others whom they trusted, would have found ways to hide the stolen art."

Bertrand purposely included the name of Steiger to see how she would react.

He saw her draw in air through her mouth and then let it out slowly. She would try to normalize herself before she would speak again. That's fine, he thought...I'll wait and let her go to whatever place she felt comfortable.

"You said Steiger. Is he the same as the other three you mentioned?"

"If you mean, is he a murderer? The answer is yes. If there were degrees of bad, he'd be as bad as it gets. He's off the screen. He was instrumental in the doctrine called the final solution. It was an agreement sanctioned by Adolph Hitler for the eradication of European Jewry."

He let it sink in. He didn't want to hurt her but he had no choice if he was going to bring her to the point where she had to be.

She seemed astonished. The look in her eyes was one of terror. Bertrand knew that her mind was processing the incomprehensible information and he knew that the horror his answer projected would be difficult for her to comprehend or accept.

Bertrand stood up and went around the table. As her head touched his chest he could hear the sobs.

Then he said softly, "I don't understand, Kathy, why are you so upset. These Germans, these Nazis have nothing to do with us. Most are long dead, although their horrific deeds live in infamy. Hitler, Goering, Gobbles and the Steigers of that world, are no longer a danger. They are probably burning in hell."

"Now come on…stop crying. If that documentary upset you, try to put it out of your mind. That was a long time ago. That was then and we are now."

Then he became silent knowing that her mind was focused on her father and the information he had related. Her analytical and legal mind was comparing the similarities between the photograph she saw in that documentary and the man she knew as a child, a teenager, and an adult. Her thought processes would vacillate between the image of her father as a young man, captured forever in the picture framed on her desk, and the man called Steiger.

Her mind would visualize the aging man, someone she knew and loved, and she would conclude that the man, so horribly described, couldn't be her father. Then she would feel a moment of tranquility before her mind reverted again to the possibility that her father and Steiger could very well be the same.

Kathy looked like she was about to speak but stopped. Bertrand waited, then encouraged her.

"Go ahead, Kathy, you can trust me."

"I don't think I can share this with you, Henri. I want to, but I can't, I simply can't. I think I have to go home, back to Illinois for a while."

Bertrand waited, but she didn't say anything more.

"Then let me go with you. I'm out of a job and have a lot of free time. You'll need a companion, an ear, and shoulder. Let me be all three."

"I have never brought anyone home. I couldn't, unless it was the man I intended to marry," then she stopped as if she said something that she didn't want to think about.

She looked at Bertrand with a sort of sadness that made him want to reach out and touch her.

"What I need to do, I must do alone. I need an answer to a question. Only my father can give me that answer."

Chapter 50

The snatch and grab was executed quickly.

As Raphael walked from 47th Street toward the parking garage located on West 45th Street, his attention was drawn to the bicycle messenger who was accelerating past him at a high rate of speed. He watched as the messenger lost control and fell across the handlebars and onto the sidewalk.

Duchant ran to the sprawled messenger and started to bend down when he felt the needle penetrate his neck from his rear. He reached up with his hand, but he couldn't quite manage to make the contact, as he started falling forward.

He felt hands roughly grab him and shove him in some type of vehicle. The last thing he remembered was his shoulder hitting a door frame and then he lost consciousness.

Duchant wasn't sure how long he was in the semi-conscious state, as he drifted in and out of sleep. He saw, or thought he saw, the shadowy figures come and go. As the effect dissipated minutely, he realized that his condition was drug induced. This was further confirmed by the soreness in his neck and his shoulder where the needle had penetrated far too many times.

He didn't know how long he'd been in this room, a room where the smell of leather was strong. He tried to concentrate on his surroundings, but nothing came into focus. He was lying on his side with his head against the concrete floor, wondering how long until the next injection.

His head hurt badly, but his mind began to clear. He chastised himself for the laxity in walking unguarded to the parking garage, instead of calling for the driver to pick him up in front of the building.

With the disappearance of Rudel and Miller, something like this should have been anticipated and precautions taken. Thinking about the Bertrand and Longrin matter might have been the cause for his laxity, but it was his stupidity that was the root cause for his present predicament.

He heard footsteps approaching, but his position precluded seeing how many or who they were. He felt a presence next to him, a foot touching his back near where the spine and buttock met. He anticipated a blow, but it never came.

He heard what sounded like a piece of furniture being dragged across the floor. Then hands picked him up and shoved him into the wooden chair like a rag doll.

The force and angle caused him to contact only the edge of the chair and he fell hard to the concrete floor. The laughter resonated off the walls, then several pairs of hands dragged him along the floor and again placed him in the now upright chair.

He watched the backs of the two men as they moved into the shadows. Then several blinding halogen lights were turned on, preventing him from seeing anything definitive.

Then a voice spoke.

"Does everything meet with your approval so far, Mr. Duchant? We hope your accommodations are satisfactory," and then there was laughter from the shadows.

Duchant thought of the words but couldn't speak them. Not enough of the drug had worn off yet.

"Does the cat have your tongue, Mr. La Monde?"

The sound of the name he used during the gallery meeting registered clearly. He forced the words out from heavy lips and a numb tongue. "Vut dis awl abot?"

"Is that a new language you're speaking, Mr. La Monde? By the way, do you prefer La Monde, or Duchant?"

More laughter erupted from the darkness. "Perhaps you should consider a second career as a comedian or ventriloquist."

Then Duchant heard nothing for several minutes.

"Now that we've had our fun, shall we get down to business? We are interested in learning the whereabouts of Mr. Garland and Mr. Miller. We believe with a fair degree of certainty that you know where they are or what has happened to them. Your life means nothing to us, Mr. Duchant. All the money you have cannot free you from the predicament in which you now find yourself. You will not be rescued, nor will you ever see the light of day unless you cooperate fully with us. Do you understand?"

Duchant caught most of the words spoken and processed them through a clouded mind. He knew what the man stated was classic interrogation verbiage. You scare the subject with the hopeless-ness of the situation, then at the end offer a caveat of hope through cooperation.

"Vot dis it you wan to kno."

"Before we go there Mr. Duchant I want to warn you that if you do not give us complete and accurate answers, we will inject you with Sodium Pentothal. Believe me, Mr. Duchant, after we shoot you up with truth serum you will become very communicative, sharing all your thoughts freely without hesitation. One way or the other, we will have your cooperation. Are you ready, Mr. La Monde?"

"Where are Garland and Miller?"

"Don kno. Left zem after duh meetin."

"What time was that?"

"Don rember."

Duchant felt a fist slam into the side of his head. He didn't see or hear the man who threw it. The force toppled him to his left and again his head hit the floor. He was hauled up and shoved onto the chair.

"Does that help to jog your memory a bit, Mr. La Monde?"

"Waz about four clock."

"That's better. Where were Garland and Miller?"

"Gal ree…waz there when we left."

"Where did you go when you left the gallery?"

"Off is…went back to off is."

"Where was Bertrand?"

"Wif me in da car, den de off is."

"And the woman?"

"Left fore us lookin for som papers back at off is."

"Who are you, Mr. Duchant?"

"Diamond d'ler und co ector of art."

Duchant's head throbbed with each reply. He knew he was still slurring some words, but his speech was improving. He decided to answer all questions, hedging where he could in an attempt to buy time until the mind fog cleared.

"We think you are much more than that, Mr. La Monde."

"I'm not more. Want to buy art, which was part of my family's collection, and stolen during the war. Not interested in who now has them, or how they came into their possession."

He was surprised at how his words were becoming more pronounceable and his lips and tongue seemed to take on a more normal feel.

"Do you think your life is worth one hundred million dollars?"

"No."

"What price would you put on it?"

"My life is worth nothing. No ransom will ever be paid. My company has specific instructions to that effect. Duchant et Compagnie de Fils will continue long after I'm gone. The only change will be that no one in the company will buy the art I'm interested in...never...and never is a long time."

"What if we told you that we can take you to where the art is located."

"That wouldn't be any significant revelation. It was evident from the beginning, with von Hoenshield, that the gallery represented the owners, Mr...err, I never did get your names."

A slap ricocheted across Duchant's face.

"We are going to take you on a little trip. I would like to extract the information from you here, but my time is limited, and my orders are implicitly clear. I regret that I am unable to show you more of our hospitality."

Another blow caught Duchant again on the left side of his face and part of his ear. He was knocked over and lay immobile on the concrete floor, hoping that there was time to clear the ringing in his head before the next blow landed.

An arm suddenly pushed Duchant over onto his stomach and then he felt a knee at the small of his back. The needle entered his neck, and he felt the sting of the liquid being pushed into him from the syringe.

Chapter 51

Bertrand returned to his apartment, showered, and changed. He intended to wait for Kathy outside the 47th Street building after she informed Duchant she was leaving. He wanted it that way and she finally acquiesced.

Kathy telephoned the office as soon as Bertrand left. The answering machine picked up.

"This is Kathy Longrin and this message is for Mr. Duchant. I will be at the office by eleven a.m. If possible, I would like to meet with you then."

She hung up and started getting ready for what she anticipated was going to be a long day. She hadn't had much sleep, but surprisingly this wasn't bothering her. She thought about the love making and the man who was her partner in it and she felt elated.

She applied her make up carefully, just a touch of lipstick and eyebrow pencil. Kathy always kept it to a minimum, believing that cosmetics were mostly hype and the chemicals clogged the pores.

Her hair was still mostly blonde with some minor highlights of brown. During all the seasons, she considered herself always the California girl, as men termed it, the perennial blonde woman that turned heads and she relished the thought.

Pronouncing herself ready in appearance and mentally prepared for Duchant, Kathy stepped through her door and went to the elevator.

A short taxi ride later, she was standing in front of 977 West 47th Street, but there was no sign of Bertrand. It didn't really matter since he was now persona non grata at Duchant and Company.

She took a deep breath and turned toward the entrance. She walked the retail floor slowly, looking at the jewelry in the display cases, but not pausing long enough for one of the overly energetic salesmen to corner her in conversation. They were a persuasive lot.

She waited patiently until she was buzzed in. Kathy approached the secretary and asked, "Has Mr. Duchant arrived yet?"

"Not yet, Miss Longrin."

Kathy nodded to her. "When Mr. Duchant arrives, would you tell him I'm in the conference room?"

Then Kathy took several steps toward the door behind the secretary and waited as the door's locking mechanism was disengaged. She nodded to the two-armed guards and walked into the sorting floor and headed for the office complex.

Halfway across the floor Shimon intercepted her. "Please come with me, Miss Longrin."

Before she could respond, Shimon had taken hold of her elbow and was moving her in the direction of his office. Once past the guard, Shimon let go of her elbow and moved toward a chair, which he pushed to the right of his desk.

"Please sit down, Miss Longrin."

It was a command, more than a request. Kathy had always been wary of this man. There was something sinister about him, but she couldn't quite put her finger on what it was.

She felt this sinister presence in others she defended, but then she knew the charges. With this man there was a void, but her intuition was never wrong.

She wasted no time, nor did she play Miss Nice. "What's this all about and by the way never touch me again like that. Never, and I mean never, place your hands on me."

Shimon stared at the woman seated to his left. He ignored what she said and asked, "Were you with Mr. Duchant last evening?"

"That's none of your business."

"Oh, but it is. Everything here...everything is my business."

The way the man spoke put Kathy on edge and unnerved her. She willed herself to maintain her bravado and not succumb to this man's arrogance.

"Well, Miss Longrin, I'm waiting."

"My personal life is none of your concern. If you're so interested why not ask Raphael?"

"He isn't here."

"Then wait until he arrives."

The man turned and moved his left leg out toward Kathy's chair. He bent his upper body and leaned forward like a snake preparing to strike.

"He won't be coming to the office...not today, not tomorrow and not the day after tomorrow. Now for the final time, Miss Longrin, I'm going to ask you, were you with Raphael Duchant at any time last night?"

She hesitantly said no. She wanted to ask what this was all about and why it concerned her, but she let her curiosity simmer.

"I didn't see you arrive at your usual time."

"I left a message on the answering machine that I would arrive about eleven a.m. Besides I'm not under any time regimen and I certainly don't account to you for when I arrive or when I depart."

"Miss Longrin, everything you do, and I mean everything, from the moment you accepted a position here, is accountable to me. You seem to have some difficulty in understanding that."

Kathy just sat there looking back at the security chief, thinking he was right but unwilling to bend to his will.

"I take your silence to mean that you understand me." Then he held up his hand in a gesture that signified don't speak.

"Last evening Mr. Duchant made a careless decision that has developed into a very precarious situation. If I was aware of his decision, I would have overrode it. What that decision was, is immaterial for purposes of this discussion. His apartment was checked as well as that of Mr. Bertrand."

"Neither residence was occupied throughout the night. Mr. Bertrand however was seen leaving your building several minutes after seven a.m. this morning and went directly to his home. You left the building at ten forty-four a.m. this morning and came directly here."

"Since you knew all that, why the questions?"

"To determine where you stand, Miss Longrin and what you would lie about. It's that simple."

He stopped talking but his eyes remained locked on hers.

"Now you know where I stand."

"I only know one thing, Miss Longrin, and that is Raphael is missing and you're a link to his disappearance."

"That's absurd. How can I be a link to his disappearance? I don't travel in his circles. He is not responsible to me. Duchant, just like I am, is a free spirit. He goes and does what he wants, when he wants and that, Mr. Security, is the long and short of it. Don't accuse me of anything you can't substantiate. I'll have your pompous ass in front of a harassment suit as fast as I can file the papers."

Shimon smiled and Kathy felt pure fear. She was pushing this man and she couldn't be sure of the consequences, but if they came her way, she knew they would be severe. She decided to soften her tone.

"Look, I don't know where Raphael is. I'm going to say it again. I don't know where he is. I left him here yesterday and you confirmed that he wasn't with me. What possible help can I give you when I haven't the slightest idea what this is all about."

Shimon spoke deliberately and enunciated each word for impact and effect. "We believe Mr. Duchant has been kidnapped. The people responsible are directly connected to the gallery, von Hoenshield, Mr. Ernst Rudel and…YOU, Miss Longrin."

Kathy felt her heart rhythm beat erratically. She heard the name Rudel not Garland clearly and she immediately knew that the man in front of her was about to expose her to something that would forever change her life. She sat there, as if rigor mortis had set in, waiting for it all to begin.

Chapter 52

The ambulance pulled up to the private hanger. The Cessna Citation was being readied as several white-coated attendants carried Duchant aboard. When he was securely strapped in a rear seat with a covering placed over his head, the attendants left the aircraft.

Schwimler spoke briefly with the two pilots, then signaled the men accompanying him and they boarded the aircraft. One of the men at Schwimler's direction checked to see if Duchant was strapped securely and still unconscious. When he nodded affirmatively, they took their seats and buckled up.

In moments, the plane was airborne.

Schwimler turned to face the man sitting across the aisle. "How much of a dose did you give him?"

"Just about three cc's. It should keep him under for the next two or three hours."

Schwimler unbuckled his seat belt, despite the sign to remain seated, and placed his hand on the man's shoulder. "I'm going to get an ale, do you want one?"

"Yes."

As he made his way to the galley, Schwimler paused to look back at the slumping Duchant and smiled.

He opened the refrigerator and took out two 750ml bottles of Sara Buckwheat (German) ale. The ale was made from black grain called Sarrasin in French and Grikki in Russian. After developing a taste for the drink, it soon became his favorite.

Holding a bottle in each hand, he headed back to his seat. He nodded to the other two seated men. "There's more, help yourself."

Schwimler passed one bottle to the other man.

"Danke," and the man lifted his bottle toward Schwimler, then took a long pull on the neck.

The man let the bottle come away from his mouth, "Sehr gut," (Very good) as he brought the bottle down to the opened seat tray.

Schwimler shook his head at the man and smiled but his thoughts were drifting back to what he had gone through five years ago. His training had been hard and long. When he finally was accepted into their ranks, his mind set was one of absolute obedience, loyalty and hatred for all things non-Aryan. His performance to date was exemplary.

Then he thought of Duchant. He wondered how these Jews were able to be so successful. How did they manage to survive? They were universally hated, yet they survived and excelled. Why?

They were everywhere, in every country, like vermin. He was taught that the International Jew was responsible for the world's ills. That

Adolph Hitler tried to correct this, but the Socialist Russian Jew Communists, together with their American and English Zionist brothers, were able to bring about the defeat of the Third Reich.

He was told that the Fourth Reich would be different. The unfulfilled goals of Adolph Hitler would at last be achieved and the world would be better for it. A world free of Jews and other sub humans like the Negroid, and olive skin mutants.

"I'm getting another ale," and he pointed toward the man.

The man held up his hand and made a motion that his bottle was still half full.

*

Bertrand arrived at the building moments after Kathy had entered. After restlessly waiting for what he thought was an inordinate amount of time, he decided to go in.

As he took the elevator up, he thought about what his appearance would provoke. On one hand he was still an employee. On the other he was off the mission and a transferred entity.

He pressed in the code and the door buzzer sounded. He nodded to the secretary and the guards and waited by the inner door until the woman pressed the release button. He wasn't sure she would, as word of his transfer was advised to all who needed to know.

As he was about to enter, the woman turned around. "Mr. Bertrand, one of the guards will accompany you. Where is it, you're going?"

"To security."

"Okay," and then she looked at the guard.

Both men walked into the sorting room and angled right toward Shimon's office. At the entrance, the guard accompanying Bertrand spoke a few words to the other guard and then after a nod, proceeded into the security complex.

When Shimon saw the two men he came around, waved the guard away with a soft thank you and then moved a chair next to Kathy.

"And before you ask, no I'm not surprised to see you Henri especially since Miss Longrin is here. The camera saw you near the building's entrance and we knew that it would only be a matter of time before you paid us a visit. That explanation was in anticipation of any question you intended to ask along those lines."

"Now that that's out of the way, shall we proceed with the business at hand. For your edification, Mr. Bertrand," the tone was deadly serious, "we believe that Mr. Duchant has been kidnapped."

Shimon watched both of them. The woman tensed as she had previously. The man sat still, the consummate professional, waiting until something tangible was provided to give him a direction, a thought process.

The security chief turned in his chair and stared off in space. His voice was modulated at a lower octave designed to force the listeners to carefully follow what he was saying.

"We know when and where the abduction took place. We have interviewed several witnesses, one a store owner, another an employee. Their account was sketchy, and the only substantial pieces of information concerned a bicycle messenger and several men in a nondescript Ford paneled van. It was a classic snatch and grab using the messenger as the decoy."

"Mr. Duchant may be in New York, or he may not. He may be alive, or he may be dead, but I don't think that the latter applies. Raphael is too valuable an asset to kill outright, although that may happen in time. With the disappearance of Rudel and Miller, the opposition will rightly assume that Duchant knows the circumstances."

Shimon turned and faced Longrin and Bertrand.

Kathy looked astonished and started to speak when Shimon shook his head no.

"Rudel, and we know the gentleman's name is Rudel not Garland, and his colleague have disappeared. Please don't look so surprised, Miss Longrin. This is a business that makes its participants obsolete very quickly."

"More than likely we are their prime suspects. And why are we the prime suspects?

Could it be because this company is a Jewish company and many of its employees are Jewish?"

Kathy wanted to speak, but again Shimon shook his head.

"All in good time, Miss Longrin," then he feigned a grin.

"The fact that the company is predominantly Jewish...well, there's nothing astounding about that. It's a known fact. What is generally not known is that the people in this Jewish company are negotiating with Nazis and surviving members of the old Third Reich. The younger ones, like Rudel, are participants in what these twisted individuals call the Fourth Reich."

"Jews and Nazis don't mix, just like oil and water are unable to coagulate. While we of course had nothing to do with any of their disappearances, we naturally would be blamed. Jews have characteristically been blamed for everything, ad nauseam."

"How do we know the owners of the art are Nazis? That's one of your pressing questions, isn't it Miss Longrin?"

"Yes, it is but I'm content to wait until you're finished."

"Good. Now, how do we know the von Hoenshields and Rudels of this world are Nazis? We, meaning numerous Jewish organizations and individuals, have compiled extensive files on the Third Reich. The Germans kept copious records and these records were meticulous. At the end of the war many of these records were recovered, copied, and the information added to, over the succeeding years."

"We have access to the detailed dossiers of high-ranking Nazi party officials, youth leaders, General Officers, Shultz Staffel, and Waffen SS unit members. We know with absolute certainty, Karta, that your father, Friedrich Buhler, and SS-Major General Ludolf Otto Steiger are one and the same."

Kathy paled at the sound of her given name, and the reference to her father as Steiger. The realization that her father and the man whose photograph appeared in the documentary could be the same, was mind boggling.

Her head was consumed with dizziness and she felt her body begin to drift to her left. Bertrand reached out and brought her upright then held her in his arms.

Once she regained some of her composure, she whispered, "I'm...I'm sorry."

Shimon pulled open one of his desk drawers and handed a small bottle of water to Bertrand. Henri twisted the cap and placed the open bottle between Kathy's hands.

She looked down at the bottle then back again to Bertrand, who smiled and moved his hand in a drinking motion.

"Go ahead, Kathy, take a long drink."

She brought the bottle to her mouth and took a swallow, then another. Some of the water dripped down her chin and Bertrand reached for his pocket-handkerchief and handed it to her.

Shimon leaned forward, elbows on his desk, "Take your time, Kathy. I know I've shocked you. Contrary to what you're thinking, I…we, are your friends. The truth is sometimes more unfathomable than fiction."

"I'm sorry. I can't believe what you've told me. There must be some mistake, some unfortunate coincidences but not the truth."

She looked pleadingly at Shimon and then to Bertrand, to bolster her wish, her desire, and her hope, that what had just been related to her was a mistake.

"If you need confirmation, Miss Longrin, please ask Mr. Bertrand."

Kathy looked at Bertrand, her mouth open and her chest heaving with each breath she took. Her eyes pleading that this man and lover would dispel what was now swelling up within her.

Bertrand hesitated, then Shimon callously said, "Go ahead, Mr. Bertrand, please go ahead."

Bertrand stared at Shimon for many seconds before looking back at Kathy.

"It's true, Kathy. What Shimon says is true. I wish it wasn't, but I could never lie to you."

She looked at him, her body shaking and then a torrent of tears flooded her eyes and cascaded down her cheeks.

Chapter 53

The plane was cleared for landing and making its final approach when Duchant started to stir from his drug induced sleep.

The man sitting across from Duchant and the man seated directly behind him didn't move as they watched Schwimler unbuckle his seat belt and side-step his way toward where Duchant was seated.

"I know you can hear me, Mr. La Monde. As your mind clears, remain still. Struggling will do you no good and any infraction will be responded to harshly. Follow the orders you are given and nothing more."

Duchant could see nothing with the covering over his head, but he did register to the restrain of the seat belt.

He shifted his body slightly and determined his confinement was limited to one seat belt and an indeterminable number of men which could easily overpower him. This translated into a situation no better than the one he left in New York. He could only wait for his mind to clear and hope for an opportunity to escape.

Duchant felt the wheels make contact with the tarmac. The plane glided along the runway at a decreasing speed until it was taxiing to the dis-charge point which he assumed would be either a private hangar, or some deserted part of an airfield.

He could feel the plane's engine decreasing vibrations and then all sound and movement ceased.

A few moments later there was the movement of feet and then he felt hands on his shoulders. The seat belt was unbuckled, and he was unceremoniously pulled to a standing position.

Then he was pushed to his left where his knee hit an adjacent seat arm, causing him to stumble into the seat itself. He was grabbed by the collar, pulled upright, turned roughly to his left again, and shoved forward.

"Okay, Mr. Duchant, we're going to take a step down. If you miss the step, you'll fall head first to the concrete. Use your hands to feel your way through the door and then the railing is on your right side. There are three steps."

Duchant gingerly started to move out the door, holding the inside portion with his left hand, while his right reached for the railing. He negotiated the first step as his hand held firmly to the railing.

He misjudged the second step, twisting his foot to the right. His body started to angle pre-cariously as he tried to maintain his grip on the railing. He bent his knees and was able to stop his forward movement.

Duchant eventually righted himself, standing sideways, one foot on one step and the other on another.

"Well done. We were hoping for a swan dive into the tarmac. One more step to go."

Duchant gingerly felt the space to his front with his toe of his shoe until he came in contact with the third and final step. He again moved slowly trying to determine the distance between the third step and the tarmac. He wasn't given that luxury as a hand on the small of his back pushed him forward.

As he stumbled, his arms extended quickly to his front as he tried to maintain some semblance of balance. Gyrating like a blind man without the awareness of what surrounded him, he fought to gain some control over his equilibrium.

When he finally managed to stop the forward momentum, he remained in place, saying nothing, and waiting for the next physical contact to occur.

An arm took hold of his and propelled him to his left.

"Stop."

He did as he was told.

"Bend down and turn to your right. That's far enough."

Duchant then heard a car door opening. "Keep your head down and move to your rear. When your leg touches metal, slide in."

The car doors closed and in moments, Duchant felt the motor shift through the gears until they reached cruising speed. He surmised they were on a highway because of the high rate of speed and the smoothness of the road.

Duchant silently began counting the minutes to himself as a way of gauging the time distance line from the landing place to the final destination. It was information that could prove valuable. This game would also work to reactivate his mind from the drug stupor he'd been in, en route here wherever here was.

After what Duchant figured was about forty to forty-five minutes, give or take five, he felt the car come to a stop on a gravel road.

He wasn't overly concerned. They wouldn't kill him just yet. The heightened possibility of his demise would probably occur after they extracted all the information they considered relevant. No one can hold out indefinitely...it was only a matter of time when even the strongest man broke.

Duchant knew he would break, too.

Chapter 54

"What am I supposed to do?"

It was a question she asked more to herself than to them. Neither of the men moved, each transfixed on the woman whose mindset was now askew.

"Is it your intention to keep me here? Keep me here under some pretense of protective custody, or perhaps as a hostage until Raphael is found. Maybe you intend to use me as a pawn in this monstrous situation, which has shaken my world to its very core…to its very foundation."

Then the glazed-over look in her eyes disappeared. She looked at the security chief, then back at Bertrand. "Do you both actually expect me to go against my father?"

Then she became still, unmoving.

Bertrand looked at Shimon, who caught the slight movement of his head.

"Miss Longrin, I have reasons to believe that your father is somehow connected with the disappearance of Mr. Duchant. Further, I believe that your father and his fellow Nazis would use all the resources at their disposal to insure that Duchant, and others who are connected with Duchant et Compagnie, meet with a swift demise."

Shimon noted how the woman's body visibly shuddered at the mention of the word Nazi.

"We are now well beyond buying paintings. We have arrived at a point where we are a presumed threat to expose the secrets that your father and his associates have managed to successfully hide since the end of the war."

"To your father and his comrades, we represent all that is considered decadent. We are the people he tried to wipe off the face of the earth. A people who have managed to survive despite the mass killing machine engineered by him and his Third Reich maniacs. That may not be very important in your world, Miss Longrin, but in ours, that survival is no less than miraculous."

"As long as Jews like Duchant et Compagnie exist and possess substantial wealth, men like Steiger, von Hoenshield, Rudel, and Miller, will look the other way for a while to get their hands on it. Then, they'll do whatever is necessary to eliminate us…the threat."

"We are certain that von Hoenshield was killed because he accepted money from Duchant." Kathy moved her body again, as if trying to physically block the words that were hurled at her like daggers.

"Von Hoenshield was getting too cozy with the Jews. It is interesting to note, Miss Longrin, that von Hoenshield's real name was Friedrich Alpers. He was an SS-Captain and he served with distinction at Dachau. Obersturmfuhrer Alpers had a significant amount of blood, Jewish blood, on his hands. That goes for your father, SS-Major General Ludolf Otto Steiger, as well."

Shimon knew the names and title descriptions shocked her to her core. They were meant to. He moved back in his seat, still looking at her, anticipating nothing and expecting everything from the woman.

Bertrand leaned in Kathy's direction and whispered, "What Shimon says is true, all too true. There is no reason to lie."

"Rudel and Miller were also Nazis. They are members of the so-called Fourth Reich, a group of young Germans who have been raised and educated in the doctrine of Adolph Hitler. These new recruits to National Socialism, with the guidance of older Nazis such as your father, intend to carry out what Hitler and his Third Reich were unable to accomplish."

. "It is a flawed dream of racial superiority that is inconsistent with most world norms today. The ideology is poisonous...the same hatreds, the same stereotypes and the same goal of world domination and eradication of what they term as the sub-human races."

"You can help us, Kathy. Help us find Duchant. Go home, go to your father, and ask him about what has been revealed to you today. You saw the documentary and the photograph that flashed across the screen...it was a photograph of your father. You know that to be true and..."

Kathy screamed, "I refuse to believe you. I know my father and he is incapable of what you claim he did." Tears welled up in her eyes, but she forced them back.

Bertrand said quietly, "All of it is true. Shimon and I held nothing back. Please ask him... ask your father yourself."

Then regaining some of her composure, she replied, "I will. I will ask him."

"And if he denies it, Kathy, does that make what we said false?"

"I expect him to deny it because my father isn't Steiger. Why should I take the word of you two over my father?"

Bertrand rested his hand on hers. "I'll tell you why, Karta Buhler, because I love you and I would never start a relationship with you based on anything else but trust. I have no reason to lie to you about what has been spoken here."

At the sound of her given name, her face ashened. Stuttering...she asked, "How could you know these things? What are you...Who are you, Henri? I'm becoming frightened and I don't like the feeling."

Henri rubbed her hand softly, as she started to pull it away. Realizing that he had to let go, he released her hand, looked at her and felt the feeling of helplessness possess him.

Shimon began to speak again. "You know what we know. What you do with it is entirely at your discretion. We hoped that we could work together toward a common end."

"And what would that end be, Shimon? The trial and imprisonment of my father under circumstantial evidence at best connecting him to this man Steiger?"

"I recall a trial not that many years ago involving a Russian or Polish prison guard at a camp called Treblinka who the inmates referred to as Ivan the Terrible. His name was Demjanjuk and he lived in Detroit. He had a family and was a retired factory worker. He was tried in Israel and despite the parade of witnesses, the Israeli Supreme Court acquitted him. Do you know why he was acquitted? He was acquitted based largely on the statements of Ukrainian guards at Treblinka who clearly identified a man named Ivan Marchenko as Ivan the Terrible. The same is true of my father...simply a case of mistaken identity. You both have made a terrible mistake."

Kathy handed the handkerchief back to Bertrand. "If there's nothing further, I think I'll go home."

"I'm afraid, Miss Longrin, that won't be possible just yet. As much as I'd like to let you go, you are far too valuable."

"Additionally, if you were to confront your father, he would simply deny the accusation and you would be satisfied because that's what you want to believe. He would then probably kill Raphael and none of us would be the wiser."

"With you in hand, we have a negotiation point. I'm sorry to put it in such a blatant way, but I know your education affords you a quick grasp of

398

the present situation. If Raphael is still alive, we want to make an exchange, simply you for him."

Kathy stared in horror at Shimon. Then she looked at Henri who remained motionless in his seat, his face expressionless and then he finally turned away from her gaze.

She could feel her heart's abnormal rhythm when she realized that he would not go against Shimon to help her.

She was now a captive in a battle that seemed to have only one possible outcome, and that would be a life changing event for her.

Chapter 55

Duchant sat in front of the desk trying to sit upright and as straight as possible to convey an appearance of confidence and resilience.

He knew his face was cut and bruised by the constant blows from his captors.

His clothes were soiled, and he hadn't eaten. The drugs clouded his mind and reflexes. Their residual effects were still with him as he tried to maintain focus.

Despite all that he encountered so far, his inner self-discipline refused to capitulate to the real, or perceived, threats. He had no doubt that in time he would tell them what they wanted to know. They had their means, and no man could withstand torture in its various forms indefinitely.

It was a pure myth to think anyone could. This situation was a far cry from the stuff of Hollywood movies and pulp fiction books.

The man standing behind the desk was military in bearing. His manner and age indicated to Duchant that he had come face to face with SS-Major General Ludolf Otto Steiger.

He looked to his left and in the shadows of the room saw several standing men whose features were not clearly discernible.

The room was purposely clouded in subdued light. The curtains were drawn and only one low intensity desk light illuminated the room.

"How nice of you to come. Do you prefer Duchant or La Monde?"

Duchant didn't reply.

"I take your silence to indicate no preference. In that case, I'll use your Christian, and given names...pardon me, your Jewish names."

There was some laughter from the corner of the room and a smile appeared on Steiger's face.

"You seem to have let yourself go, Mr. Duchant. Your hygienic habits are quite unbecomeing of a man of your stature and wealth."

There was additional laughter.

Steiger turned his back to Duchant and faced a window, staring intently at the texture of the drawn curtains. He placed his hands behind his back as he was standing at parade rest and then began to speak.

"Mr. Duchant...I remember reading an article in Der Sturmer...in case you've forgotten, or never knew, Der Strumer was a publication whose editor, Julius Streicher, knew the Jew all too well."

"I remember the article precisely because it made such an indelible impression on me. The comments were contained in issue number 14, in

1937, and the statements were from the former chief Rabbi and later monk Teofite."

"The monk declared that ritual murder of Christians takes place on the Jewish holidays of Purim and Passover in memory of the murdered Christ. The Jews pour small amounts of blood into the dough of their matzos and into the ritual wine. Then the head of the family cries out, 'Sfach, chaba, moscho kol hagoyim.' May all the Gentiles perish as the child whose blood is contained in the bread and wine."

"Herr Streicher refers to your Holy Scripture correctly as, and I am quoting here, A horrible criminal romance abounding with murder, incest, fraud and indecency. This Talmud is the greatest Jewish book of crimes that the Jew practices in his daily life."

Steiger turned to face the seated Duchant.

"Is it any wonder therefore, Mr. Duchant, that we, the German people, did what was necessary to eradicate the Jew and their perverted influence from humanity?"

"Very eloquent, Steiger, and of course absurd...do you prefer to be called Steiger or Buhler?" Then Duchant smiled and suddenly felt the pain above his upper lip as it cracked open, releasing several drops of blood that dripped slowly into his mouth.

"What you neglected to state in your warped soliloquy, is that Streicher died on the gallows at Nuremberg along with ten other insane dreamers of

402

a perverted regime called the Third Reich. When the Berlin garrison surrendered to the 1ˢᵗ White Russian and 1ˢᵗ Ukrainian Armies on May 2, 1945, your dreams of a master race of German Aryans went down in flames and we Jews are still here."

"The blood libel you referred to has been around for centuries. It's simply one of many attempts by those who have hated us throughout recorded history, to demonize the Jews."

"What you and your ilk can never fathom, is that we are an indestructible race. While we suffer and die, we can never be destroyed. But if by some twist of fate, the impossible should happen where Jews disappeared from the earth, then the universe itself would disappear as well. The only reason for the existence of the universe is that it provides a place for Jews to serve and worship the almighty, Hashem, the Lord of Legions."

"Look around, Steiger, our numbers remain the same. We are twelve million, give or take a few. We were never meant to be large in number although our influence is without measure. We have returned to our homeland, Israel, and the desert blooms again because of our presence."

"And you, and your kind, Steiger, are reduced to a shadow world living a dream that has long ago been shattered. You try to maintain the semblance of that perverted world with your militaristic garbage. Your distorted mind still thinks that the world ruled by a master race could still exist. If that wasn't so sad, it would be laughable."

"Laughable, Duchant? It is not laughable now, nor was it then. We gave the world an idea, an idea of racial purity. We exposed a vermin, a disease to the world, and we attempted to stop that vermin from continuing to spread its evil ways."

"It was your people, Duchant, who corrupted German society. It was your people who were the direct cause for our defeat in the First World War. It was your people who took advantage of the aftermath of that defeat to prey on true Germans with your money grabbing ways. It was only after the rise of Chancellor Adolph Hitler that you Jews were put in your place. The only true tragedy is that we didn't have enough time to finish our work."

"How does it feel, Steiger, to always look over your shoulder, wondering when your past is going to catch up. And sooner, rather than later, Brigadefuhrer, you will crawl before those who will judge you. Die stunde nul (Zero hour) is closer than you think."

"If that is the case, Mr. Duchant," and Steiger smiled broadly, "we should not waste any additional time. Shall we proceed with the matter at hand... you."

Chapter 56

A male and female member of Shimon's security staff escorted Kathy to her apartment. Shimon reasoned that it was the safest place to hold her and the last place her father would consider.

Soon after Kathy Longrin was removed from the premises, Shimon instructed the internal security operator to dial the gallery's number. When the connection to the answering machine was made, he handed the receiver to Bertrand, who didn't immediately place it against his ear. Instead, he looked at Shimon, knowing what was expected of him, but hesitated anyway.

Shimon motioned with his hand and Bertrand started speaking.

The monitors in Illinois listened and watched as the device began recording.

"This is Henri Bertrand. We have the daughter of Ludolf Otto Steiger as our houseguest. We want to affect an exchange for Raphael Duchant. We will telephone with instruction shortly. If any harm befalls Duchant," then his voice trailed off, the meaning clear.

He handed the phone to Shimon, who replaced it on the receiver, cutting the connection.

"Where is she, Shimon?"

"At a safe house and in anticipation of your next question, the location is on a need to know basis and you don't need to know."

"It's that simple?"

"Yes, Henri, it's that simple."

Shimon rubbed his left eye with his knuckles and then looked back at Bertrand. "You need to go underground. They will have their operatives canvassing and you're a known entity."

"Any suggestions?"

"Use the facilities here. You'll have enough company. My office will be the focal point of this operation."

Bertrand shrugged. "It's as good a place as any."

"We're meeting with Pincus and Phil Goldman in about an hour here. Why don't you get something to eat, wash up or whatever until then?"

Bertrand nodded and left.

Chapter 57

The knock caused all heads to turn in the direction of the door.

Schwimler moved and opened the door just wide enough to see the man standing on the other side. The note was passed through the minimum opening and then the door quickly shut.

Schwimler started walking toward the Doctor when he halted in place and waited as the Doctor raised his hand, stood up, and went to where Schwimler was standing.

As he came abreast of Schwimler, Steiger called out, "Keep your head and eyes straight ahead, Mr. Duchant. This is nothing that concerns you."

Steiger took the piece of paper from Schwimler's outstretched hand, opened the paper, then read and reread the transcribed conversation before he handed it back to Schwimler.

"Please read it."

After reading the message, Schwimler, without saying anything, handed the paper back to the Doctor.

Steiger folded the paper, then placed it in his pocket. He walked back to his desk, sat down and looked at Duchant.

"We do not have sufficient time to play games, Mr. Duchant, or argue the morality of the

Third Reich. You know that we possess the means to extract any information we want from you. I will guarantee that if we must resort to these means, it will be a very unpleasant experience. I encourage you to answer my questions. Shall we begin?"

"What happened to Rudel and Miller?"

"What happened to von Hoenshield?"

"Mr. Duchant. You don't seem to understand. It is I, who asks the questions."

Then Raphael felt a blow at the base of his neck which propelled him forward.

His unbound hands allowed him to cushion the impact with the floor, however the pain from the blow still resonated at the back of his head.

Hands lifted him up roughly and slammed him into the chair.

"The last time I saw Rudel and Miller was at the Madison Avenue gallery, I guess a few days ago. I've no time reference at present so I think it was a couple of days ago. We, that is our side, had a screw up with a cashier's check and some papers. It made no sense to continue the meeting, so we agreed to end it. Bertrand and I left and returned to the office on 47th Street. Rudel and Miller were still in the building when we left."

Duchant was waiting for the blow to strike his neck again. After a few seconds passed and nothing happened, he allowed himself to relax slightly.

"While it sounds plausible, why is it, Mr. Duchant, that I don't believe you?"

"I can't help that, Steiger. It's what happened."

As Duchant finished the last syllable, the blow came.

"Why are you Jews so obstinate? How did you kill Rudel and Miller?"

"When we left the gallery, Rudel and Miller were alive. If you look at the timeline logically, Steiger, it's not possible that Bertrand and I could kill Rudel and Miller, dispose of their bodies and arrive back at our office approximately fifteen minutes later."

"Further, when I was taken by your people, I was walking alone. That's hardly something some-one who has just committed a murder would do. If I was the killer, assuming both of your men are dead, I would be shielding myself from retribution by surrounding myself with protection."

"A careless mistake perhaps, Mr. Duchant?"

The words sliced through Duchant and he thought if he only knew how right he was.

"We're getting nowhere, Mr. Duchant. I think we've reached an impasse and more stringent methods should be applied. Don't you agree?"

Before Raphael could reply, two pairs of hands hoisted him up and dragged him out of the room.

He was in a hallway and now standing before an open door. Then hands pushed him roughly forward.

As he fell headfirst, he felt the searing pain as a bone in his right wrist cracked.

Duchant remained motionless, trying to bring in as much air as possible through his open mouth. He could taste the blood on his lips and felt the need to run his tongue over his teeth to assure himself that they were intact.

Suddenly hands were lifting him up and then he was dragged across a concrete floor.

The hands let go and he fell the few feet to the concrete floor. When his right wrist impacted with the floor, the pain reverberated up and down his arm and he let out a soft moan.

He was rolled onto his back, his left sleeve pushed up, and a hypodermic needle inserted into his vein. The yellowish liquid which had an alliaceous, garlic-like odor, flowed into Duchant.

As the Sodium Pentothal liquid surged through his arteries, Raphael slipped into unconsciousness. After sixty seconds, Schwimler nodded to the Doctor who bent over a now awakening Duchant.

"How are you feeling, Mr. Duchant?"

Duchant was looking up at a ceiling and feeling the dampness of the floor against his back. Then his mind formed a picture of being thrown down a flight of stairs, but his mind somehow couldn't remember all the details.

As he moved his left arm, he felt severe soreness just below his bicep muscle. It registered that he had been injected again badly and the needle probably damaged his vein during penetration. Since Steiger and the others were here, the dosage wasn't the usual knock out amount.

Then he faintly remembered something that Schwimler said about using truth serum, or was it Steiger?

He knew from his early training that when someone is injected with Sodium Pentothal, he may very well lose some inhibition, but he doesn't lose all his self-control. Although the subject becomes very communicative and shares thoughts without hesitation, the common misconception is that the serum forces the subject to tell the truth completely. The opposite is in fact the case. The subject will not tell the truth if he chooses not to do so.

He relaxed as much as possible, knowing that he was in partial control, not them, despite the physical injuries and abuse. He'd have to play it carefully, let his training kick in...use what he was taught and with a little luck, he just might pull it off.

As he stared at the ceiling waiting for the questioning to begin, a deluge of memories came flooding back. Images of the Yom Kippur war, the fourth Arab-Israeli War flashed by in a vivid panorama.

He saw himself as a young twenty-year-old paratrooper in the 31st Paratroop Brigade under Northern Command's Major General Yitzhak Hoffi, fighting at the bloody battle of the Chinese Farm. And again, attacking and securing the bridgehead over the Suez, where he was wounded. He saw the hospital bed, weeks of convalescing, then the Mossad recruitment and training. He saw the missions in places whose names he'd forgotten and then a fast forward to the present as a deep cover operative, using his family's company as cover.

The images disappeared as the voice of Steiger resonated.

"What happened to Rudel and Miller?"

Duchant fought within himself to maintain control. "I can't say I liked Rudel. A little too militaristic and too sure of himself for my taste, but that seems to be a German trait...that feeling of superiority. Too bad you couldn't manipulate that feeling into results. The last time I looked, you lost the war," and then Raphael chuckled.

"I don't know what happened to Rudel. Why not call the police and file a missing persons report?"

Then he laughed and stopped abruptly as a foot came down on his broken right wrist.

412

Duchant screamed. The pain was excruciating. Someone grabbed his hair from behind and smacked his head against the concrete floor.

He looked up through eyes that couldn't clearly see the forms that now hovered over him.

A voice other than Steiger's began speaking. He thought it might be Schwimler's voice, but he couldn't be sure and what difference did it matter anyway?

"What happened to Rudel and Miller?"

Duchant could feel his heart beating at an accelerated pace and tried to get his breathing under control before answering the question.

He evidently waited too long, and a foot pressed down again on his broken wrist. His screams echoed off the basement walls.

"Well, Jew, answer the question."

"I told you before, Bertrand and I left both of them at the gallery. The meeting didn't work out because of some missing papers and there was no use to stay any longer so we…"

Before he could speak another word, hands grabbed his index finger on his right hand and pulled it back until it cracked. Duchant screamed again.

"You sons of bitches, you fucking schmutzige Nazi schweine." (Dirty Nazi pigs)

There was laughter. "Our Jew speaks the mother tongue," then more laughter.

"We have plenty of time, Mr. Duchant. We will continue breaking your extremities and adding to your growing discomfort until you tell us what we want to know. We are not interested in your idle thoughts, only facts. Is it possible for that Jew brain of yours to comprehend that?"

"I am telling you what you want to know. I left Rudel and Miller at the gallery."

"Let's leave that question for the moment. Who are you, Mr. Duchant?"

"I am the son of Edmund Duchant, grandson of Solomon Duchant and now the President of Duchant et Compagnie de Fils."

"Very good, Mr. Duchant, but not quite good enough. Please elaborate further."

"I am a patron and collector of the arts. I am seeking to recover paintings that were stolen from my family and I am willing to pay reasonable sums of money for their acquisition, no questions asked."

"Again, very good, Mr. Duchant, please continue."

"There is nothing else."

"Oh, but there is, Mr. Duchant. Tell us about your connections…shall I say, your working arrangements with a foreign government."

414

"The company has a presence in France, if that's what you mean."

"You know what I mean, Mr. Duchant. Perhaps we can help you recall."

A hand reached down and grabbed another finger. The crack sent the pain shooting up Duchant's arm. He screamed and then whimpered trying to convey a feeling of hopelessness. The pain could be compartmentalized, but he wondered for how long.

"Your left hand, Mr. Duchant, seems to be lonely. Shall we let it participate in our game?"

A hand grabbed his wrist while another took hold of the index finger of his left hand and jerked it back with so much force that Duchant thought it had been pulled off. Then a blow struck his broken wrist and he screamed until he lost consciousness.

Chapter 58

"You're getting a reprieve, Henri. No vacation in France just yet. You'll stay here for a while longer."

Shimon handed Bertrand the telephone. He nodded then listened to the ringing until the answering machine at the gallery picked up.

"An exchange will take place in Manhattan on Monday evening at 2200 hours (Ten p.m.) precisely. That is four days from now. Specific instructions will be left on this answering machine before then. Any deviation, no matter how minor, will negate the exchange. We are not adverse to writing Duchant off, but if we do, I can assure you we will have our way with your daughter before we bury her alive."

Bertrand handed the phone to Shimon.

Pincus and Phil Goldman sat quietly eyeing both men.

"You have a sadistic streak in you, Mr. Bertrand."

Bertrand just stared at Shimon before his eyes moved to the two men who remained motionless. Then he looked back at the security chief.

"I'm not entirely comfortable with the location. I'd opt for someplace open on the Jersey side. The New York harbor is too congested, with too much traffic and too many streets to negotiate."

Pincus spoke up. "I don't share the same concerns. We'll have snipers in place and Phil and I will be in the water with scuba equipment. They're not getting details to the final location until we are set. They won't have time to bring in cover for themselves. They'll be vulnerable and that's what we want. We'll take them out."

Bertrand looked at Shimon. "How do you feel about it?"

"I'm comfortable. Pincus and Phil will handle the water part, I'll be with the snipers and you'll be on location watching and handling the General, and to dispel any doubts you might have, the General will come. He wouldn't trust this to a subordinate, not when his daughter is involved."

"How can you be so sure and what happens if he doesn't?"

"We'll neutralize whoever they send and keep the girl."

Then Shimon leaned back in his chair, brought his left hand up to the back of his neck and massaged it with his fingers.

As he moved his head around, he looked back at Bertrand. "Steiger is a dead man and maybe the girl as well."

Bertrand felt the contraction of his chest as the words were repeated across his brain.

"What has the woman done?"

"She is expendable. It's that simple. Our objective is to recover Duchant and vacation the Nazi killer of our people. The woman is immaterial. She is an afterthought, is that clear, Mr. Bertrand?"

"It's clear, but not acceptable. I want her salvaged."

Shimon stood up, "YOU WANT! I'm not concerned about what you want."

He lowered his voice and softened his tone.

"I know that you're not neutral when it comes to the woman, but I want to believe that you are professional enough to put aside personal feelings. If you are not, I need to know that now. This is an ongoing concern of mine, and it's been mentioned before. I will not let you screw up this mission."

Three sets of eyes bore into Bertrand. He waited only a moment before replying.

"I'm a team member. Nothing comes before the mission. If we can salvage the woman without compromising the…" and then he let the words trail off. He looked at Shimon, "I'll do what has to be done, no exceptions."

The stark look on Pincus and Goldman's faces lightened up a bit. It was only Shimon who held back.

It wasn't wasted on Bertrand. Henri knew Shimon questioned his dedication, despite the words he spoke. The look Shimon gave him caused

418

him to wonder what he would really do if Kathy was placed in harm's way.

*

The buzzer sounded and Schwimler moved to the wall phone. He held the phone in his two hands as he motioned to Steiger.

The Doctor brought the receiver up and listened to the voice on the other end.

"Ja, once again, more slowly this time."

After a minute, he hung up and turned to Schwimler. "It will take place in New York City on Monday. Additional details will be left on the gallery machine. Continue to work on the Jew until we know what happened to Rudel and Miller. I'll be in my study. Contact me there when you have the information."

Schwimler tilted his head forward toward his chest and assumed a rigid stance as the Doctor turned and left the basement room. Then he turned his attention back to the unconscious Duchant.

He motioned to one of the men to lift Duchant off the floor and strap him in a chair.

Once Duchant was secure, Schwimler removed a small leather case from his pocket. He held the case in his left hand as he slapped Duchant across his face with his right. He continued the slapping until the moaning sound from Duchant's mouth grew louder.

Duchant opened his eyes. The pain of his broken and damaged wrist and fingers resonated throughout his body. He had heard that pain had its own nirvana. Enough pain brings on a euphoric haze, a sort of out-of-body experience, but he wasn't feeling anything except misery.

He looked at the man standing in front of him with a detachment he reserved for things that couldn't be categorized immediately.

He knew that his Nazi tormentors weren't finished. He reasoned that he would not leave wherever he was alive, so he became resolute to hold out as long as possible. It was a test of wills. He didn't try to fool himself. He knew that the future pain would increase in intensity and his will would be broken.

Schwimler placed his hands at Duchant's eye level and opened the black case slowly. He removed a titanium surgeon's scalpel and ran it carefully across the back of his wrist. He turned his wrist on an angle so Duchant could see the smooth hairless area the scalpel had crossed.

"I think it's sharp enough, but perhaps another test will confirm this."

Schwimler moved to the seated Duchant, and slowly cut across his right shoulder. The scalpel tore into his soft body tissue soaking his shirt with blood.

At that exact instant, Duchant's body was experiencing electrical and chemical events. The pain receptors were triggered, and the pain signal was transmitted through the nerves to the spinal cord and then to the brain.

Duchant tried to suppress the scream but the pain overrode his attempt.

"I think the scalpel is sharp enough. Wouldn't you agree, Mr. Duchant?"

Duchant's broken wrist and fingers throbbed. The cut to his shoulder was excruciating. He wondered how long and deep the cut was and then thought, what does it matter?

His body tried to normalize itself, but the areas of pain alternated so that his discomfort was a continual torment. He made an effort to make himself breathe slower, then he went into a reserve mode where he made a mental commitment to himself, I'm going to live.

Duchant took a deep breath and let it out slowly, trying to bring his breathing rhythm back to normal.

"I know you'll cut me to ribbons with that thing and eventually I'll tell you something about Rudel and Miller and anyone else including Hitler."

"I'm going to tell it to you at some point...so you'll stop. But what I tell you will be pure bullshit because I don't know what happened to Rudel, Miller, Hitler, or anyone else after I left the gallery. Check the timeline. There is no way Bertrand or I could be involved. No way."

Schwimler moved closer to Duchant.

"I don't believe you. Jews are born liars."

Then he pressed on Duchant's broken wrist.

Duchant's body shuddered in pain but clamped his teeth down so that no sound came out.

"I see you are enjoying our little exercise session," and then Schwimler pressed down harder.

Duchant couldn't restrain himself any longer and his screams ricocheted off the walls.

"Now, now, Mr. Duchant, you'll disturb the neighbors."

Duchant heard the laughter come from his rear.

"You want to know about Rudel, okay I'll tell you. He probably had access to von Hoenshield's bank account and looted it. We gave the money to Manfred for services rendered to our company during the negotiations for the painting, Woman in Black. Rudel was handed a cashier's check in the amount of twelve million which covered the amount agreed on for the painting. It was, and is, a significant sum. That's the best I can do. I don't know what happened to them."

"Oh, but you do and that's what we're trying to find out."

Schwimler pressed down again on Duchant's broken wrist and held the pressure until Duchant was screaming at the top of his lungs.

When he let go, Duchant's body went limp, his head resting on his uninjured shoulder, saliva coming out from the corners of his mouth and his chest heaving erratically.

The German walked to the phone and asked to be connected to the Doctor. Once the voice came on line, Schwimler's body stiffened and he began to speak slowly.

"We have inflicted considerable punishment on the Jew but his answers are unwavering, both under the influence of the serum and the torture. It is possible, Herr Doctor, that he doesn't know what happened to Rudel and Miller."

Schwimler waited for a response.

"I'll be there in a few minutes."

Schwimler hung up the telephone and walked back to a slumping Duchant.

"Your end may be near. The Doctor is coming perhaps to administer the coup de grace," then he smiled. "Before he arrives, I'll give you one more chance to tell me where the two are."

Duchant looked up from the angled position of his head. "I've told you I don't know."

Without another word Schwimler stroked the scalpel lightly across Duchant's chest opening a gash that turned the remainder of his shirt crimson. His body shook with tremors as the pain registered in the nerve center of his brain.

As the pain reached its apex, it forced Duchant to involuntarily lift his head up, open his mouth and release a guttural scream from the depths of his lungs.

The sheer magnitude of the scream forced Schwimler to back away.

When the pain finally dissipated, it left Duchant weak and in a cold sweat.

The Doctor arrived in time to see Duchnat's head fall and assume an awkward angle against his chest. Raphael tried to suppress the whimpering, but he couldn't completely negate the sound.

The Doctor looked at the blood-soaked man and said, "You are a stubborn lot, you Jews. It would be so much easier for you to cooperate. I asked you only a simple question and you refuse to answer it. You subject your body and mind to pain for no reason. A simple answer stops it all."

Stuttering and gasping for breath Duchant managed to say, "Know...nothing...can't...tell...you ...what...I...don't...know."

The Doctor waved off Schwimler who was moving on Duchant again with the scalpel.

He grabbed Duchant's head by the hair, forcing it up at an odd angle. Then Steiger bent down almost face to face with his victim.

"Our Mr. Schwimler loves to play games. The more blood, the more heightened the games become. He is not adversed, in fact he welcomes the opportunity to spill Jew blood. But between you and me, why give him the opportunity? Tell me what happened to Rudel and Miller and you can consider yourself a free man."

Duchant fought to remain alert but he floated in and out of consciousness hearing only part of what Steiger asked. His mouth was parched and what concentration he could maintain, was now exclusively centered on his continuing pain.

Steiger looked at Duchant with disgust, then motioned to the two men standing behind the chair.

"Watch him."

Then he motioned to Schwimler to follow him.

Steiger walked out of the room and toward the stairs. When he stopped, he turned and faced Schwimler.

"Check the Jew's wounds. I don't want him to die before we make the exchange. We fly to New York tonight. Keep him here until we're ready to move. Before you inject him, give him a minimum amount of food and water. Meantime, do not let him sleep. Keep him awake, continue to interrogate him regarding the whereabouts of Rudel and Miller and find out if the Jew bastard is connected with Mossad."

Steiger shook his head and quietly said as he walked away, "There's linkage somewhere."

Schwimler stiffened and clicked his heels as the Doctor started up the stairs.

Chapter 59

Duchant was carried off the plane and to a waiting Mercedes Benz, where he was shoved into the back seat. The duct tape across his mouth muffled his screams.

The drive to SoHo was a blur.

His wounds remained untreated. His injured wrists and broken fingers were haphazardly strapped to his side. The cuts and lacerations bled often when the clotting was reopened. The clothes he wore were the ones he was captured in. He hadn't bathed since that time and his body smelled of sweat, dried blood, bodily functions, and fear.

He received only a minimal amount of food and water and had been denied sleep which caused him to hallucinate frequently.

He was carried into the Prince Street address and taken below the retail floor, to where it all began.

He was kept in a vertical position several feet off the floor by straps that circled his body and looped over a hook embedded into the ceiling.

As Duchant slowly came out of the drug induced stupor, he had little recollection of events. As far as he was concerned, he was still at the same location where he first saw Steiger but one thing had changed...his resolve had diminished.

He knew he had reached his limit and resisting any longer would be foolish. He needed sleep. He had nothing to be ashamed of. He held out as long as he could, now he'd cooperate to a degree in an attempt to stop or minimize the pain.

As Duchant tried to lift his arms he realized he was bound with something that constricted his movements.

When he did manage to shift his legs to one side, the movement caused his body to contact with the wall behind him. His pain sensors responded to the contact and he moaned.

He felt the exhaustion take hold and his eyes closed. He pictured himself falling from a great height, steadily downward through a midnight black canyon. His body seemed to shake because of the canyon's frigid air which grew progressively colder and damper the further he fell.

Then his eyes were jolted open as he realized the coldness, he felt was from the shock of cold water hitting his face and that the falling feeling was a result of hallucinatory dreams.

He feebly looked at Schwimler's chest, unable to lift his head or eyes above that point.

"You've been sleeping on us, Mr. Duchant. I hope you had pleasant dreams, but no matter, it's time to go to work again. Are you ready?"

"Wait. I'll tell you what you want to know."

"That's very sporting of you, Mr. Duchant. You've wasted a lot of our precious time. We'll begin once again but there will be no more opportunities after this one."

Schwimler paused and when Duchant said nothing, he asked again, "What happened to Rudel and Miller?"

"Both Rudel and Miller are our prisoners. They are being held at a safe house, one of several that the company maintains."

Duchant stopped and raised his head up, but still not far enough to look directly at the standing Schwimler. "May I have some water?"

Schwimler turned to one of his associates. "Bring some water, a small amount."

The man handed the glass to Schwimler who placed the rim to Duchant's lips. Duchant took a large swallow and then began to gag. He spit out the water and said with a voice that cracked as he spoke, "The water is hot, damn you."

"Be grateful for little pleasures," then Schwimler began to laugh and the others joined in.

"Now back to Rudel and Miller. How was this done?"

"What done?"

"How did you overwhelm them?"

"We had weapons and the assistance of one additional man who entered the gallery as a UPS messenger. There was nothing they could do."

"Where are the safe houses?"

"New York…Manhattan and Fort Lee, New Jersey."

"At which one are they being held?"

"I don't know."

Schwimler began to move on Duchant with the scalpel in his hand.

"You can cut me, but all I'm going to tell you is I don't know for sure. If the pain intensifies, I'll tell you an address and then the other over and over again, because I simply don't know which of the safe houses will be used."

"What are the addresses?"

"Whatever addresses I give you will not be the right ones…the operational ones. The safe houses are rotated every three to five days. Since I've been kidnapped, Rudel and Miller have been taken to a new safe house used only when a situation like this occurs. Only the company's security chief and his deputy know the locations. I'm not privy to this information because of my vulnerability."

"Give me their addresses anyway."

"One's at 348 71st Street, and the other is the Cape Horizon House in Fort Lee. I don't remember the exact address."

"Do you work for Mossad, Mr. Duchant?"

"Hardly! I doubt if any of their personnel would be sitting where I am right now. I'm a principal in Duchant et Compagnie, nothing more. We have security to protect our diamonds, personnel and premises."

"Why were Rudel and Miller taken?"

"To ensure that the negotiations would continue and as a form of protection for Bertrand, Longrin, and myself."

"Why would you need protection?"

"The painting I recently purchased was stolen from my family's collection. We have reasons, good reasons to believe that the theft was in cooperation with high-ranking German military and party officials when Paris was occupied in 1941."

"When the new list of available paintings was handed to us by Rudel, several of these, seven as I recall, were again from my family's collection. We surmised that we were dealing with those who stole these works of art and felt that having Rudel and Miller under protective custody gave us, likewise, some measure of protection. Once the second transaction was completed, Rudel and Miller would be released unharmed."

"The amount of money that would have been involved in the second round of negotiations would have been substantial, upwards of one hundred million. If our suspicions were correct, and these were heightened after the disappearance of von Hoenshield, we couldn't walk blindly into a trap, so we decided to take Rudel and Miller as insurance."

"That's it. Since the moment I was taken I know nothing of Bertrand, Longrin, or what anyone else connected with the company is doing. You can continue to torture me but the story I've just related won't change."

The effort took all that was left out of Duchant. His head slumped to his chest and his eyes closed. He was asleep. One of the men started toward where he was suspended when Schwimler held up his hand.

"Let the Jew sleep, but not too much. Watch him carefully. Give him some water and food when you wake him up. I'm going to report to the Doctor."

Chapter 60

Kathy Longrin slammed the bedroom door. She hadn't taken two steps when it was opened, and the female guard walked in.

Kathy turned to face the woman. "I need some privacy. We're four stories up. I don't plan on jumping."

"My orders are specific. I go where you go and that includes the bathroom."

"Suit yourself. I'm going to take a shower."

The guard didn't divert her eyes from Kathy as she stepped out of her clothes and went to the shower. After she regulated the water flow, she stepped in and closed the shower curtain. The guard leaned against the doorframe and waited.

Kathy stepped out after she'd wrapped the towel around herself. Then she stood in front of the mirror brushing her hair. She moved toward the bathroom door saying, "Excuse me," as she pushed on the door and retrieved a set of silk pajama shorts and a t-shirt from the hook.

She walked out, brushing against the unyielding guard and went to her bed.

She turned on the TV and leaned into the pillows.

The guard sat in one of the bedroom chairs and continued to watch her charge without saying anything.

The primary thought occupying Kathy's mind as she stared blankly at the TV screen, was how to distance herself from her captors. She might be able to overpower the woman but the male guard now sleeping on the living room sofa was another story.

She knew the woman was armed. If there was some way to get the weapon away, she had a chance. Kathy realized that the larger area, like the bedroom, presented greater difficulty in confronting the guard.

The close confines of the bathroom presented the best place to make her move. She needed something, a weapon to use against the woman. She remembered seeing the curling iron in an open box.

She thought about how she'd do it. Each step calculated like a summation in front of a jury. She'd wait a little longer, maybe another ten or twenty minutes. The change in shifts between the woman and male guard took place about every three hours. The woman had shadowed her for at least two.

Kathy moved the pillows to one side then leaned back with her head touching the headboard. She tilted her head slightly and closed her eyes. She counted to herself and after ten minutes, pushed herself up and out of bed.

As she stood, so did the woman. Kathy walked back to the bathroom, lifted the toilet seat while eyeing the curling iron.

She dropped her silk boxers and sat on the toilet.

The guard took up a position just outside and braced her shoulder against the right door frame.

When Kathy finished, she stood up, angled slightly right toward one of the walls and with her back to the door looked down at the toilet bowl.

Her hand moved to cover her mouth. "Oh my God...look," and she pointed toward the bowl.

The guard moved quickly into the room and looked into the toilet bowl as the curling iron connected solidly against her skull.

The guard let out a whimper as Kathy reached out and grabbed the slumping body with her left arm. She gently let the body slip to the tiled bathroom floor.

A search of the guard's pockets and waistband revealed nothing. She turned the woman over and saw the weapon tucked into a concealed holster worn inside her pants.

She took the weapon and holster and went back to her bedroom, then dressed in jeans, sneakers, and a cotton sweater. She removed her wallet from her purse and placed it in one of her pockets along with a canister of pepper spray.

Kathy picked up the pistol from the bed and walked toward the half open bedroom door. She placed her hand on the doorknob, stepped back, and opened the door quickly.

The guard wasn't sleeping. He was sitting up reading a magazine and his eyes instantly moved in her direction, locking onto the pistol in her hand.

He started to get up.

"Keep your hands on the magazine and stay seated. Your partner is in slumberland on the bathroom floor. Place your feet on the coffee table."

The man did as she asked.

"Now take your left hand and pull up your left pant leg."

The man hesitated.

"Do it!"

The man's left hand went to his pant leg and he pulled it up. Good, no ankle holster. "Now do the other."

The man complied.

"Now stand up, interlock your fingers behind your head and move away from the couch to your left."

"Now turn around with your back facing me."

Again, the man did as he was instructed. When he turned away, she saw the pistol holstered at the small of his back.

"With the index finger and the thumb of your left hand, reach behind your back, pull out the pistol and let it drop to the floor. Keep your right hand on the top of your head."

The man reached around and after several tries, lifted the pistol out and let it drop to the floor.

"Now kick the weapon away, gently."

The man's foot moved sideward as if he was kicking a soccer ball and the pistol moved toward the far end of the rug, about ten feet from where Kathy was standing.

"Now your cell phone. Remove it with the same two fingers."

"I won't be able to get at it. It's in my right-hand pocket."

Kathy moved her left hand underneath the pistol grip cupping her right hand. She remembered seeing this done in many movies. It was supposed to steady the shooter's hand.

"Okay, place your left hand on top of your head and with your right hand, take out the phone...slowly...very slowly."

The man complied with the command, looking for any opportunity to tip the situation in his favor.

Kathy backed away several feet, sensing something in the way the man looked at her. She watched as he pulled out the phone and held it by his right side obstructing her view.

"Bring the phone around to your front with two fingers only. Toss it in front of where I'm standing…slow and easy."

The man instead tossed it end over end at her midsection. Kathy instinctively took a step back, keeping the pistol pointed at the man's chest. She let the phone hit the rug, and bounce without averting her eyes from the guard.

"Now move back between the couch and the coffee table. Don't sit… stand and make sure your fingers are interlocked."

Kathy watched the man move, as she kept a respectable distance away.

She paralleled his movements. As he moved closer to the couch, she moved closer to where the weapon had been kicked.

She stood over the pistol, her eyes still on the man and her weapon pointed at his center mass.

She moved one step to her right, squatted down without altering her line of sight. Then she wrapped her fingers around the weapon and resumed a standing position.

After placing the guard's pistol at the small of her back, she squatted down again and picked up the cell phone and pushed it into one of her back pockets.

The thought crossed her mind that if she got too close to the coffee table, the man might kick the table distracting her just long enough to regain control. He was a professional. She had to neutralize him somehow.

"Move to the bathroom and shut the door. If your friend is in the way, move her."

The man did as he was told but his movements were slow.

He was probably calculating what he could do to reverse the situation before he reached the bathroom door.

Kathy hung back far enough to prevent the man from overpowering her if he decided to turn and rush at her.

"Move faster."

He reached the bathroom and walked in. He leaned down and examined his partner's head, then looked back up.

"I think you've killed her."

Kathy took a step toward the bathroom, then stopped.

"Shut the door and do it now."

The man looked at Kathy, his eyes clearly revealing the hatred he held for her. He complied with her command and moved the body of his partner away from the doorway, then he closed the door.

Chapter 61

After locking her apartment door, Kathy ran down the hallway toward the fire exit. Turning the doorknob and shouldering the door open, she took the stairs two at a time until she reached the bottom landing.

Stopping momentarily to catch her breath, she realized that she was still holding the pistol. She tucked the weapon into her waist, pulled the sweater down and then opened the door.

Once in the alleyway, she turned right and started to run. She frequently looked back, expecting to see the man chasing her but there was no one. When she saw a cab turn the corner, she flagged it down.

"Where to, Lady?"

The only place she could think of was the coffee shop near where she once worked. She told the driver the address and settled back into the seat.

Her thoughts were of survival and she needed a sanctuary, someplace that her pursuers wouldn't think of, but where?

The cab pulled up in front of the coffee shop. She paid the driver and then stood curbside looking around and wondering why she decided to come here.

She hesitated only a moment longer before she started toward the door.

There were a few people at the counter and several booths were occupied. It was late, but these people seemed to be the neighborhood regulars or workers beginning their late-night shift.

She knew there was a heavily populated nighttime world, people who worked the graveyard shift at various jobs from janitor to computer techie.

She walked toward Oscar and before he saw her, called out softly, "Hello, Oscar."

"Kathy...hello! I'm seeing you at odd times, and odd hours. Sit down, over there in that corner booth. I'll bring you some coffee and something to eat."

"I'm not hungry, Oscar, but a large cup of coffee would be perfect."

Oscar busied himself with several of the counter customers and then brought over a cup of coffee and a plate consisting of a slice of meatloaf, some spinach, and small roasted potatoes. He set it down in front of Kathy and slid into the seat opposite her.

"I want to make sure you eat something. You look a little pale. I think the food could help."

Kathy reached over and placed her hand over his. "You're a kind man, Oscar. Thank you! It looks delicious."

"It is delicious. Go on try it."

Kathy picked up the fork and cut through a small corner of the meatloaf. She dipped it in the gravy and then brought it to her mouth.

Oscar saw the smile on her face. "See, I told you it would be good. Now eat. I'll be back in a bit and will have a cup of coffee with you."

Kathy was surprised when the plate was empty. Despite the late hour, she was hungry, remembering that she hadn't eaten since breakfast, her choice, although food was offered to her.

Kathy was sipping her coffee when Oscar walked over with a cup and pot.

"Let me freshen that up a bit, Kathy."

She pushed the cup toward Oscar. He filled it to the rim and then poured some into his cup.

Then he picked up her empty plate. "I'll be right back."

He placed the plate and coffeepot on the counter and returned to the booth.

As he sipped his coffee, he looked over the rim at Kathy. She didn't move her eyes away from his.

"What's wrong, Kathy? I can sense these things but with you it is obvious. Do you need help, money or something?"

Oscar noticed her eyes well up and a tear trickled down her cheek. He waited, just staring at her, wanting to help but realizing that she had to provide the opening.

"You're a kind man, Oscar. You have endured more than most people I have ever come in contact with and you still open your heart. I don't want to burden you. You've been through enough."

"I am a survivor of hell and all its fury. You cannot burden me but perhaps I might be able to assist you in some small way. Why not let me try?"

Kathy felt exasperated as the full weight of her problems tugged at her very being. There was nowhere to turn at the moment. They would already be looking for her and she needed to find a safe haven, someplace to stay. Maybe this man could provide one.

"Oscar, if I told you I need a place to stay for a while, no questions asked, would you do it?"

"Yes, but that won't help you solve your problem. It would only delay it a bit and maybe it would grow worse."

She took a deep breath and let it out slowly.

"Remember when I asked you about a man named Steiger, someone I'd seen on a TV documentary about the death camps?"

Oscar nodded his head yes.

"Well, that photograph…" She took another deep breath and started to cry, the sobs racking her body. Several of the customers turned to look and then turned away. Oscar handed her a napkin.

"I'm sorry. I don't know what came over me. Nice fix for a lawyer, huh?"

"Take a moment. It's time to close up and then we'll talk some more."

He slid out from the booth, talked briefly with the two waitresses who were getting the counter and booths ready for the next day and then announced to the several remaining patrons that he was closing in five minutes.

After the last of his customers left, Oscar placed the closed sign in the window and returned to Kathy.

"Now where were we, Kathy?"

Kathy smiled at the old man.

"Why do you want to help me, Oscar? You don't know me. Just because I was a regular when I worked near here and I exchanged a few words here and there with you, you really don't know me. Why would you want to help? Why do you want to get involved?"

"I've seen evil personified in my lifetime. I know when I see good also. You are a good person, Miss Kathy. Do I need more of a reason than that to offer my help?"

Kathy felt like crying again as the old man's words registered deep within her. She brought her fingers to her lips nervously then leaned forward, elbows on the table and began.

"The man Steiger, I think he's my father."

She saw the shock clearly in the old man's eyes. He pushed backed into the seat as if he was trying to distance himself from where he was. Then he sat deathly still as if frozen in place. His eyes glazed over and he drifted to some distant point at the far end of his mind, a place that was only his to access.

As his eyes refocused, he weakly asked, "How is such a thing possible?"

Kathy began hesitantly, wary of reopening memories for the man seated opposite her. But she quickly concluded that there was no way to tell it without hurting the man and herself in some way.

Oscar sat quietly through it all, her words and the images they projected had a mesmerizing effect on him. When she used certain terms and mentioned certain names, she saw him stiffen and his face assumed a pained look.

She tried to stop but each time he said a word or two of encouragement, she found the inner strength to continue.

She spoke of her childhood memories of Gerta the nanny and Udo the chauffeur, bodyguard, and confidant and about life on an Illinois farm and the frequent visitors, aging men, who spoke to her only in German.

She related her teenage years, growing up as an only child, her university days and her graduation from law school.

She told him about her job as an attorney at the firm around the corner and the Jewish company known as Duchant and Son, the painting and the negotiations. Kathy held back momentarily, then decided to reveal the existence of the underground room where masterworks of art were on display.

The hardest part was relating the events of the last few days and her escape only hours ago.

She didn't mention anything about Henri Bertrand. That was something that wasn't for public consumption, at least for the moment. She skipped over the woman guard who was dead on the bathroom floor. The thought of killing another human being sent a chill through her body.

She leaned her head back into the leatherette seat covering then brought her hands up to her eyes and rubbed them trying to clear away the tiredness and heaviness that lay behind them.

She wondered why she had opened up so freely and in so much detail, but it was now out and the why wasn't worthwhile thinking about.

"That's it...that's my life or what's left of it. I feel like I'm in quicksand and sinking fast."

Kathy brought her hands away from her eyes and refocused on Oscar who sat quietly. He hadn't moved a muscle, sitting rigid through Kathy's entire story.

When he began to speak, he had trouble getting the first words out and coughed to clear his throat, or maybe to gain some additional time while he formulated his thoughts.

"You are in considerable danger. Your father may or may not be the infamous Steiger. Whether or not he is, he will do whatever is necessary to secure your safety. The others, this Duchant group, will do whatever it is that's necessary for them to recover their principal, most likely at your expense."

"Please come home with me. I have a spare bedroom. It's comfortable and you can relax. I must get up early to open the shop, but you can sleep late and you can come back here when you're ready. We'll talk more and then decide on a course of action. Give me a few minutes to finish up here and we'll be on our way."

Kathy looked at the man as he slowly moved out of the booth, stretched and started walking toward the kitchen. He stopped part way and turned around.

"To put your mind at ease, I have no ulterior motives," then he laughed.

Kathy smiled and then replied, "Oh well, another dull night," then they both laughed as much as a release from the tension as from the comment itself.

Chapter 62

The guard left the bathroom the moment he heard the outer door close. He fumbled with the bottom lock of the apartment door, then opened the door.

He shifted his body from foot to foot as he stood watching the elevator light indicator move to the fourth floor. In moments he was standing in the lobby. He moved quickly toward the doorman who was sitting just inside the front entrance.

"Did Miss Longrin come down this way?"

Arthur, the doorman, looked strangely at the man who he saw enter earlier then remembered he was with Longrin and another woman.

"No, is there something wrong?"

"Just a mix up. Is there a rear exit?"

"Yes, but it's secure after five p.m. and it's not opened again until eight thirty a.m. the following day."

"Is there an emergency exit in case of fire?"

"Yes, it's at the end of the mail alcove over there. Turn right," and he pointed.

"Thanks. I'll take a quick look."

A few moments later the man was standing in the alley holding the door and looking quickly in both directions. There was no sign of the woman.

He went back to the lobby and walked out the main entrance to the sidewalk. He saw a taxi stopped about two blocks north of where he was standing.

He watched as the cab pulled away and made a U-turn.

He moved to the curb and then stepped into the street. As the cab passed, he locked onto the license plate and the name of the taxi company.

He kept repeating the license plate sequence to himself as he re-entered the building and walked to the elevator. Once back in the room he took a pen off of the desk and wrote the license plate and the name of the cab on an unopened envelope. He put the pen down, picked up the phone and dialed.

As soon as the connection was made the man began to speak in short sentences. When he finished, the voice on the other end asked, "Is she dead?"

"Yes."

"Remain where you are. We will send some cleaners immediately and run a trace on the license plate," then the connection was broken.

In twenty minutes, the ambulance was parked in front of the building and two white suited attendants carrying a portable stretcher rushed past the doorman. A third stopped and stated that they were going to an apartment on the fourth floor.

"What's the name?"

"Longrin, Kathy Longrin."

All three entered the elevator and were in the apartment less than two minutes.

Two men placed the woman on the stretcher, covered her with a sheet and moved into the hallway toward the elevator.

The third man called out to the guard, "Get some towels and start wiping the doorknobs, phone, coffee table glass and any plates, cups or glasses either one of you used. Be quick about it."

They covered the living room, bedroom, kitchen, and bathroom quickly. They worked in opposite directions, then crisscrossed each other and began sanitizing the previous areas until they met again. Then they moved on to the next room and went through the same drill.

"Okay, that should do it. Get your jacket, pick up the dead woman's purse and her coat, and let's get out of here."

They walked out, locking the apartment door behind them, and made their way to the fire exit.

Out in the alley they entered the passenger side of the waiting ambulance. It pulled away, turned right at the corner, and drove two blocks until it reached a one way street heading south. The driver turned on the siren and flashing lights as he sped away into the night.

Arthur was dialing the police as the sound of the siren faded.

*

Within fifteen minutes, the man was sitting before Shimon waiting to be admonished or worse. The security chief spoke in a normal voice and his cadence was modulated to reflect his displeasure.

"The woman escaped, there's one asset dead and you were neutralized."

Shimon paused and stared at the man until he averted the security chief's eyes.

"We're knee deep in shit because of you and I don't like the smell. The cab company is located at 161st Street, not far from Yankee Stadium. Get over there and find out who picked her up and where they left her off. Don't screw up again, or you'll be walking sentry duty for donkeys somewhere on the Golan Heights."

Forty minutes later, Shimon picked up the phone. He listened then said, "Meet me there. I'm leaving now."

*

The car pulled up in front of the darkened luncheonette. Shimon and the driver got out and walked to the waiting man.

"This is where he dropped her off."

Shimon nodded, "She came here because she knew someone and by simple deductive reasoning, that someone is the owner. Okay, let's call it a night. These places open early and we'll be back here by four a.m. Let's get some sleep."

Chapter 63

"I've been thinking about what you said since we left the restaurant. If your father is Steiger, being with him will place you in danger. I know it is difficult that something so impossible could be true. It's beyond one's imagination to realize that some-one, who is flesh and blood, is a mass murder. But, dear Kathy, if Steiger and your father are one and the same, you must stay away. From what you have confided in me, there are forces at work, avenging forces perhaps and the times now, these times, will become very dangerous."

Kathy felt as if she was going to faint. The weakness in her legs signaled that she had to sit down.

She walked the several steps to the cot and sat, then placed her hands over her eyes.

Oscar walked over to her and placed his hand on her shoulder.

The touch caused Kathy's emotions to spill over and the tears flooded down her cheeks. She didn't remove her hands from her eyes. It was as if she were trying to hide herself from everything.

Oscar took his hand away and stood quietly until Kathy regained control. She rubbed her eyes then asked, "May I borrow your handkerchief?"

He handed it to her and waited until she dabbed her eyes before he spoke again.

"Perhaps I can be the go between."

Kathy looked startled.

"No, not with your father but with the others. I could make a telephone call to them and find out what they want. You said they are Jewish, and I am a Jew. We have some common ground if for no other reason than that."

"Sleep on it. I must get up early to open. There are eggs and stuff in the refrigerator and coffee in the pantry. Make yourself something. Telephone me at the restaurant when you're ready. I'll leave the number on the kitchen table."

"You can wash up first. I'll get some towels and soap and leave them on the sink. Good night, Kathy."

"Thank you again, Oscar, for everything. God bless you."

"He already has." He smiled and waved as he turned to his right and walked out of sight.

Kathy got up and closed the door.

She went back to the bed, pushed the pillow against the single metal rod at one end of the cot and laid down. She started to think about her options before she fell into a deep, exhaustive sleep.

Chapter 64

Duchant was dragged to a corner of the room and told to take off his clothes. His broken fingers and wrist couldn't respond normally, making his progress miniscule.

Impatient with Duchant's slow movements, one of the men ripped off his clothes, indifferent to the pain it caused.

Duchant screamed and rolled over on his side. The same man grabbed his hair and pulled until Duchant righted himself. His head lolled to one side and he closed his eyes, asleep despite the pain.

The cold water splashed over his head and body. He screamed on impact, more from fright than from the effects of the water. He stared at Schwimler and watched as he signaled for another bucket which was placed near his right side.

"Wash yourself. This is all the water you'll get. Try to wash off that Jew smell."

From off to his left, a towel was thrown and landed at Duchant's feet. He bent forward trying to extend his left arm with its broken index finger and move the towel closer. He couldn't.

With difficulty he shifted his body to his left and tried to trap the towel with his left heel. On the fourth try he succeeded in bringing the towel close enough to grab it with two fingers.

The effort was exhausting, and he leaned back trying to draw in quantities of air which he hoped would somehow stop the pain reverberating through his arms, chest, and shoulders.

The towel rested on his outstretched legs. He felt the stickiness against his skin. Upon closer examination he saw that the towel was covered with oil, probably motor oil.

He spread his legs, pushed at the towel until it fell between his knees and onto the concrete. Then he reached over and with two fingers took hold of a piece of his ripped shirt.

Holding the cloth piece gingerly in his left hand, he dipped it in the bucket, which was clouded with a dark film. Unable to hold on, the piece fell to the bottom. Exhausted by the effort, he let himself lean back against the wall. He closed his eyes involuntarily but was quickly awakened with a hard slap across his face.

When he opened his eyes, Schwimler hurled the bucket's murky contents at his head. Duchant gagged as some of the putrid liquid managed to get into his throat.

"You might not smell much better, Mr. Duchant, but the rats won't know the difference."

There was laughter as Duchant once again fought to stay awake but succumbed to a body that had a will of its own.

*

Shimon, the guard, and the other man sat in the car, which was diagonally parked across from the restaurant, a large Dunkin Donuts coffee cup in each of their hands. As the front window became fogged, Shimon rolled down the passenger's window letting the cool early morning air invade the car's interior.

At four nineteen a.m., an old man with a slow gated limp, made his way to the front of the restaurant. He fumbled first, before he was able to insert the key into the double lock.

Then he bent down, grabbed hold of the wire mesh grating and with some difficulty raised it. He secured the lock to the bottom of the grate before he moved to the front door and opened it.

With his left hand he pressed the light switch on the inside wall and instantly the interior was bathed in fluorescent light.

The old man closed the door behind him, locked it, and disappeared into a rear area.

He reappeared in a chef's hat, white shirt, and apron. The three men watched as he busied himself setting up for the restaurant's opening.

After a final look around the old man picked up a large cup and walked to one of the coffee pots. He carried the coffee around the counter and sat on a corner stool. Then as an afterthought, he shook his head, got up, and walked to the window where he turned the sign around to open.

458

As he started to turn away, one of the waitresses waived and Oscar unlocked the door.

After a few words, the old man went back to the stool and his coffee.

Shimon turned toward the guard in the back seat. "Show time."

The guard opened the curbside door and slid out with the coffee cup in his hand. He emptied the contents into the gutter, crumpled the cup and let it fall. He put his hands in his pocket, crossed the deserted street, and entered the restaurant.

"Good morning. Seems I'm your first customer."

The waitress didn't lift her head up from filling sugar canisters but replied, "Someone has to be first. It might bring you luck."

"Well, I need all I can get."

"Don't we all. Booth or counter?"

"The counter is just fine."

Without asking, the waitress poured a steaming hot cup of coffee and placed the cup in front of the man with a smile.

He looked at a woman who he figured was in her late forties, still somewhat attractive but with her best years behind her. He smiled back.

"How about some rye toast with margarine."

"Do you want some eggs to go along with the toast?"

"No thank you, just toast."

The guard turned his head toward the seated man at the end of the counter. "Good coffee. You have the touch."

The man smiled but didn't say anything.

The guard faced front and stared down at his coffee.

Shimon turned away from watching the restaurant, took out his cell phone and dialed a series of numbers. Then he placed the phone to his right ear and waited.

*

Kathy heard the jingling but couldn't focus on where the sound was coming from. Still half asleep, she tried to block it out. Then as quickly as it began the jingling stopped.

Kathy pushed her head deeper into the pillow, trying to return to that moment of sleep. She was almost there when the jingling started again. As she picked her head up and looked around, she wasn't sure of her surroundings and then slowly she began remembering it all.

She pushed the curtains away from the small window seeing nothing but the darkened night.

She felt the vibration in her jeans' pocket, then realized that it was the cell phone she'd taken from the guard.

She rubbed the back of her hand across her mouth debating whether she should answer it.

Still unsure, she reached tentatively into her pocket and tugged gingerly at the phone as if it were a piece of white hot metal. She flipped the cover and pressed the connect button. The voice asked, "Kathy?"

She dropped the phone as if it seared her hand. Wide-awake now, she realized that the guard briefed his superiors regarding the loss of his weapon and cell phone. It wasn't exactly surprising that they would try to make contact this way.

She bent over and picked it up. Then cradling it with her right hand she answered, "Yes," and waited.

"We'd like to talk, only talk. Is there someplace we can meet?"

Kathy didn't believe that cell phone locations could be traced, but she'd make this conversation brief anyway. She took a deep breath, "What's wrong with this way?"

"Well for one thing it's somewhat impersonal."

Kathy laughed sarcastically. "I hardly think anything positive could come out of a personal meeting, but I can think of a host of negatives."

"We want to get Raphael back in one piece. We need your help."

"I have no intention of helping you or anyone connected with you," then she pushed the end button and let the phone drop from her hand.

She began to take off her clothes, aware that she had fallen asleep in them. As she undid the top button of her jeans, the two pistols at her waist fell to the worn carpet. She stared transfixed wondering how she was able to fall asleep with both of them pressing against her body.

Then she lost the thought as she walked to the small 1950's tiled bathroom. The small shower stall was a tight squeeze, and she wasn't able to direct the nozzle to the places she wanted. Still, she stayed under, letting the water cascade over her body.

After more minutes than she planned on, Kathy stepped out and dried off with one of the towels Oscar placed on the sink. It was old and worn, just like its owner.

She looked around and saw a comb and brush set. She dried her hair with the towel, then brushed it over and over again, letting her mind try to fix on her next course of action.

When she tired, she went to the kitchen and opened the wooden pantry door, scarred from years of abuse. She took down the tin coffee container and moved the four-cup aluminum coffee pot closer.

In a few minutes, Kathy was seated at the small kitchen table drinking the dark, rich brew.

She saw the small slip of paper with the restaurant's telephone number and began rolling it back and forth, as she entertained thoughts of leaving just on the outside chance that the cell phone could be traced.

Then she thought, leave sure but where to?

She made a conscious decision not to answer the cell phone if it rang again. What purpose would it serve? She looked at her wrist where her watch would normally be and said out loud, "Left it at the apartment, damn!"

She looked around the kitchen and saw a small electric clock encased in yellowing plastic, sitting on top of the refrigerator. It read five forty-one a.m.

Kathy unrolled the paper and looked around for a telephone. There wasn't one in the kitchen or the room she had occupied. She thought about using the cell phone, then discounted the idea.

She reluctantly walked into Oscar's bedroom. The room smell was musty, and she couldn't immediately locate a light switch.

She moved her hand toward the right of the doorframe and found it.

The room was bathed in a low intensity light from a single lamp on a night table, holding a low wattage bulb. The bed was unmade but everything else was in surprisingly neat order.

Kathy slowly looked around the room, her eyes stopping when they focused on the photographs in tarnished silver frames sitting atop a bureau.

She moved into the room and toward the bureau. Feeling like an intruder but continuing anyway, she picked up the closest photograph. The photograph was of a family, a young boy, his sister, two older brothers and a seated woman with a man standing to her rear, hand resting on her shoulder.

Kathy replaced the photo and picked up a frame containing a brown stained photograph with a crease running through the bottom portion. It was the same man in the family photo but years younger. He wore the uniform of a World War I German officer, with a ribbon proudly displayed around his neck. The black ribbon with two white bands held the four-pointed black Iron Cross First Class, awarded for bravery in combat.

She recognized the medal for what it was, having seen it before in her father's home. She recalled the instant clearly. She saw herself as a little girl playing hide and seek with Udo. In her excitement she opened the door of her father's study, a place where she was strictly forbidden to be, unless he accompanied her.

She hid beneath his desk. After a while she felt it was safe to come out and when she stood up, she noticed several medals resting at the center of his desk. The one with the black cross trimmed in white fascinated her and she picked it up. Then realizing where she was, she placed the medal down and quietly went out of the room and into the hall.

As she tiptoed back toward the kitchen, Udo jumped out and scared her so badly that she started to cry. He picked her up and carried her to the kitchen where Gerta was preparing something for her father and his two visitors.

"Let's get some strudel and milk for Karta. She had a bad scare from mean old Udo."

She giggled as he tickled her and they both sat at the pantry table dipping strudel into their milk and laughing. As she chewed the milk-laden strudel, she looked up at her father's bodyguard and asked, "What does a black cross with white around the edges mean, Uncle Udo?"

"Where did you see such a thing, Karta?"

"If you promise, cross your heart never to tell, I'll tell you?"

"Okay little one, I swear."

"I saw it on Papa's desk. I was hiding under the desk so you couldn't find me. Now remember you promised. Now tell me what it means, please."

"It is given, Karta, to a soldier who is very brave in battle. It's called the Iron Cross First Class."

"Was my Papa the brave soldier?"

"Yes, Karta, he was very brave, but that's a subject we'll discuss when you grow a little older. Now no more talk, let's eat more strudel."

She smiled at the memory, but it quickly disappeared as she thought of what Udo's words now meant and how they added substance to what she didn't want to believe.

The final photo showed several aged men dressed in black coats and wearing black hats. The beards and dress were in the style of Eastern European Jewry.

She saw the telephone on the nightstand. She unfolded the paper and dialed.

When Oscar's voice came on line, she said, "I think it's better if I stay here until you close tonight. Leaving here might present a danger to both of us."

"If that's what you want to do, fine. I'll see you later tonight. By the way I was thinking. What about your previous law firm…the one you worked for. Could they help you?"

"It's a possibility. Oscar, can I ask you for another favor? Before he had a chance to answer she continued. "Would you ask one of the waitresses to buy me several changes of underwear and a skirt and sweater. I'm a size five. I'll reimburse you when I see you tonight."

She waited and finally asked, "Are you there, Oscar?"

He answered, "Yes. It's a little awkward but I'll manage it."

"Tell her it's for your new girlfriend."

"At my age, hardly," then he chuckled. "I'll bring the stuff home with me unless you need them sooner."

"No, when you get here is fine."

Kathy cradled the phone and walked back to the kitchen picturing Mr. Higgins and wondered why she hadn't thought of him. After all, he did extend an open offer of assistance…maybe, just maybe he could help. His resources were infinitely better than anything she could muster and that included Oscar.

She refilled her coffee cup at the kitchen table and debated with herself whether she should contact Higgins. At nine thirty a.m. she decided it was the right move and walked back to Oscar's bedroom and the telephone.

She sat on the bed, again feeling as though she was taking liberties she wasn't entitled to take. When the receptionist's voice came on line, she responded with, "This is Katherine Longrin, may I speak with Mr. Higgins, please?"

"Hello, Miss Longrin, this is Mary Ann, how have you been?"

"Just fine, Mary Ann, how about you?"

"I'm doing well. We've missed you around here."

"Thanks for the kind words."

"One moment, Miss Longrin."

The operator's voice came back on line. "I'll connect you now, Miss Longrin."

The voice of Mr. Stanley Randolph Higgins came through with the same authoritative tone Kathy remembered.

"What a welcome surprise, Kathy. I hope this call is to inform me that you want to return to our hallowed halls of Law."

"In a way yes, Mr. Higgins. You made an offer to assist me if ever I needed help. Does that offer still stand?"

"Certainly."

She began exactly as she felt at that moment, "I believe I'm in personal danger. I can't go to the police and I can't return to my apartment. I'm staying with a friend, but it's temporary at best, maybe a day more at the most. I need help and I think you're my best and last hope."

"Can you come to the office now?"

"I only have jeans, a sweater, and sneakers, not exactly the attire for an attorney once associated with the esteemed firm of Higgins, Blackstone, and Randall," then she laughed.

468

"I like your sense of humor, Kathy, in the face of your adversity. It always helps. Why not come over now."

"I'll be there in thirty or so minutes. Make sure security is alerted to a gal in jeans that's coming to see you."

It was Higgins' turn to laugh. "Will do. I can assure you, you'll be welcomed," and then he hung up.

Chapter 65

The guard smiled at the waitress. "The coffee was great but I've gotta run. He placed a five-dollar bill on the check in front of him and stood up.

The waitress walked over to the cash register and the man followed. She handed him his change and he handed back two dollars.

"Do you have a card with the restaurant's name and phone number on it?"

The waitress pointed to the side of the register. The man picked up a card and looked at it.

"It doesn't have the owner's name on it."

"No need but since you're curious, it's Oscar, Oscar Steinheim."

The man smiled and started to walk out, then stopped and retraced his steps. "Do you happen to have a telephone book I could use?"

The waitress reached under the counter and handed him a thick Manhattan telephone directory. Then she walked away as another customer entered.

The man leafed through the pages until he reached the page containing the name Steinheim. There were several but only one Oscar. He wrote the address and telephone number on the back of the card, closed the book, and left it on the counter.

He walked out, turned left until he was half a block away from the restaurant then crossed the street.

As he entered the rear of the car, he handed the card to Shimon.

"The owner's name is Oscar Steinheim. That's his address and telephone number."

Shimon looked at the driver. "I want you to stay here. Watch the restaurant in case she decides to come back here. We'll go to the address and try to take the pigeon out."

The man nodded his head then opened the door and took up a position across the street from the restaurant.

His attention was diverted back to the car as it pulled away from the curb. He watched as it negotiated the early morning traffic and then he turned and faced the restaurant.

*

Within nine minutes the car was parked on the opposite side of the street and its occupants were looking at the building's entrance.

It was nondescript and atypical of most of the buildings that housed New York's teaming working class. A brick, multi-storied building with fire escapes placed in the front and at the rear. A few window air conditioners signaled the more successful of the renters and the iron window bars gave notice to all, of the constant danger that lurked throughout the decaying neighborhood.

Shimon looked at his watch. It read six twenty-two a.m.

"I'm going to take a look at the mailboxes. I'll be back in a few minutes. Tap the horn once if someone is about to enter the building."

Shimon exited the vehicle, crossed the street quickly and walked up the five steps to the door, which would open into the building's inner foyer.

The lock was a deadbolt, a pin and tumbler designed cylinder lock. The pins were designed in pairs of varying lengths resting in a shaft running through the central cylinder plug and into the housing around the plug. When no key was inserted, the bottom pin in each pair rested completely inside the plug while the upper pin stayed halfway in the plug and halfway in the housing. The positioning of these pins kept the plug from turning and ensured the door remained locked.

Shimon took out a leather case from his pocket and extracted a stainless spring steel tension wrench which resembled a thin flathead screw-driver.

He inserted it into the keyhole and turned it in the same direction that a key would be turned. This movement turned the plug so that it was slightly offset from the housing around it. Then Shimon slipped in a thin piece of metal, curved at one end like a dentist's pick.

He maneuvered the pick into the keyhole and lifted the pins individually into the housing. He turned the handle and opened the door.

He stepped into the foyer, scanned the mailboxes noting that Steinheim was number 319, then he walked out of the building and back to the car.

"He's in 319. I'm not sure how we'll take her, assuming she's there and I want to believe she is. I need a few moments of quiet to think about it."

Shimon slouched down in the seat wondering whether he should chance taking her on the street or in the building. Then he turned to his associate, "Okay...let's see what she does. Let her lead us. If she comes out or if she stays put, we'll react accordingly. We'll give her some time, not too much, just enough to set a pattern. Then we'll move...meantime we wait."

They watched from the car, shifting their bodies from time to time.

Shimon got out and moved away from the car but maintained a visual on the building's door. The early morning foot and vehicular traffic started to pick up as several hours went by. There were a number of people who came through the building's door heading in various directions, but not the target.

"It's almost ten a.m. We'll give it another thirty minutes, then go in."

The other man nodded but said nothing.

At ten after ten, the building's door opened and the target appeared.

Kathy took her time, first looking to her left trying to spot something out of sync.

Satisfied, she looked to her right then back to her left. When she moved down the steps, she again looked in both directions then started walking.

Shimon got out of the car and crossed the street so that his position paralleled the woman. When Kathy turned the corner, Shimon crossed quickly and watched as she flagged down a cab.

Waving at the guard who was following with the car, Shimon stepped into the street as the car cut across traffic and came to a stop.

He got in and pointed to the cab that was now distancing itself from them.

They were six cars behind the taxi when they saw it pull curbside in front of a massive marble-faced building.

The building's location was only several blocks away from where she hailed the cab.

Shimon opened the door and was in the street before the car had come to a complete stop.

Smart, he thought, taking a cab for a few blocks rather than chance walking. He jogged toward the cab which was now discharging its passenger.

When he gauged, he was close enough, he stopped and turned away.

As Kathy stepped onto the sidewalk, Shimon angled his back toward the cab knowing that the woman would look in both directions to see if she was followed before she would start walking.

Trying to decide if he should turn around, Shimon heard the toot of the horn which he figured correctly, signaled that the woman entered the building.

He waved to the driver and then started through the revolving doors of the building's entrance.

He began making a 180-degree visual of the lobby, trying to spot the woman. She wasn't there. It could mean that the building was used as a flow-through where the target went out the back, or she could have taken an elevator before he got to the lobby.

Shimon walked to the window board which listed the various occupants. There were several law firms listed, government and state offices, as well as commercial enterprises.

He remembered the first initial of the law firm indicated on her résumé and started scanning the "H's." It was nine names down. "Higgins, Blackstone, and Randall," occupied the entire fifth and sixth floors.

Shimon turned, went out of the building, walked to the parked car and got in.

"She's at her former law office. Now we have the circle expanding again and another consideration in the equation."

The guard turned to face Shimon. "I don't know if you're aware of it, but we're not far from the restaurant."

Shimon shook his head, "What?"

"Yeah, the restaurant is back there and to the left."

"Stay here and I'll get Aviv. I doubt if she'll be out for a while."

Shimon hurried around the corner, crossed the street, then quickly walked several long New York city blocks until he reached the standing man who was idling near the brick building.

The man straightened up as Shimon reached him.

"She hasn't shown up yet."

"In a way she has. She's in an office building a few blocks from here. The car's parked there, let's go."

The two men jogged back to the car and got in.

"Aviv and I are going back to the apartment she used. We'll take a cab. You stay here and tail the girl when she comes out. She might go to the restaurant or back to the apartment, or who knows where. If it's the apartment, we'll take her there. Park the car in front. You'll keep us informed by cell. Let's not screw this up. Time isn't on our side."

"My cell was taken by the girl."

Shimon shook his head, then nudged Aviv, "Give him yours."

*

Kathy stood in front of the receptionist quietly chatting and feeling somewhat self-conscious about her attire when the voice of Stanley Higgins caused her to stop in mid-sentence.

She smiled back at the receptionist and then started walking toward the old gentlemen.

He embraced her and took her elbow as they moved in the direction of his wood paneled office.

Once inside, Higgins pointed. "Let's sit over there, Katherine."

They moved toward comfortable chairs and a coffee table arrangement, positioned at one corner of the room. She waited until Higgins had seated himself and then sat in a leather club chair which faced him.

"May I offer you something, Katherine?"

"Yes. Some help."

"Ah, it's that serious, is it?"

"I'm afraid so, Mr. Higgins. I mentioned that my life might be in danger. It seems I'm caught between two forces, one of which involves my family."

Now that she had begun in this vein, she knew she couldn't stop.

"As I've just stated, one of these forces is my family. Information I received, and this information seems highly credible, states that my father is a…" and then she stopped as she tried to contain the tears. When she started again she said. "a Nazi war criminal." Then she started to cry and between sobs asked, "Oh my God…how could it be?"

Higgins got up, went to his desk and opened a drawer. He retrieved a box of tissues, carried them back and placed them on the coffee table in front of Kathy.

Higgins sat down diverting his eyes away from the woman and patiently waited until she was ready to continue.

Kathy looked up at Higgins and said in an almost inaudible voice, "I'm sorry for the break-down."

Higgins smiled and answered, "There's nothing to be sorry for. Take your time and continue when you're ready."

Several moments later Kathy began again.

"The other concern is the company I'm now working for, Duchant et Compagie de Fils, is engaged in recovering stolen art taken from the family during the war years. The bridge here is that Duchant and Company are negotiating for these paintings with my father and his representatives."

"Additionally, since the disappearance of the company's principal, Raphael Duchant, I have become a bargaining pawn. I was being held at my apartment under guard but managed to escape yesterday."

She started to say that she has been hiding at an apartment whose owner ran the restaurant near here but decided, for some unknown reason, to hold back.

"I know the Duchant people are looking for me. I can't go to the police because of my father."

Kathy paused and dabbed her eyes with several crumpled tissues. "That's it…at least all the important details."

Kathy moved back into the chair and stared at Higgins who sat quietly trying to absorb the enormity of what had just been revealed to him.

"Who were the people holding you, Katherine?"

"Security from Duchant Company."

"How did you get away?"

"I hit the woman guard, took her gun and managed to get the drop on the male guard. I've been walking the streets ever since, then decided to call you."

While Kathy was leaving out salient parts and lying about other events, she somehow knew that too much information now was counter-productive.

"Do you have the weapon with you?"

"Yes, two."

"May I have them?"

"I'm reluctant to give them up just yet. They're my comfort dolls."

Higgins looked quizzically at the woman. "It can only get you in serious trouble."

Kathy thought about the curling iron and the dead woman on her bathroom floor then replied, "Maybe, Mr. Higgins, but until I'm safe, away from the men chasing me, I think it's better to hold on to them."

Higgins, sensing that further dialogue about the pistols would be fruitless, went on to another subject.

"What we need to do is get you a place to stay. Please wait a moment and let me make some arrangements."

The old man smiled, stood up with some difficulty and walked gingerly back to his desk as Kathy followed his movements.

Higgins leaned over and started writing on a pad of seven by five-inch white paper. Then he stopped abruptly and began crossing out some words. Dissatisfied, he ripped the paper from the pad, crumpled it, and threw it in the wastepaper basket. He started writing again, tore off the sheet, and walked toward the door.

"I'll only be a few minutes. I want to talk with my secretary and an associate. I'll be back shortly."

Kathy's eyes didn't leave the man until the door was closed behind him.

She got up and uncharacteristically walked to the wastepaper basket and retrieved the crumpled paper. She opened it, spreading out the creases with her fingers and stared in shock at the written words.

Connect me with… then several words were obliterated by numerous horizontal pen strokes followed by the name F. Buhler. The note went on that he'd take the call in…but Kathy couldn't make out the words after, in.

She stared in disbelief at her last name and knew that the F stood for Friedrich, her father.

How was it possible that Higgins knew her father? Was the crossed-out name Steiger?

Kathy felt panic well up within her, raw, sheer panic. Higgins' office became claustrophobic. The more she stared at the paper, the more the enormity of the inexplicable situation became.

Kathy crumpled the paper and threw it back in the basket. Then she walked to the door, opened it carefully and noted Higgins' secretary at her desk holding a telephone to her ear.

Stanley Higgins was nowhere in sight. She mouthed the words ladies' room as she walked past the secretary.

She continued to the reception area and waved to the receptionist as she pushed the down button. She stepped in and fidgeted impatiently as the elevator stopped at each floor before arriving at the lobby level.

Kathy pushed the revolving doors forcibly. Standing just steps away from the entrance, breathing heavily and holding her hands to her face, she started to cry.

Regaining her composure, she took her hands away from her face, dried her eyes with the sleeve of her sweater, and then began walking.

She passed the guard who was watching from the car, then stopped at the corner and looked to her left. Instead of hailing a cab as the guard anticipated, she started walking again and disappeared from view.

Losing sight of his target, the guard was out of the car and moving quickly toward the corner. He reached it in time to see the woman running in the direction of the restaurant.

He took out his cell phone and dialed.

Shimon and Aviv were in the apartment when the call came through.

Chapter 66

Bertrand went to the Security Chief's office and again found it empty. He hadn't seen him in over twenty-four hours.

He moved behind the desk and removed a blank sheet of paper from a pad. He picked up the pen which was leaning against the telephone and scribbled three words.

"Be back shortly," and signed his name.

He placed the paper on the seat of Shimon's chair and walked out and onto the main sorting room floor.

He passed the guards and secretary in the reception area and took the elevator to the retail floor. Once he reached the street, Bertrand walked north in the direction of Fifty-Seventh Street, figuring he'd get a cab before then and if not, it would loosen up some inactive muscles.

He hadn't gone two blocks when he saw a cab whose roof light indicated empty. He flagged it down and was at his apartment in another fifteen minutes.

After taking out his pistol, the small caliber one he wore on his right ankle, Bertrand listened for anything that would break the quiet.

He removed his shoes then inserted his key.

Pushing lightly on the door, he braced himself at the right edge of the doorframe. After waiting about thirty seconds and hearing nothing that alerted him to a possible danger, he stepped inside.

Bertrand left the lights off. There was enough light coming through the plantation shutters to provide the illumination he needed. He stayed close to the narrow hall wall as he made his way into the apartment's interior.

A slow canvass of all the rooms revealed that he was alone.

He went back to the door, bolted it from the inside, then walked back to his bedroom and looked down at the answering machine.

There were no messages.

Bertrand got out of his clothes and went to the bathroom.

Still dripping water from a quick shower, he returned to the bedroom and dialed Kathy's apartment for the hell of it.

After four rings the answering machine came to life.

He hung up. The guards were there and so was Kathy, but they wouldn't answer the phone and certainly wouldn't let her.

He got dressed slowly, thinking of the predicament that he had gotten into with this woman and wondering how it all came down to the present. But of course, he knew, he was a professional with a piece of baggage that was pulling him along and down at the same time.

An ominous feeling came over him. He tried to shake it off by thinking of the more pleasant aspects of his life, up to this point, but his mind came back to the woman and the myriad circumstances that surrounded her.

Bertrand started packing a small bag with clothes and personal items when the telephone rang.

He picked it up on the second ring. "Yes."

"Henri."

He recognized the voice before she said, "This is Kathy," and his mind filled with the numerous questions he wanted to ask.

He slowed his breathing but felt his heart pound with excitement at the sound of her voice.

"Are you okay?"

"I'm not sure. I'm not hurt but I need to see you."

"Where are you?"

"I'm in a small restaurant…" then Kathy gave him the address and added, "The owner is a friend of mine."

"You'll have to assume, Kathy, that you're being watched. Despite any precautions you've taken, you're under surveillance. See if you can borrow a jacket from your friend, maybe a hat, anything that can alter your appearance somewhat. Go out the back of the restaurant and take the subway to Grand Central station. Go through the lower-level concourse towards the 44th Street exit. Just before the exit, you'll see the entrance to the Roosevelt Hotel which borders 44th Street and Madison Avenue. I'll be in the lobby. Something like hiding in plain sight."

"Okay, Henri. Thank you. I'll hurry," then she hung up.

Kathy handed Oscar his cell phone. "I need to meet someone, and I need to alter my appearance. Can I borrow something that can change me a bit?"

Oscar called over a waitress. "I'll take over your station for a few minutes. Please talk with Kathy."

The waitress smiled at Kathy. "I guess you want that change of clothes now?"

"Were you able to get them?"

"Yes," then she reached under the counter, and brought out a brown bag imprinted with the name Stella's Fashions and handed it to Kathy.

"The bill is in there, too."

Kathy spread the bag open and pulled out the invoice. She reached into her jeans pocket for her wallet and handed the waitress the money with a thank you and a smile.

"I need to take advantage of your kindness just one more time. Could you possibly let me borrow your wig? I know what I'm asking is stretching it to the limit but I'm in a pretty bad situation. I can't leave here as the woman who entered."

The waitress shook her head and smiled back. "Don't worry, dear. If you're a friend of Oscar, you're a friend of mine. Give me a moment and let me see what I can do with what's underneath," and she pointed to the wig.

Kathy watched her disappear into the ladies' room. In a few minutes, the waitress opened the door, pointed to the brown bag and motioned Kathy to come in.

Kathy used one of the stalls to change into a skirt and sweater combination. Then she placed the two pistols between her waist and the skirt's elastic top. After pulling on the sweater so that it covered several inches below her waistline, she stepped out from the stall and asked, "How do I look?"

"You look good and you're going to look even better after this," and she pointed to the wig.

The waitress placed the wig on Kathy's head and began brushing it into place. After pronouncing her ready, the waitress opened the door and let Kathy lead the way out.

Kathy reached into her pocket for her wallet. "This should cover the cost of a new wig." She smiled, gave the waitress a hug, and then pecked Oscar's cheek. "I'll call you at the restaurant before you close."

She turned and left by the rear entrance. Once in the alley she walked quickly past the rear entrances of several adjacent buildings before she turned toward Pearl Street. She took the subway to Grand Central station and then followed the concourse to the Roosevelt Hotel.

She walked up the stairs to the lobby and looked around. She spotted Henri who was already walking toward her from a corner of the room.

*

Schwimler stood before the Doctor, waiting for a reply. Steiger had listened to his discourse without interrupting and was now looking at his subordinate with curiosity.

"While it sounds plausible, my inclination is that his entire statement falls into the realm of fantasy. It's difficult to believe these Jews. They lie with such ease, lie about everything and to anyone. We must go on the premise that both Rudel and Miller are dead. While I would relish killing this Jew, we must wait a while longer. Has any further message been received?"

"Nein, Herr Doctor."

"Has the Jew's condition deteriorated further?"

"He is in considerable pain and his injuries remain untreated, but his condition is stable."

"Good. Let's keep it that way. Do not let him sleep to any degree. Keep the physical torture to a minimum. I don't want the Jew to die on us. Let me know as soon as another message is received regarding the meeting."

As Schwimler left the room, the telephone rang on the doctor's desk. Steiger reached across with his right hand and picked it up.

"Yes."

"A call for you, Herr Doctor. The call was placed to Illinois and we are re-routing it to you through the secure line. Please wait."

The voice on the other end came through clearly.

"Ludolf, this is Herbertus."

Steiger hadn't spoken to the Colonel since Karta left his employ. Unknown to his daughter, her employment there was carefully engineered.

Stanley Randolph Higgins was in fact SS-Standartenfuhrer, Herbertus Bikker, and a fellow member of the Organisation Der Ehemafigen SS-Angehorigen, The Odessa.

"It's good to hear your voice again, Herbertus. What can I do for you?"

"I must apologize, General. Your daughter was here, at our offices. She is obviously in some difficulty and came to me for help. It seems she is being pursued by unnamed parties and stated that she was concerned about her safety."

"I left her in my office in order to place this call to you. My secretary informed me that your daughter came out of the office and indicated that she was going to use the ladies' room. When she didn't come out for many minutes, my secretary went in to see if there was a problem. She was gone and I am unaware of her whereabouts, Brigadefuhrer…"

Higgins paused for only a moment then added, "There is one thing more. During our conversation she mention the possibility that you could be a…and I am quoting her Brigadefuhrer…a Nazi War Criminal."

Steiger stood in stunned silence. Finally, he said, "Thank you for the information, Herbertus, at least I know she is alive."

"Even with the suspicion…if I may take the liberty, Herr General, why hasn't she contacted you?"

"That, Herbertus, is what I would like to know. Please keep me posted if anything further develops at your end. She may contact you again."

"You will be advised the moment anything tangible develops, General."

"Danke," and Steiger cut the connection.

He stood thinking that her escape had shifted the advantage to his side. First, he would secure her safe return, then in time he would right the confusion confronting her regarding the man named Steiger...the man who he was and who he would always be.

Chapter 67

They embraced, kissed, and reluctantly Bertrand disengaged.

"I wasn't sure it was you. The wig had me second guessing myself."

He still held her close and looked deeply into her eyes. "Let's go to the mezzanine floor. There are some chairs and sofas there and it's deserted, at least it was ten minutes ago. It'll give us some privacy and we can watch the main floor at the same time."

Bertrand stood at the railing of the mezzanine floor and gave the lobby a three hundred and sixty-degree visual before he sat down on a sofa across from Kathy. He leaned forward. "I've missed you."

She touched his hand and repeated his words to him, adding "too."

"I'm in deep trouble, Henri. I think I've killed one of the guards…one of Shimon's people, the woman. I hit her with a curling iron, then took her gun. That's problem number one."

"The second problem is that Shimon and his boys are probably still after me. I've been camping out in the apartment of a restaurant owner. He runs a luncheonette not far from my old office building. He's a sweetheart of a guy and a survivor from the death camps. He's not the problem, but I'm concerned that his involvement with me will spell trouble for him."

"The third problem is that I went back to my old law firm. That kindly old gentleman, Higgins," and Kathy paused, "knows my father."

"After I told him my story, he offered to help me, including a place to stay. He scribbled something on a piece of paper, then discarded it in the wastepaper basket and re-wrote whatever he was trying to convey on another paper."

"He left the office with the rewritten paper and asked me to wait. As soon as the door closed, I went to the wastepaper basket and picked out the paper he'd tossed. It read in part, F. Buhler, my father's name. It is inconceivable to me how Higgins knows my father. Just another part to add to an already screwed up equation."

"Does Higgins speak with an accent?"

"To be perfectly honest, I've never really paid any particular attention, but now that you mention it, yes, he does but it's very slight."

"How would you categorize the accent, Kathy?"

"It sounds somewhat like German," then Kathy brought up her hands and covered her mouth with the palms. "Oh my God, can it possibly be?"

"It's true, Kathy. Higgins is surely a member of Odessa, the organization Shimon mentioned when discussing your father's back-ground."

The questioning look on Kathy's face revealed that she couldn't, or didn't want to, remember.

"It's the clandestine organization of former SS members and high-ranking Nazi party function-aries. They're tight knit and their tentacles and members seem to be everywhere…yes, even the United States."

"But Higgins…him…I'm shocked."

It was going to hurt her, but he had to say it. "Any more shocked than finding out about your father?"

Kathy didn't answer. She still didn't want to believe it was possible, but the impossible was beginning to unfold in all its clarity.

"Yes, Henri, him, too. You've got to understand where I'm coming from. He's my father, not some intermediate acquaintance like Higgins. It's far easier for me to believe the accusation against Higgins than it is for me to accept it about my father."

"Before you say anything more, I think my father and Steiger are the same. I don't want to believe it, but all that's happening around and to me, says it's so."

"I know you're hurting. Please believe me, Kathy, I'm hurting with you. I can't feel your pain, but I can see it. Seeing it hurts me a great deal, especially when I can't take that pain away from you."

Several tears ran down her cheeks. She brushed them away with the back of her hand.

"I seem to be crying more these days and they're not tears of happiness. What am I going to do, Henri, what am I going to do?"

*

The guard pressed the button of his cell phone on the second ring.

"No, she's still in the luncheonette. Sure, okay I'll go in for a visual."

The guard entered the restaurant and looked around as he slowly walked to the counter. The woman wasn't there. He caught the waitress's eye.

"I'll have a cup of coffee. Where's the men's room?"

She pointed and then turned toward the coffee urn, holding a cup and saucer in her hand.

He walked toward the bathroom and stopped in front of the ladies' room. He knocked softly, then turned the knob and opened the door. It was empty.

He returned to the counter and sipped some of the coffee. Pushing the cup away, he stood, placed two dollars next to the cup, and walked out.

He dialed and waited for the connection.

"She's not there."

Shimon held himself in check. This was the second time the target disappeared, but it was as much his fault as the guard's. There was no one watching the rear of the building.

He gave the guard the address and number of the restaurant owner's apartment with instructions to fill in as the second man on the stake out team, while he returned to the office with the car.

Once back at 47th Street, he sent word for Pincus and Phil Goldman to meet at his office.

*

Bertrand was conspicuously absent as the security chief huddled with the two men, reviewing what had transpired.

"The plan is scrapped. Until we get the girl back, we're behind the proverbial eight ball."

Both men nodded.

"I'm concerned for Raphael. We're hiding behind tissue paper... find Bertrand," and he waived Henri's note back and forth. "I'll concentrate on getting the woman back."

Chapter 68

The guard got up from the kitchen table and walked out to where Aviv was seated.

"It's claustrophobic in here."

Waiting for a response which didn't come, he continued. "I feel like getting some outside air and before you comment, it's only a passing thought."

Then after an extended pause said, "I can't help wondering whether anyone in this family photograph escaped the Nazis?"

Aviv turned around, "Doubtful."

The guard shook his head. "After all this time our enemies still abound, the old ones and the new ones. These perverted imbeciles never learn. It's always someone, isn't it Aviv? If it's not the Palestinians or one point two billion Muslims, it's the Nazis, the neo-Nazis, and their ilk."

"We're still around, aren't we? Our numbers are small because that's the way we're supposed to be. We weren't meant to be any other way. Despite our limited numbers, we've outlived our enemies for thirty-three hundred years. Does that tell you anything?"

"Yes, it says it all."

*

Bertrand held her hand in silence as he looked back at her and wondered how he could answer her question.

"Right now, it's imperative that you're out of sight and stay that way. You can't go back to your apartment and my place won't work either. I was thinking about a hotel, but the credit card could be easily traced and no hotel I know will accept cash. Going back to the place you stayed last night is chancing it."

"It's a tenement building, nondescript, one of a hundred like it in New York. The place is one step above seedy. Who would look for me there?"

"Never underestimate Shimon or for that matter your father. After the phone call from Higgins, your father knows you've escaped and has operators in the field looking for you."

Kathy sat in silence and Henri gave her the space and time to retreat within herself. He sat there looking at her, waiting until she felt comfortable again to start talking.

She seemed to regain some composure and Henri smiled at her trying to let her know it was okay. When she still didn't speak, Bertrand began.

"It's okay, Kathy, to be confused and it's okay to be scared. Those are natural emotions. You've been through a lot and hopefully it will end soon."

"I've got to get back to 47th Street. You can't wander the streets. Let me take you back to where you stayed last night. I'll make sure you're okay, and then leave."

Kathy moved her shoulder up in an act of indifference.

Bertrand reached out to her. "It's not that bad, Kathy. It's all going to come together soon. It's just that I'm not sure how, but everything has an ending, and this will too. We can't panic. It only leads to mistakes. We know a lot, but not everything. The bad has a way of changing. It either gets better, or worse. We'll face whatever direction it takes together," then he squeezed her hand.

They stood up and came together. He kissed her passionately and she returned it with equal passion. Then he took hold of her hand and they made their way in silence to the elevator.

*

Bertrand paused and looked up at the building. Then he followed Kathy up the five steps to the foyer door.

She turned around. "I don't have a key. I came in last night with Oscar and didn't think about getting back in after I left for Higgins' office."

Bertrand nodded then said, "Going back to the restaurant to get a key borders on insanity. I have a friend in Soho that owns an art gallery. The living quarters are in a loft above the gallery. It's a possibility."

"No choice, I guess. I'm having trouble thinking clearly, Henri. I need you to get me through this."

They walked to the corner stopping in front of a small bodega. "Let's go in."

"Where's the phone?"

The clerk pointed to his right. "It's gonna cost you a dollar to use it."

Bertrand handed him a couple of dollars and said, "Buy yourself a car with the extra money." Then he instinctively looked around before he picked up the receiver and dialed.

The phone rang in the loft and after four rings was re-routed to the gallery below. A familiar voice answered the phone.

"Tom?'

"Yes, may I help you?"

"Tom, this is Henri Bertrand, is she there?"

There was a moment of silence before the voice said, "I'll tell her."

The silence grew heavy as he continued to wait impatiently for the voice he remembered so well to come on the line. When he finally heard it, he seemed momentarily at a loss for words. When she repeated the hello, he finally answered by saying her name.

"Yes, Henri, what can I do for you?"

Her voice was strong and her words, while not friendly, were not cold. Bertrand thought, perhaps she answered for old times' sake.

"I need a place for a female associate of mine to stay for a few days. A hotel won't do and I'm simply out of options. I need a favor. I know it's a complicated matter to ask you, but I have no one else."

After more silence, the voice began to speak.

"It's more than a complicated matter, Henri, it's an outrageous request which you have no right to make under the circumstances. Why should I do anything for a strange woman and you," her voice raising an octave, "Especially you!"

"I think you've caused me enough grief. Let her stay at your apartment. You've always seemed quite able to accommodate women there before without difficulty."

Her words, biting, rang true and Bertrand felt revulsion as they registered. The words conjured up some long-ago memories that had been relegated to a far corner of his mind, reserved for the stupid things he'd done.

Bertrand inhaled and replied softly. "Let me stop by…meet her. If you still won't help her, I won't persist, and I'll leave immediately. I'm asking this favor for old times' sake."

She laughed cynically. "Don't waste my time, Henri. You've done enough of that in the past."

"I never meant to hurt you. I know I did, and I can never make that up to you. I have no right to ask you for anything, but I'm not asking for myself. I'm asking for someone else. I would never have telephoned you if I had another option, but I don't have another option. You're my last hope. I'm asking you to please help, meet her and then decide."

He held his breath waiting for her to reply. When she finally did, he let out the air in a rush.

"Thank you. We'll be at the gallery shortly. Thank you."

Bertrand hung up, and walked to a large beverage refrigerator, opened the door, and took out several bottles of water. He paid the clerk and walked with Kathy back to the street.

Twisting the cap, he handed her one of the bottles. He watched as she took a long drink then he lit a cigarette.

When she brought the bottle away from her lips, she smiled. "That tasted great."

She reached up and took off her wig. Shaking her head back and forth, he watched as her blonde hair flew with each movement. She placed the wig in the brown shopping bag and looked up.

"Okay, Henri, I'm ready to meet your friend."

He stepped off the curb and waited for a passing cab.

Chapter 69

The introduction was strained. Kathy saw the hesitation and reserve in the woman and knew, as a female, that Bertrand and the woman had been intimate. The extent of the intimacy was pure speculation, but she concluded quickly that at one point it was very serious.

"We need your help, Janis. We need a place where Kathy can stay for a few days."

Bertrand wanted to believe that it might be more difficult for the woman to refuse his request once they were seated in front of her, once she saw him again and met Kathy. He was banking on the past, the good part, to somehow win over the situation for the present.

He sat and watched the exchange between the two women. It began tentatively at first and then expanded. Kathy related what she felt necessary and held back other salient details that she was reluctant to reveal, or felt the woman didn't need to know. The woman's questions were pointed and attempted to test the validity of the answers she heard.

Finally, the woman stood up. "I don't think I can help you."

Then she faced Bertrand. "Stay out of my life," and with that walked out of her office and into the gallery. Tom saw her, and moved in her direction, excusing himself from a browsing couple.

"Is everything okay, Janis?"

"I think so."

They both watched as Kathy and Bertrand came out of the office and into the gallery area. They walked toward the standing pair and stopped several paces away.

Tom, anticipating trouble, tensed. The woman remained relaxed.

Kathy smiled at the woman. "We both appreciate your time. Thank you for meeting with us."

Bertrand stood there saying nothing. When Kathy finished, they walked out the gallery's door, paused on the sidewalk in front, and then walked to their left.

Betrand didn't want to believe how the meeting ended. He was so sure the outcome would be different. As a result, they were still dangling without a safety net.

Since he left 47th Street, he hadn't checked in for hours, violating every rule he'd been trained to observe. His career was over anyway, one way or another, it was finished.

As they passed a leather shop, Kathy pulled on Bertrand's arm bringing him back to the moment. She pointed toward the window.

"We were here before, Henri, although it seems like a long time ago. Do you remember?"

"I do. You mentioned that you'd like to come back here when they were open. How's that for a memory?"

"It's good, let's go in."

"Sure, why not? At least we get off the street."

Bertrand held the door open as Kathy moved past him and into the store. A matronly looking woman came from behind the counter.

"Good afternoon. Is there anything specific you're looking for?"

"Just looking," and both women smiled at each other.

Kathy moved to the several lazy Susan display tables in the center of the room, each holding a number of leather purses and accessories.

Bertrand's attention was directed to several small, tinted glass globes placed in the ceiling. Then he moved to one of the two leather chairs that flanked the door and watched as Kathy examined several items. Placing his chin in one of his hands, Betrand tried to think through a solution to their ongoing problem.

Eventually Kathy handed the saleswoman a black leather purse, together with her credit card.

"The leather is as soft as butter."

"It's our signature trademark, Miss. The leather is finished here, on site. Until it's perfect, it's not brought up to the retail section. Our store has been discovered by the Japanese tourists who make us a mandatory stop when they visit New York."

Kathy signed the receipt and handed it back to the woman. "When the Japanese consider your leather goods a must have, you've definitely made it. Thanks for the help."

The saleswoman smiled as she handed Kathy the gift-wrapped purse.

The dialogue between the two women refocused Bertrand's attention. He stood up as Kathy reached the door and then started following her out. When she stopped suddenly, they collided.

"What's the matter, Kathy?"

"I paid for this," and she pointed to the wrapped purse, "with my credit card."

"It would have been better if you hadn't, but if a trace is made, so what. We're not coming back here."

"I think that I ought to get the key from Oscar."

"What key, who's Oscar?"

"He's the restaurant owner...the place where I stayed last night."

"Okay. Did you tell me his name before? I can't remember."

"I don't know…maybe. I'm not sure."

Then they both laughed, not really knowing why.

"I don't have anything better to suggest. It's chancy but…"

They walked an additional block and then Kathy stopped and turned toward him. "Henri, I have two guns that I took from the guards at my apartment. I don't want them anymore."

"Where are they?"

"Tucked in my waist."

"Okay…move into me."

As their bodies touched Bertrand's hand moved to Kathy's midsection. He took one of the pistols and placed it at the small of his back. The other he tucked into the left side of his waist.

He decided they'd take the F train rather than a taxi. It was a mistake. The subway was crowded with school kids, New York's teeming underclass, who played their boomboxes loudly, indifferent, and uncaring for the feelings of their fellow passengers.

Kathy and Bertrand watched as they swung on the poles and danced in the narrow aisles. A

Puerto Rican, marked with several tattoos, dodged an oncoming associate, and fell into Bertrand's lap.

Henri shoved him up and with the sole of his shoe propelled him forward. The force drove the boy into several dancing kids who in turn fell onto several seated passengers.

Bertrand watched as the boy righted himself, turned, and stared. The boy was debating whether to make something more out of the situation, when a girl grabbed his arm and pulled him away.

Several stops later, at the Cortlandt Street station, the majority of the kids started to exit the train car. The boy hesitated then came over to Bertrand and hovered over him.

As he was about to swing, Bertrand's right foot came up with as much force as he could garner from his seated position and smashed it into the boy's crouch.

The Puerto Rican screamed in pain as he fell to the floor. Several of his companions started toward the seated pair when Bertrand stood up and straddled the withering boy on the floor.

Then he opened his jacket just wide enough to reveal the butt and part of the blue steel casing of the pistol's receiver.

He pointed down at the boy and with a head and hand motion, indicated they should take their friend away.

They grabbed the screaming boy by his legs and dragged him through the opened subway car doors.

Bertrand sat down to applause from several seated passengers.

He turned to Kathy. "Whose idea was it to take the subway?"

She just smiled.

Bertrand shifted his eyes away from Kathy and watched the few kids who still remained in the car. They were eerily silent.

Bertrand heard Kathy let out a sigh when they reached their stop. They took a cab from the station, instructing the driver to let them out a block before the restaurant.

"I have the number." Kathy brought out the crumpled paper and handed it to him.

"Please telephone Oscar and tell him a man who will introduce himself as George will pick up the keys." He handed the paper back to her along with his cell.

She spoke, then listened and ended the conversation with a "Thank you."

"Wait here. I'll be back momentarily. Don't panic and don't leave."

Kathy smiled hesitantly and moved back against the building's wall. "Hurry please."

Bertrand started to jog then slowed down, trying not to attract undue attention from peering eyes.

*

The man watched the traffic in and out of the restaurant, unaware of the two passengers who were discharged from the cab a block away. But he did notice the jogging man who slowed down about a hundred feet from the restaurant's entrance.

As he turned toward the wall, he placed the cell phone to his ear and waited. Shimon's voice came on the line.

"Bertrand just entered the restaurant."

"Is the woman with him?"

"Negative."

"Does he know you?"

"I don't think so, but I can't be sure."

"Okay, let's not spook him. Don't go in, but when he's on the move, get close enough to keep him in lockstep. The woman is around...close by."

Then remembering the woman used a rear exit, Shimon added, "There's a rear exit that the woman used. I'm betting the man will use it as well. Get positioned so you've got a visual on it and do it now."

The man slipped the phone into his side pocket as he ran in the direction the man had initially come. If the woman was around, she would be somewhere in that direction. Bertrand would eventually come back to her. If he guessed wrong, he'd make a u-turn at the end of the block and take up a position where he could observe the rear of the restaurant.

He slowed down as he neared the corner, then crossed on a diagonal. As he reached the sidewalk paralleling the cross street, he saw her huddled against the wall.

He retraced his steps back to the corner and when he was out of her line of sight, took out the cell phone.

"She's here. I've got her in a visual. No sign of Bertrand yet...probably still at the restaurant."

"Don't lose them."

The man pocketed the phone, then moved several steps behind a double-parked truck, which provided cover and gave him a line of sight in three directions.

He watched as the woman, obviously nervous, paced, stopped, then leaned against the building's wall.

She kept repeating the jittery sequence until a taxi slowed and pulled to the curb. The door opened and she was inside within seconds.

The man watched as the cab pulled away and merged into the flow of traffic.

He took out the phone cursing silently as he realized that he was losing his target.

"Bertrand used a taxi for the pickup. Longrin is with him and I'm out of the loop."

"Come in," and then the connection was broken.

Chapter 70

Steiger listened to the transcribed message, and the unfamiliar voice, as it was re-routed from Illinois. The voice outlined the order and conditions of the exchange scheduled for ten p.m.

When he hung up, he smiled, knowing that the caller did not have his daughter. Wherever she was, she wasn't with them. That thought provided some minor consolation.

*

The cab discharged Bertrand and Kathy in front of Oscar's building.

"I'll go up with you, just to make sure everything is okay."

"That's not necessary, Henri, once I'm inside the building, I'm fine."

"No, I'm not leaving until I know that apartment is sterile and you're locked in tight."

She shrugged her shoulders and started toward the steps. They moved up through semi-darkness until they reached the third floor landing which was shrouded in subdued light.

"I don't remember so many lights out at one time."

"Be careful, Kathy. Someone should get the manager clued in."

515

Bertrand motioned her to one side of the doorframe of the apartment as he slipped the key into the lock. He turned the key slowly and then gave the door a push. As it creaked open, he stepped back.

He held up his hand as Kathy took a step toward the doorway. She backed off and remained motionless.

Bertrand listened and then took a tentative step into the room. He moved in further assuming a crouched position with his pistol held horizontally in front of him.

His eyes quickly scanned his surroundings, then he moved to the small kitchen, the smaller den-like bedroom, and the tiny bathroom.

Three rooms had been cleared with only the owner's bedroom remaining. He cautiously entered, then stopped, as the musty smell hit him. He put his hand to his mouth and moved toward the small closet.

Seeing nothing, he turned around anxious to get out of the room. As Bertrand started back toward the entrance, he called out, "It's clean, Kathy. Come on in."

Kathy didn't respond. He raced to the hallway and felt his heart pound as he stared into emptiness in both directions.

He moved to the staircase and looked down at the landings, then took the steps two at a time, until he reached the foyer. He pushed the door open, as his inner rage was building. He took hold of the handrail and using it for balance, leaped the five steps to the sidewalk.

There was no sign of her, nothing in either direction or across the street. She'd vanished. Bertrand decided to go back in the building, retrace his steps and do a systematic search from the top of the building down. Then he remembered the keys were still in Oscar's apartment door lock and there was no way to re-enter the building.

*

Minutes before, as Bertrand entered the apartment, two men immediately moved on their prey from the shadow of the hallway. There was no opportunity for evasive action on the part of the woman. It happened too quickly. The guard cupped his hand over her mouth and with the other hand brought it to her forehead and tilted her head back.

Aviv grabbed her around her chest and locked her arms to her side. As they carried her down the hallway, she tried to free herself.

Aviv let go and slapped her with a glancing blow to her face. Her eyes widened, revealing the pain and shock of the blow and then they slowly registered on the man who held his index finger to his lips.

He whispered, "The next time will be substantially harder. Do you understand?"

She nodded.

The guard still maintained his grip over her mouth as he pushed her forward. They descended the steps like Siamese twins. Every time Kathy tripped, the guard applied pressure to his grip until she managed to painfully regain her footing.

They were out on the street in less than a minute. He released his grip and pushed her forward.

"Dead or alive, it makes no difference to us. Keep your mouth shut and run to the parked car."

Aviv opened the rear door and motioned for Kathy to get in. The guard went quickly around to the other side sandwiching the woman in between them.

The driver turned around. "Miss Longrin, you've caused us some very real problems."

She gasped as she saw Shimon's face.

"How did you know we'd...I'd be here...how?" Then her voice went quiet.

Shimon turned back to his front and pulled away from the curb. In forty minutes, they were parked in front of 47th Street.

In another ten minutes Kathy Longrin was seated in Shimon's office surrounded by the guard and Aviv.

"Please relax, Miss Longrin. Mr. Bertrand will be here shortly."

Hearing the words caused her face to reveal the feelings she was experiencing, despite her attempt to maintain a neutral look. It was a combination of concern and fear, as much for Bertrand as herself. She knew that she would not be able to escape from these people again.

She wondered how the security chief was so certain Bertrand would show up and why didn't he mention the dead guard...the woman she killed at her apartment? Maybe he was saving that for the final mea culpa.

Her thoughts were diverted as she watched Shimon write something on a piece of paper. Then she followed his eyes as they came up from the paper and looked directly at her.

"We're going to make a phone call, Miss Longrin. You will say what's written on this paper, nothing more and nothing less."

Kathy took the paper from the outstretched hand, turned it around, and started reading.

'Papa, this is Karta. Please help me.'

She held the paper with both hands as if she were afraid to let go. Then she slowly moved her hands to her lap and sat staring at Shimon as he dialed.

After a moment, he handed her the phone. At the same instant, Aviv moved closer and placed his hand on her shoulder.

When the connection was made, she spoke the first word and then her mouth went dry. She immediately felt the hand squeeze her shoulder and she winced in pain. A whimper escaped as the pressure on her shoulder was increased. Then she began speaking again and the pressure subsided.

"Papa, this is Karta." She took a deep breath before continuing. "Please help me."

Aviv yanked the phone from her hand and held it out to Shimon.

"Very good, Miss Longrin. You're a quick learner."

Kathy stared back feeling nothing but hatred for these people.

"You are to be exchanged for Raphael tonight."

Kathy sat motionless.

"In the meantime, we'll wait for Bertrand. Please make yourself comfortable. Oh yes, Miss Longrin, Bertrand will be here shortly."

Kathy didn't answer him. She stared through him, lost in her own thoughts.

*

Bertrand got out of the cab hurriedly, hooking his jacket on the door handle and tearing the pocket.

He walked quickly across the ground floor, then shifted his weight back and forth as he waited impatiently for the elevator.

At the secretary's desk he was instructed to wait. The secretary handed the phone to one of the guards who nodded then handed it back to her.

He faced Bertrand with his Uzi leveled at his midsection.

"Please hand me your weapon, Mr. Bertrand."

Bertrand took out the pistol from his waist, and handed it to the guard, butt first. The other guard moved in front and began a pat down. The weapon at the small of his back was quickly detected, as was his ankle holster. Satisfied, he motioned Henri through the doors and into the sorting room.

"Where to?"

"Shimon's office."

Bertrand led the way with the guard trailing.

At the entrance, the guard reversed direction and another guard accompanied Bertrand into the security chief's office.

As Shimon stood up, Kathy turned around. Seeing Bertrand, she began to cry silently, only the tears streaked her cheeks.

He started toward her, but Aviv moved quickly in-between.

Henri tried to push him aside, but Aviv grabbed Bertrand cross-handed by the collar driving him back and at the same time applying pressure to his throat. The more he struggled, the more the pressure cut off his circulation and his breathing.

He let his body relax and felt the pressure loosen. Aviv looked at Bertrand while still holding him cross-handed by the collar. "We understand each other, don't we?"

Bertrand nodded yes.

Shimon had moved around his desk and taken up a position next to the two men.

"I want you to sit down in the chair next to Miss Longrin. Say nothing unless you are spoken to. Is what I've just said clear?"

Bertrand didn't immediately respond, and Aviv tightened his grip again. Bertrand nodded and the hands came away.

He brought his right hand up to his neck, rubbed it and then moved his head from side to side slowly. He coughed and then moved to the chair. Once he was seated, he took hold of Kathy's hand.

Shimon went back to his desk and sat on one of the corners facing Kathy and Bertrand.

"The exchange will take place tonight. You will be taken to the conference room and will remain there until tonight. If you try anything, Mr. Bertrand, I will have you killed."

Shimon slid off the desk, nodded his head to the two men and turned his back on the seated pair.

Aviv touched both their shoulders and they stood up. He pointed to the door.

Chapter 71

Shimon dialed the gallery.

"The message left by your daughter should dispel any speculation regarding her whereabouts. You will be advised of the location shortly," and then he replaced the phone.

He picked up the phone again and touched two buttons. "Inform Pincus and Phil to come to my office immediately."

Once the two men were seated, Shimon began speaking.

"We have Longrin back along with Bertrand. They're under guard in Raphael's conference room."

"The situation has stabilized, but we're altering the plan away from the 28th Street dock. Since Bertrand can't be trusted, the location has to change. We have to assume that he's revealed something, or everything to the woman."

"The exchange will take place in Battery Park, at the old Fort Clinton. You'll station her off on the left side near the pathway that runs in front of the Fort. There's good cover on both sides of the fort and the river to its rear."

"I want Pincus to be zeroed in on her at all times. Phil will concentrate on Steiger. I'll be with the two snipers, and Aviv will be near the woman."

"Longrin and Aviv will be visible from each of the six paths leading to the fort. I want both of you set up and ready before their arrival. Aviv will accompany you and the woman to the park. It goes down as we discussed except for the location change. We'll be along shortly after you leave. Once we're in place, we'll signal...you acknowledge."

Kathy was taken down the service elevator. Her hands were bound, and she was taken to a waiting car.

They made their way through surprisingly heavy traffic for that time of night and when they reached the West River Drive, headed south toward the southern tip of Manhattan.

The car stopped at the Lafayette Street entrance to Battery Park. While the three stood by the front passenger's side, Phil Goldman went to the trunk and removed two large canvas bags.

Aviv touched Kathy's arm, "Cry out and we'll finish you here."

He pushed her forward.

As she walked, Pincus and Aviv took up positions flanking her with Phil Goldman bringing up the rear. They moved along one of the paths leading to Fort Clinton.

Foot traffic was minimal, but that was changing with the influx of the usual nocturnal visitors composed of the drug seekers and sellers, the prostitutes, homosexuals, and a few uniformed and undercover cops.

Aviv couldn't help but wonder about the location change. It was definitely Shimon's backup plan, but it was too open and presented too many possibilities for a classic screw up.

It was a short walk to the bricked fort. Off to the left were several heavy wrought iron and wooden park benches. Aviv tapped her shoulder and pointed to one. "Move."

Kathy stood in front of the bench waiting for the next command. She felt a hand take hold of her wrists and the plastic straps that bound her hands fall away. Aviv turned to his two companions. "Watch her."

He moved to the bench and slipped the straps between two horizontal wooden planks in the seating area.

"Sit down, Miss Longrin, at the end of the bench and place your hands behind your back."

She felt the plastic straps being re-attached. The way the straps were looped through the seating area, her hands were locked to the bench itself.

Aviv moved back to where he placed one of the canvas bags and took out a four-inch wide hemp belt with Velcro tabs. Molded around the hemp belt was a half-pound block of C-4 plastic explosive. Inserted in the C-4 was a blasting cap and twenty-five inches of primer cord.

Aviv leaned into the seated woman and wrapped the belt around her waist. He took up the slack and then pressed the Velcro ends together. He buttoned her jacket covering the belt and primer cord except for about three inches that hung loosely outside the jacket.

"A little something to make the night more interesting."

"What are you doing to me? What is this?"

"Shut up, Longrin."

Kathy felt the tears again. She was literally falling apart. She had no reserve left.

She looked down at the exposed tip of the primer cord, which she concluded was a fuse of some kind.

Her mind formed image after image of the unimaginable. She was strapped to a bench with some type of explosive device around her waist.

Shimon picked up the telephone and re-dialed the gallery.

"This is the last message you'll receive. Your daughter will be at Battery Park near the old fort. She will be wired with an explosive device." Then Shimon paused for effect.

"Steiger is to take Duchant to the area where the eight stone slabs memorializing the World War II dead are located. It's to the south of Fort Clinton abutting the river. At ten p.m. you will walk along the path toward the Fort. When you see your daughter, you stop and at that point you release Duchant. He will walk unassisted to where your daughter is. After we have Duchant, you will wait five minutes, three hundred seconds, before you approach your daughter."

"If you do anything that is contrary to these instructions, your daughter will light up the night's sky like the Fourth of July. The ultimate decision is yours. If you want to test us, you're as dead as your daughter."

With that, Shimon hung up, motioned to two men waiting by the door. Then all three left the building.

Chapter 72

Schwimler listened intently as the Doctor repeated his instructions. After he finished, Schwimler clicked his heels, bowed slightly, and left.

At nine p.m., Duchant, supported by two of his torturers, walked unsteadily to the van. Unable to climb in under his own power, he was hoisted up by two sets of hands and pushed into the rear seat. He fell on his right side causing new waves of pain to reverberate up and down his arm.

The van reached Battery Park's West Street entrance at twenty-five after nine. One of the men handed Schwimler a portable wheelchair, which he unfolded in one fluid motion and locked in place.

Duchant was pulled from the van and shoved into the wheelchair. Then he was strapped in, his arms immobilized, and a blanket placed over his lap.

Schwimler, dressed in the uniform of a New York City policeman, went to the rear of the van, grabbed a dark green polyethylene bag and walked to the back of the wheelchair.

He opened the bag and removed a MAC-10 machine gun with silencer and a thirty-round magazine. He placed the weapon in the pouch compartment behind the wheelchair's seat.

"Try to be a hero and you're dead."

Duchant heard the words clearly. He was too tired, too weak, and too physically damaged to present much of a threat.

A man dressed in Steiger's clothing, his face obscured by the minimal light and a gray fedora pulled down so that the brim rested just above his eyebrows, started pushing Duchant up the path that would lead to the East Coast Memorial.

Schwimler walked to the passenger's side of the van, listened as the seated man spoke, then started walking in the same direction as the wheelchair. After sixty yards he turned off on a path that would lead to the front of Fort Clinton.

As he neared the Fort, he saw the woman and a man seated together. Schwimler continued walking toward them at a slow pace, ambling along, and appearing like a bored New York city cop on the eight to twelve graveyard shift.

"Getting chilly tonight folks, isn't it?"

The man answered, "Yes," and smiled back at the officer. He moved closer to the woman and started to place his arm around her shoulders.

Kathy thought about screaming, then thought about what was strapped to her waist. If it was a fuse...an explosive, he would have to light it wouldn't he, and he couldn't in this position.

She decided to chance it when she felt something sharp press against the side of her neck.

"I wouldn't plan on staying here too long folks. You never can tell who might be loitering about."

"We'll only be here a little while longer, officer, and then we're off."

Schwimler nodded and then started off in the direction of the granite pylons that composed the East Coast Memorial.

When he was out of sight, Aviv took his hand away from around her shoulder. He moved his hand in front of her face so that Kathy clearly saw the razor blade that was held between the man's middle and fourth finger.

"I would have cut your throat if you did what you were thinking, and I'd have been forced to kill the cop."

Kathy shivered, but said nothing.

Aviv placed the razor blade on the bench to his left. Then he took out a pack of cigarettes and tapped one out. He placed it in his mouth and lit it with a Zippo lighter cupped between his hands. He blew out the smoke without inhaling.

"Smoking is so bad for your health," and then he laughed quietly.

He reached over toward Kathy and opened her jacket. His hand moved to the C-4 belt and her stomach muscles contracted instinctively. Without saying anything, he took hold of the primer cord

531

and moved it across her lap, extending it to its full length.

"The cord doesn't burn, it explodes. You'll only get out of this alive after we have Duchant. Even if I don't get to light the fuse, others will make sure you're dead before anyone can reach you."

As Aviv reached for the razor blade, he heard the sound of a cricket. The sound was repeated twice more. He reached into his pocket and pulled out his clicker. He pressed once, waited several seconds, then pressed again. Shimon and his men were in place.

He pushed the clicker back in his pocket, then moved his hand to the razor blade and maneuvered it again between his fingers.

Satisfied, he looked back at the woman. She was staring at his face and watching the smoke rise from the cigarette dangling from his lips. Her hatred was evident.

Aviv stared back at her and then felt the need to respond. "The cigarette…I'll light the primer cord with the cigarette. The razor blade will be used to cut the cord before it detonates, but who knows if I'll succeed or want to."

Then he turned his head away and looked around the immediate area, knowing that his words caused the woman more anxiety. He could care less. The only feeling he felt for the woman was revulsion. She was the daughter of a Nazi SS-General who was part of the final solution and a woman who probably harbored many of his sentiments. As far as he was concerned, she existed only as means to recover Duchant.

He heard the sound which resembled a moving cart, off to his right. Then he saw the wheelchair and the man pushing it.

Aviv remained motionless as the wheelchair came closer. He whispered to the woman, "Keep silent."

His hand went to the weapon in his waistband. He fingered it, then moved his hand away. He took the cigarette away from his mouth and held it near the primer cord.

The man pushing the wheelchair stopped in place approximately twenty yards from the seated pair.

Aviv nodded his head, and the man moved to the side of the wheelchair.

The bound, seated figure slumping forward was Duchant.

Aviv called out softly, "Untie him."

The man leaned into Duchant and began removing the straps. He braced Duchant with his shoulder and then lifted the man to a standing position.

He moved his mouth close to Duchant's ear and whispered, "Your freedom awaits you twenty yards from here," and the man pointed.

"Walk!"

Duchant heard the words and willed his legs to take the first step toward the bench. Despite squinting to focus his eyes, he couldn't clearly distinguish who the two seated figures were.

After several steps, Duchant fell. He tried to get up, but his weakened condition prevented him. He remained on the cement pathway in a semi-conscious state.

Aviv, still holding the end of the fuse, called out, "Pick him up, and place him back in the chair. Then shove the wheelchair in this direction."

The man did as he was instructed but didn't re-strap Duchant. As he pushed the chair, Duchant's body shifted, and fell out, stopping the chair's forward moment about ten yards from the bench.

A thin smile crossed the man's lips as he started to move toward the sprawled body.

He was beside the chair and stooping down to pick up Duchant when Aviv said, "No further. Leave him there and move back."

The man moved quickly behind the wheel chair, and with one hand on a handle started moving it backward. The other hand secured the MAC-10 machine gun.

"Leave the wheelchair where…" Aviv never got to finish the command.

The swing moment of the MAC-10 was fluid and the short burst of .45 caliber rounds hitting Aviv's chest made his body dance in a grotesque fashion. The woman shrieked as the blood, bone and sinew splattered her face and neck.

The man ran several steps toward the woman, spun around, then fell forward. His body hit Kathy full force, then crumpled to the ground by her feet.

She was screaming hysterically and struggling to free herself. Her fear and anxiety heightened at each passing second, unable to comprehend what was happening and realizing that she could not get free because of the plastic restraints.

The blue uniformed New York City cop came running along the path, his pistol drawn.

Schwimler reached the woman and said in German, "I am here to help you."

He pushed Aviv's body away and then saw the dangling end of the fuse. He opened her jacket and saw the Velcro explosive belt. Deciding to leave it in place momentarily, his hands reached behind her back and undid the plastic handcuffs.

As Schwimler straightened up several soft pops sounded, and he toppled to his right. His body hit Kathy's legs on its downward descent, then came to rest partly on top of the other dead German.

She brought her hands around to her waist and pulled off the Velcro belt. Peripherally, Kathy saw several figures coming toward her.

She started running, her fright fusing her adrenaline rush and propelling her forward beyond what she thought she was capable of. She had no sense of direction, she just ran blindly ahead.

Kathy cut off the path into some vegetation and continued to run when she became aware of the sound of broken twigs behind her.

She ran on, silently praying that she could distance herself from her pursuers or find someone to help.

Then she saw them…the figures that stepped out from the underbrush, but her momentum caused her to run headlong into both knocking one to the ground.

The standing man grabbed Kathy by the shoulders and quietly said, "This way, Karta."

The woman struggled at first then recognized the voice. It was the voice of her father.

Chapter 73

The man with Steiger picked himself up quickly and assumed a crouch position while Kathy and her father made their way back to the park's West Street entrance.

As Pincus and Phil Goldman moved through the underbrush, the German fired off several rounds. The quiet thuds burrowing into the trees and ground around them indicated that their attacker was using a silencer attachment.

Both men dropped to prone positions and began crawling. There was no sign of the attacker and in the darkness, they couldn't be sure if they were even near the location the attacker used.

The immediate ground didn't reveal any spent shell casings. In the darkness, it would have been blind luck if any were found.

They moved to a path on their left.

"I'll head toward the fort to hook up with Shimon and Duchant, then move to the Lafayette Street entrance. Take the right quadrant, Phil, and meet us at Lafayette."

Phil nodded and started off in a slow jog.

Pincus ran back along the path that led to the fort. As the fort came into view, Shimon and Duchant were gone as well as the bodies of Aviv, the policeman, and the German who pushed the wheelchair.

He started running toward the Lafayette Street entrance when he came upon Shimon pushing the wheelchair. Shimon was bent forward in an awkward position.

As Pincus moved closer he saw the chair held the body of Aviv with Duchant strapped in and sitting on top of the dead man.

He moved to the chair and started pushing.

"What happened to the other bodies?"

"In the tree line next to the fort. We need to get out of here." Then pointing to Duchant, "He needs some medical help and we're still in the shit ourselves."

A hooker started toward Shimon and Pincus when she noticed the overloaded wheelchair. She reversed direction and was quickly out of sight.

As they neared the Lafayette Street entrance, they were approached by two drunken panhandlers, who couldn't or didn't want to make sense out of what they saw. Pincus cursed them out, then turned back toward Shimon who had moved the wheelchair next to the parked van.

They loaded the body of Aviv and the wheelchair into the rear, then took Duchant to the front passenger side. They lifted him onto the seat then Pincus climbed in and held Raphael upright until Shimon slid into the driver's side. Once he was inside, they were able to brace Duchant between them.

Shimon pointed to the windshield.

Pincus looked and saw the parking ticket.

"Lucky we didn't get towed."

Shimon mumbled to himself, "Come on, Phil, get here damn it."

Then said more loudly, "We'll give him several more minutes, Pincus, then we're gone."

They sat in edgy silence both anxious to distance themselves from the park. Then without saying anything to Pincus, Shimon started the engine, put the gear shift in drive and began pulling away from the curb, when something hit the van's rear quarter panel.

Shimon jammed his foot on the brake pedal and held onto the steering wheel as the front right tire bounced over the curb. Pincus looked out his window and saw Phil Goldman standing mid-way back.

"He's here," and then inched over on the seat as Phil opened the door.

"Close the damn door, get in the back, and let's get out of here."

The door closed with a thud as the van picked up speed.

"I didn't see any sign of Longrin. I made a canvass around the right side as far as the ticket booth. The woman is long gone."

Shimon kept one hand on the wheel as he hit the speed dial on his cell.

"Doctor Barab, sorry to wake you, it's Raphael."

Shimon listened and then replied, "No… this is not Raphael calling. Raphael is the one that's hurt. We should be at your home in twenty-five minutes."

He listened again then said, "I can't be sure, but he doesn't appear to be shot. Look Doc, just get ready. We'll be there shortly."

The van made its way up the u-shaped driveway and stopped in front of a doorway at the far left side of the house.

The door opened before they reached the first step.

"Bring him in."

Phil and Pincus carried Duchant through a hallway which led to an examining room.

"Place him on the table."

Duchant let out a groan as his right arm made contact with the metal table. The doctor cut away Duchant's clothing and began his examination as Shimon and the other two men moved in for a closer look.

The cuts on Duchant's chest were still oozing blood. Shimon started to say something, then stopped.

The doctor kept his eyes on Duchant as he began speaking. "He has a broken wrist, several broken fingers, his chest and arm has been cut with a sharp instrument and will require stitches. He is dehydrated, and probably hasn't eaten or slept in a while. His face shows signs of blunt trauma. Outside of that and a few other items, he's in perfect health."

Phil and Pincus looked toward Shimon who motioned them with his head. "We'll wait outside, Doc, and let you do what you have to do."

Shimon turned and, followed by the other two men, walked out of the room.

When they were outside, he said softly, "They've worked him over pretty good. We've lost the woman and didn't get Steiger, but we have Raphael back."

"What do you mean we didn't get Steiger? I know the two rounds I put in the Nazi were all in the kill zone. I saw him take a few steps, drop, and he didn't get up. He was dead."

Phil kept looking at Shimon, waiting for him to reply. Pincus stared as well, confused, and unsure as he shifted his weight.

"You killed the man pushing the wheelchair, but it wasn't Steiger. There was no way to confirm it, one way or the other, until I examined the body.

He was the approximate height, build, and weight, but he wasn't Steiger."

"Shit," and Goldman looked at Pincus who just shook his head, then turned away staring into the night.

It was a number of seconds before Phil Goldman spoke again.

"Okay, Shimon, we didn't get him, now what? I don't want the Nazi to get away," he paused, "especially now," and he pointed back at the house. "And I don't want to turn it over to the authorities through a discreet phone call or note. I want to settle it…I want us to finish what we've started. Aviv was my friend, he was a friend to all of us."

His eyes bore into the security chief.

"I feel the same way as both of you do, but right now we need to get Raphael mended. Aviv will be sent home for burial."

Shimon saw the look on both their faces.

"Look, I hurt just like you both do, but now is not the time to feel sorry ourselves or swear revenge. We need clear heads. Any future course of action will be free of emotion. Let the Doc finish and we'll get Raphael to a safe house and then get some sleep. It's already another day, time enough to hack out a plan. Agreed?"

Both men nodded, then moved slightly off from each other to be alone in their own space.

As Shimon sat on a porch step, he let his mind freewheel. The mistakes were evident. It was always that way. Hindsight was always twenty-twenty. One of his crew was dead. Duchant was battered, but alive, and the target was heading for sanctuary with his daughter.

Shimon came awake with the sound of the door opening. He looked up from his sitting position on the porch step and nodded to the doctor.

The doctor simply said, "I'm finished. Please take him."

Shimon motioned to the two men who had come over to the porch as soon as the doctor appeared. "Get him and be gentle."

Then he stood up and asked, "What's the status?"

"I've set the broken wrist and fingers and stitched up the cuts on his body and face. It took thirty-nine stitches. I've given him a small quantity of water. He needs food, gradually at first, then build the intake up until his eating pattern becomes normal. The dressings should be changed every two days. The splint stays on for six weeks minimum."

He handed Shimon several bottles of pills. "The instructions are written on the label. Make sure he takes them until the bottles are empty."

Shimon nodded. "The money will be wire transferred into your account as usual."

Both men stepped aside as Pincus and Phil Goldman carried Duchant to the van.

Raphael smiled weakly as he passed Shimon, who reached out and touched his arm.

"Thanks, Doc," then Shimon followed his men to the van.

Chapter 74

Kathy clung to her father. The man's arms gave her the reassurance she craved. At that moment, she was beyond the realm of rational thinking. She was again that little girl of so long ago, seeking comfort and reassurance in the arms of someone she trusted and loved.

As the vehicle moved through the night, Kathy was oblivious to everything except the nearness of her father.

When the vehicle stopped, she lifted her head from his shoulder, apprehensive, but comfortable in the feeling that she was protected.

She stepped out with the aid of her father and another man and saw that she was in front of the same leather store that she had visited with Bertrand.

She didn't fully comprehend why they were there, then her father's voice, which sounded so far away, said, "Karta, please come."

She moved, not really feeling that she was in control. It was as if her body was in suspended animation and she was watching herself walk in slow motion.

They entered the store and turned to their right, where two armed men stood guard. After a brief exchange which Kathy didn't pay attention to, they took the stairs up until they reached the second floor.

The entire floor was an open loft with three closed rooms, a lavatory at the far end, a seating area, and an ample kitchen.

They walked to the seating area, then the man who accompanied them in the vehicle asked if her father would like a drink.

"Ja, I'll have a whiskey."

Then he turned to Kathy who replied. "I'll take a double scotch on the rocks."

The man clicked his heels and turned away.

Kathy looked across at her father who stared back but said nothing. The man returned with the drinks and set them down.

"Danke, Rolf."

The man bowed slightly, clicked his heels and walked several paces away taking up a position behind her father's chair. One of the guards from the floor below assumed a position in the doorway.

Kathy stared at the drink which she held in her lap, prompting her father to speak. "It's been a long journey for you, Karta, and that journey has taken you full circle. We are going home tomorrow. I will explain everything to you then."

As she listened to her father's words, she was overcome with both a feeling of dread and relief.

"By noon, Karta, you will be home and safe, now drink up. It will help."

Kathy moved her eyes from the drink to her father. He sat there smiling at her and holding his glass out as an act of encouragement.

She smiled weakly and lifted her glass.

His smile broadened as she watched him sip his drink. Then she brought her glass up to her lips and took a long swallow. The scotch burned her throat, made her feel lightheaded, and had an immediate numbing effect.

She took another long swallow, then brought the glass back to her lap.

"Papa, I need to wash up and sleep. Will you please excuse me?"

Her father said nothing in reply, just smiled.

Then he turned his head toward the man he addressed as Rolf, who immediately approached Kathy.

"If you follow me, Miss Buhler," then he paused as he watched the woman set the glass down and start to rise.

Her father stood up as well, moved several steps toward his daughter and embraced her. Kathy responded in kind, a natural act which had taken place countless times over the years.

Her father moved slightly away. "Sleep well, Karta. We are leaving very early."

Kathy smiled again weakly, then turned toward the other man who motioned with his hand.

"That door over there, Miss Buhler, is your bedroom and the one on the left is a fully equipped lavatory. There are towels and a robe, plus other items that you'll find useful."

Then Rolf turned and followed her father down the stairs. The guard remained at the doorway.

Kathy turned back toward the door and pushed it open. The bedroom was adequate.

She walked out and into the bathroom. It contained a shower, toilet, and a large sink. A robe was hung behind the door. Towels were sitting on a small table to the right of the sink and above the sink was a medicine cabinet with soap, shampoo, shaving items, cologne, perfume, and several feminine hygienic products.

There were several lipstick containers and manicure items. She acted with mild surprise, then realized that this room and the others here were obviously used frequently by both genders.

The shower didn't relieve the tension but at least removed the grime and sweat accumulated over the past hours. She pulled down the bed covering, curled up on top of the blanket and was asleep in seconds.

*

The security chief opened the rear door of the apartment building, then moved aside as Phil Goldman and Pincus hurriedly carried Duchant to the service elevator.

They rode up in silence.

When they were in front of the apartment door, Shimon knocked once.

It was opened immediately, then the man moved against a wall as Duchant was carried directly to one of the bedrooms.

Shimon spoke briefly to the man at the door who nodded and followed the security chief into the living room area. When both men were seated, Shimon started outlining the sequence of events.

The man listened without speaking. When Shimon finished, the man moved his left hand to his lips and shook his head.

Pincus and Phil Goldman came out of the bedroom, looked at Shimon, then walked out the door.

The man looked up. "Where are they going?"

They're taking Aviv to the undertaker. After arrangements are made, he'll be flown home."

The man again assumed the position where his left hand rested against his lips. His eyes were cast down as if he was staring at something that required his full attention.

He didn't look up as he spoke. "It was a poorly handled exchange. An open area at night with insufficient assets in place, is hardly ideal."

Shimon remained calm although he wanted to pounce.

"It was for those very reasons that the area was chosen. We wanted Duchant recovered and Steiger dead, but the primary focus was on getting Duchant back. We had what we needed in place. We all realize that someday our number is up. It's part of the business we're in. Aviv knew that. I'm sorry to lose him...we all are."

He stopped, looked at the man, then felt the need to continue.

"Duchant is back and he'll mend. As far as I'm concerned, the mission is a success. We lost a good man. They lost four of theirs. Four of them doesn't equate to one of ours, but..." and Shimon let his voice fade.

"Perhaps, Shimon, you should get some sleep. We can continue later."

"No, I'm fine, let's continue."

"Good. Time is important. The girl and Steiger are or will be heading to a safe area. That area in my estimation is Illinois, but they won't be there long. Odessa will assist them, and they'll be taken to a safe haven somewhere in South America, Central America, or maybe Europe.

"Some of our men will be operational in Chicago in a few hours. I want to capture or kill Steiger at his farm. Are you interested?"

Shimon smiled. "Count me in. I want to bring along Pincus, Phil Goldman, and Bertrand."

The man nodded. "Where was Bertrand tonight?"

"It's complicated."

"Isn't everything! Break it down for me in a few sentences."

Shimon related the background, then sat back into the chair.

"So why do you want to bring him along?" The mission is fraught with uncertainties and you want to add one more."

Shimon raised his hands indicating that he wasn't entirely sure himself, then responded, "He's a good man, if he can keep focused."

"That's not the part that concerns me."

"It's my judgement call. I'm going back to 47th Street, meet up with Phil and Pincus, and catch a few hours of sleep. Make the plane reservations for four on the first flight out from JFK. Have someone pick us up at baggage. Who's heading up the unit?"

"Mozar."

"I've worked with him in Teheran in '75. Does he lead?"

"Yes."

Shimon shook his head.

After a moment he started walking toward the door when he stopped.

"Take care of Raphael. Shalom." (Goodbye in Hebrew)

Chapter 75

Images and scenes of carnage flashed constantly across her mind. Kathy Longrin's attempt at sleep was nothing more than an effort in futility. So much so, that well before the first light of dawn, she was fully awake and staring at the ceiling.

Image after image cascaded across her mindscreen.

She saw the death camp scenes replayed and the pictures of her father, now so clearly visible. The word description of her father and what he did resounded in her mind. She saw Bertrand reaching for her hand and assuring her that her father and Steiger were the same. She again felt the explosive belt around her waist and the horror it projected suddenly consumed her. She shivered at the thought of the dead men and that park bench.

Kathy reached down and pulled the blanket around her legs. Then she closed her eyes, squeezing them shut to dispel the images. It didn't work. When the knock came, she was fully awake.

"Good Morning, Miss Buhler. There is coffee and some pastries in the kitchen. I was instructed to inform you that we will be leaving in forty-five minutes."

The door didn't open, but she recognized Rolf's voice.

She dressed in the same clothes she wore the previous night and felt self-conscious as only a woman as fastidious as she was, would.

She was in the kitchen within fifteen minutes.

She noticed the guard at the door was different from the one who manned that post the night before and her father was conspicuously absent, as was the man, Rolf.

Kathy brought the coffee and one of the croissants to the seating area and sat in the seat she occupied previously. The coffee was strong and hot and worked to relieve some of the tension.

She looked around the loft, at its simplicity, and wished her life were as uncomplicated.

She knew that her father would place a protective cordon around her, and that protection was all that she was concerned with for the moment. Everything else, including Bertrand, would be pushed to the side, at least for the time being.

Kathy sipped the coffee and tried to relax. She wasn't in the mood for food but forced herself to eat the croissant.

Although she had garnered little sleep, she didn't feel tired, only apprehensive at what lay ahead. She wondered whether Shimon would come after her even though they had Duchant back?

Then she wondered, is revenge a thing for the Jews that outweighed everything else when it came to the camps, or one of their own?

For a moment she didn't feel safe and looked around as if she expected to see something that would endanger her. But that feeling quickly dissipated when she saw her father and Rolf reach the landing and start toward her.

"Good Morning, Karta. Did you sleep well?"

Kathy smiled, stood up, and moved toward her father. They embraced.

"I'm sorry I overlooked a change of clothing for you, but that will be remedied when we get home. Are you ready?"

"Give me another five minutes."

*

Kathy rejoined her father and Rolf and walked to the waiting black Mercedes Benz.

The car moved quickly toward Kennedy airport. About a quarter of a mile from the main entrance, the MB veered off to its left and followed a narrow road that led to a private hanger.

Rolf opened the rear door for her father and then helped her out.

A man in a pilot's uniform standing near an aircraft lifted his hand and then started walking toward her father. After a brief exchange, Steiger motioned to his daughter to follow him.

They boarded the aircraft, a Dassault Falcon 50 Business Jet. She saw the two men in the rear passenger area turn and assumed a position of attention as they entered.

"Sit here, Karta," then her father moved past her to the standing men.

Kathy assumed correctly that these men were part of her father's detail and were an added layer of protection in addition to Rolf and the driver, who was now seated across from her.

Steiger took the seat next to his daughter and signaled the pilot to take off.

Kathy watched through the open cockpit door as the pilot and co-pilot completed their internal pre-flight check.

Her gaze was transfixed on the pilot as he pushed the control lever slowly forward. As the aircraft began taxiing to the far end of the runway, Kathy's mind again reflected on what her future might hold. Her attention span was broken as the reverberation of the jet engines reached their apex.

She felt her body press into the back of her seat as the aircraft thrust forward and reached take-off speed.

In a few minutes, the jet was airborne and turning to its left as it moved steadily upward toward its cruising altitude.

She continued to watch as the pilot corrected the airspeed and then her eyes shifted to the co-pilot who turned around, smiled at her, and then shut the cockpit door.

*

Shimon, Phil, and Pincus walked through the guarded reception area of the 47th Street building and went directly to the security chief's office.

Shimon turned to Phil. "Get Bertrand."

In minutes they walked in together.

Before the security chief could say anything, Phil said, "I've filled Henri in enough so that he's in the loop."

Shimon looked at Bertrand momentarily, then focused on his two men. "We're going to Chicago on the first plane out tomorrow…" Then he shook his head, "Damn, it's already tomorrow, better get a few hours sleep. Be ready to leave at zero four thirty hours."

The security chief looked back at Bertrand. "You're going too, Henri. We'll receive the operation's plan once we've hooked up with the others. I'm going to make some coffee in case anyone is interested."

They shook their heads and started to leave when Shimon called out. "Phil, can you wait a moment?"

Phil Goldman turned back to his chief with questioning eyes.

"Watch Bertrand, watch him well."

Goldman nodded and left.

*

Kathy felt a wave of relief as the jet's tires touched the tarmac. While the apprehension still persisted, the distance now separating her from her adversaries was welcomed.

As she stepped from the plane, she broke into a broad smile when she saw Udo standing beside the station wagon.

Another vehicle, a silver Mercedes Benz S class, was parked next to the station wagon and a man she recognized as someone who was a frequent visitor to the farm, was leaning against the rear fender. He straightened to a standing position as his eyes became fixed on her father.

"I want to talk to that gentleman, Karta. Please go with Udo. I'll follow you in the other car." He smiled and patted her hand.

As an afterthought, he turned back. "Rolf will go with you," then he turned and walked away.

During the entire forty-five minute drive, her mind was at ease. The journey was exhilarating as it always was. Kathy loved to watch the scenery drift by, the level fields, the grazing animals, the barns and farmhouses. She felt her body and mind relax as she thought, I'm back...back where I belong.

Then thoughts about her father's past came flooding back. In moments, those thoughts were replaced by something she remembered him saying... it would all be explained.

She was brought back to the moment as the tires of the station wagon contacted the gravel road that would lead her to her childhood home. As she listened to the sound the tires made, her exhilarating feeling was suddenly replaced by a feeling of foreboding.

As Rolf helped her from the station wagon, she shivered. She was about to say something but was distracted by someone calling her name.

She turned and saw Gerta moving down the steps and running in her funny way toward her.

When the nanny reached Kathy, she threw her arms around her and kissed her on both cheeks. When the old woman released her, Kathy saw the tear-stained cheeks.

The woman had been a surrogate mother to her. She loved this woman as she would have loved her own mother, a mother whom she identified with only through a photograph that rested on a desk in her New York apartment.

Kathy embraced the woman again. "No need for tears, Gerta."

"They are tears of joy. I'm so happy to see you, Karta."

They began walking arm in arm to the main house. When Kathy reached the porch, she turned and waited for her father, who together with the other man were moving slowly, engrossed in what appeared to be a deep conversation.

She called out, "Papa, I'm going to freshen up and change. I'll see you in a little while."

Her father nodded and then Kathy looked at Gerta. "I'm hungry, Gerta, could you fix me some buckwheat pancakes and bacon?"

Gerta smiled, "How soon can you be ready?"

Kathy broke away and opened the door, then walked up the stairs to her room. After she showered and changed into a black cotton sweater, tan britches, and short black riding boots, she started down the stairs and toward the kitchen.

She passed the dining room and noted that the doors were closed.

Seated around the large butcher-block table in the pantry/kitchen were Gerta, Rolf, and Udo. Kathy stopped a few steps into the doorway. "Am I intruding?"

Both Udo and Rolf got up. Gerta smiled. "It's never an intrusion when you appear, little one. Take a seat at the table. I'm making enough for you and these two starving men as well as your father and his guest. Would you like some coffee?"

Kathy nodded, walked several steps to an old scarred wooden farm table and took a seat.

Rolf and Udo left the small butcher-block table they were sitting at and took seats opposite her. In seconds Gerta set three cups of steaming coffee in front of them.

As Kathy picked up her cup, she looked over the rim and saw Udo staring at her.

"Is anything wrong, Oheim (Uncle) Udo?"

"Nein, kleine (No, little one). I'm only pleased you are safe and back with us."

"It's good to be here again, Oheim Udo," and Kathy reached for the back of the older man's hand. His smile broadened at her touch and he clasped his hand over hers, rubbing it softly.

Kathy wondered how much Udo knew of the events encapsulating her recent life. Then quickly deduced, as her father's trusted confidant, bodyguard, and chauffeur, he knew it all.

Rolf appeared indifferent to the physical and emotional interplay taking place between the two. Then Kathy's eyes momentarily locked with his before she quickly looked away.

*

Gerta kept placing pancakes on Kathy's plate until Kathy, laughing loudly, pushed the plate away. "You'll get me so fat, Gerta, that none of my clothes will fit."

The old woman, who seemed smaller in height than Kathy remembered, walked toward the table with a skillet heaped with pancakes.

"Never mind with all that kind of talk. You're withering away to nothing. You need some meat on those bones of yours."

Kathy laughed and Udo joined in.

"Absolutely no more for me. Udo and Rolf can split my portion. I think I'll freshen up a bit and take a ride."

Kathy turned to Udo. "Could you get the Palomino ready for me?"

"It will be saddled and waiting for you, Karta."

Chapter 76

The four men walked through the baggage claim area at Midway Airport, Chicago, and out to the sidewalk. The fifth man, the one who met them, held back, went to the bank of telephones, and dialed a toll-free number.

The man spoke briefly, hung up and went to join the others. In a few minutes, a shuttle van stopped and the five boarded. The van drove to a secure parking facility and discharged its five occupants.

They got into a Buick four-door sedan and proceeded west on 46th Street. The driver made a right onto Cicero Avenue and followed the road until he came to the onramp for the I-55, exiting at Central north. They took Central to Ogden Avenue West and then turned onto 34th Street.

The Buick finally pulled up in front of an eleven thousand square foot concrete warehouse with a sign that read Tela Food Purveyors.

Once inside, Shimon, Phil Goldman, Pincus, and Bertrand followed the man to a small alcove that led to an office complex. The man knocked, and then opened the door.

He moved his hand in a way to motion the four into the room. Then he closed the door.

The four faced a standing man, who was extending his hand toward Shimon.

"Nice to see you again, Shimon."

The Iranian Jew's voice was strong and sincere.

"Likewise, Mozar. These are my men," and he pointed to Pincus, Henri Bertrand, and Phil Goldman, and introduced each by name.

"We're a bit worn, but you can count on us when the time comes. Can you bring us up to speed on the operation?"

"Please come over here," and the Iranian moved toward a metal table whose surface held a series of enlarged aerial photographs.

"These are all high resolution, eight-megapixel digital images. This is the farm of Ludolf Otto Steiger. Notice the guards at the four corners, here," and Mozar pointed to the red circles.

"The green circles here are roving patrols, usually two to three men going in opposite directions and crossing at some point. There are several that patrol the path here," and the Iranian moved his finger back and forth over an area on the photograph. "I will come back to this path in a few moments."

Mozar paused and looked at the four men gathered around him. "Please forgive me for not asking whether you cared for coffee."

"We'll wait, Mozar, until we're finished," then Shimon looked back at the aerial photographs and three other heads moved in tandem.

Mozar nodded and continued.

"This wooded area to the east is constantly patrolled around the perimeter, but the gorge about two hundred yards away is somehow overlooked. There are trip flares and light activators from twilight through dawn that will be set off by any movement through the woods. Only the patrolled path is clean. The house has guards on duty around the clock on rotating shifts, both internally and externally and the perimeter lights are activated from the moment daylight recedes."

"There are two roads leading to and from the main house and, as mentioned, this walking/riding path through the wooded area." Mozar again pointed to the path.

"All the information I've just related to you has been collected, evaluated, interpreted, and correlated from the moment we received the first message from you, Shimon, that Steiger is the owner of the farm."

"The mileage from Chicago to Carthage is approximately two hundred and nine miles. We don't have the time to spare. We are going to jump in."

Mozar looked at Shimon and then each of the men individually. "We don't have a choice."

No one said anything, but Bertrand felt his heart skip a beat. He looked toward the others and assumed they experienced the same jolt.

All four men had completed parachute training in Israel and served in various Israeli Airborne units, but for all of them, it was a long time between then and now.

"We will be departing here within the hour. We will drop approximately two miles from Steiger's farm. The place we've chosen for the DZ (Drop zone) is a recently cultivated field whose owner is about to plant his winter wheat crop. The pilot of the plane thinks we're a parachute club and the field is an authorized drop zone."

"Steiger's guards wear distinctive black cargo-like pants and blouses, with black boots reminiscent of the SS. We have duplicated these as closely as possible, and we will wear these on the jump. It will look, for all intents and purposes, to the pilots and ground crew at the airport, as a uniform of our parachute club. It will also aid en route and when attacking the house. You'll notice a small strip of whitish tape on the back collar and above the left front breast pocket of the blouse. These strips will glow at night enabling us to identify each other."

Mozar saw the look on Shimon's face.

"It's not going to be so bad, my friend. We old paratroopers never forget how to make a soft PLF." (Parachute landing fall)

He turned back to the aerial photographs, "Once on the ground, we'll split into three groups. Two groups will make their way to this gorge," and Mozar traced the two routes with his finger. "At the same time, we're moving toward the gorge, another

566

group composing two teams of two men each will secure the two entrance roads, here and here, both of which lead off Illinois-94. Their mission will be to stop any vehicular traffic moving away from or to the main house at the I-94 junction."

"I want you and your men, Shimon, to envelop left until you reach the path that cuts through the woods, here. You'll appear to anyone who will have a visual on you and your men as just another patrol. You'll take out any guards that you come across as silently as possible. No automatic fire, use the pistols with the silencers."

"When you come out from the path, you'll be approximately fifty yards from the front of the house. You'll signal me by radio with two squelch breaks. Once I acknowledge with one in return, you'll double time across the open space to the house and go through the front door. My men will break through the rear and take out as many as possible, until we have the house cleared. I don't care if Steiger is killed or taken alive. Either way is fine by me. I will augment your group with several of my men."

"If Steiger and his people decide to leave earlier, we'll hit them on the way out. Our transportation away from the operations area will be by their vehicles. Any questions?"

"Good, no questions. Now let me introduce you to the others who are waiting for us. Please follow me."

Behind the closed doors of his study, Steiger listened intently as Obersturmbannführer Herbert Kappler began speaking.

"We have secured Vatican passports for you and your daughter, as well as others that make up your primary staff. These passports will enable you and your party to travel unencumbered. Our friends at the Vatican have a propensity toward us, and the money we pay them."

Both men laughed, and Kappler lifted his whiskey glass. Steiger followed and touched his glass to Kappler's rim. The bell-like sound of the fine crystal glass resembled the sound of a church bell. Steiger thought about the connection, a bell and the Vatican and laughed louder while trying to explain what he was laughing about to Kappler.

"What will happen to the paintings below, and this farm, Herbert?"

"Nothing will change. There will be someone appointed to continue the New York gallery, watch over the paintings and this farm. The important thing now is your safety and your daughter's. Everything else is immaterial," then Kappler smiled.

"Am I at liberty to know where our new home will be?"

"But of course, Ludolf. This is not a secret among us. You will be returning to the Fatherland, to Germany."

568

Steiger smiled broadly and lifted his glass toward the other man who stood up, clicked his heels and said, "Zum Vaterland." (To the Fatherland)

Steiger repeated the toast and drained his glass. He walked to a small table and poured himself another drink, then brought the bottle over to where Kappler was now seated and handed it to him.

Then he sat down, still smiling.

"That's good news, Herbert. When do we leave?"

"Tomorrow morning. Everything is arranged. Please take only one valise with you. You and the others can purchase what you need once you're back on German soil."

Steiger nodded, then took a long sip from his glass.

"Please make yourself comfortable, Herbert, while I retrieve some personal belongings that I must take with me. In fact I'd like to show them to you. I'm sure they will bring back some pleasant memories of our glorious days during the Third Reich."

Steiger walked to his desk and inserted the key. He watched the colored lights move from red to yellow and with the reversal of the key, turned the small light to green. He pulled open the drawer and took out the metal box that held the pictures and documents that covered all the lifetime that he cared to remember.

He closed the drawer and reset the lock, then walked toward Kappler.

*

The plane, a DeHavilland DHC-6 Twin Otter, circled over the plowed field after a twelve-minute flight from the private airport.

The twin engine turboprop, capable of carrying twenty jumpers, held sixteen men, all anxious to exit the aircraft as quickly as possible.

Leaning out of the plane's door was Andre Elazar, a dark-skinned Algerian Jew and former member of the 2nd Regiment Etranger Parachutiste (2nd Parachute Regiment) of the French Foreign Legion. After completing his five year Legion contract, he emigrated to Israel where he joined the controversial deep commando unit 101, which was later merged into Battalion 890 to form one of the Israeli Defense Forces elite infantry brigades.

He was recruited from this unit to serve under Mozar as directed. He was now acting jumpmaster on this mission as well as the rigger (Packer) for the Elliptical Ram-Air parachutes they were using.

On Elazar's signal, sixteen men stood up. On the plane's first pass, three large rubber containers were tossed out, their respective chutes immediately inflating, slowing their descent.

As the Twin Otter banked into its second pass, the jumpmaster gave the signal to move to the door. When he motioned again, sixteen men at one-second intervals exited the aircraft from twelve hundred and fifty feet.

At that height, the men were descending at a rate between eleven and seventeen feet per second. It would take each man approximately ninety seconds to reach the drop zone.

Shimon assumed a parachute landing altitude when he was approximately one hundred and fifty feet above the DZ. (Drop zone) With his knees slightly bent and his arms holding onto the front risers, Shimon waited until the balls of his feet touched the plowed earth, and then rolled onto his right side.

Unencumbered by equipment, he was up quickly. The wind was minimal, and his chute collapsed off to one side. He hit the quick release latch at the center of his chest and the chute's harness unbuckled.

As he pulled the risers away, he looked around and saw men scattered over a hundred-yard radius. Several were running toward what he assumed were the rubber containers.

He bundled up his chute and jogged toward the assembling men.

Mozar nodded to Shimon then looked at the group. "Everyone okay?"

After a few wise cracks from several of the men, Mozar said, "Good, once a paratrooper always a paratrooper...you never lose it," then he motioned to several of his men and they opened the three rubber containers.

Sixteen Israeli Uzi sub machine guns were distributed. Each man was handed four, 40 round magazines of 9-mm parabellum cartridges and a .45 ACP pistol with a silencer attachment plus several 8-round clips. Small radio/telephone units were handed to Shimon and the other team leaders.

Four men with entrenching tools began digging a trench as others stuffed the parachutes into the three empty containers. Then the containers were shoved into the trench and the trench covered over.

After another four minutes, sixteen men moved away from the drop zone and split into several groups, all heading by different routes toward Steiger's farm.

Shimon, Pincus, Phil, and Bertrand stayed with Mozar and two of his men as they made their way toward the gorge. They covered the two plus miles in just over seventeen minutes.

When Mozar called a halt, they were at the gorge at the eastern edge of the property, with the main house still another two hundred yards away.

Another group of five men joined them, almost immediately.

The remaining four men who took up positions along the two entrance/exit roads acknowledged being in position.

Mozar motioned Shimon closer, then he whispered, "Tell me what you're going to do."

"From here we move left until we reach the path cutting through the wooded area. Then we continue straight forward stopping at the end of the tree line. I'll signal you with two squelches. You acknowledge it with one. After receipt we move across the open area to the house and enter through the front. You come through the back. We clear it room by room."

Mozar shook his head up and down, then patted Shimon's shoulder.

"Okay, go. Good luck."

Shimon moved to the rear motioning to his men to come over and then pointed at the two men Mozar had allocated to him to do the same.

He reviewed the plan and concluded with, "Make sure your pistols have the silencer attached, and the safety is off. Follow me."

They enveloped left keeping low. When they reached the path with the lake to their rear, all five men stood erect and started moving north toward the house with Shimon, Pincus, and Bertrand leading.

Hearing movement to his front, Shimon raised his arm with his fist clenched...a signal to halt in place.

He motioned with his head and whispered, "We have company."

Moving along the path in the opposite direction were two black-clad guards approximately sixty yards away.

"I'll take the one on the right, and Pincus will take the other one. Henri shoots both. Play it cool."

The two guards hesitated a moment and then started walking again.

When they were about twenty yards away, one called out in German, "We were not informed that there would be any other patrols here until we were relieved, which is still…"

The guard never finished the sentence as three pistols fired. Shimon, Pincus, and Bertrand emptied their clips into the shocked guards. The sounds they made as the bullets impacted them were indiscernible as their lifeless bodies fell to the ground.

Shimon pointed. "Dump them over there."

After the two bodies were taken off the pathway, the five men jogged toward the tree line. When they were in place, Shimon squelched his radio twice. A single squelch was returned. He looked back at his men, nodded, and started out of the tree line, on the run, toward the farmhouse.

Chapter 77

Kathy was walking toward the stable area when the gunfire erupted behind her. She stood frozen for a moment unsure whether to return to the house or continue toward the stable.

Frightened beyond what she thought was possible, she began running toward the stable. She burst through the unlocked door and into the stall area when she tripped on some recently deposited excrement and fell hard on her right side.

She heard a horse whinny and looked up to see the saddled horse standing nervously between the stalls. At the same time, a hand reached toward her.

Kathy looked to her right and saw Rolf standing there, a pistol in the other hand. "Please Miss Buhler, get up. We must get away from here."

Kathy reached up and took hold of his outstretched hand. He pulled her up and immediately let go.

She started brushing her side when her hand became encrusted with excrement. Rolf pulled a soiled towel off one of the stall doors and handed it to her. Kathy started wiping her hand when she felt the tug on her arm.

"Please, Miss Buhler, time is of the essence."

The staccato ring of gunfire prompted Kathy to follow the man carefully past the horse, who was now pounding his hooves against the flooring and swaying erratically back and forth against the nearest stall.

The three other horses were bolting against their respective stall enclosures as each exchange of gunfire registered.

Once out the rear door, Rolf motioned to his right. "There are two jeep vehicles near the service road which we keep there for emergencies. We will take the back road to the highway and notify your father as soon as we are safely away from here."

The German began running in a crouched position. Kathy followed his lead. In minutes they were beside the jeeps.

Rolf opted for the enclosed Jeep Cherokee instead of the topless military style one. He motioned her in and, once he was situated in the driver's seat, reached under the floor mat for the key and started the ignition.

He put the Jeep in drive and hit the gas pedal too quickly. The tires spun but couldn't grab the soft road surface.

He shifted back to neutral, turned on the four-wheel drive, and then slowly depressed the pedal again. The jeep moved forward and began to pick up speed as it negotiated the ruts and depressions of the back road's surface.

The gunfire muted as they distanced themselves from the stable. Rolf had the 9mm Pistolen-08 (Luger pistol) under his left thigh while his hands gripped the steering wheel tightly.

As the vehicle bounced in and out of the ruts and depressions that covered the road surface, he struggled to keep the vehicle from turning over.

The road widened and improved slightly as they neared the intersection with Illions-94. Rolf braked and slowed the jeep to a crawl as the black-top of the interstate became visible.

Suddenly, two men stepped silently out from the underbrush on both sides of the jeep. The man on the left moved obliquely to one side so that he was facing Rolf full frontal and fired twice through the driver's side window.

One of the .45 caliber bullets hit Rolf in the left temple and the other penetrated his upper chest slightly above his heart. Kathy screamed as Rolf's dead body toppled onto her.

The shreds of glass flew through the forward compartment cutting her face, neck and hands.

She felt the stickiness of blood seep through her riding breeches, adding to the pandemonium welling up within her. Her hand instinctively reach-ed for the door handle as she made an attempt to squeeze her body away from the dead German.

Before she could apply force on the door handle, the door swung open and she faced a man dressed in a guard's black uniform and holding a sub-machine gun pointed at her chest.

For a moment she felt relief as she thought the guard was one of her father's men, but that feeling disappeared instantly as the man spoke.

"Get out carefully. Keep your hands where I can see them and no sudden movements."

She climbed out of the passenger's side and stood still as she blotted her face and neck with her sleeve. She felt the man's hand move over her body searching for non-existent weapons. Her eyes quickly darted toward the other man as he moved in their direction.

The man with the sub-machine gun straightened and moved his head in a motion toward the jeep.

The other man replied, "He's dead. Secure the woman and move the jeep off to the side. Keep it out of view from the highway."

The man nodded, took out plastic straps and bound Kathy's hands then walked to the jeep. With her hands bound behind her, she shivered, remembering clearly the park bench and the explosive belt around her waist.

Her attention was redirected to the moment as the man grabbed her arm roughly and pulled her toward the underbrush.

Chapter 78

Shimon saw several guards take up a kneeling position off to his left and opened up on the run with a burst of 9mm rounds. Bertrand, who was running slightly behind the security chief, fired as well.

As the dead men dropped in place, two more guards rounded the farmhouse from the right. The bullets from their weapons peppered the ground directly in front of the two running men and then abruptly stopped.

The two guards then focused on Pincus, Phil Goldman, and Mozar's two men, who were closer and fired.

Shimon and Bertrand continued to run, firing off short, ineffective bursts at the guards until they reached the porch area.

Bertrand dove headfirst and skidded along the floorboards until his body smacked against the house wall. He moved his body position until he faced the right side of the house and then squeezed the trigger until his weapon was empty.

He pressed the magazine release button and inserted another forty-round mag.

Shimon took up a position behind the steps facing to the right of the house. He fired off a short burst, but the two guards moved out of sight.

He called out to Bertrand, "Are you okay?"

"Yes, you?"

"Okay…I'm going to move to the porch."

Shimon maintaining a crouched position, placed his foot on the first step just as one of the guards reappeared and fired.

Bertrand watched as Shimon fell, not sure whether he was alive or dead, then leveled his Uzi at the right corner and fired off half of his second magazine.

He knew he couldn't reach the security chief and had to move before he was killed.

He fired off a short burst toward the right corner of the house, stood up, and then drove his shoulder into the front door.

The door didn't budge.

He took two quick steps back, then emptied his magazine into the door lock and again hit the door with his shoulder. The door sprung open and he dove inside just as the whoosh of bullets passed behind him.

As he made contact with the floor, he rolled onto his side then stood up and braced his back against a wall.

He ejected his magazine unsure of how many bullets remained and inserted a new one.

Then his mind registered on the firing coming from various sections of the house. He knew Mozar was inside.

After dropping to a prone position, Bertrand crawled to a sofa that was situated near a fireplace and moved behind it, waiting for what he anticipated would come through the front door.

The firing in the house was sporadic now, one side or the other was gaining the upper hand. Then he heard firing from outside and thought about Shimon and the other men.

Still looking at the open door, Bertrand saw an outline of someone who swayed in place for several seconds before toppling over.

He moved from behind the sofa, hugging the wall on his left and angled toward the prostrate body. Whoever it was lying there appeared dead.

After he confirmed the dead man was one of Steiger's men he retraced his movements past the couch and through an archway that led to a narrow hallway.

He stood up, pressed his back against one of the walls, and side stepped his way slowly to his right.

He stopped at the first door, shifted his Uzi to his left hand and then extended his right toward the doorknob. He turned the knob slowly, applied some pressure against the door, but the door was locked.

Bertrand removed his hand and pressed his back into the wall just as bullets from inside the room tore through the door.

Inside, Kappler changed the magazine of his German machine pistol, an MP-40 Schmeisser, then looked toward Steiger who was motioning him toward the far wall.

"We'll use the escape hatch," and he quickly yanked back the small oriental area rug, revealing a wooden trapdoor.

Steiger grabbed the metal ring and pulled the door up. A blast of cold, musty air flowed into the room from the air conditioning units pulsating below.

Kappler started down the wooden steps followed by Steiger who let the door fall quickly into place. As the trapdoor closed, the tunnel was thrown into total darkness.

"Once your foot touches the floor, move left and stay there for a moment." Steiger took a lighter from his pocket and flicked the striking wheel, lighting the wick.

After moving into the tunnel, Steiger saw the electrical switch on the right side of the wall. He moved the switch up and the tunnel was immediately immersed in subdued red light.

Then Steiger turned toward the stairs.

"Stay here...I've left the box. I can't go without it. I'll be right back."

Kappler grabbed Steiger's suit jacket by the collar. "Are you out of your mind? They're in the room already. Forget about the box. We've got to get out of here."

Steiger let out a sigh in frustration, nodded his head knowing that his friend was right, and then started down the tunnel.

*

Outside the door, Bertrand listened intently. No sound was coming from the room.

He angled his Uzi toward the door lock and pulled back on the trigger. The locking mechanism shattered and then he waited, listening for any movement inside. Satisfied, Henri pushed the door open with the barrel of his submachine gun.

Then he dropped to the floor and into a prone position. He crawled slowly into the room, stopped, and fired a short burst into the backs of several chairs scattered around the room.

He moved up on one knee, transversed the Uzi in a sweeping arc around the room, then stood up. After several seconds passed, he went back to the open door, or what was left of it, and closed it.

There was no sign of who fired through the door. The windows were still shuttered, and the curtains drawn. He looked slowly around the room for any sign of an escape panel, doing a three hundred and sixty-degree search of the room's walls. He found nothing to indicate an exit mechanism.

His foot crunched on metal and he looked down at the large number of spent shells. Henri kicked at some of the shells near his foot, caught part of an area rug with the metal reinforced toe of his boot and lifted it away. He looked down but there were only wooden floorboards.

He let his eyes move slowly over the floor and then he saw it, a rug that was partially folded over and at an odd angle.

As he moved closer, he saw the trapdoor.

He pulled up on the ring and as the door opened, he saw the dim red glow from below.

As the firing continued intermittently in the house, Henri descended the steps into the tunnel.

Chapter 79

Steiger and Kappler ran through the tunnel and past the door leading to the underground gallery. Steiger stopped a few steps past the door. "There are grenades in there," pointing back to the door.

The response from Kappler came quickly. "No time. We'll make do with what we have," pointing to his Schmeisser machine pistol and Steiger's Luger pistol. "We must get out of this tunnel, Ludolf. It will become our coffin."

When they came to several forks in the tunnel, Steiger moved to his extreme right, and Kappler followed.

They reached a wooden ladder leading up the stone wall. Steiger climbed quickly and pulled down on a d-ring handle dangling from a wire.

There was a pop sound and then a metal covering opened, revealing a three by five-foot hole to the surface.

The sporadic gunfire now seemed distant.

Both men climbed out quickly.

Once outside, Steiger went to his knees, pushed the metal lid closed, but held onto the d-ring handle so that it remained on the outside.

The two men ran toward the far-left side of the stable area. As they ran, Steiger pointed off to one side. "There are two vehicles nearby, over that way."

Both ran on weakening legs. The years and their age had taken their toll. Steiger pulled up. "I've got to take a breather."

Kappler shook his head, no but Steiger didn't move.

"Ludolf, we're in the open. The Jews are after us. We cannot stop."

Steiger nodded and started walking at a faster than normal pace, sucking in quantities of air with each step. He wanted to run but couldn't.

By the time they reached the jeep, both men were exhausted.

Steiger noticed that there was only one vehicle, the opened canvass military jeep.

He got into the driver's side, reached under the floor mat and inserted the key into the ignition.

Kappler placed the machine pistol on the canvas seat, grabbed hold of the windshield frame and metal bar behind the passenger's seat and hoisted himself into a standing position on the small running board.

With his left hand he took hold of the SMG, and then maneuvered himself into the seat.

Steiger placed the floor-mounted gear shift into first gear and moved the jeep forward.

Then he double clutched it into second gear and headed for the dirt road that would lead to Illinois Interstate-94.

Steiger thought about the other vehicle and then said what he was thinking. "I hope Rolf and my daughter are the ones who took the other vehicle."

Then his hand went to the Luger at his waist. The coolness of the metal somehow conveyed a feeling that things would turn out all right.

Kappler turned in the General's direction, but said nothing, his mind thinking of only one thing. That he was distancing himself from the area and the gunfire. He was not in the least concerned about Steiger's daughter.

*

Inside the tunnel, Bertrand came to the forks that faced several pathways. Standing there for only a moment, he opted to go to his far left. After another hundred yards he came to a dead end, a stone wall that offered nothing in the way of a route to the surface.

He cursed, turned, and started running in the opposite direction.

Again, back at the fork, he turned toward his far right. He ran until he reached a ladder braced against a dead-end stone wall.

He climbed several rungs, saw the wire and followed it up until he touched the side of the metal closure.

Bertrand pulled on the wire, but it remained taut. He moved up another couple of rungs and pushed up with the palm of his hand. The lid refused to move.

He climbed two more rungs on the ladder, bent his head forward so that his right shoulder pressed against the metal lid, and shoved upward. The lid didn't move.

After several more attempts, he went back down the ladder and moved toward the fork again.

Once back at the fork, Bertrand retraced his steps slowly through the initial pathway, stopping at a door he inadvertently missed when he passed the first time.

He fired off several rounds into the intricate lock system and shouldered the door open.

Stepping into the darkness, he began searching for a wall switch. When the lights came on, Bertrand sucked in air. His eyes widened as the paintings and sculptures came into focus. He moved slowly, then quickened his pace, as he walked past several of the chamber's walls lined with master paintings encased in their ornate frames.

Then he saw the two small crates stacked one on top of the other and partially hidden behind several paintings leaning against one of the walls.

He moved closer, lifted the lid, and saw the grenades.

Bertrand thought, one hell of a combination, works of art and grenades. He shook his head and let a smile form as he left the room and returned to the stairs leading back to Steiger's study.

Bertrand moved up and out quickly, then braced himself against one of the walls moments before the study door was peppered by gunfire.

The hail of bullets tore what remained of the door away from its hinges.

Henri dropped to one knee as he aimed his Uzi at the open doorway.

A voice from the hallway called out, "Identify yourself."

"It's Bertrand."

"What's your first name?"

"Henri."

Shimon appeared in the doorframe followed by Phil Goldman and one of Mozar's men. "You okay, Henri?"

"Yeah."

Bertrand saw the blood spot on Shimon's right leg. Goldman had been hit also, his left arm dangling by his side as he held his Uzi with his right cradled against his hip. Mozar's man seemed unscathed.

Shimon looked toward the tunnel opening. "What's that?"

"That," and Henri motioned over his shoulder, "is an escape route. I followed it to the end but whoever it was made sure that the escape hatch couldn't be opened from the inside. Is the house secure?"

Shimon shook his head, "As far as I know, yes."

"Is Steiger dead?"

"No sign of him, Henri, but we have his daughter."

Bertrand's eyes widened. "You have Kathy?"

Shimon nodded. "They were stopped before they reached the I-94 by two of Mozar's men."

"They?"

"Yes, the man with her is dead."

Bertrand breathed a sigh of relief. He hadn't thought about Kathy since the mission began, concentrating solely on remaining alive.

His attention diverted to the doorway as Mozar and several of his men entered. He looked at Shimon, "It appears that most of the guards have been captured or killed. Some are probably still around, others are trying to distance themselves from this place. Something we should be doing shortly. For all practical purposes, Steiger's men have been neutralized and the house has been cleared, but there's no sign of the Nazi."

Shimon pointed to the opening. "That's where Steiger escaped. His daughter has been captured by two of your men guarding the road leading to the I-94."

Mozar twisted his lips into a semi-smile. "I heard the transmission as well. At least that's one of them anyway. How many casualties do you have?"

"I have two dead, Pincus and one of your men. Goldman and I are hit, but we'll live. How about you?"

"One dead, one wounded. There are seven of Steiger's guards alive, and they're all wounded. Their dead are scattered all over the area and inside the house. I've been hit, but I'll live as well."

"That leg," and he pointed toward Shimon, "doesn't look good. Better get off it."

Mozar motioned to one of his men.

Shimon and the man moved toward Steiger's desk. The security chief leaned on the desk's edge and then maneuvered into the leather chair.

"I'm going to re-check the house. Stay here." Mozar pointed to Goldman, "Stay here with him."

Goldman acknowledged with a nod of his head.

Then Mozar looked at Bertrand. "You come with me."

Bertrand moved out through the doorway followed by Mozar and one of his men.

After they left, Phil took a seat on one corner of the desk. "How's the leg?"

"It's a nasty wound, but I don't think the bullet broke anything. Rip me a piece of cloth so I can tie off the blood flow."

Seeing nothing adequate, Phil reached down and undid his bootlace. He handed it to the security chief.

As he watched Shimon begin to make an impromptu tourniquet, Phil inadvertently began to spin the metal box resting next to his leg with his good hand.

He stopped spinning the box and lifted the lid. He saw photographs and papers. He removed several of the photographs and stared in disbelief.

"Look at these, Shimon."

Shimon finished tying the bootlace around his upper leg when he looked up, and said, "What?"

"These pictures…there's one of Himmler…and here's one of Himmler and Steiger holding a baby. Oh my God, there's a picture of Eichmann…"

Shimon reached for the photos and turned them around. He stared in abject horror at the murderers of his people. "What else is in there?"

"Some paper, documents, official looking ones, all with the Nazi seal."

"Let me see one."

Goldman reached into the box, brought out several papers. and then handed them to Shimon.

"I can't read German, but I'd be willing to bet a tidy sum that they're authentic. I'm sure one of Mozar's men can translate these. Put them back in the box and keep the box closed. Now let me take a look at that shoulder."

*

One of Mozar's men guarding Kathy Longrin looked up as he heard the whine of a motor coming from the dirt road.

He moved his hand away from his body as a signal to his companion to move back into the tundra. He then moved his fingers to his eyes and pointed at the girl.

His companion nodded and said quietly, "If you call out, you're dead."

Kathy's eyes widened.

He grabbed her arm and began pulling her awkwardly into the tundra.

The other man watched as the two disappeared. Satisfied, he ran across the road and made his way through the tundra until he was about thirty yards from where he had left the woman and his companion.

He crouched down, looked at the selector switch on his Uzi and pushed it to full automatic.

The whine of the engine, and the shifting sound of a vehicle's undercarriage as it negotiated the rut-covered road, made it clear to the Israeli what was coming his way. What he had to determine was whether the driver and his passengers were friendlies or hostiles.

As the vehicle came into view, he saw it was an open jeep with a driver and passenger.

The Israeli, like all the members of his team, had seen a photograph of Steiger, and immediately recognized him as the man driving.

The passenger who sat gripping the metal bar on the dashboard was an unknown.

The Israeli aimed at the passenger's side front tire and in seconds the quiet was replaced by the sound of automatic gunfire.

Steiger tried to maintain his grip on the steering wheel as he fought to control the jeep. The shredded tire made the jeep veer awkwardly toward the right, finally coming to a stop several yards in front of where the Israeli was standing.

Kappler tried desperately to steady himself enough to get the weapon pointed at their adversary but was unable.

The Israeli moved quickly to the passenger's side, knocked the SMG out of Kappler's hands and smacked him on the side of his head with the metal stock.

The German slumped forward hitting the front of his head against the metal u-bar, then fell to the right so that his body was hanging partly out of the jeep.

The Israeli grabbed him by the collar, while still aiming his Uzi at Steiger and pulled the unconscious Kappler roughly out of the jeep and onto the ground.

Steiger sat staring at the man whose black battle dress resembled one of his guards. He knew full well that the man was not one of his, but one of the hated enemy. He reasoned that he would be dead before his hand could reach the Lugar, so he kept both of his hands on the steering wheel and continued to stare back.

"Get out of the vehicle slowly…keep your hands behind your neck, fingers interlocked."

The Israeli watched as Steiger complied.

"Now move to the front and stand there."

Steiger moved to the front of the vehicle and stood with his body at an angle to the man.

"Get over here next to the other swine."

Despite being called a swine, Steiger's face and body remained composed.

He moved slowly toward Kappler, who was starting to regain consciousness.

As Steiger came closer, the Israeli moved away, lengthening the distance between them in anticipation of a possible lunge.

Nothing could have been further from Steiger's mind. He was beyond the years when he could have taken the younger man. His only hope rested with the Luger at his waist.

He knew Kappler's SMG was beyond reach on the floorboard of the jeep.

The Israeli stood motionless, watching as Kappler regained consciousness. He first looked up at the Israeli, then towards Steiger.

The Israeli called out, "Get up."

As he started up, Kappler fell back, his legs buckling under him.

"Help him up, Steiger."

It was the first time the man had used his name. Hearing it erased any minimal doubt that remained regarding the nature of his attackers and whether they knew who he was.

He bent over, grabbed Kappler under the arms and struggled to lift the squat, heavyset man. When he was almost erect, Steiger motioned with his head and eyes. At first Kappler didn't understand the movement, then he remembered.

Kappler leaned into Steiger, reached into his waist and pulled out the Luger concealing it with a shift in his body position.

He turned around quickly and fired off two rounds into the center mass of the Israeli's chest.

As the Israeli's body started crumpling downward, his finger in a delayed reaction, pulled back on the Uzi's trigger. The exploding 9mm cartridges made the weapon dance in the man's loosening grip and forced the Uzi to move independent of the Israeli's hand.

Rounds tore through the front fender and hood of the jeep in a vertical line, ripping the metal apart as if it were attacked by some alien beast. Then the weapon, as if by its own will, moved left and several rounds tore into the left side of Kappler.

The effect on his body was devastating. He crumpled into a sitting position as if forced there by some unseen hand.

He sat there, eyes wide in disbelief, as his body quickly went into shock, blood spurting from his wounds with each breath.

The Uzi became silent as it rested just out of reach of the dead Israeli's hand.

Steiger stood on rubber legs but quickly regained mastery over his shaking body.

He reached into the jeep and grabbed Kappler's Schmeisser SMG, then crouched behind the jeep and waited for an onslaught that didn't come.

Chapter 80

Shimon picked up the mobile telephone and listened as the caller first identified himself, then related the events of the past few minutes. His dialogue was concluded by a request for instructions.

"Is the vehicle operational?"

"Yes sir, minor damage only."

"Take the vehicle and the woman and drive to the I-94. Head to the main access road that leads to the farmhouse, it's the gravel road. I'll instruct the other team you're en route. Stay there until we advise further. Is that clear? Under no circumstances deviate from these instructions and make sure the woman is secured."

The caller acknowledged and the connection ended.

Shimon lifted his head toward Goldman. "You know my side of the conversation. They," and he pointed to the mobile now resting on the desk, "heard a vehicle approaching and one of them went to investigate. There was gunfire and then silence, that's it…probably Steiger…the other Israeli's fate is unknown."

Shimon looked back at the mobile telephone and then called Mozar. He briefed him on the conversation.

"Wait, where you are. I'll be there in five minutes. Just several more rooms to recheck."

*

Mozar walked in, followed by Bertrand and two more of his men.

"We're down to what you see. Counting the three guards at the main road, we're nine in total."

Mozar pointed to himself as he brought his mobile phone to his ear. He listened for a moment then replied, "Stay there. We'll regroup shortly. There's no guarantee we've neutralized all the guards. There are probably some in the general area...Steiger is on the loose as well. Stay alert."

Goldman handed Mozar the box.

"What's this?"

"Some photographs and documents... Steiger's treasure chest. We can't read them, but the photos tell a pretty good story."

Mozar opened the lid and saw the top photo of a smiling Steiger, together with Himmler. A short rush of air escaped Mozar's lips.

He picked up another photograph and stared at the images. He went through the others, one by one, then picked up several of the documents and studied the embossed Nazi eagle at the top and Himmler's signature below the body of the documents.

The Israeli looked back at Goldman, then Shimon. "I can't read German, but the photographs tell a compelling story." He looked behind him, at one of his men.

"Arno, come here please."

Arno Rosenfeld took several steps closer, moving his Uzi to one side as he took the documents from Mozar's outstretched hand.

He noted the photographs on the desk and then moved his eyes back to the documents.

Mozar and the others stood motionless as the man scanned each of the documents. All their eyes were glued on the Israeli as he lifted his head from the papers and refocused on Mozar.

"This document," and he held it with his left hand, "says that a baby girl was adopted. It is an official adoption document signed by Reichsfuhrer-SS, Heinrich Himmler."

"And this document," he held up the paper with his right hand, "contains a list of the names of German Jews, men, women, and children, who were executed on the date indicated by order of Oberstrumbannfuhrer, Otto Adolph Eichmann, Gestapo Department IV, B4. Jewish Affairs."

"The three names circled, Joseuf and Sophia Ullman, are the girl's biological parents. The third name, Tova Ullman, is the baby's given name. The note at the bottom of the document confirms this. Further, this document states that the baby was spared by orders of Reichsfuhrer-SS Heinrich Himmler. The parents were exterminated."

Bertrand listened with a light-headedness that came from the realization that the woman known as Kathy Longrin and Karta Buhler and who was raised as the daughter of SS-General Ludolf Otto Steiger, was in fact Jewish. A child who was taken away from her exterminated parents and raised as a German Catholic.

The men assembled in the room looked at each other. Mozar broke the silence. "Thank you, Arno. Please hand me the documents."

As he placed them back in the box together with the photographs, he said, "If it's alright with you gentlemen, I'll hang onto this box."

Bertrand looked at Mozar, then back to Shimon.

"We have Kathy. She's safe. She's a Jew, a treasured survivor from the Holocaust."

Then Henri looked at Shimon. "You know what exists between the woman and me. Life takes unusual twists and turns, mostly bad, but this time it happened right. I want to go to her."

He waited with pleading eyes.

Shimon turned to Goldman. "You okay?"

Goldman nodded.

"Go with Henri. Take the Mercedes sedan. I'll phone the guards that you are on your way. Signal me when you're in place and watch out."

Bertrand smiled and passed Phil Goldman on the run.

*

While his eyes were directed to his immediate front, Steiger's thoughts were of his daughter and then the metal box.

He decided to backtrack, moving through the woods to the gravel road and then paralleling the road toward the stable.

He knew he couldn't remain in place. They'd be looking for him as soon as they discovered the bodies of the Israeli and Kappler and he estimated that would be very shortly.

He calculated that they wouldn't figure that he'd return to the house.

Steiger looked first to his left, then his right and then as an afterthought, looked to his rear.

He listened intently, aware of only the quiet. He turned around again, keeping the SMG pointed to his front and then started moving carefully and painfully to his rear.

He soon distanced himself from the area and paused frequently as he tried to catch his breath as well as to let the pain from his joints subside.

His mind continued to focus on the metal box and its contents. He couldn't let it fall into their hands. His world, his daughter…and then he knew what he must do.

Without further hesitation, he moved quickly ahead, ignoring the pain.

He had walked through these woods for years. He was comfortable here and his direction was certain. As he neared the edge of the tree line, he held back. Then slowly moved into a prone position, his body racked by wave after wave of pain.

He touched his side, and felt the warm, sticky liquid that he knew was blood and realized that he had been shot…probably a ricochet.

The position gave him a clear view to the stable and a semi-obstructed view of the right side of the main house. Bodies, unidentifiable from where he was, were scattered around the house and adjacent areas.

He wasn't sure whether he had the stamina to crawl across the open area, but he saw no other alternative. He couldn't run. He knew moving across the open area was inviting sure death at the hands of anyone watching, but he had to retrieve the box.

Steiger moved slowly from his concealed position dragging the SMG by the sling. He tried to use the shadows to his advantage, moving forward at infrequent intervals.

He wasn't sure how long it took him to transverse the area, but he finally reached the stable.

He moved behind one wall and leaned his back against it. The pain was constant now.

He cradled the SMG and breathed deeply trying to rejuvenate himself. His clothing was filthy, blood-stained, and his face and hands streaked with sweat and dirt.

As he looked at his trembling hands, he painfully realized that his youthful vigor, which once projected an invincible image, had left him. He was old, very old, and his mind could no longer will his body to the tasks that once were taken for granted.

When he felt he was ready, he moved to his right, around a corner of the stable which gave him a direct line of sight to the tunnel.

He needed to cross the short distance quickly and decided to run. He strapped the SMG across his back, held his hand against his wounded side and with his head down, ran with all the speed he could muster.

His legs crackled at the knees and the joints sent waves of pain to his brain. As his feet rose and fell with each step, the blood oozed out between his fingers.

Seeing the tunnel lid directly in front, he slowed and fell to his knees and then rolled onto his side, mouth open sucking in as much air as he could. When he regained some strength, he crawled the remaining distance and again fell forward.

Steiger pushed up to his knees and lifted the lid. He threw the wire, with its attached ring, into the opening then slowly maneuvered onto the ladder.

When his foot missed a rung about half-way down, he toppled to the concrete flooring below. The contact sent waves of pain reverberating through his body. He screamed in pain then whimpered like a child, until the throbbing subsided.

As his mind cleared, he saw that the red subdued lighting was still on. He took a deep breath and willed himself to move forward dragging the SMG behind.

As he neared the far stairway, he saw the yellowish light shining through the opened trapdoor.

He heard voices in muted conversation but couldn't discern what was being said. He knew, unequivocally, that the voices belonged to his enemy. He stood still, contemplating his next move. Had they found the box? If they did, why were they still in the room?

The questions came rushing at him and he closed his eyes tightly, trying to clear everything away. When he opened his eyes, he reached down and took off his dirt caked shoes.

Then he moved toward the wooden steps, looked up and saw that there were no shadows blocking any part of the light. He knew that whoever was up there was standing away from the opening.

Steiger leaned into the wooden steps and painfully started to inch his way up. He paused after each step to listen.

When he reached the third step from the top, he stopped and placed the stock of the SMG into his shoulder, keeping the barrel pointed upward at a forty-five degree angle.

Then he stood straight up, allowing his upper body to move through the opening, pointed the SMG in the direction of the voices, and fired off a short burst of eight rounds.

*

Mozar toppled forward and was dead before his body reached the floor.

Shimon dove behind a chair and felt the pain instantly as his right side made contact with the floor. He reached down and touched the warm, sticky wetness on his leg.

Shimon aimed his Uzi in the direction he thought the firing had come from. Then his eyes locked onto the open trapdoor.

The Israeli, who was standing by the shattered doorway, dropped automatically when the gunfire erupted. He called out, "Anyone hit?"

Shimon yelled back, "Mozar is hit. The firing came from the trapdoor."

The Israeli quickly moved his eyes in that direction. "I'm going to fire a burst above the hole, then move toward it. Keep me covered."

The bullets passed over the hole and embedded in the wall splintering the wood paneling.

The Israeli crawled past some furniture and stopped just short of the hole. He kept his body flat against the floor as he moved the barrel of his weapon into the opening and then fired a sustained burst.

Steiger had dragged himself away from the stairs and retreated further into the tunnel. As he sat with his back against one of the walls, he saw the bullets impact the stairs, the area directly in front of the stairs and ricochet off the walls.

He screamed as he felt the searing pain to his leg, as the bullet tore into soft flesh. His mind immediately pictured Kappler bleeding to death and he didn't want to experience the same fate.

He called out as loudly as he could, "I'm wounded. I need help."

His breathing came in waves, alternating with the pain. He took a deep breath and pleaded again.

The voice above called out, "Crawl to beneath the opening. If you don't, you'll die where you are."

Steiger let go of the SMG and painfully began to crawl toward the opening, inching his way to the stairs.

The Israeli looked down at the bleeding German.

"Stay face down with your hands extended straight out."

Then he turned to Shimon. "Cover me."

Shimon moved slowly to the trap door dragging his leg behind him.

Once he was in place, he nodded to the Israeli, who started down the ladder, his Uzi pointed at the German.

Chapter 81

Bertrand insisted on driving, which was fine by Goldman. He put the gear shift in drive and floored the accelerator.

The rear tires spun, kicking up gravel as they tried to bite into the loose stones. He eased up on the accelerator and the tires gained some traction.

As soon as the short block engine began pulling the 280S sedan forward, Henri pushed steadily down on the pedal until the car was traveling precariously toward the I-94.

Shimon had alerted the group of three men regarding who would be in the vehicle. At the sound of the Mercedes approach, two men stepped out on either side of the road, their weapons held loosely and pointed toward the oncoming car.

Bertrand jammed his foot down on the brake pedal, spinning gravel in all directions. The car rocked and then veered to its left, sliding on the gravel like it was moving on ice.

It made a one hundred and eighty-degree turn, finally coming to a stop facing back in the direction it had come.

"One great ride, Henri. Maybe we can do it again when we have some free time," then Goldman laughed.

As Bertrand started to move out of the driver's side, he was hit with a beam of light. The light dropped away, and he saw the Uzi pointed in his direction.

"I needed to make sure."

"I understand. Where's the woman?"

"Down the road a bit. I'll take you there."

Bertrand followed the Israeli and then saw Kathy, her hands behind her back staring into the darkness and looking petrified.

Bertrand called her name and ran toward her.

"It's all right now."

He moved behind where she was standing and undid the plastic straps.

As soon as her arms were free, she turned around and flung them around his neck. She buried her face into his chest and sobbed.

He just stood there, knowing that she had to cry herself out. The Israelis moved off and Goldman joined them.

The tears turned to a torrent and then she became still as she clung to him.

When she looked up, her cheeks were streaked with tears. He moved his hand up and gently brushed some of the wetness away with his thumb.

"Oh, Henri, I'm so scared. What is happening? I want to die, just simply die."

"Now is the time for living, Kathy. Come with me, please. You'll be safe so help me."

Kathy looked into his eyes, hesitant even to trust this man.

"Please, Kathy."

He took her hand in his and they started toward the Mercedes. When they came abreast of the Israelis, she shivered, and pressed closer to him. Her eyes averted theirs, afraid to acknowledge their presence.

"I'm accompanying the woman back to the house. Are you coming Phil?"

"Sure."

Goldman nodded to the other men and then caught up with Bertrand and the woman.

The ride back was at a slower pace. Kathy was leaning against Bertrand, her eyes shut and unaware of the bodies scattered around the house.

She became aware of the carnage when she entered the house and saw the first body. She pulled away from Bertrand and started to run.

Both men chased after her and stopped her before she passed the parked Mercedes.

Kathy dropped to the ground and placed her head in her hands. She started to cry again.

"Kathy darling, some terrible things have happened here, but now you're safe. Please come back into the house. There is something that I need to show you."

She looked up at Bertrand. "How can I be safe? I've lost my father and Shimon and his people are trying to kill me."

"You're safe. Come, please come."

Her mind reeled, but in the end, she was overwhelmed by a feeling of indifference. Maybe it would all end shortly. Let them kill her. What difference did it make when it happened?

Bertrand nodded to Phil, who came over and then both men helped her into a standing position. They walked together back to the house. Once inside they made their way toward the study.

When they entered, Arno moved several paces back from the doorway and pointed his weapon toward the floor.

Then they focused on Shimon, who was leaning over a man, his back blocking the seated man's face.

When the security chief turned around, Kathy saw the man was her father. She let out a scream when she saw the blood and then ran to him.

He put his arms weakly around her.

She looked back at Bertrand, then to Shimon. "What have you done? What have you done to him?"

In the gentlest tone she ever heard from Shimon, he said, "He is alive and will recover. That's more than I can say for him," and he pointed toward Mozar's body.

She looked at the dead man and then back at her father. She slowly moved away from the seated man and stood on trembling legs.

The room started to spin, and she felt her body drifting backwards, when Shimon's arms moved up.

He helped her to the chair in front of the desk, then turned to Goldman. "Phil, please get some drinking water and a wet towel."

Goldman returned with a glass and a washcloth dripping water.

Shimon squeezed out the excess and handed the washcloth to Bertrand. He kneeled next to the chair and placed it against Kathy's forehead. "Hold it there for a few minutes."

When she looked up, Bertrand was holding the water glass. "Take a few mouthfuls. It'll help."

She took a long swallow, as the men watched her.

Shimon smiled down at her.

"This has been a very long day, Kathy, and I know you are frightened, and confused. There is no reason to be frightened any longer. No harm will come to you...I swear on my parents' graves."

"As far as being confused, there are some things that we need to show you. The documents are in German, a language in which you are fluent in..."

Before Shimon could finish, Steiger rose from his chair and screamed, "Nein, Nein," before he fell back down, exhausted by the effort.

The only sound was his whimpering as he stared down at his shoeless feet.

Kathy looked at him, one part wanting to rush toward him, the other willing her to stay where she was.

The security chief opened the metal box. He took out the photographs and handed it to her. Shimon looked back at Goldman and pointed toward the water glass.

Kathy stared at the pictures, looking first at one then another, then back again until the tears welled forth like a broken dam.

Shimon gently pulled the photographs out of her hand and replaced them with two documents.

Goldman, returning with a pitcher of water, stopped abruptly at the sound of Kathy's heart-wrenching scream.

He and the others watched as the woman's eyes rolled back into the recesses of her eye sockets. Then, as if in slow motion, her limp body began to slump forward.

Bertrand reached out and stopped her forward movement.

The documents drifted away from her open hand, coming to rest on the blood-stained floor.

Chapter 82

Kathy never imagined that she would return to the 47th Street building, but as unreal as that seemed, she was there, seated beside Bertrand in the conference room.

Kathy had entered a vacant reception area and walked across the sorting room, which was devoid of people.

Several sorting tables, all that remained of many, were askew, which might indicate to the casual observer that some work activity had previously taken place here.

The office was deplete of furnishings. The banks of computers that monitored both the inside and outside activity of the building were gone. All that remained of any semblance of what was, was the conference table and several chairs.

Opposite her sat a bandaged Duchant. To his right was Shimon and on his left was the Israeli, Arno, and then Phil Goldman with an arm splint. Bertrand sat in the chair next to her.

At the head of the conference table was a man she estimated to be in his late seventies, maybe eighties. His skin was chalk-like, complimenting his white beard and contrasting with his black suit and black skullcap.

As she sat there, her mind drifted. Kathy recalled the shock that transcended her body after seeing the photographs and the feeling of light-headedness at the revelation of what the documents contained.

She remembered being taken to the Mercedes sedan. Goldman drove while Bertrand sat in the rear seat with his arms around her. The boarding at the private airport was a blur, as was her arrival back in Manhattan.

For several days, Bertrand didn't leave her side. He fed her and comforted her as only someone so enamored with another living human being could do...forgetting totally about himself and dwelling completely on the other.

Duchant smiled at Kathy. "Welcome home, Tova."

The name sounded strange and foreign, as if Duchant were addressing someone other than herself.

For an instant, Kathy was unsure whom Raphael was speaking to. Then vividly, she remembered the documents, the circled names on the documents and her name...the name of a child so long ago forgotten...Tova Ullman.

"I know...it takes some getting used to, but all in good time. The man to my left is a Rabbi, a survivor from the camps. He's here to try, in some small way, to start putting your world back together again."

Kathy stared at the old man wondering what he could offer.

The man lifted his head and looked at the young woman sitting to his left.

Kathy immediately noticed his blue eyes, so blue they seemed glass-like. She wanted to look away but couldn't. It was as if some force possessed her and she was powerless to resist or divert her head.

Then in a clear, strong, accented voice, he began.

"My name is unimportant. What is important is that we, you and I, have two common and indestructible bonds that forever connect us. First, we are survivors. We are living proof, a testimony if you will, to man's inhumanity to man. As long as we live, we carry with us an enormous burden for we are the lucky ones."

"The second bond we share is our Jewish heritage."

Kathy started to say something, but the blue eyes seemed to plead, willing her to wait. She held back.

"Like you, I too have lost my parents to the camps. I was much older when the Holocaust happened. I have asked myself countless times why I was spared, and my family murdered. I have but one answer. It was His will."

"When it began, I was at an age of understanding, but I understood nothing. I witnessed slaughter and depravity beyond what the human mind is capable of processing. Their savagery was perpetrated on our people not only because of who we were, but because we were...we existed, which for them was reason enough to eliminate us. Those who passed judgement on us declared us, a people, unfit to exist."

"Their perverted sense of reason was seeped within the crevices and corners of coerced and bastardized history...in lies, innuendoes and century old blood libels."

"They enjoyed their work of extermination, and at night joyfully returned home to their wives, and children, relishing in their accomplishments of murdering us in ever increasing numbers."

The old man lowered his head for a moment, breaking contact with Kathy. In a millisecond his blue eyes were again focused and staring at the woman.

"One day among countless days, Himmler and one of his Adjutants inspected the camp. I was assigned to the showers, the gas chambers on that day, to remove the corpses to the crematoriums for burning. There were just six of us."

"As the Reichsfuhrer and his Adjutant entered, we were whipped away by the SS guards. We cowered in a corner afraid to make a sound. My head was bowed, eyes to the ground as always, but I could still see them...their shiny black boots, their black uniforms with the death head insignias and their arrogance...an arrogance that comes with knowing that they hold the power of life and death."

"They watched through small windows as the naked men, women and children screamed inside. They laughed and pointed, their excitement heightened with what was about to take place."

"Then the command was given to drop the Zyklon B pellets (Hydrocyanic acid) into the chamber through special air shafts in the ceiling. As the pellets vaporized, they gave off a bitter, almond-like odor. When these vapors were inhaled, they combined with the red blood cells, which in turn deprived the body of oxygen. Soon the victims became unconscious and eventually died through oxygen starvation. Some of the victims held their breath, trying to extend their lives just a little longer. Others welcomed a quick death and inhaled deeply. Through it all Himmler and his Adjutant smiled, joked, and then complained that the process was too slow."

"As Himmler and his party turned to leave, someone in our group let out a sob. It was a sound that was highly unusual, since we all had seen and endured more than any one of us believed we were capable of. We became devoid of tears and emotions long ago…yet one of us sobbed."

"Who did that?"

"I cowered lower. I didn't want to die, not after all I had gone through."

"The Adjutant repeated his question."

"No one said anything. Then the Adjutant in an almost inaudible voice said, if the Jew swine who made that sound doesn't identify himself, I will have you all gassed."

"No sooner did he finish his statement, then three of our group stepped forward. In this bottomless pit of hell, three Jewish men took it upon themselves, individually, to step forward so the others could live. I'll never know whether one of them was the man who sobbed, but the Adjutant, after smiling at Himmler, instructed the guards to place all three inside the gas chamber. In moments they were dead."

"The Adjutant moved in front of us...the three who remained. Our eyes were staring at the floor when he instructed us to look up."

"I have enjoyed this little visit and we don't want to keep you from your work. Perhaps when you're next in Berlin, you'll pay me a visit."

"Then he laughed loudly. He started to leave with Himmler when he turned toward us again and said, Ask for Brigadeführer Ludolf Otto Steiger, then laughing and joking with Himmler, they walked away leaving us trembling."

"The SS guards soon reappeared and opened the gas chamber door. We began removing the bodies to the crematoriums. It was something that I had done hundreds of times and still could not put up a wall of indifference toward these dead landsmanner (Countrymen). These were my people."

"And, Tova Ullman, you are one of my people, a living testimony to our enviable ability to survive. Your parents were murdered in my camp...

maybe they were murdered on that very day. The name of that camp was Buchenwald."

"You were raised a Catholic and baptized. You have lived your life believing in what you were taught and understood to be true. I, we, understand. In our religion, every one of us possesses a Jewish soul. Regardless of one's repudiation, rejection, assimilation, or acceptance of another religion or their idyllic rituals, the soul remains Jewish."

"We hope in time, you will be able to open yourself up, and learn about who you are. We are people of the book with over three thousand years of recorded history. I am always available to help you. The others assembled here are likewise disposed to doing anything they can to reunite you with your people."

Then the old man pointed toward Henri.

"The man whose hand you now hold is not Henri Bertrand and he is not a Catholic. He is my son, and his name is Ariel Kellerman."

She looked strangely at the man she knew as Bertrand. He squeezed her hand gently, then began speaking.

"A name is only something that identifies someone and separates them from everyone else. It is meaningless otherwise. If I've offended you or hurt you in any way, I ask your forgiveness. My feelings for you were the same whether you were called Kathy Longrin or now Tova Ullman. Nothing has changed. I know it will take time for you to readjust and that's fine…take all the time you need. I'll be waiting for you when you're ready."

Kathy looked at Duchant. "What has happened to my fath…" then she stopped. She removed her hand from Bertrand's grip and looked down at the table.

Raphael knew that the question would be asked. No matter how he answered it, the answer would be hurtful.

"Your father has been taken to Israel. He will be judged before his accusers. The woman known as Gerta and the man, Udo, were among the dead."

Despite what she knew to be the truth, the memories of her youth, Gerta, Udo, and the man she had called father, came flooding back. Her eyes welled up with tears and she cried.

Sensing some movement toward her, she called out, "Please do not come near me or touch me. I'm okay."

Bertrand looked at her but said nothing.

He just sat there watching, knowing that the last thing he could do was offer comfort. Kathy would have to fight these demons alone. If she could overcome them, there was a chance that they would make a life together. Otherwise, it would simply be a chapter in his life that would scar him until the day he died.

When Kathy regained control, Duchant continued. "These premises and everything that took place within it, was a ruse. Our sole purpose in being was to recover stolen works of art confiscated from European Jewry by the Nazis and hidden by Odessa."

"We had identified a former SS Officer operating a gallery in New York. He was the late Manfred von Hoenshield. We knew he would lead us to others, and he did. Money speaks volumes."

"Duchant et Compagnie de Fils is real and does exist, but not at 47th Street. Everything you saw here was set up to validate who we were. Our legends, that is our assumed identities, which were constructed and put in place years ago, worked well. Whether some of us are who we claim to be…well, only they know for sure."

"Prior to leaving the farmhouse, we returned to the underground room. We removed the paintings from the frames and packed them in whatever was available along with the artifacts. Then we loaded them into the station wagon, the jeeps, and the sedan and drove them to the airport. They were placed on the plane that brought you back to New York. They are now in Israel where our people will attempt to locate the rightful owners and return these works of art to them or their heirs."

"By the way, the woman guard you struck in your bathroom was severely hurt but she'll recover. That should ease your mind a bit."

Then Raphael placed the metal box on the table's surface and gently pushed it toward Kathy.

"This belongs to you, Tova."

He smiled, stood up, then turned and walked out of the room.

The others followed one by one, leaving Tova Ullman and Ariel Kellerman alone.

ABOUT THE AUTHOR

Harris L. Kligman

Born and educated in the "City of Brotherly Love," the author left Philadelphia, Pennsylvania in his early twenties. For over thirty-five years, he interacted with various military governments and business entities who dominated the spheres of influence throughout the Far East, Africa, and South America.

A linguist, a devotee to the Martial Arts (holder of a Black Belt in Hapkido, earned while living in South Korea) and a retired United States Army Intelligence Officer who is also cross-trained as an Infantry Officer, the author brings his varied experiences to these writings.